THE HUNDREDTH WOMAN

To the Maywood Public Library ~ always remember who you are! 100th

Kate Sear

The Hundredth Woman

Kate Green

iUniverse, Inc.
New York Lincoln Shanghai

The Hundredth Woman

iUniverse, Inc.

For information address:
iUniverse, Inc.
2021 Pine Lake Road, Suite 100
Lincoln, NE 68512
www.iuniverse.com

ISBN: 0-595-27958-9

Printed in the United States of America

For you, the reader.

Contents

Acknowledgments

I am profoundly grateful to Nancy Bancroft, my dear friend of many years and the author of *The Feminine Quest for Success.* Nancy patiently sifted through each draft, provided crucial feedback, encouraged me every step of the way and insisted from the beginning that these ideas had to get out there. Nancy, I think you know that a simple thank you isn't enough. I don't see how I could have written this book without you.

Thank you to Ann Anderson, my editor, who helped polish the final draft and whose friendship and encouragement heartened me.

I'm grateful to those who have pioneered and made available new ways to think and feel, among them Starhawk, Mary Daly, Alice Walker, Sonya Johnson, Ted Andrews, Barry Kaufman and Oprah Winfrey. For the millions—mostly women—who have responded to these (and many others) and to their own spirit's calling, I am so glad you are here and doing your work. What a time to be alive!

So many native people have contributed to the understandings in this book. I am especially grateful to Sandy Frary for the treasure of our friendship, laughter and richly textured journeys together. Tyson Sampson and others in Cherokee, North Carolina, and the surrounding area were also helpful at key points in developing this book.

I'm grateful to each client I have worked with over the decades, especially those who stayed with the work for years as their quests continued to unfold. Thank you for sharing your deepest selves, thereby continually reminding me how magnificent the human spirit can be.

I received invaluable help from many readers along the way and am especially grateful to those who provided detailed commentary on every chapter: Marj Boyer, Stephen Schilling, Paul Hellwig and Betsy Bickel. Other readers include Jane Norton, Barb Smalley, Andi Elliot, Angela Williams, Catherine Nicholson, Elizabeth Brownrigg, Melissa Delbridge, Jody Eimers, Amber Taylor, Elizabeth Saria and Cara Benedetto. My thanks to all.

A special thanks to Sandra Stanton. The image on the front cover was derived from her amazing painting, Eve©. To view her impressive body of work or to purchase prints, go to goddessmyths.com. The epigraphs that begin each chapter are by contributors to *We'Moon* from 1994 to 2003. I am so grateful to them for their evocative expressions of the female spirit and for the profound gifts that *We'Moon* so generously provides, year after year, to support women's spirituality. And thank you to Whitehorn—gifted artist and technowizard—(whitehornwebdesign.com) for creating my website at **hundredthwoman.com** and to Susan Baylies for doing whatever it took to overcome technical snafus and take my concept for the cover design to heights that tickled me giddy. Check out Susan's powerful, spunky, and heartfelt work at snakeandsnake.com Rani Gil generously contributed technical support during the final moments.

And then there are those I love. My greatest blessing is the enduring, tangible love of the most wonderful beings I have had the thrill to know. I am profoundly grateful to each of them. I didn't know such powerful, nurturing connection existed until we found each other and fanned the flames. First, my tribe. They are my sanctuary—huge-hearted, questing, truth telling, protective, clear-eyed visionaries all: Patrick, you are my angel—thank you for standing fast; Honey, you sassy girl, thank you for your jokes and boundless love; Darcy, thank you for your courage, your vision and for seeing me—generosity is too small a word for your wide-open heart; Marjorie, your get-the-job-done spirit is exceeded only by your integrity, core of giving and fascination with life; Paul, you rascal, your big bear presence, love of the earth, and rolling laugh steadies me; Marj, wise crone, lover of the green world, your quiet communal spirit fascinates and inspires me. And then there are the rest of my angels: Pat, Kathy, Scott and Tessa—as well as Ruth, Jon, Jessica and Madeline—thank you so much for always making me feel integral to your wholesome, loving families; Barb, quirky, brilliant and always at the ready, I love your ever-increasing willingness to let your buzz-cut down; Sharon—how to you do it? and how do you know so much?—you've been there every single time; Nancy and Sue, thank you for our love and understanding that spans a quarter of a century; thank you to my loving, soulful, and watchful neighbors; and my dear son, I love you.

To the lovely, loving earth and to divine wholeness—the sacred spirit of all that is—thank you for nourishing and guiding me step by step and for nestling me, always.

And many, many thanks to you, dear reader. We are in this together.

And let's not forget the magnificent soul with two bumper stickers, "Oh, EVOLVE!" and "Do not meddle in the affairs of dragons, for you are crunchy and good with catsup."

CHAPTER 1

crawl

Reflect on the darkness,
where fear is lost.

Reflect on the darkness,
where light begins.

Reflect on the darkness,
where gold is dancing.

—Janine Canan

Where are you?
Why won't you answer me!
For once, can't you tell me what to do?

Morgan Forrester screamed silently at God, the universe, whoever was out there to listen. She felt as if the blasts of rain that rattled her office windows were thrashing the raw tissues inside her chest. She was an experienced woman—a counselor, a mother—but in this moment, she knew nothing.

Why wasn't God someone you could grab around the neck and throttle the truth from? Or at least set an appointment with and get some answers, as her therapy clients tried to do with her.

Speaking of whom… reel it in!
You're at work.

Ignoring the undulating rumbles of thunder that challenged her resolve, she hauled her awareness back to the present and anchored herself to the comforts of her office with its pale golden walls, richly patterned furniture, and cloisonné vases overflowing with every variety of flower that bloomed in her garden.

When she greeted her four o'clock appointment, the woman shook out her umbrella and dragged herself to her usual perch on the couch. Morgan met her client's eyes with what she hoped was the open compassion she felt two layers up from that clenched place in her gut that longed to scream, not listen.

The woman's chin jerked. "I'm losing myself." Lightning sizzled behind the window nearest them, followed by an explosion of thunder that resonated through their bodies and heightened the fear in the woman's dark eyes. "My job is wearing me down, I can't do enough for my kids, and when it comes to the house… my husband never even breaks a sweat. Where am I in all this?"

Morgan gazed at her hands through her tumbles of silver-streaked auburn hair and fingered the gold fringe that edged her velvet chair. The woman's words throbbed in her temples.

This was the same yearning she'd heard from three clients in a row that afternoon. But how could she help them when her own rebel angels were screaming that she was a workaday drone with nothing to show for her life except good kids, a job well done, and an unfortunately long list of relationships she'd fought to keep alive but eventually had to take off life support? Where was she in all this?

Were she and her clients self-absorbed head-cases, jamming the works of what could be a better world? Were they as indistinguishable from one another as the countless candies hurtling down Lucy Ricardo's nightmare conveyer belt?

But we can't be suffering like this—striving, reaching—for no reason.

Morgan sucked in a jagged breath, smoothed the flowing dress that fell across her plump thighs and wished her legs were long enough to stretch across the floor, as her client's did. She flipped off her sandals and pulled her tapestry footstool closer with a brightly pedicured foot. "Let's take these concerns one at a time, so they're not overwhelming. Which one troubles you most?"

"My job is the worst. It's a vulture convention." The woman grinned before her mouth went tight. "Everyone is circling. There's no creativity, no vision, no mission, just a weirdly passive hacking away at whatever comes along."

Her words hit Morgan in the chest and reverberated like a gong. How long had she herself been in a holding pattern, ravenous for something new but unable to envision what that might look like? Her life was good. But it wasn't right. Whatever her path was meant to be, she wasn't on it.

"What is it you want from work?" Morgan said. She plucked at the sunny swirls on the arm of her silk dress, unable to stop the chant running through her head.

Where am I going?

Why am I here?

What do I want?

It was like an advertising slogan she couldn't make herself forget, but more ominous. She seized control of her attention and worked to suppress the last line. It echoed in her awareness anyway, wrapping its well known chill around each vertebra in her back.

What if I never find out?

But she wasn't going to let that happen. It would be a living death. Besides, she'd never let anything stop her before. She'd fought her father's groping hands and the emptiness of her marriage and divorce. And she'd had the courage to move to the South and make a normal life for her kids in Grandmama's old Victorian. So she certainly wasn't going to give up now. She drew a deep breath, pushed her feet into the footstool, and straightened her spine.

How would it feel to be certain—in my heart, my soul, my body—that I'm fulfilling my life purpose exactly?

"Morgan?"

Morgan flicked her hair off her shoulders. "I'm sorry. I was wondering how many other women—throughout the world—share your hunger for something more. I know I do. Yet each of us is alone, isolated by the circumstances of our lives, pecking at the walls of our prisons like baby birds struggling to break free from their eggs. I wonder—could we be poised on the edge of a transformation as profound as the one the chicks are fighting toward?"

"You've always told me there are wings on the other side of our pain."

"Right. But what if the whole flock takes flight and discovers that together we can change the world?" Morgan sank back in her chair. She was losing herself in questions she could barely ask, let alone answer. "Let's get back to your situation at work."

Weren't these patterns of experience, these coincidences—her clients reflecting her own agitation—supposed to mean something?

But where's the meaning in restlessness, dissatisfaction, yearning?

"I hate my job because I want my work to fill me up—and it doesn't."

The pastel light from the Tiffany lamps flickered, then died, along with the air conditioning. Morgan rose, lit a candle, and placed it on the table between them.

"Sorry," she said. "This is one of those old Hopewellen buildings that's been around since before the Civil War. I think it's morally opposed to electricity." She glanced outside. "At least the rain has quieted."

But the sky was still boiling blackness. She was grateful her son's plane had gotten off safely this morning. It would have been agony to know Ian was in the air during this storm. She could barely see the wide stream of water coursing through the parking lot and down the residential street before pooling around the overworked sewer. At least the massive willow oaks that lined the road had stopped tossing and stood in their usual repose, lacing fingers with their companions across the way.

Inside, the rising heat and humidity wrapped the women in a dark sanctuary, a womb of gray velvet light. The warmth had coaxed open the gardenia buds she'd picked this morning in the prickling Carolina damp. They floated in a jade lotus-shaped bowl next to the candle, suffusing the room with their exotic scent.

Morgan stared into the candle's pulsing flame. "Perhaps the answers you seek lie in your unhappiness, like seeds, waiting for you to find and water them."

Where did that come from?

Her words drifted up from a place so deep it was beyond understanding, as did the peace that gently filled her body. Were her prayers being answered in the messages beginning to flow through her?

"What do you mean?" her client said.

"Exactly what are you unhappy about?"

The woman began to speak, but Morgan put her finger to her lips. "Don't settle for the first answer that comes to mind. Close your eyes and breathe. Drop your awareness from your head into your feet. Good. Now put one hand on your heart and the other on your belly and ask your troubles what they're here to teach you, what gifts they bring, what they need from you."

As her client looked within, Morgan tried to follow her own instructions, to reach the source of her pain and learn from it.

But something stopped her. Ancient fingers, icy and familiar, coiled around her spine and a voice whispered that she'd never find her calling.

This voice felt alien, as if it belonged to someone else. But she'd received enough counseling and training to know better. She'd thought she was past this yet here she was again, projecting her feelings, trying to pretend she didn't have to take responsibility for them by imagining they weren't part of her.

The only way to create a shift was to own this dread, the same terror she used to feel when she'd startle awake to find her father leering above her.

Her stomach lurched as the thing gripped her harder.

❧ ❧ ❧

The next morning, Morgan awakened slowly. She was tangled in a damp mass of seldom-laundered polyester sheets in the bed of Adam Mandrake, the most recent man with whom she'd tried to find a corral for her soul.

Sweat prickled along her hairline, pasting her hair flat against her head, and the mingled odors of mildew and unwashed male laundry assaulted her senses. Even above the futile clatter of his air conditioner, she could hear his pet pig, Sheila, snorting and rooting outside. The night before, Sheila had shown her more affection than Adam had. Now he was stirring, and it took only two words out of his mouth to confirm her suspicions that she'd wasted the year she'd spent with him.

Suddenly they were on their feet, naked, arguing, hurling words across the room at each other faster than she could think. Yet she was experiencing their fight in slow motion—like a dream in which the action was underwater.

He was usually so quiet, his tall, tight body so controlled. But now he was a trapped animal, frantic and wild. She could imagine him thrashing against the bars of a cage, the whites of his eyes flashing and great white loops of spittle trailing from his mouth.

He wouldn't hurt me.

But then why were her calves tensed, the balls of her feet poised to flee? And why did she feel nervous each time his pacing cut her off from the door?

This isn't happening.

Her first summer without the responsibilities of children was beginning today. It was supposed to be a respite, a retreat, a chance to discover her true path—the woman she was without children tugging at her time.

Had she ever faced such freedom?

Certainly not since college, when she got pregnant with her daughter Sierra. Childbirth had launched her into a maze of marriage, mothering, graduate school, work, and divorce. Life became simpler fifteen years ago when Grandmama suggested she bring her kids to the South and move in with her. But they'd lost Grandmama, Sierra married Rich last fall, and Ian needed her less and less.

Still, Morgan hadn't had a real break since she was a child.

If you could call that a break.

Hiding from my father's hands and my mother's hollow eyes.

And their fights.

She shuddered.

This felt like a bad rerun of her childhood.

She tried to calm Adam, as she had her parents. Her heart felt as bare as their bodies. But nothing in his face told her that her words were hitting home. His eyes were narrow pinpoints of brilliant black light. They held her, bored into her.

Morgan taught the rules of a clean fight to her clients and she always followed them. She could say what she meant, even raise her voice, and still behave respectfully. But when he called her a fat bitch, she lost it.

"Ever hear of Viagra? It's not my fault you can't keep it up anymore."

Later, she wondered why she happened to notice his hand at the exact moment his thumb locked around the handle of the iron. She watched each individual finger curl around the handle, beginning with the smallest. The image of a chorus line flashed through her mind, rows of legs fanning down from a kick.

He paused. Then his lower lip curled down oddly. He drew his arm back over his right shoulder and lifted his left leg as if he were about to pitch a fast ball.

The iron sailed toward her skull, pointed end first, like a missile. She seemed to watch it forever as it flew toward her, heading straight between her eyes as though guided by a built-in homing device, the cord trailing behind like a blaze of rocket fuel.

She actually had time to think that if she put her arms up to shield herself, she'd be admitting this was happening. Their year together was ending in less than a second. It would be more dignified to remain motionless and simply look at him. Let him see what he had done.

❧ ❧ ❧

Of course that crazy alarm never did go off. Yet Clarissa Albright jumped out of bed, eyes wide, at the exact moment her digital clock read seven a.m.

What am I?

Time's slave?

But if she hadn't awakened, Frankie and Martin wouldn't have made it to their Y.M.C.A. camp. And she wouldn't have had their cramped apartment to herself so she could figure out how to stop the nuclear dump.

Still, Clarissa hated belonging to the clock. Back on the reservation, Big Mom would have leaned back in the old porch rocker, opened her face into that toothless grin, and chided her softly, calling her a fish—flop, flop, flopping on the river bank.

"Time is a river," Big Mom would have said, her obsidian eyes drifting into other worlds while her round hands danced like otters. "Slip into the water, Granddaughter. Give yourself to the current. Let it carry you. Listen to the river's whisperings and let her help you find your way."

The laugh that rumbled through Big Mom's body would have come up through her belly from somewhere deep in the earth as she patted Clarissa's cheek with a warm palm, the black pools of her eyes disappearing in a smile as furrowed as caked clay.

But she wasn't on the reservation anymore with it's tall pines, domed mountains, and hooded valleys.

I'm a city girl now.

If you could call Hopewellen, North Carolina, a city. Clarissa blinked hard. Big Mom was dead and she was alive. And whether she liked it or not, the nuclear dump wouldn't be built in the forgiving fluidity of Indian time—or stopped that way, either. But she wouldn't stand for the threat of a nuclear accident that could poison all the beings and destroy the land for her children's children.

Her boys' raised voices snapped Clarissa's attention back to the present.

"Only girls bring stuffed animals to camp." Martin's back was arched, his butt protruding, as he brought his face tauntingly close to his little brother's.

"Shut up, Martin." To keep his lip from trembling, Frankie stuck it out at his older brother. He'd never slept without Snowy, his threadbare stuffed kitten.

"Boys, boys," Clarissa said. "Breakfast is ready. Come on, now. I'm counting on you two to get along."

At the table, a tear slid down Frankie's cheek, so she took him into the bedroom and closed the door. When she pulled him in for a hug, inhaling his warm, little-boy smells, he began to cry.

"Frankie, I bet all the other nine-year-olds are worried about the same thing. Look. We can wrap this shirt around Snowy and no one will see him, but you'll know he's there."

"I don't have room for all my stuff then." He drew a ragged breath.

"Sure you do, Baby. Let's see what you've got here."

Quickly, she helped Frankie consolidate. Then she spent a little extra time with Martin, whom she knew was going through a similar struggle in spite of his manly twelve-year-old posturing. By the time they got to the Y, the bus was already loaded with kids and gear. It was just as well—prolonged goodbyes wouldn't have helped.

As the bus pulled away, Clarissa squared her shoulders and set her jaw. She had almost two full days to figure out what to do about the nuclear dump slated to be built not far from Hopewellen. Nuclear waste was to be hauled in from seven states, inviting nuclear accidents on every major thoroughfare in North Carolina and encouraging terrorist attack. She knew she had to stop it. What she didn't know was: how?

With the boys away, she could think.

The morning, however, brought no inspiration, no ideas, not even the germ of a plan. The walls of her steaming second-floor apartment closed in and her efforts yielded nothing but a slamming headache. Without telling herself why, she put on a crisp white halter-dress and went for a walk. Now she was massaging her temples in a dark, chilly, neighborhood lounge while outside the sun was melting even the air.

How can one woman stop a nuclear dump?

Perching primly on the barstool nearest the wall, she tried to look as if she were at home in the Back Street Bar. Eight years ago, she'd have blended in perfectly.

"I'd like a brandy, please," she said. "In a snifter."

No matter how hard she tried, she hadn't come up to her own expectations. So she might as well go back—all the way back—to her old ways. But when her brandy arrived, she stared into it and didn't drink.

Sometimes I feel like a motherless child, a long way from home.

Which I am.

She pulled herself down with the familiar words of the old spiritual, a remnant from her Bible-thumping ex-husband, Ray. The Ray of Hope who turned out to be Ray the Dope. Ray was probably out there witnessing right now, one hand around the waist of a woman half his age, the other fingering the flask in his suit pocket. He'd be carrying on about the Lord but his mind would be due south, wrapped around his Johnson.

What did Ray have to complain about? He thought he was oppressed because he was black. And he probably was. But at least blacks accepted him.

Try being black, Cherokee, and white. Nowhere, nobody, and invisible. Indians used the "n" word to describe her, white people just knew she couldn't be one of them, and blacks thought she was too white.

Of course black people thought Cherokee blood was cool. And, judging by their seldom-discussed pecking order, a certain amount of white blood had its advantages too—but only up to a point that Clarissa's strange mix seemed to cross. So they called her "zebra" and "honky."

She swirled her brandy and watched it glide back down to the bottom of the glass. The first sip would burn at the back of her throat.

... a motherless child... .

Clarissa longed for the mother she couldn't remember, the one who'd left her with Big Mom as a newborn, the woman who had the skills to help her in the ways of the world as Big Mom couldn't.

After all, her mother had sent money to the reservation for her and her Cherokee grandmother. Regularly. Plenty of it, too. To have that much to give away, her mother must have at least figured out how to stand up for herself. But then again, why not?

She was white.

~ ~ ~

"Hey there, Serenity!"

Serena hated surprise visits from the neighbors, but this time an interruption might be a good thing. She'd been fretting about her daughter all day.

How am I going to find out where you are, Clarissa?

I can't ask anyone on the reservation.

Every relative you have would call you before I got the chance.

I want to be the one to tell you I want to see you.

Travis bumped along Serena's driveway on his vintage John Deere tractor, then crossed the field to where she was spreading compost in one of her vegetable gardens. Sunlight glinted off his tanned forearms and the fringe of white hair that stuck out straight below his cap.

Serena straightened from her work and threw down her hoe. She flipped her thin white braids behind her, arched her wiry back, and dug her knuckles hard into the base of her spine. Like a rain soaked hound, she shook herself from head to toe. Then she growled.

Fifty-nine is too damned old to be working this hard.

She moved toward Travis in her best imitation of an easy stride. In her eight years on Mother's Mountain, she'd proudly resisted hiring help, installing electricity or a telephone, or putting in running water. Of course she could easily afford to build an extravagant estate on the ridge and light up every tree on the mountain like Christmas at Macy's. But living simply had been a relief and an adventure—especially after the disturbing entanglements of academia. She was no longer under attack by brain-dead academics for her "radical" ideas and "uncooperative" ways.

And she was proud each time she filled her odd assortment of containers at the spring and loaded her wagon with water for herself, her garden, and her dogs, cats, chickens, and rabbits. When she lit her kerosene lanterns and stoked the fire in her wood-burning stove, she felt superior. "If the rest of the monied world learned to live as I do," she often thought, "humanity would not be blindly hurtling toward extinction."

But now her back hurt and her joints creaked in the morning like the old barn door swinging on its brittle hinges. Farm work was becoming more a burden than an adventure. She was slowing down like her old Australian Shepherd, Virginia Woof, who didn't do much of anything anymore except follow patches of sunlight around the cabin floor.

Though she'd rarely admit it, Serena longed for an easier life. A life in which one could put one's feet up at the end of the day and read a book or attend to the evening news—and soak one's joints in a hot bath.

What am I grumbling about?

Look at Travis.

He's got fifteen years on me and works from dawn to dusk.

"I brung you your mail." Travis cut off his motor.

"That's kind of you."

"Couldn't help it. I took a notion when I drove by your mailbox and all. Kinda give me the allovers to see it stuffed to bulging past noon. I was afeared you'd up and done it."

"Done what?"

"Took off on your broom. Folks said they seen you." Travis's eyes crinkled. His laughter sputtered into a series of dry coughs.

"Nope. Tell them to watch out on Halloween, though."

"Best not."

"Whatever you think."

"Well, I'm mighty glad to see you up and around. Plumb near scared the fire outta me when I thought you was laid up, what with you being alone up here and all with no water and no…" Travis spit a long arc of tobacco juice. "No nothin'."

Serena couldn't help smiling. "How's Elsie?"

"They ain't a bit a tellin'. She run off to that Wal-Mart with her sisters." Travis wheezed and cackled. "Hope she saved something out. It's more'n a week before the next Social Security."

Travis's grin exposed a patchwork of tobacco-stained teeth as he leaned down and plunked her mail into her hand. Jane's letter was on top. The envelope was addressed on a computer. Good news would have been jotted exuberantly on a handwritten envelope, so Morgan had refused to see her again. She felt her face flush with anger.

Damn you, Morgan Forrester!

~ ~ ~

Halfway through his meal, Jake Miller shoved his food back in the cooler and dug his back into the old chestnut tree he was leaning against. He picked up the leather-bound journal Morgan had given him for his thirtieth birthday and ran his fingers over its buttery surface.

Staring out over the grounds of the Buchanan sisters' estate, Jake watched his mind circling back to thoughts of Morgan—though he knew he should be finishing his lunch, going over the books for his landscaping business, and placing orders during the gathering heat. Then he'd have time during the cooler evening hours to work on the ponds the Buchanans wanted done yesterday.

At first, he'd tried to discourage the sisters' plan to build an upper pond joined by a curving stream to a lower one, with the water collected in the lower pond and then pumped back up. To his way of thinking, that was trendy and contrived. Why couldn't the two ponds be separate, the larger one for swans and the smaller one for a water garden and goldfish?

But then he understood what the women had in mind. Connecting the ponds would give them a path beside a stream, a smooth walkway each could navigate on her own, Dixie with her walker and Merilee with her motorized wheelchair. Dixie had had a stroke over the holidays and was facing her first summer of being unable to push Merilee along the public path by the river.

So now Jake wanted the sisters to have their pond, even though undertaking a project of that size during peak growing season meant he'd need to hire a third worker in order to keep his other clients happy. That's another thing he should be getting on with this afternoon. Good help was hard to find, especially in the heat of summer.

He'd decided to cut a wide path along the stream so the Buchanans could move side by side for a change. The walkway would be the color of the red clay along their beloved river. When he duplicated a section of their favorite path, they'd be delighted. He envisioned sycamore, river birch, hackberry, mimosa, and green ash for the trees; spice bush, elderberries, and hop tree for shrubbery; willow grass and river oats for ground cover; and flowers of jewel weed, green-headed coneflower, and green dragon. He loved believing the sisters would look forward to the future growth of the new plantings and stretch themselves to keep going so they could make elderberry jam when the bushy shrubs matured.

But as much as Jake willed himself to stay focused on his projects, his heart kept returning to its favorite subject. Hoping to free himself of the emotions that claimed him all morning while he staked out the ponds, the stream, and the walkway, he picked up his journal and began to write.

Saturday, June 17th, noon

Morgan. Morgan, Morgan, Morgan. I should tell you.

But I know what you'd do and I hate it.

You'd say I should find someone else to love, someone my own age. You'd say you love Adam—though any fool can see he doesn't deserve you. You'd say you're flattered, and you love and trust me as much as anyone in this world. But, you would say, the rest is impossible.

I say, nothing is impossible. We've stood by each other for years. Who better to love?

For as long as I can remember, your sensitivity has been my cushion. It's in how you treat the life around you.

With your children, you provided support from underneath, the way a whale does when she nudges her calf to its first breath. You placed what they needed within reach, yet far enough away to require a stretch. So they felt supported and loved, yet independent.

I wanted a mother like you.

But I never wanted you to be my mother. Even then, the soft curve of your hips would stir feelings in me that had nothing to do with a child's longings.

How many times have I ached to feel the weight of your breasts in my hands, to touch the rhythm of your heart beneath their softness? To caress the back of your neck with my lips, to press my tongue into the hollows at the base of your throat, to quietly coax you to want me, to finally feel myself inside all that intensity?

All I want is to hold your face in my two hands and tell you I love you.

CHAPTER 2

there is no away

My aunt kept a bucket with a stick in it under the rain gutter. The stick is for any critters who may have fallen in, so they can crawl back out.

—Sara-Lou Klein

With the iron flying toward her skull, Morgan's instincts kicked in. She ducked and wrapped her arms tightly around her head. The iron struck both forearms before crashing to the floor. Her right arm, which took the hardest hit, instantly became some numb, useless weight that hadn't been there before. The plug snapped around and stung her leg.

Engulfed by a tidal wave of feeling, she gasped for air. Her familiar world washed away in the undertow. There were other women drowning with her, tumbling end over end, their long skirts snaking like seaweed. Then the ocean became uncannily still. One woman's legs moved lifelessly in the current like the stamens of a flower in a gentle spring breeze, her head and torso invisible beneath the flowing petals of her skirts.

Morgan blinked and came back to herself.

"How could you?" she said, her voice as quiet as the deep sea. "I gave you all that I am, Adam. I loved you."

"Then why did you make me do it?"

Why did you make me do it?

I've been with a man who could resort to that twisted cop-out?

For an instant she stood staring at him, swaying and faint, consumed by an intense desire to disappear, to die, to be swallowed up by the sea. Instead, she drew a lungful of air and willed herself to act.

She nailed Adam in place with her eyes. Keeping her distance from him, she moved swiftly around the periphery of his house, gathering up her things. Hairbrush, diaphragm jelly and case, toothbrush, deodorant, underwear, bra, panties, purse, everything from last night shoved in her overnight bag.

She was stuffing her dress in the bag when she realized she was still naked. Swiftly, she pulled the dress over her head, cramming her large breasts into a rough approximation of the right position. Her wounded arm throbbed, but was following orders.

I can't think about my pain right now.

He stayed quiet, so she dared to glance over his piles of junk to see if there was anything else she needed. Morgan made sure nothing was ever between her and the door. She wanted to believe he wouldn't attack her again, but animal instinct told her not to bet her life on it.

I won't ever be back.

They'd never recapture those lazy days tangled in the sheets, laughing until the tears came. Or press their nakedness together and join forces in an almost desperate need to be so close that nothing could come between them. The sandy feel of his face, the tilt of his head, the square line of his jaw, the tiny, vulnerable sound he made just before he came… it was all gone.

How could she, who prized peace, have chosen a man who could assault her? Just yesterday, saying goodbye to her fuzzy-faced boy as he left to spend the summer with his father, she'd gently rubbed circles into his chest the way she had since he was a baby. For fifteen years this had been her way of reminding Ian's body not to close off his sensitivity as he grew into a man. Then there was her daughter Sierra—strong and fine—now gloriously pregnant with her first baby.

I exposed my children to this man!

On the outside, Morgan was moving decisively. But inside, she struggled against an overwhelming undertow. She was pushing to behave as though she were steady, on course, while internally she was being tossed like a doll in the waves. She had to hold it together until she got home. She could drown then.

Pack.

Get to the car.

Be safe.

Her cobalt blue vase. Not in a million years would she leave that with him. With a swift, disgusted motion, she seated the vase quickly but carefully in her bag. Three books off the bookshelf. She held his eyes. His keys were on the shelf by the door. She snatched his key to her place off the ring and stuffed it in her bag.

"Oh, right," Adam said. "Make a scene as if you're leaving forever. You think you're threatening me. But guess what? I'm not buying it."

He took a step forward. She stopped him by pointing her finger like a gun.

"Go ahead," He said. "Play your little game. When you're ready to talk this over like a big girl, let me know."

Get me out of here.

Her eyes inventoried the dozens of gifts she'd given him. Mostly they were only bits of nature from walks they'd taken. A rock here, a shell there. The hurt little girl inside wanted to snatch all these tokens away. But something deeper wouldn't permit that indignity. She would take the feather. It was the only truly big feather she'd ever found.

Why did I give it to you?

You never cared about it, and it means so much to me.

She backed toward the door.

"I can't believe you're doing this," he shouted. "We have a boat reservation at the lake. I've already paid for it!"

Suddenly it was easier to leave.

"I can't sail alone!" He was actually whining.

The slow motion film clip of an approaching tidal wave began to play. She had to be in her car, down the road, and home before it hit.

When her heel hit the threshold, she risked one last sweep of his home and a silent goodbye. The light outdoors was blinding after the dark interior of his place and the crushing heat of the Piedmont engulfed her. She backed a few steps in the direction of the car.

Now that she was out of his sight, she sensed his anger gathering. She remembered how the women at the battered women's shelter spoke of the buildup to violence as a gradual accumulation of tension, like sex. Once the explosion was over, they'd be safe, maybe even in a honeymoon period, until the tension built again. Unless, of course, they left. That was the most dangerous time, the time when a woman was most likely to be killed.

She turned and ran, terrified he'd come tearing out of the house and rush her, overpowering her before she could get away. Her gold Saturn was her salvation. She leaped in, her right arm pounding, praying she could make it out of the isolation of Adam's long wooded driveway before he came after her.

Her jaw relaxed at the sound of the locks snapping shut when she turned her key in the ignition. Drawing a long breath, she backed the car to turn around.

But before she could complete the motion, Adam exploded out of the house naked—his penis waggling—wielding a fireplace poker.

Morgan floored it, but not in time. The poker smashed through the glass on the passenger side, sending shards flying across the car at her.

She sped forward. Her tires kicked up a spray of gravel, causing Adam and his pet pig Sheila, who had joined in the fracas, to cry out. She almost got ahead of them. But he launched himself at the car and landed on the hood, his nose, chest, and penis momentarily flattened against the glass.

He was blocking her view. If she slowed down, he'd have a chance to raise the poker again. But if she didn't, she could hit a tree get stuck in the ditch. Either way, he had her.

No he doesn't!

His weird, crazed eyes stared into her.

Sheila, Morgan's only support, was galloping through the woods beside the driveway, squealing. Like flashing strobe lights, the glare of sunlight danced crazily through the pine saplings that flanked the rutted path on which Morgan steered her car more by instinct than by sight.

When she got to the highway Adam raised his poker to smash the windshield and her skull. Not daring to stop to check for oncoming traffic, she prayed for clear access to the road and slammed her foot on the gas pedal as she cut sharply to the right.

~ ~ ~

Had Clarissa been swirling the same glass of brandy for hours? Though the Back Street Bar was vast compared to her apartment, she felt even more closed in here. The stink of stale beer and dead cigarettes sickened her, so she brought the liquor close and inhaled deeply again and again, willing the fumes to grab her. When the familiar compulsion to drink finally kicked in, her hand shook as she brought the glass to her lips. But an image from Big Mom's dying jolted her and she lowered the glass without drinking.

Last November when she got the call that Big Mom was gone, she had made the long drive back home to the mountains during an ice storm. She arrived to find the funeral paid for and a huge display of Calla lilies positioned on each side of Big Mom's casket. More mysterious gifts from her mother.

Even without Big Mom, Clarissa had been comforted by the sight of the rusty-roofed log cabin, chinked with river rock, and the wisteria that was pulling down the front porch while roses tugged at the back and spread across the low-slung roof.

Inside the cabin, she noticed immediately that two enormous double-woven, lidded baskets were already gone. Those two baskets were Big Mom's best work. Created with pale, undyed strips of river reed interwoven with strips dyed in walnut, butternut, and bloodroot, the geometrically patterned baskets were smooth to the touch and so tight they could hold water. Some auntie or another must have snatched them already.

But the old corn gathering basket was still there, the one Big Mom's grandmother had woven and used in the field. Big Mom always made everyone call it Clarissa's basket, making sure they all knew she was to have it one day.

On top of the things stacked inside was a piece of paper with "Clarissa" written on it in big letters drawn in Big Mom's shaky scrawl. Underneath, carefully folded, was her fringed white shawl, the one she wore to every ceremony and powwow. In her tiniest and most intricate basket of all, which was carefully protected by the shawl, was a white rose bud, the last of the season. Clarissa's eyes filled when she saw it. Big Mom's last thoughts had been of her.

To one side of the small basket, reverently wrapped first in red cotton cloth, then in hand-beaded buckskin, were two tail feathers from a red-tailed hawk.

She had been amazed that Big Mom had passed this medicine on to her instead of to one of her full-blood daughters. And now Big Mom came in dreams, urging her to wield those feathers to protect the earth. Somehow she was supposed to stop big money and the government from destroying the land for future generations.

But how?

She laughed out loud, causing the bartender to look at her.

Go wash glasses.

Keep your pity for some poor drunk who needs it.

She brought the brandy to her nose and sniffed.

I bet my mother would never catch herself sitting alone in a bar, bitter and confused.

And if her dream was to fight this damned nuclear dump, she would just go ahead and do it.

When she gazed into the tawny liquid, she saw Big Mom reflected in the brandy and snorted at the irony of this illusion. What would the patrons of the Back Street Bar think of this so-called sister, this honey-skinned zebra, if they knew she was haunted by an ancient, round, Cherokee elder? A woman with two hawk feathers she used to heal the neighbors and white hair that had once fallen to her knees in thick braids the color of a raven?

What patrons?

Clarissa looked around and realized it was still early afternoon. She began eating from the bucket of peanuts in front of her. The only other customer was a hunched little man with skin like a raisin and white stubble. Through blood-shot, rheumy eyes, he stared at her over his bottle and shot glass from a small table at the back of the bar.

He's trying to figure out what race I am.

She hated her fine, black ringlets that refused to go either straight or nappy and therefore had to be kept short, like a dark cloud around her head. She could never find a stylist who knew anything else to do. She knew her broad nose and lips told the old man she had Negro blood. But her caramel skin told him she was more white than black.

As if I'll ever be able to cash in on that.

Her thoughts drifted back to Big Mom. Now there was a woman who would never set foot in a bar. Too worried about turning into a drunken Indian. But then again, Big Mom wouldn't exactly be out there getting the job done with this stupid dump, either. She had all the aggression of a mourning dove.

Why did you have to die on me?

How am I supposed to raise two boys on my own?

How can I bring them up to be fine black men when I was reared on an Indian reservation and the only man they know, their father, is off carrying on with any woman he can get his hands on?

How am I supposed to teach in an overcrowded, drug-ridden public school, raise two children, and keep it all together with no family behind me?

And how am I supposed to stop the creation of a nuclear dump when no one else seems to care?

Guilt stabbed Clarissa's heart like an arrow.

Her mouth tightened and she fought back the burn of unshed tears.

Suddenly she could swear she felt Big Mom's strong hands on her shoulders, propelling her away from the bar.

"Talk to your elders," she heard Big Mom say in the round, measured tones of a tongue more accustomed to Cherokee than English. Her tone, though gentle as always, had the quiet force Big Mom used when she insisted that Clarissa pay attention.

She had always wondered how Big Mom's voice could resonate with so much power and at the same time be reassuring and… innocent. It was a voice that stopped your soul. She'd never gone against Big Mom's wishes when she used that tone.

Through the dark veil of her pain, Clarissa felt the steady beacon of Big Mom's loving spirit. She pushed herself away from the bar, went to the pay phone on the wall, and called Flo, her sponsor from Narcotics Anonymous.

"Girl, you get your black ass to a meeting!" Flo yelled so loudly Clarissa wondered if the bartender heard. "And don't you stop there, Miss Thang! You need you some counseling."

She had to hold the phone away from her ear.

Counseling?

"I'm talking about now." Flo's voice was even louder. "You've got a lot of shit with you, Honey. You better fix that dump in your head before you worry about the nuclear."

Clarissa was silent.

"Who you gonna call?"

She found herself focusing on the pattern in the paneled walls.

"I'm waiting!" Flo's normally deep voice was shrill. She could almost hear Flo drumming her fingers while Clarissa pulled open the yellow pages.

Big Mom, guide me.

Her hands were shaking, but she let her finger fall on one of the names listed under counseling, Morgan Forrester.

"Now, I've heard of her. She supposed to be good. You call her the minute you hang up this phone, hear? Monday, girl, Monday. You see Miz Morgan Forrester first thing Monday morning."

"I don't feel right leaving the boys."

"Don't you be talking that stuff with me, Clarissa. I mean it. You up to your skinny neck in fry grease. And you know it. Mm, mmm, mmmm."

She could hear Flo's breath blowing across the receiver.

"And you get yourself up out of that bar. What you thinking about? Eight years clean and sober, sitting up on a barstool with nothing but a big old brandy?"

Clarissa felt the sting in her eyes as she pressed her forehead against the cool metal of the telephone box. "I didn't drink."

"Good. See that you don't. Now you go home and make you a gratitude list." Flo was still shouting. "That's what you need, Baby. An attitude of gratitude. I'll see you at the meeting tonight."

Reluctantly, Clarissa wrote down Morgan Forrester's number. Something had gotten into Flo. Whoever heard of a black woman going to therapy? Or an Indian, for that matter. Fear gathered in her throat like a thirst.

Does Flo think I'm crazy?

Or is she just sick of me?

She had only this one weekend to decide whether to trash her life or try to save it one more time. Martin and Frankie would be back tomorrow night. She shouldn't be thinking the way she was, with two boys to raise. Good mothers don't sit in bars contemplating suicide. And suicide is exactly what it would be if she picked up that drink. She'd never stop drinking and her life would be as good as over.

The bartender had cleared away her brandy, which hardly made it feel like a choice, so she ordered another. She ceremoniously cleared the peanut shells from the space in front of her and put the drink on one side of her and Morgan Forrester's phone number on the other.

❧ ❧ ❧

With a stride that made her tiny frame feel seven feet tall, Serena headed for her compact cabin. Hermaphrodite, her elegantly tuxedoed cat, scooted in the door just ahead of her. She picked up her stack of mail and pitched the catalogs and junk mail into the wood stove, tossing all correspondence labeled "Revocable Trust of Serena" into a box in the corner.

I wonder if Travis knows I'm a trust baby.

Frowning, she fingered her unopened letter from Jane, the one with the news about Morgan. She wanted to fling it in the wood stove almost as much as she wanted to tear it open and devour it whole. But she made herself do chores first.

A few years back, she had made a rain reservoir on the roof out of an old barrel and rigged up a hose that brought water down to the kitchen sink. Because of the plentiful rainfall in the mountains combined with her own moderation, she almost always had enough water for her daily dishes and sponge bath. She filled the huge iron kettle with the hose and seated it heavily on the back of the wood stove to warm for her bath later.

Serena decided on spaghetti for dinner. Something easy. It would take awhile to heat water for the noodles since the fire was just getting started, so she pulled down a large frying pan. Its larger surface would boil the water more quickly.

Using drinking water from the plastic jugs into which she decanted water after she brought it up from the spring, she filled the fryer half full. She then dished up food and water and set them out on the porch where her black lab, mutt shepherd, and five cats had already gathered. Hermie and Virginia Woof she fed inside.

The most urgent tasks out of the way, she grabbed Jane's letter from her end table—an overturned cable spool she'd saved since the sixties—and plopped herself down on the royal purple leather of the Danish modern rocker.

She had paid eight thousand dollars for the rocker and accompanying ottoman on a rare shopping binge in Manhattan the day her mother died of breast cancer. That day, Serena also bought an original Degas in a six-inch wide gold frame and twelve cases of Italian hand-painted ceramic tiles that still stood in a corner of the barn in their original boxes, gathering dust.

She laid Jane's letter across her thighs and smoothed it with both hands. Her mind drifted back twenty-five years to her sunlit office at Temple University where she had pored over papers while her favorite student—the one for whom she had such plans—studied beside her.

Morgan.

If only she could go back, capture one of those seemingly endless days, and rewrite the history that followed so she never lost Morgan's friendship.

Either that, or fix it so now she didn't care.

But she couldn't let it go, so she had to make it right. It was as if they were goddesses in a myth, she and Morgan, with the fate of the heavens resting on whether or not they reconciled. The two of them and her lovely daughter, Clarissa.

My Pearl.

Pearl was her pet name for Clarissa, her pearl of a girl, locked away from her in a shell of Serena's own creation.

But I can't think about Clarissa now.

She carefully opened the letter and began to read.

June 12th

Dear Serena,

By now you must be very busy with your vegetable garden....

"Come on, come on!" she thought as she skimmed down the page.

I'm sorry, Serena, but I can't help you. I keep trying to get Morgan interested in seeing you, but it's not working....

She leaped up from her chair.

"Are you insane, Morgan Forrester?"

Hermie dove under the bed.

It was as impossible to patch things up with Morgan as it was to make herself go hunting for her daughter. The irony was that the last time she'd heard, Clarissa lived in Hopewellen, the same town where Morgan had established her counseling practice. But that was years ago when Clarissa first got married—she could be anywhere now. If only she'd acted back then, she could have simply marched into Hopewellen and made both Morgan and Clarissa deal with her instead of burying herself alive on this stupid mountain and refusing to allow Big Mom to tell her anything about Clarissa except whether or not she and the boys were all right.

Serena sank back into the rocker.

Big Mom. Clarissa would still be mourning her death. With two boys to raise. Alone.

Clarissa, I'm so sorry.

You need your mother now, and all I can think about is how devastated I'd be if you rejected me.

I'm as selfish as ever.

She wadded up the letter and threw it across the room. It ricocheted off the wall and bounced off Woof, who looked up with concern in her dark eyes.

I'm a coward.

She sighed deeply, glanced sideways at Woof, buried her head in her hands, and tugged on the hair at her temples.

Do you hate me for leaving you, Clarissa?

Things were so different then. Unmarried Irish Catholic girls, New York society debutantes, never got pregnant. Never.

A colored baby.

That's what they would have called you.

Back then, a child with your luminous skin, your complexion like a golden pearl, was unthinkable.

There would have been no place for us.

And hate me for this if you want to, but I wanted my doctorate more than I wanted to breathe.

It was my one-way ticket out of hell.

Her eyes darted across the tiny room. Barely registering the leaning bookcases and the piles of papers, books, and assorted junk strewn across the grayed pine floors, she suddenly felt young, afraid, and alone. She'd been terrified of giving up her dreams and falling in line the way her mother had. Her mother always said that having Serena robbed her of the opportunity to be somebody.

I had to live with her bitterness every day of her miserable life.

She sat up straight and squared her shoulders.

I couldn't do that to us, not once I tasted freedom at the university and with your father and Big Mom.

There hadn't been many female academics back then, and it had been a long, hard climb each step of the way.

If I'd kept you, I never would have made it.

I had to leave you with Big Mom, where you'd fit in.

I did it for you.

Serena released a long sigh and leaned back.

Hell, I did it for me.

She had stayed out of Clarissa's life so her presence wouldn't confuse either of them and took care of Clarissa the only way she knew how—she'd sent money. A continuous stream of money. What choice did she have?

Clarissa, is it too late?

Can you forgive me for not wanting to keep you?

Can you give me a chance to make things right between us, to learn how to be the mother you need?

We could be something to each other now, I think.

After all, I am your mother—how different can we be?

CHAPTER 3

steps

There's no away to throw things to…

—Jean Mountaingrove

"What about the pig?" It was the female cop talking. Officer Briggs, according to her badge.

On her drive home—during which Morgan had scanned her rear view mirror as religiously as she'd willed herself to focus on the road—she used her cell phone to report Adam to the police. Then she called her dear friend Jane.

Now one officer was searching her property, the other was trying to tell her what the police had already discovered at Adam's place, and Jane was standing beside the car, her eyes tight with concern behind coke bottle glasses. Jane's lank black hair twitched as she scanned the wide sweep of Morgan's front lawn, searching for any sign of Adam.

Morgan turned off the ignition. Suddenly overwhelmed by exhaustion, the throbbing in her arm, and the knowledge that she was finally safe, she flopped back on the car seat.

"Watch out for the glass shards, Ma'am," Officer Briggs said.

"Thank you." She'd forgotten that Adam smashed the window, even though steamy air blew at her all the way home. "The pig you're talking about is Sheila, Adam's pet."

"Not anymore, Ma'am. Skull's bashed in. The pig is dead."

The color drained out of the greenery and people surrounding her and the image of drowning engulfed her again. In the film clip that flickered in her mind, she was one of many, lifeless women thrashed by a violent sea.

The vague but unmistakable sense of a dark, shadowy presence next to her in the car startled her. This was that old feeling, the one that used to come in times of dread, first when she was a child and then later, when she remembered the real reason she hated her father. Invisible eyes were boring into her and the thing grabbed her heart and twisted hard.

"Back off, Shadow," Morgan said.

"Ms. Forrester?" Officer Briggs said.

"Breathe, Morgan." Jane was crouching next to the car. She laid a steadying palm on Morgan's thigh.

"Ms. Forrester, what can you tell us about the pig?" Briggs said. She'd been joined by Sinclair, a male officer.

"She was wonderful." The tears were coming now, slowly, from some well deep in her chest. "I loved her."

The officers exchanged looks.

"Mandrake's not at his residence. His car's missing," Sinclair said. "We put out an APB on the Mercedes."

Inside her vast Victorian, the officers positioned Morgan in front of the opulent display of white gladiolas Jake had placed in her foyer the morning before. Then they photographed the wounds the iron made on her arms and the tiny nicks from flying glass that peppered her face, neck, arms, and hands.

How exquisitely ironic.

Nothing but the best—an elegant floral backdrop for the battered woman.

She, the victim—not the criminal—was posing for mug shots. They even had her holding a number. Whoever trained these two really ought to know better.

Jane grimaced, then made soothing noises. Even with her support, Morgan was losing it. After the third flash went off, she shifted her focus to how the officers' bellies protruded below their belts. The man was shaped like Humpty Dumpty, except where his belt cinched him in.

The police were going to arrest Adam. He'd be in jail for the night, at least.

Below her belt, the woman's belly formed two soft mounds that aligned with her breasts. Maybe she'd had a Caesarean that divided her like that.

There would be a trial and Morgan would be asked to testify.

It must be so uncomfortable to wear polyester in summer.

The police would double up on their rounds by her house. They'd let her know once they had Adam in custody.

How can she feel attractive in those clothes?

Morgan held it together until the officers left, then bolted the door behind them and sank to the floor, sobbing. She shook her head from side to side but couldn't escape the image of her body floating face down on a shimmering, sunlit sea, while the bodies of other women gently bobbed on the small ripples around her.

Jane crouched close beside her, stroking her hair.

"My god, Jane, why did I report Adam? He hates the police."

"I think you're safer this way."

"What if he comes here?"

"Do you think he will?"

"I don't know."

Jane stood and offered Morgan her hand.

"Let's take care of that arm."

She let Jane lead her to the bathroom.

"Thank you, Jane. Thank you."

Fifteen years ago, when Morgan left Pennsylvania and a marriage that had slowly fizzled into a tedium that was sucking the breath from her body, she'd scooped up her children and moved to Hopewellen, seeking refuge with Grandmama, her savior. Jane, who had been her college roommate, was too traditional for the California scene she'd been putting up with since graduation and landed a job at the university in Hopewellen shortly after Morgan moved here. Now Jane was married, childless, and thoroughly entrenched in academia.

But though their lifestyles had taken them in different directions, they thought of each other first in times of trouble or celebration.

Once her cuts were disinfected and the raw flesh on her right arm bandaged, they entered the cool forest green sanctuary of her living room. Jane scurried off in search of cold packs and Morgan sank into the velvet cushions that lined Grandmama's couch. Though she expected Adam to kick down the front door at any moment, Morgan took off her shoes and pushed the soles of her feet into the cool oak floor, soothing her psyche with the swirling designs and rich colors of the ferns, flowers, and berries that decorated the fabric on the recently upholstered furniture across from her. Jungle ferns filled every corner and swayed gently in response to the fan high overhead.

I'm home.

In Grandmama's sanctuary.

Surely Adam's evil can't follow me here.

Bit by bit, she'd painstakingly created this house exactly to her liking after Grandmama died three years ago. For the first time in her life, she hadn't had to consider anyone's wishes but her own. She'd redone every room in the old Victorian except Grandmama's bedroom, which she kept exactly as it was when Grandmama was alive, including the old canopy bed, settee, secretary, and the massive key that hung in a frame on the wall.

Grandmama always said the key was to the family plantation, "before the war," words that in Grandmama's rich accent rhymed with "boa." She was referring to the Civil War. Or, as Grandmama called it, the War of Northern Aggression.

Throughout the rest of the house, Morgan pulled off the ancient floral wallpaper and added strong, vibrant colors. Grandmama wouldn't have begrudged her that, even though she was replacing the gentile tradition of the worn and ancient with an upscale look.

"You young people do things differently," Grandmama would have said, her voice resonant with pride and understanding.

When Jane returned, she brought one towel to spread across Morgan's lap and another to wrap an ice pack. Morgan sank her arm into the welcome coolness and Jane snuggled in beside her on the couch.

"I've been forking my heart over to a sociopath," Morgan said. "But I thought I'd evolved past this kind of mess. So why am I still here?"

"Nature abhors a vacuum?"

"What do you mean?"

"Is it enough to release the old emotional pattern? Don't you have to put something new in its place?"

"Touché. You should be the therapist." She was silent for a long time. "My life is supposed to mean something, Jane."

"It does!"

"You don't understand. I'm a thoroughbred racehorse, stuck plowing fields. Good honest work—true—but I ache to run the Derby. I was born for it. Don't you see? I need to be totally used up." Morgan arced her arms high above her head, forming the shape of a large bowl, though she couldn't help wincing at the pain the gesture brought. "And I don't mean by men. My life has to count for something. I want to make a difference more than I want to breathe. I must. I have to."

"You make a difference to me! And to your children and your clients, your friends—"

"Thank you." Her eyes moved to the framed photograph on the table beside her, a light-filled black and white of herself with Ian and Sierra on a whale watch. An elongated clay sculpture of a pregnant woman stood next to the picture, her belly as taut and swollen as her beautiful daughter's soon would be. "I'm grateful for the life I have, and I don't take any of you for granted." She drew a long breath. "But it's not enough."

They were silent. Then Morgan said, "There's something I was born to do, to know, to give, to experience. And I'm not doing it."

"Maybe you should give up sex for awhile," Jane said.

Morgan whipped her head around and stared at her friend. "But I love sex! It's my religion."

"Have you eaten anything today?"

"No." Morgan caught the irritation in Jane's voice but didn't want to get into it.

"I'll go fix us something."

Morgan reminded herself of what she told her clients. Even when you're down, you need to nourish the ones you love, especially when they're supporting you. Stay involved at the very time when you feel like snarling and retreating to your den. Connect. It keeps you in the game.

"Thanks." She paused. "Jane, I love you."

Jane smiled.

They drifted into the kitchen and Jane began chopping vegetables.

Great.

A healthy meal.

Just when I need some serious junk food.

"Maybe the universe closed this door so I could open another," Morgan said.

Jane's chopping became too hard, too fast.

"What is it?" Morgan said.

"There's something I can offer you, but I know you'll refuse."

"What's that?"

"Serena. She could help."

"Serena? I don't think so." Morgan tried to keep her voice light.

"You'd be surprised." Jane stopped chopping and studied her face. "Serena is very knowledgeable about the imbalances between men and women."

"Come on." She tried to be soft from the inside. Jane was being so generous, she didn't feel comfortable indulging the irritation she always felt when Jane raised the subject of Serena. "How could I bring up something that hurts so much to a woman I haven't spoken to in years?"

"Try to keep an open mind. Serena still cares about you, more than you know. And she's easier to get along with than she used to be."

"Ha! How easy can she be? A multimillionaire who hordes all her money except for one minor purchase, a *mountain?* Talk about pushing people away! And living in a shack?"

"I never said it was a shack. It's a cabin. It's simple."

"With an outhouse,"

"And an inhouse."

Morgan tried not to sneer. But she couldn't suppress a flood of warmth at the memory of how good it used to be to talk with her old mentor.

"The point is, she could help you with this," Jane said.

Who says I need help?

"Shouldn't you stay at my house tonight?" Jane said.

"I'll be okay. I need to stand my ground."

"The idea of you here alone scares me."

"Adam will probably spend the night in jail."

"Yeah, but what if he doesn't."

Suddenly three loud raps echoed through the house. The doorbell began to ring repeatedly. Someone banged on the door with something bigger and harder than a hand.

They whipped around and searched each other's eyes.

"My God," Morgan said, "the police haven't called. Adam's still out there."

They reached out to each other and stood transfixed, like two does in the headlights of a rapidly approaching vehicle.

❧ ❧ ❧

Still angry about Jane's letter, Serena grated Parmesan cheese over her spaghetti and tried to be interested in her food. What right did Morgan have to turn down her olive branch?

After all these years, you'd think she might give a little.

But then, why am I obsessed about seeing her?

It's as if some weird destiny is pulling us together.

I don't like it.

In her mind, the image of the Morgan she'd known—a quarter of a century ago—was as vivid as the layered blue mountains on the horizon she gazed upon. She could still see sunlight slanting in through the window of her old office at Temple University, catching the red tints in Morgan's long waves of auburn hair and causing them to crackle with fire.

They had tossed ideas back and forth with electrifying intensity. Following unexpected twists of thought, they darted like kayakers in white water, plunging dazzling depths of insight, cold water splashing their faces and clean air filling their lungs.

Or they would turn over their impressions slowly, savoring them with lazy precision like two cats stretching themselves on the back of a sun-drenched couch. Sometimes Jane would join them.

Serena chased a broccoli leaf around the rim of her plate.

There had never been another student like Morgan, before or since. Secretly, Serena had been paving the way for Morgan's graduate work. She'd have had a brilliant career in philosophy ahead of her.

Morgan approached history from unique angles, speculated about the future with rare intuitive ability, and had the skill to interpret the present in its pivotal relationship between the past and the future. Together, they would have taught the world to think.

If only that clod Rex hadn't come along. Rex wasn't bad to look at, she'd give him that. But that was the extent of it. She never dreamed he could cause so much trouble. Serena raised a forkful of spaghetti to her mouth. But instead of eating, she returned it to her plate.

God, I wish I hadn't slept with him!

Who would have dreamed that Morgan would actually take him seriously?

Once before, they had inadvertently come close to sharing a lover. They both thought it was funny—certainly not significant enough to interfere with their intellectual bond. They met on higher ground.

Serena thought then, as she did now, that monogamy was an antiquated, stifling system, a mere contrivance to keep women in line and shackle them to homes, children, and dishwashers.

Monogamy would have no place in the new order in which all we have is now. Now. Now. And now. The ever new, always changing, now. That's what she'd told herself and her students.

It was very Zen.

She had discussed her thoughts about monogamy with Morgan countless times. She thought they were of one mind.

So when Serena blundered into her brief encounter with Rex—whom she considered to be a pretty boy with a nice body but not much going on upstairs—it hadn't occurred to her that Morgan's getting there first might be a problem. She'd thought she and Morgan would compare notes on Rex and have a good laugh. By the time she grasped that Morgan was seriously involved with him, it was too late.

The air from the open window moved across her arms, raising goose bumps. But she didn't get up to pull on a sweater.

Eat this damned spaghetti before it gets cold.

She shuddered with a memory that chilled her more than than the breeze, the memory of the day everything between her and Morgan went up in flames.

Morgan had discovered she was carrying Rex's baby on the same day she found out about Serena's affair with him. She quit coming to Serena's class, switched majors from philosophy to psychology, married Rex, and never spoke to her again. Morgan hadn't even cared enough to have it out with her. She had refused Serena's calls and marked the letters Serena sent her with large, block letters, "Return to Sender."

It's all my fault.

If I hadn't made her so angry by sleeping with that drone, maybe she'd have listened to me and gotten an abortion or put the baby up for adoption—something.

Then she wouldn't have wasted her life on a husband and kids.

And switching to psychology!

What a colossal misuse of her talent.

The only thing the field of psychology had going for it was the money, a pedestrian concern if ever there was one. Morgan had abandoned the lofty realm of ideas for the messy cesspool of human emotion. Serena jumped up and paced the tiny room, skirting piles of junk and assorted projects, then came back to the table.

For years, she'd had nightmares about Morgan with her hair in rollers, ironing Rex's shirts and washing diapers in between showing up in some dingy office to nurse along a flock of headcases who had nothing more productive to do than ponder themselves and their misery.

Morgan would be fixing dinner for her robotic husband and a horde of noisy, demanding children. For her evening break, she'd balance the family checkbook. Serena blamed herself for causing Morgan's free spirit to drown in the rancid stew of marriage, children, and psychology. It was her fault Morgan's broken dreams were scattered and forgotten.

"There isn't much time," Serena said to Virginia Woof, who was sitting at her feet gazing up at her.

Woof thumped her tail.

"No, Woof, I'm serious. For some reason that's bigger than both of us—don't ask me what—Morgan and I must work together again."

Woof cocked her head.

"I know you think I'm crazy, but I know—better than I know I'm sitting on a mountain all by myself talking to a dog—that all of creation wants Morgan and me together. Now."

Woof lowered herself to the floor and let out a long sigh.

"But I don't know how to make that happen."

While Woof snored softly, Serena sat shivering with her head bent, twisting strands of spaghetti round and round on her fork without bringing them to her mouth.

~ ~ ~

Morgan got 911 on the cordless, crept to the front door, and peeked through the peephole.

"My God," she said, backing up and tripping over Jane, who was hovering at her shoulder. "Are you ready for this? It's Aunt Lee."

They collapsed on each other's shoulders and snickered with relief. The doorbell began to sound again, along with the incessant rapping, and Morgan—who felt extremely foolish—got rid of 911.

"She's banging on the door with her cane." They went weak with laughter.

She recovered somewhat and opened the door. Aunt Lee Montrose pushed her four foot, ten inch frame past her, pale wig askew and "Jesus Saves" rhinestone pin twinkling on the collar of her navy and white polka dot dress with white ruffles. It was the attire of a demented schoolgirl in the days of black and white.

In one hand Aunt Lee grasped her cracked and peeling white patent leather purse and the rhinestone-studded maroon cane she leaned on. In her other hand was a pie carrier she handed to Morgan.

Aunt Lee patted her face. "I just love to see my Peach Blossom laugh." Her dentures dropped and smacked as she spoke in her tinkling, musical drawl. "Mighty pleased to see you, too, Jane. I got me some Elberta peaches up from Georgia." She glanced at the bandage on Morgan's arm and the small cuts that dotted the right side of her face, looked piercingly into her eyes for a second, frowned, then seemed to put what she saw out of her mind.

"My cousin William, twice removed, and his wife Amanda Lynne brought them by my place on their way to Virginia. Naturally, I had to make me a peach pie for my Peach Blossom." Aunt Lee pinched Morgan's chin, then tapped her way into the living room. "Minty green! I do believe your Grandmama would have approved of that."

She was about to seat herself when Morgan suggested she come to the dining room and eat with them.

"Y'all go ahead, I couldn't eat a bite. I'll sit down with you, though. Now what did you say that color was?" Aunt Lee said, pointing her cane at the walls of the dining room.

"That's brick." She raised her voice to be sure Aunt Lee could hear her. "And the trim is pewter gray."

"It's mighty nice. Yes indeedy. Modern. Better than that old Wisteria vine print, I imagine. Why, it had stains from when your grandmama was a girl! Besides, it was peeling." She smiled, but her voice was wistful.

They were just getting seated—with steaming rice, stir-fried vegetables, peach pie, and tea laid out on the table—when Morgan heard something at the front of the house. This time the knock on the door was quiet, like a test to see if anyone was listening.

CHAPTER 4

what she takes

i move through fogs of mystery
with tiny steps
on the way to meet myself.

—Pandora

Morgan crept to the front door, grabbing Ian's baseball bat. Jane followed, cell phone in hand. Morgan's head told her the sound at the door was what to expect from Adam as predator—probing and intelligent, gathering information before making his move.

But her sensory radar—the ball of energy in her belly that was relaxed and breathing instead of clenched and hard—detected help, not danger, on the other side of the door.

The peephole revealed a round distortion of Jake Miller's face. Jane returned to Aunt Lee and Morgan swung the door wide.

"Vidalias?" Jake said, intentionally adding honey to his drawl. He held up a heavy sack of onions on his forefinger and raised one brow. He knew she craved the seasonal treat. Vidalias were sweet and she ate them like apples.

"Did you know you left your car window open?" With the crisp clarity of an autumn sky, Jake's eyes leaped out of his sun-toned face. She felt her throat close at the sight of him. His scent, warm and woodsy, was so comforting she almost lost it.

"It's not open, it's broken."

He dropped his smile. "Are you all right?" He glanced at her arm and face and moved toward her protectively.

She stepped back. "Better than I was. Do you mind covering the window with plastic before you leave?" She wanted to let go, fall into his arms. But she didn't.

"Of course not. Were you in an accident?"

"No."

He double-bolted the door behind him, nodded a quick "hey" to Aunt Lee and Jane, and went to the kitchen to drop off the Vidalias—an excuse, she knew, to check the back door. After he covered the car window, he seated himself easily beside Morgan and stared at her from under the waves of sun-streaked blond hair that fell across his brow and shoulders.

With Jake beside her, she could finally breathe. He'd been a member of the family since they moved to Hopewellen. Morgan and Jake had bonded deeply and immediately, doing things for each other no one else ever thought to. In the beginning, he was Ian's baby-sitter and Sierra's defender. Later, he coached Ian in sports. The boy adored him and he understood Ian's need for older males, so he visited frequently.

For her part, she'd helped him study for his S.A.T.s, complete his college applications, recover from countless heartbreaks, and accept himself when he didn't want to join the corporate world his father tried to force on him. He still took care of Grandmama's elaborate garden, a task that had become the nucleus for the interior and exterior landscaping business he developed with her help.

"Peaches, aren't you going to eat anything?" Aunt Lee said.

Morgan realized she'd been dissociating on and off since she got home, leaving her body and tripping off into the horrors—and, in this case, the comforts—of the past. She busied herself with her food while Aunt Lee worked her way through her third helping of rice and vegetables.

When Jane finally served the pie, Aunt Lee winked at Morgan, her head bobbing. "This recipe was used by my grandmama, and her grandmama before her, long before the War."

Aunt Lee was, of course, referring to the Civil War, which she often discussed as though it happened two months ago. She told them how Jesus helped her bake the pie with just the right amount of brandy. "You have to marinate the peaches for a little while. How long depends on the peaches, the temperature, and the brandy. Of course I don't drink, but the Good Lord forgives me for tasting them now and again until they're right."

Jake covered his need to laugh by asking Aunt Lee how her roses were doing. She answered him, then turned to Morgan and glanced at her arm. But she pretended not to notice.

Jake picked up on her discomfort and tried to divert Aunt Lee. "Morgan's yellow roses are coming down with black spot and she doesn't want me to use chemicals. Is there any other way?"

"Oh my yes," Aunt Lee turned reluctantly away from her and gave her a look that seemed to say, "I'm not dumb, you know."

"My mother always used that baking soda," Aunt Lee said. "You mix it with water, about a quarter cup to the gallon, and spray that on the leaves. I always mixed in a little dishwashing liquid so it would stick. Of course, you can get more work done with the one application if the water has some tobacco in it. You know, like a tea. You just take the butts from three, four packs of cigarettes and there you have it. The tobacco keeps the bugs off."

"Thank you, Ma'am, I'm mighty grateful for your help." Jake was slipping into the more traditional Southern manner of speaking he always used with his elders. "I never would have thought of that. But since no one in this house smokes, is there anything I could substitute for the tobacco?"

"We've used garlic from time to time and it works real good. Just get the powder, you know, the cheap stuff."

"How much should I use?"

"Enough so it smells." Aunt Lee threw him a look that was both shrewd and mildly sharp, as if to signal that this game was now over.

She turned to Morgan. "Peaches, I have been sitting here waiting for you to tell me about your arm."

Morgan looked into the whiteness of Aunt Lee's much loved face, with its deep lines and liver spots, and decided to tell her the truth.

"Child, you called in the law?" Aunt Lee said after she finished her story. She hadn't been able to bring herself to tell her about the dead pig.

"I may be an old woman, but I say why not just stay away from him? Lord help me, I'd be scared to death to call the law on my man, afraid he'd do me in. Besides, it was just the one time." Aunt Lee smacked her dentures and thought. Then she leaned forward, stretched her skinny arm across the table, and patted Morgan's cheek, the one which hadn't been nicked by flying glass. Her thin hand with its translucent skin was tender and cool.

Jane stirred, ready to step in. But Aunt Lee's question was a relief. It clicked on the professional part of her brain that was reliably clear. "Aunt Lee," she said, "If you and I were out for a walk and a man drove by and threw a brick that almost hit you in the head, what would you do?"

"Why, I reckon I'd have a mind to call in the law." Aunt Lee nodded to everyone present.

"Exactly. So why should I allow the man I loved to go unpunished for something I'd have a stranger arrested for? Adam committed a crime."

Aunt Lee was silent for some time. "I never thought of that," she finally said. "Still and all, isn't it dangerous? Won't he get angry and come after you?"

"Actually, it's more dangerous to do nothing. This way he knows that if anything happens to me, he'll be the first suspect. I figure Adam spending a night in jail is my best protection." She bit her lower lip.

Aunt Lee told her how clever she was and turned to Jane to elaborate on the correctness of turning Adam in, giving Jake an opportunity to whisper to Morgan. "There's more. For god sakes, tell me."

"After I left, he killed his pet pig."

He let out a hiss of breath, causing Aunt Lee to regard them with knowing concern. But she didn't press them for more information. Instead, she continued talking with Jane.

"You're getting a restraining order?" he whispered.

"I could, but I don't think I need one. I think that when Adam realizes the full implications of the number of charges he already has against him, and when his lawyer tells him how his behavior now could affect the outcome of his trial, he'll stay away from me."

"So he's in jail?" He spoke too quietly for Aunt Lee to hear.

Morgan shook her head. They exchanged a deep look.

"I had no idea he had such violence in him," Morgan said.

"It doesn't surprise me, the way he snapped at you and the kids. He's a control freak."

Morgan sank. "I was so addicted to him, I couldn't see it.

He leaned in toward her and laid one finger gently on the crook of her elbow. "Sugar, if you're addicted to something, I'd say it's to being hurt."

Her breath caught in her chest.

Is that really how it is with me?

Do I still have so far to go?

Aunt Lee turned to her. "You did the right thing, Peaches," she said. "Bless your heart. I'll be down on my knees every day asking the Good Lord for your safety, and I'll get you on our prayer list at church."

"Thank you, Aunt Lee."

What else can you say to that?

Suddenly she felt exhausted. Her guests must have picked up on it, because in no time they cleared the dining room and finished the dishes. Everyone left at once except Jake, who insisted she let him stay until she heard from the police.

"Jake, I know you're worried, but I need to be alone. I'll be fine."

When she closed the door behind him, the sound the bolt made as it slid into the doorframe seemed too loud. At the same moment she cringed from the sound, she felt a chill enter her spine from behind. She turned and leaned her weight against the door, pressing her back into the wood and using its familiar solidity to work out the fear that gripped her backbone the moment she realized she was alone.

Ian had always been in charge of generating noise in their household, with his music blasting and friends roving in and out—often in large, unruly bands. When Ian and his friends were gone, the quiet was a friendly relief that would be broken the moment he burst through the door again. Whenever he left to visit Rex, the house roared with silence. But this was the first time the stillness of her home frightened her.

I wish the police would call.

She made herself move into the living room. Even though she felt it knocking on her spine with fingers like knives, she refused to allow the dark, disapproving presence she'd felt in the car to overcome her again.

Quit it, Shadow.

I have enough trouble without you.

She was on her way to the sofa when she heard a soft thud at the back of the house. Something had dropped.

No.

Someone was there.

Her hand flew to her throat. There was another way to get to her house. In the back. Through the woods. She'd forgotten to tell the police about it.

Adam.

~ ~ ~

"It wasn't 'til I put down the drugs," James J. paused for effect, pointing his slender finger at no one in particular. "And the jugs," he went on, pounding out the beat in the air with his finger. Some members of his audience tittered. "That I got the hugs." James grinned broadly, crouching to hug the podium with his long black arms. More people laughed. "And lost the mugs." He posed, deadpan and slouching, first to the side, then to the front. Everyone in the old church basement laughed and applauded.

Except Clarissa.

These people are pathetic.

All anyone in Narcotics Anonymous seemed to care about was staying clean, sober, and out of jail.

What about the rest of the world?

What about the seventh generation to come?

If everyone worries only about themselves, what will we leave for our children?

James left the podium and was returning to his chair near Clarissa. People high-fived him along the way. When he passed her, he dropped down to her for a hug. The warmth of his cheek on hers brought her back. She was happy for him. He was a mess when he first came into the program two years ago and now he'd been working the same job for over a year and had his kids back in his life. He was a good person. She didn't begrudge him his pride in his accomplishments.

But she wanted to be clean and sober and making a contribution in the world. There was no support for that in the program. Every time she tried to get out there and do something, she got stuck. Then she hated herself for getting stuck. Then she wanted to drink.

And there wasn't anyone in N.A. who had any idea what she was talking about, except to counsel her to take things one day at a time. But one day at a time, the world was going to hell. No way was she going to stand by and watch that happen.

My mother wouldn't.

I'm sure of that.

N.A. was no help whatsoever on this one.

And that Morgan Forrester was probably just another honky do-gooder with her head up her ass.

~ ~ ~

Morgan grabbed her portable and crept silently to the back of the house to investigate the sound she'd heard. Wanting to remain unseen, she moved the curtains imperceptibly and peered out. But it was only Jake, checking the grounds.

She dropped her shoulders and rubbed the back of her neck, rolling her head. What did she want? To be clean. She filled the downstairs bathtub with warm water and herbal essences, lit candles all around the room, and put on a selection of pieces by Bach.

"This is never going to happen again," she said after her bath, looking into her own serious eyes in the mirror.

My life is going to be bigger than this, no matter what I have to do.

She was speaking both to herself as an adult and to the child she once was.

"My mother keeps an eye on me," her daughter, Sierra, used to say when she was little, her young voice ringing with the security of being a loved child. With her therapist, Morgan had tried to instill that kind of confidence in herself. It could be a lifetime job, for it seemed that old fears resurfaced whenever life jostled her sleeping ghosts.

She wrapped her long, graying curls in a towel and pulled her yellow satin robe close.

What's that noise?

A key in the door.

Did Adam make a second key?

She grabbed Ian's baseball bat, positioned herself in front of the door, and raised the bat high in the air.

Sierra swung the door open and laughed. Morgan dropped her eyes to her daughter's belly, which looked bigger than the last time she saw her but still not big enough for six months, and realized how ridiculous she must look with her baseball bat held high, her robe gaping, and the towel with which she had wrapped her hair draping askew.

"Bases are loaded, Mom, and your team is down at the bottom of the ninth. Two outs, two strikes. No pressure or anything."

Morgan straightened and leaned Ian's bat against the wall.

"Knock next time you drop by, will you please? Better yet, call first. I do have a life of my own, you know."

"Yeah, playing baseball in the front hall. But you're right. I'm sorry. I had a few minutes and I wanted to see you, that's all."

Sierra gave her mother a quick hug and headed for the living room, then turned for an explanation of the baseball bat. Morgan hesitated. But she wasn't going to hide the truth from her daughter, so she led her to the couch and told her what Adam did.

"Oh, Mom." Sierra hung her head.

"Talk to me, Honey," Morgan brushed Sierra's long strawberry blonde hair away from her face. "Truth."

"Truth? I wish you'd stop chasing after these loser men. Good job calling the police, though. You did the right thing."

She studied her daughter's face—skin both luminous and touchable, like the inside of a seashell, full lips, classic profile, liquid, hazel eyes—and wondered where such beauty came from. Beneath her cocky sophistication, Sierra was an angel, all her surfaces illumined by some sweet and rarefied essence glowing within.

But lately Sierra was holding it all together. Since she got pregnant, she often seemed to be trying too hard, as if she had to play-act the adult mother-to-be. Morgan wanted to wrap her in her arms the way she had when she was a little girl and tell her she was going to be a wonderful mother. And someday she would. But she sensed that doing such a thing now would somehow undermine Sierra.

"I thought you liked Adam," Morgan said.

"Not really."

"Why not?"

"You're so giving. So warm. He sponged it all up and didn't give back."

Sierra's words stung. Because she was right.

Why didn't I see it?

"A man is supposed to be crazy about you," Sierra said, "or he's not worth it. I have a husband at home preparing a gourmet, candlelit dinner. Salmon with caper sauce, asparagus with lemon, Arugala salad with sherry vinaigrette and slivers of yellow pepper, and poached pears."

Sierra's expression was level, challenging. "Dinner is running late because he waxed the kitchen and bathroom floors earlier and they were still drying."

"Geez… ."

"That's okay. I fixed the washing machine and washed both cars. The thing about Rich is, he tells me he loves me several times a day and lets me know I'm the most beautiful woman he knows, baby-belly and all. He worships me."

"Rich is terrific."

"Yeah, Rich is great but hey, that's how a man is supposed to act. Otherwise, they aren't worth the trouble. There are too many compelling things to do to in this world. Why waste time with a man who doesn't treat you like… like silk?"

Sierra dropped her head again. "Maybe we should talk about something else."

"Maybe we should talk about this." Morgan lifted Sierra's chin. "I want to know how you feel."

Sierra drew a breath. "Okay. It's better to be by yourself than with someone who doesn't treat you right. Why don't you try it? I've never seen you alone. There's always some guy around."

"I keep thinking I finally found a good one."

"Yeah, I know. But what about you? When are you going to stop worrying about men and concentrate on your own life?"

She couldn't stop her eyes from filling. Sierra, who appeared to not notice, relaxed back into the couch, leaned her head on a pillow and patted her belly. Morgan knew her daughter had said her piece.

Still, she couldn't help feeling Sierra had inadvertently stolen her thunder, speaking to her with such force about issues she was just beginning to face on her own.

I'm overreacting.

"So my baby brother is in Philadelphia now, with Dad?"

"He left yesterday. Fifteen minutes before we went to the airport, he buzzed the hair under his ponytail on the theory that girls like that."

Sierra threw back her head and laughed.

"Before summer's over," Morgan said, "he'll have time for at least two more incarnations in his style of presenting himself to the female universe. I hate to miss even one of his looks."

"Naw. He'll be too busy organizing Dad. He'll spend the next week cleaning the kitchen before he moves on to the rest of the house." Sierra's mouth formed a tight line. "I'll tell you one thing. I love Dad and I want his grandchild to spend time with him, but he's going to have to hire someone to clean up first."

"You're scaring me. I just sent my baby up there."

"Ian's not a baby, Mom. He's almost a man."

No way.

"He'll whip Dad into shape within a couple of weeks. It's only until then that there's any real health risk."

"Oh *that's* reassuring."

While they talked, she stroked Sierra's hair and scratched her head. As she had since she was a baby, Sierra arched into her mother's massage like a cat. They chatted about names for the baby, colors for the nursery, and how Sierra's high school boyfriend—the one who used to call at all hours—had organized Gay Pride this year. Then Sierra glanced at her watch and announced it was time to go back to Rich.

The last rays of the setting sun had streaked the sky with colors like peacock feathers and the insides of mangoes while she and Sierra were talking. But now the window panes stared back at her like black ice on the pond near her parents' house in Chestnut Hill. The thought chilled her. She moved around the house swiftly after Sierra left, lowering blinds, closing curtains, and trying not to wonder where Adam was.

She was exhausted, so she turned out all the lights and went to her bedroom, where she started to turn back the bed. But that was where she had hoped to be with Adam tonight. The thought was too much, so she pulled on a nightgown and made her way down the hall to Grandmama's old room.

She pressed her forehead into the dark, cool wood of the post at the foot of the bed and ran her fingers first along the carved wood, then over the quilt Grandmama's grandmother made. That quilt—or comforter, as Grandmama called it—had always covered the old bed in which generations of the Forrester family had been conceived and born.

Comforter.

It was one of the many words—like, "veranda," or "garden"—that Grandmama would wrap her mouth around reverently and slowly, as if what it named were something so delicious, so rich and sensual, there was a whole feast to be savored just uttering the word. From earliest childhood, Grandmama's cadences convinced Morgan there were secret veins of knowledge about pleasure and sensuality she might never mine.

It was as if Grandmama were intimately acquainted with some vast, enchanted garden, enticing and shadowy, where warm honey slid off exotic fruit with a sound like drops of water echoing in a cave pool. And Morgan, no matter how hard she tried, could never find the entrance to the labyrinth leading to the center of that garden.

Ever since she was a little girl, Grandmama had spoken to her as if the two of them as women, as Southern women, shared the secrets of this garden. But Morgan wasn't Southern. And there was something about Grandmama that made it impossible to tell her, "No, I don't know. I want to, though. Please, Grandmama, teach me. I have to know what you mean."

But all was shrouded in gentle, impenetrable mystery. Her Southernness, or more precisely her Southern womanliness, was Grandmama's only point of inaccessibility.

She pulled Grandmama's picture down from the wall and held it to her breasts, the coolness of the glass consoling her. Then she carefully arranged Grandmama's picture on the night table. She sank into the solace of the feather bed that topped the old horsehair mattress and was about to turn off the converted gas lamp when the phone rang. It was Officer Briggs.

"Mandrake's in lockup," she said.

"That's it?"

"Think about coming down Monday for a protective order. He looks like the type who can make bail and hightail it out of here, quick. He already has an attorney with him."

Morgan eased the phone into its cradle, turned off the light, and allowed the indigo velvet night to embrace her. That's when the tears came, a tsunami that reared up in her bowels, tore through her intestines, and twisted her face before breaking into into a long, howling release. When she finally stopped sobbing, she found that she had forced Grandmama's crocheted pillow between her large breasts and was gripping it as if it could stop her from drowning. She eased her hold on the pillow, stroked its nubby surface, and willed her mind to be blank. With dark voices barking just outside of the perimeter of her attention, she released herself to sleep.

Later that night, she jolted awake with a man sandwiched behind her, his arms and legs immobilizing her. Fear gripped her throat with hard, strangling fingers. This had to be a dream, but it was so real she couldn't be sure.

If only she could move just one part of her body. She concentrated hard on her thumb. It took her a long time, but she forced herself to move it. Then she could move her hand a little. The thing gripped her harder. Calling up all her strength, she made herself shudder with her whole body and roll over.

When she flicked on the light, the room was the same as always. It had been Shadow gripping her.

In the darkness again, she pulled the quilt up around her face even though her body was drenched in sweat. At last sleep overtook her, bringing more dreams.

This time the struggle was over and she was beneath the surface of the ocean, drowned. There were other women there too, drifting by in the shimmering light of their underwater prison. Their bodies waved like seaweed and their hair billowed in the current. The women's colors were cool and watery—greens, grays, blues and purples—except for the lovely golden globes glowing in their bellies.

Their eyes were disturbing—staring and unfocused—but the glow in their bellies, which was strangely warming, fascinated her. One of the women looked like Serena, of all people. Grandmama was there, and a very old Indian woman. There was a long, willowy woman with black ringlets and skin the color of honey.

Most of the rest were barefoot peasant women from another time, one of whom stopped drifting, took Morgan by the shoulders, and looked into her eyes with an expression that communicated both strength and urgency.

Then she saw herself float by, blank and unseeing, tiny bubbles gathered around her lips.

Wake up!

She was yelling, shaking first the limp form that was herself, then the bodies of the others, fighting to elicit a response, driven by an imperative she didn't understand. All she knew was that life depended on the awakening of all these women. And not just her own small, personal life.

All life.

Everywhere.

CHAPTER 5

brewing

What she takes is hard to do.
What she does is hard to take.

—Gentle Doe

If Serena were a frying pan, drops of water would scuttle across her. She crashed through her morning chores by the light of a kerosene lantern, alarming the dogs, cats, chickens, and rabbits, who were accustomed to sleeping in.

Back in her bedroom, Serena slammed her fist into the wall, hard. She blew out her exhale, shook out the pain in her hand, and grabbed some silver items from the bureau that she wrapped in a stained bandana. She tossed the bandana and a few items of clothing into a paper grocery sack, muttering to herself in some unintelligible language.

She loaded the sack into her faded blue Chevy pickup and headed for the next farm to find Travis's grandson Ron, the teenager who did the chores when she had to leave.

~ ~ ~

Jake stretched his arms, legs, and back, which were stiff from his all-night vigil beneath Morgan's window. He had completed his last patrol of the grounds just before dawn and was again hidden in the hedges, his jeans damp from the fragrant earth beneath him. Now that it was light, he pulled out his journal.

Sunday, June 18th, dawn

It's as if a bomb has gone off inside her. She won't let me help. But I'm not going to leave with Adam on the loose.

How can I tell her I love her? It would add to her burden.

But I know her. It won't be long before she finds another man.

I missed my opportunity a year ago, and look what it cost me. And her. I'll have to tell her somehow.

Today.

Goddess, what will I say? "Mornin' Ma'am. Pay me no mind, but I'm in love with you."

Think, Jacob.

❧ ❧ ❧

Morgan felt the morning sun on her face and almost bounced into the day with her customary lightness of spirit. Then she noticed there was a brick where her heart used to be and her arm throbbed.

And what did that dream mean? The floating women were lifeless and bruised—the way she felt.

Water-logged.

Out of it.

Gone.

The sun's rays illuminated the rainbow intricacy of a spider web on the windowsill next to the bed. Near the center, a spider meticulously wrapped a captured insect in strands of silk.

How simple.

Why can't I eliminate my problems that way?

She turned her back on the spider and the sun and chose the oblivion of sleep.

When she finally pulled herself up, she checked her voice mail. There was a message from a Clarissa Albright. Morgan returned her call and set up an appointment for Tuesday morning. Clarissa was very businesslike and not at all enthusiastic.

She's nervous.

This would be Clarissa's first experience with therapy. She had an interesting accent—educated, but with a trace of mountain twang. And something else, something about the roundness of her words and the slow, meticulous rhythm of her speech.

After her conversation with Clarissa, Morgan took Grandmama's photo to the table by her bed—where she was determined to sleep that night—so it would face her while she slept, then peered at her reflection in the freestanding full-length mirror, her gauze and lace nightgown revealing the peach tones of her flesh and the fullness of her body, framed by the royal purple walls behind her. With an approving nod, she wrapped herself in a cream satin robe the color of her nightgown.

In the kitchen, she poured herself a glass of half-turned orange juice, and got out a box of stale powdered sugar doughnuts, a bag of chocolates, a jar of peanut butter, and a spoon. Staring into the garden from the window at the breakfast nook in the kitchen, she noticed that—between doughnuts—she was bringing one spoonful of peanut butter after another to her mouth.

This is disgusting.

She swirled orange juice in her mouth to free her teeth from their coating of peanut butter, brushed the powdered sugar from her face, nightgown, and satin robe, and pressed her spine into the wooden back of the built-in booth.

She longed for the presence of Spirit to comfort her but all she could sense was the echoing whiteness of her Victorian kitchen. She stared into the ornate design molded into the lacquered tin ceiling high above her head and counted cobwebs. Four big tears spilled down her cheeks. She was just settling in for a quiet cry when a knock on the kitchen door interrupted her.

Adam?

So what.

If he gives me any more crap, I'll just have to kill him.

The headline would read, *Shrink Slays Shit-head.*

Morgan took her time getting to the door. It was Jake.

When he noticed she'd been crying, his eyes grew soft, like a mother. He reached out to her and she melted in his arms. Jake's embrace was solid, like a sun-warmed pillar, yet tender. She wanted to lose herself there, to let him erase what Adam had done, to remind her body that touch is a kind thing, a connecting thing.

What am I thinking?

This is Jake!

Am I an infant rooting at the breast?

She pulled back. "So, how's your songwriting coming along?"

He looked as if someone had slapped him, but he produced a crumpled piece of paper from his pocket. "I wrote this earlier today," he said, carefully smoothing his paper. "Of course it will sound better with music."

He began to read. Morgan noticed his voice was trembling.

Silver

Silver, you are all I see.
Silver moonlight on the sea,
Waves of silver, flying, free—
Love yet to be.

Silver in your golden touch
For all of those you love so much.
Silver in your sunlit hair
And in your air.

Your clear eyes have held my soul,
Warmed me, when life took its toll.
For fifteen years, your faith in me
Has set me free.

Interrupted by a banging on the front door, he jumped up protectively. But it was only Jane, dropping by to invite her to dinner that night at MaMa's, their favorite Italian restaurant.

Jake shuffled outside to tend the garden.

"He has a crush on you!" Jane laughed.

"Don't be ridiculous."

"What's this?" Jane picked up his poem, which he'd left on the counter. "Oh my god Morgan, listen to this!"

First they come and then they go,
Men whose love you'll never know.
But every single time I knew
That I'd be true.

Silver, hear me, this must end.
That sweet boy, your dear young friend?
The child who's now become a man
Needs you again.

Silver, will you listen now?
Let go our past, start fresh somehow?
Trust my love is right for you?
You need me too.

Or will my hair turn silver, too
Before I speak my love to you?
And silver tears fall from my eyes
As life flies by?

"This is a love poem to you, Morgie!"

Her mouth fell open. She straightened her robe and cleared the breakfast nook. "Get a grip, Jane! I'm old enough to be that boy's mother!"

"That's not the way Jake sees it, Honey." Jane was giddy with laughter. "Heigh ho, Silver!"

Morgan gave Jane her best scowl.

"Look at him!" Jane said. "What a hunk. Don't tell me you never noticed."

She looked out across the garden at Jake. Actually, he wasn't himself this morning. He seemed tired and confused.

Isn't that the same shirt he had on yesterday?

"This is insane. He's my friend. He's my gardener!"

"Well shut my mouth, Lady Chatterly." Jane said in her best imitation of highbrow Southern. She put her hand to her mouth, cocked her head, and raised one eyebrow. "And now your gardener wants to plow your fields." She shimmied her hips.

"I doubt it. What's with you? First you tell me to stay away from men, then you throw me at Jake, who's practically a member of this family."

"Right. Someone you *know.* Someone who adores you, who's decent, who respects you." Jane glanced out into the yard.

Morgan followed her gaze. Jake had pulled off his shirt and his bare back was gleaming with sweat. Muscles rippled beneath his tan as he pulled up long trails of Virginia Creeper.

"You could do worse," Jane said. "Hell, you have done worse. Pretty consistently, too. Look at those bee-stung lips."

Bee-stung lips?

"The heat simply rises off that man." Jane fanned her neck with her hand.

"What do you expect? It's ninety-three degrees and *humid.* He's not a salamander. Have you had your hormone levels checked lately?"

"The way he moves is so… fluid. Kind of androgynous. The New Male. Perfect."

"Maybe you should take up with him. Never mind that you're married."

"Not that I think you need a man right now—"

"A man? Jake is still a boy."

"Really? Is Sierra still a girl?"

"No." Morgan was not liking this. "She's a grown woman with a baby on the way."

"I see. How old is she?"

"Sierra is twenty-four."

"Oh. And how old is Jake?" Jane seemed to be thoroughly enjoying herself.

"He's six years older than Sierra."

"So he's thirty."

"Barely."

Jane started counting on her fingers.

"Stop that!" Morgan said. "Stop counting!"

"If you were a man and Jake a woman—these things happen all the time!"

"Get off it, Jane. What does a strapping young man need with a middle aged, fat, brokenhearted woman?"

"Whoa! How about experienced, voluptuous, and vulnerable?" Jane paused. "You're blushing!"

"I most certainly am not!"

"You are. And look at you! Hair tousled, satin robe gaping, peekaboo nightgown revealing naked flesh. Pretty sexy. I can even see where your muff is! No wonder poor Jake is so confused."

Morgan wrapped her robe tighter.

Damned satin never does stay together.

But it feels so *good.*

Morgan waved Jane off. "Good god. First you want me to give up men, now you want me to rob the cradle. Which is it?"

"Hey, did you ever just have fun with someone? Someone nice? Instead of falling head over heels before checking out the dude's credentials?"

She nudged a laughing Jane to the door and resisted the urge to crawl back into bed and pull the covers over her head. If she were going to stay up, she needed to be outside, so she wandered through the house and back to the kitchen. The instant she opened the door, she was blasted by a wall of heat and humidity.

Honeysuckle was creeping into one of the flower beds, its scent drifting lazily toward Morgan. Its delicate white flowers, hot in the sun, smelled like Grandmama. The grass springing up between her toes helped her sink her center toward the ground, away from the congestion in her mind. Even in this heat, the earth was cool. She allowed its mineral strength to enter her body like an answered prayer.

She floated through the garden, drifting on currents of hot, heavy air. The mimosa tree drew her to it with its newly burgeoning clouds of pink and cream. Brushing her palm over the long, fine hairs that formed the mimosa flowers, she plunged her face deep into a cluster of blooms and salved her soul with their beauty. The blossoms brushed her softly with a fragrance like watermelons and jasmine.

This is my life.

Touch.

Shimmering, essential beauty.

Heat.

And I will have it.

But that's not all—I'll find my life purpose and be whole.

Peace entered her body with the penetrating heat of the sun, extending the embrace she'd longed for.

Beyond the mimosa was the crape myrtle. Her satin robe fell open and warm, wet air caressed her skin through the fine cotton of her lacy nightgown. The garden captured her and she half danced toward the myrtle, then fondled the fuchsia flowers and glided her fingers along the the twists of the smooth, peeling, tangled trunk. So fine and old, this tree.

Morgan remembered how Grandmama had come alive in this garden, drinking in the heat that warmed her bones and watered her memories. She caressed the curves and dips of the crape myrtle, lost in the spell of the garden. She began to shed her robe, but then she remembered Jake.

He was leaning on his shovel, watching her from the opposite end of the garden with an expression that caused her throat to constrict and somehow made her aware of the rivers of sweat moving along her waist and her inner thighs.

But it was a moment she quickly dismissed and forgot. Pulling her robe in closer, she smiled at him and turned inside.

~ ~ ~

Serena pulled the hot, rattling pickup off the interstate to top off the radiator. Now that she was well out of the cool mountain air, she greeted the relentless heat and humidity of the piedmont with annoyance. Driving on the interstate with her windows rolled down was noisy, smelly, and unnerving. She tore through her paper bag, searching in vain for something cooler to put on. After more than three hours of driving, her rage had been replaced by determination and apprehension.

She placed a call at the pay phone. At the other end of the line, Jane seemed shocked to learn she'd be seeing her in an hour or two.

~ ~ ~

Jane picked up Morgan for dinner. Morgan was pleased to have found the energy to pull herself together. She was bathed, groomed, and wearing a long, flowing jade dress with multiple gauzy layers that reminded her of ancient Greece. To complete the effect, she wore her hair down and tousled, tamed only slightly by narrow, crisscrossing bands of dark green ribbon just above her hairline. Billowing sleeves covered her wound. Her dress was cut low and she wore Grandmama's cameo at her throat.

She carried herself in triumph, not defeat. To do this was important to her. Close beneath the surface of her composed exterior was a fragility she needed to honor yet not submit to. She would comport herself like a queen tonight. Adam would not dethrone her. She would taste and feel what she had in this present moment and mourn later what she'd lost.

Jane seemed withdrawn during the ride to MaMa's.

I hate perimenopause.

It's a frigging emotional roller coaster.

Just let us have a nice dinner.

Please?

They pulled up at MaMa's, a medium-fare Italian restaurant with an intimate atmosphere: deep red walls, low lighting, and widely separated tables. Morgan was comforted by the routine familiarity of this choice. But Jane led them to a booth in the corner instead of their customary table for two.

As the waiter approached, Morgan said, "I know—you want portabello soup, salad with Italian dressing on the side, a roll, and water." It was a game she and Jane played, mimicking each other ordering dinner.

She felt one eyebrow go up as Jane eyed her back and firmly recited to the waiter, as if from memory, an order of linguine with scallops, sun dried tomatoes, portabello mushrooms, shallots, olives, capers, and yellow peppers in a light wine sauce, along with a warm spinach salad with roasted garlic and a mineral water with lime.

Morgan stared at Jane.

What's going on?

The waiter had to remind her to order. She requested stuffed clams, Veal Parmigiana, cheese garlic bread, and sweet iced tea. She inquired about the freshness of the pastries and whether or not cappuccino would be available that evening.

Suddenly a small, charismatic woman wearing stained dungarees and a faded denim shirt strode into the restaurant. Her long, thin, white braid bounced and her eyes penetrated the room like a blue jay scanning for prey. She had heavy contemporary silver and turquoise jewelry flashing at her ears, throat, and wrists that was obviously worth many hundreds of dollars.

The restaurant grew still except for the tinny, oddly misplaced sound of "O Sole Mio." The patrons stopped eating and stared at the eccentric, commanding figure.

It was Serena.

"She called me from the highway on her way here," Jane said as she swiftly rose from the booth and came around to Morgan's side, sliding in and thereby blocking her from leaving. "I had no idea she was coming. She was on her way to your house. I thought this would be better."

Morgan resented this trap.

Haven't I been through enough in the past twenty-four hours?

But now Serena was seated opposite her.

"Look, I know being corralled in here with Serena is the last thing you want right now." Jane was speaking in low tones only Morgan could hear. "But I think it's serendipity that she came. Give her a chance. This could be exactly what you need."

Great. Now I don't know what I need.

But oh boy, Jane does!

Serena too, apparently.

Jane slid back out of the booth and said to Morgan, "Eve, meet Lilith," and to Serena, "Lilith, meet Eve."

"What? I'm Eve now? As in Adam and Eve?" Morgan felt her voice growing shrill. People were staring.

Serena snickered.

Jane shot Serena a nasty look and said, "You, behave." Then she glanced at Morgan. "And you, stay put."

Abruptly, Jane was gone. Morgan noted to herself that she was now without a ride.

CHAPTER 6

yearning

we have been

collecting
sorting
memorizing

Brewing

Distilling
and running

our issues

underground
since prohibition

moonshine

of potent

portent information

—Terilyn Milke

I can leave if I have to, Jane or no Jane.

But how many times can I summon the strength to say no?

First Adam, now this.

Besides, Morgan hadn't had a real meal in two days and comfort food was on its way. The thought made her salivate, even with Serena staring at her.

There was nothing she wanted to do less than meet her former mentor's eyes. But she squared her shoulders, raised her chin, drew a deep breath, and stared straight at her.

The waiter appeared with the first course and asked if Serena wanted to order. Serena told him the food Jane ordered was for her, then reflexively lectured him about the effect of too much air conditioning on the environment.

The stuffed clams looked and smelled fabulous. She took advantage of Serena's tirade and tore into them. Maybe Jane was right and fate had engineered this meeting.

But I refuse to let this become one more drama to distract me from finding my path.

If it works to see Serena, fine.

If not—oh well.

When the waiter left, Serena turned to her, her neck flushed and her breath-stopping blue eyes suddenly shimmering with unspilled tears.

"I'm so sorry I got involved with Rex, Morgan. You can't imagine. If I knew he mattered to you, I never would have boinked him. I mean, oh my god, I mean goddess, I mean… ."

"Let's not talk about Rex." Morgan had dispatched the first three clams with great satisfaction in spite of the circumstances. Some deep part of her wanted to laugh. It was the same old Serena, her speech as imperious as royalty except when she was at ease or beside herself. Then the New York street kid came out and she blurted whatever slang she thought was in vogue.

She was moved by Serena's discomfort. Besides, she'd traveled so far to see her. Serena appeared to notice her softening and slowed down.

A good sign.

She isn't thinking only of herself.

The last of her anger dissipated—for the moment at least—and she realized how good it was to see her old friend.

"Relax, Serena. We're both here and no one's dead yet. I don't know why I put you off for so long anyway, at least where that bow wow Rex is concerned. He was… boring."

Serena smiled. Her eyes rested on Morgan's arm. Part of the fresh dressing she'd applied was peeking out from under her sleeve.

"Jane told me you've been having a hard time."

"That's one way to put it."

She looks the same but more so, more Serena.

And those hawk eyes.

It almost hurts when she looks at me.

Shall I talk to her, really talk to her?

But of course there would be no ho-hum, cordial relationship with Serena. Either they'd get back to their former intensity or they'd be over for good. It was the law of the chemistry between them.

"I was battered by my lover yesterday." Morgan looked hard at Serena. "I also went through the ordeal of having him arrested, so I'm on a short fuse."

"Morgan, I'm not here to—"

"I didn't say you were."

She told Serena about Adam's violence and was immediately satisfied by the familiar intensity with which Serena listened. Their long estrangement began to melt away.

~ ~ ~

Serena thought it was as if they were back at Temple and Morgan had burst into her office and flopped across the worn leather couch, unburdening herself as she always had.

But this time twenty-five years had passed and they were probing, tentative. She could see Morgan juggling shock, caution, bravery, and need.

And maybe even her own desire for our old friendship.

Morgan opened, unfolding and contracting in cycles like the petals of a flower in time-lapse photography. The tight bud slowly gave way to a generous fullness. Then the bloom closed as her emotions shifted, soon to open again with the dawn of new feeling.

How did she keep herself so fluid—so present—for all these years?

No wonder men still want her.

Morgan's auburn hair had faded and was sprinkled with gray. Her features sagged a little and she'd put on a good deal of weight. But like the Morgan she remembered, the woman across from her pulsed with the intensity of… jungle hibiscus. Yet she was also plain, like dirt, with some ancient knowledge shimmering just beneath the purity in her eyes.

"So he's in jail?" Serena finally dared to speak.

"He was. I imagine he got himself bailed out by now."

"Are you all right?"

"I'm getting there."

"How did the fight start?"

Egad.

Why do I have to go straight for the jugular?

Morgan looked at her quietly for some time. "He wanted me to fix him something to eat. It was the way he said it. He actually nudged me with his foot to get me out of bed to feed him." Morgan paused. "I was furious."

"I should hope so."

A look of annoyance flashed across Morgan's face that Serena thought she saw her quickly erase.

Careful!

She thinks I'm being condescending.

"We used to be so free," Morgan said. "In the beginning, we lived in a world of ideas, as you and I once did. It was magic. We were right here, right now." She thumped the table twice with her finger. "Our bond was intense, hot. But the sex drained out of our connection and he started to treat me like a wife."

"And you hated it."

"Damned straight. I felt as if I were kicked out of bed, where I once reigned as queen of heaven and earth."

"I can't believe you said that."

The waiter arrived with their entrees. Serena had been looking forward to the yellow peppers because she couldn't get them in the mountains until her own were ripe. But these were limp and faded. She tested the scallops by pressing them lightly with her fork. They were tough. The linguine beneath them, however, gave way too easily. Normally she would have sent the order back, but her time with Morgan was too precious.

"Why?" Morgan was digging in to an exceptionally unappealing conglomerate of cheeses rimmed by a thick ring of oil.

"Because Inanna was called Queen of Heaven and Earth. Do you know her?"

Morgan maneuvered her food to one side of her mouth. "I don't recognize the name. Is she from around here?" She raised her eyebrows and scanned the room with feigned innocence.

She plays through the pain.

That's good.

"Inanna is an ancient Sumerian goddess. When you said you felt like the lover turned wife, I thought of Lilith, the independent woman."

"I don't know her, either," Morgan said between enormous, greasy bites.

"Lilith appears in mythology for the first time as one of Inanna's priestesses, a guardian of the sacred temple of sexuality.

"All that, huh?" Morgan laughed.

This was so familiar even now, Morgan teasing her about going from life to myth and back again.

"Oh yeah." Serena grinned.

"Is that the Lilith Jane was talking about?"

"Yes."

Morgan flinched, but she said, "I love that, a sacred temple of sexuality."

Serena explained that later in mythology, Lilith appeared as Adam's first wife whom the Hebrew God created from the earth, just like Adam. Lilith's idea was that they were partners, equal. But Adam wanted her under him, so Lilith magically disappeared and went to live far away where she could be free and where she gave birth to numerous children by her many lovers. Adam was lonely, so God made Eve from Adam's rib. Eve willingly traded equality for protection for herself and her children.

Morgan looked deflated.

What's wrong with her?

They were playing "O Sole Mio" again.

"I heard a joke about that," Morgan said.

This place is inexcusable.

"Oh?" Serena consciously relaxed her shoulders.

"God said to Adam, 'Suppose I told you I could give you an ideal partner, a loving woman who was your equal mentally, physically, and spiritually. In exchange you would have to give up one testicle.' Adam pondered and said, 'What could I get for a rib?'"

"Exactly," Serena said. "Ever since the time of the so-called 'Garden of Eden,' Lilith has been banished. She's been coveted and vilified but, unlike all the other goddesses, she was never worshipped."

Serena tried to choke down a bite of pasta. It gave way in her mouth, like gelatin.

"Ever since Lilith left Adam," Serena said, "which was when the matriarchies were conquered by patriarchy, the independent, sexual female has been an outcast. Women became housewifized in order to survive."

"What century are you in?" Morgan gulped down her third glass of sweet tea. "The bras were burned back in the sixties. Not that you ever needed one." She was reviving an old joke about the disparity between their breast sizes. "Aren't you being a little black and white? And angry?"

"Oh, and you don't think you're angry? The day after you almost got killed? By an iron, yet."

Can they afford only one CD in this damned greasy spoon?

And turn that frigging air conditioning down or I'm going to scream!

Morgan ignored Serena's comment and tore into the last piece of cheese garlic bread. "I'm an independent, sexual female, and I'm not an outcast," she said, still chewing.

"Oh really? You're alone. Hurt and alone."

Oops.

Did I blow it?

Jane says Morgan needs to hear these things, and I haven't even gotten to my main points yet.

Serena dropped her head low and took a deep breath, reminding herself that she needed to reconcile with Morgan to fulfill the destiny she felt calling them.

"God, Serena, why does everything has to be some big deal archetypal myth? You make Eve sound like a wimp. I'm not a wimp. Haven't you ever loved anyone?"

The waiter appeared to refill Morgan's sweet tea and Serena's water. Morgan ordered more cheese garlic bread.

"I'm sorry. I didn't mean to upset you. I simply meant that when Adam threw that iron at your head, it wasn't personal."

"Tell that to my arm."

"Men have been controlling women through violence for thousands of years."

"Let's stay on earth."

"I'm serious. You said something he didn't like, and he hurt you. You don't think that was about control?"

Get your head out of your plate and listen to me!

"Every woman carries the experience of thousands of years of oppression," Serena said. Her breath was becoming shallow. "It's in every cell of our bodies!" She pinched at her arms, her hands, and her face.

"Yeah, right. In every cell of my body is—"

"It's not just the rape, the incest, and the spousal abuse that we're finally hearing about in the last decade or two," Serena said. "This goes way back. Take the women's holocaust, for example."

"The what?" With her fresh order of greasy cheese bread, Morgan was sopping up the horrible oil in which her entrée had been floating.

"The Inquisition, what is referred to as the witch burnings. Did you know that during the so-called Age of Enlightenment, eighty percent of the people killed were women?"

"Come on, Serena."

"It's true. This isn't some esoteric, controversial feminist theory. Look it up in the encyclopedia. We're talking up to nine million people. The wonder is that no one knows exactly how many women were killed. Accurate records weren't kept. Apparently we weren't sufficiently important to tally whether millions or hundreds of thousands of us were slaughtered."

"Why haven't I heard about this before?" Morgan said, although her mouth was too full to speak, really.

"Good question. Ask yourself why history books don't highlight this information the way they do the Jewish holocaust. Could it be because men weren't being tortured and slaughtered? If it weren't for women scholars—painstakingly and in the face of tremendous opposition—unearthing this information bit by bit over the years, we'd still be in the dark about it."

Morgan shifted and opened her mouth to speak.

"I digress," Serena said. "The Church wanted to expand beyond the cities. To do so, it needed more land and a broader power base. But the rural people still embraced the old goddess spirituality. The earth was sacred to them. It was the mother of all, so it never would have occurred to them to divide land—their mother—into segments and own it. They lived off the land communally. Women—because they, like the earth, were the lifegivers—were revered and villagers turned to them for their abilities as counselors, midwives, herbalists, and healers."

Morgan's brow creased and her eyes were thoughtful. She had finished that horrible bread and seemed to be taking in what Serena was saying.

Am I finally getting through?

Then listen to this!

"For the church to dominate the rural areas, the existing system had to be overthrown. The most efficient way to accomplish that was to get rid of women, so women were accused of witchcraft."

"I'm having trouble with this."

"Good! We should all be having trouble with this." Serena felt her jaw set. Her heart sputtered in her ears like the drum roll at an execution. "If you were thrown into the water and you drowned, that meant you were innocent. But if you survived, that meant you were guilty and had to be put to death. There were villages where the entire female population was tortured and killed, from infants to old women. It took five hundred years of concentrated persecution—more than twice as long as our country has even existed—to beat down the last vestiges of feminine power."

"That sounds crazy to me," Morgan motioned to the waiter and asked him to come around with the dessert cart.

"What I'm saying is that most women don't have our history straight. It's been kept from us—barred from the textbooks—and we've allowed ourselves to remain ignorant. It's still going on. In Arab countries, in Africa, over a hundred million girls and women have been genitally mutilated—their clitorises hacked off—in order to be marriageable. A girl gets butchered every fifteen seconds! Girls and women are imprisoned or killed if they dishonor their families by being raped, maimed or killed or for seeking divorce—"

"Whoa. This is too much." Morgan had actually stopped chewing her current mouthful of bread.

But Serena couldn't stop. "Why do you think women have to be coached in assertiveness? In our cells, we remember being tortured for being who we are and we're terrified. Otherwise, why would we put up with the way our lives are structured? Our husbands sit around and watch T.V. while we do all the housework and childrearing—"

"Taxi!" Morgan inserted two fingers in her mouth and made a low whistle.

"In our jobs, we butt our heads on the glass ceiling. We're paid a fraction of what men make for the same work. The worst of it is, most men aren't even conscious of how much they use us and how dependent they are on their male privilege."

"What's all this 'we' stuff, anyway? You never had a husband, or children! Where do you get off speaking for all women? You're a woman of privilege alone on a mountain. You're talking to a mother." Morgan pointed at her own chest. "A working woman, a former wife. No doubt you assume I've been shuddering in the dark with the mindless masses, firmly ensconced under the middle hump of the bell curve, without you to enlighten me. Is that why you flew your broom down here, to save the Stepford wife? Besides—"

"Meanwhile, what do we do?" Serena refused to be interrupted. "We cling to men as if we can't live without them—"

"Calling Planet Serena! Anybody home?"

"And do you know why? Ever heard of the Stockholm Syndrome? Alternating cruelty and kindness is the best way to brainwash the human animal."

Pay attention, Morgan.

Because according to Jane, I'm talking about you.

"That's what marriage is!" Serena said. "A little good stuff thrown in with all the crap. And we buy it, because it's our history. At a cellular level, we expect to be controlled."

"I've heard enough! You make it sound as if men are the enemy. Haven't you ever seen the gentle side of a man? Held him in your arms while he cried? There are good men, kind men, everywhere. Can't you see them?"

For the briefest moment, the image of Lloyd, Clarissa's father, flooded Serena's with overwhelming intensity. She could almost feel his huge, soft shoulders shaking and the dampness of his tears on her neck when they said goodbye. But Serena swept the image from her mind.

"Never mind that—" Serena said.

"Besides, what's with all this solidarity with women? Like you're in there with your sleeves rolled up with the rest of us."

Goddess.

I've lost it.

When did I stop reading her?

Have I blown this whole encounter?

Damn it though, look at her!

Defending men after one tried to kill her.

Yesterday.

The waiter appeared.

Serves me right to be saved by a man.

He was rolling a creaking cart on which the display desserts were arranged. Each was uniquely disgusting. Especially the cannoli, which had a yellow crust forming on the ricotta. Didn't everyone know you don't fill a cannoli until just before serving? Basic.

And you don't leave dairy sitting out.

Morgan, however, was most interested.

In New York, this place would fold in a week.

Where do they get off calling this food Italian?

Sixth generation Italian, crossbred with Chucky Cheese.

From Iowa via Little Rock.

"You should write a book, Serena," Morgan said, having made her selection.

She's dismissed everything I said.

Damn, I've got to get back in the game.

On the other hand Morgan, who was furious only moments ago, was now attempting to lighten the conversation.

A cue I would do well to follow.

Next time she might bolt altogether.

Serena paused. "I do have a book in progress."

Shit, am I going to have to talk about that grand fiasco?

"Well, stick with it," Morgan said. "Get yourself some readers though, before you approach an editor. I'm guessing you might be having a little problem with tone. You put your message out there—raw as sushi as you did with me—and the world will treat you like a... ." Morgan rolled her hand in the air, searching. "Like a cat hacking up hairballs."

Serena laughed. "The fact is, I am stalled on my book. And as you said, why should any woman listen to me, from my perch on the mountain?"

"Yeah, well—what kind of a therapist gets assaulted by her lover? You'd think I'd know better."

Serena thought for a moment. "Have you ever heard of Chiron?" she said.

Morgan laughed. "I'm afraid to go there after that last round. But okay, I'll bite. Who's Chiron?"

"A planetoid discovered in the late seventies was named Chiron, after another figure from mythology. This means, according to astrologers, that Chiron's influence is now in our collective consciousness. He's an archetype for our times."

"Yeah? There's always room for one more archetype, I suppose."

"Chiron was a centaur. Half man, half horse—"

"I know what a centaur is, Serena. Well hung, in other words. But of course you're going to tell me he was a horse's ass, right?"

"Just the opposite." Serena grinned. "Chiron is referred to as the wounded healer because he performed miraculous healings, but he had an injury in his own foot he couldn't mend. Because he couldn't heal himself, he lost his status as a god and became human. Still, he did a tremendous amount of good and helped countless others. He even helped the gods."

"Now there's an archetype I can buy," Morgan said. "Did you happen to notice Chiron is a guy?"

We're sparring again, like old times.

The bond is still there.

The waiter was bringing Morgan's dessert and cappuccino, with decaf for Serena.

She actually ordered that cannoli?

I hope she doesn't get food poisoning.

"There is one thing we need to clear up," Morgan said. She was ignoring her dessert.

This must be the big one.

"Okay."

Let me handle this well.

Please.

"You always spoke so condescendingly about women having children. And when I got pregnant, you thought I should have had an abortion."

Oh god.

I mean goddess.

This is it.

"You weren't supposed to hear about that."

"But I did. You'll never know how much it hurt me, because you never carried a child in your body."

Serena felt as if she'd been slapped.

What if Clarissa still lives in Hopewellen?

Her heart ached for her Pearl. At the same time, it closed in fear.

"Underneath," Morgan was saying when Serena was able to bring her attention back to the conversation, "I always knew Rex was a mixed bag. But that little girl of mine, who has become such a remarkable young woman—my daughter… ."

Morgan looked down. Time passed.

Shit, she's going to cry.

I'm going to cry.

I didn't want you to go through what I did, choosing between keeping your baby and having a career.

"Sierra's life is more precious to me than my own," Morgan finally said, raising her head and looking at Serena levelly. "You can never understand how important my children are to me. How could you, with no children of your own?

If only she knew.

"I hated you for wanting me to abort my child. It's why I never forgave you."

"What can I tell you?" Serena was about to blurt again. She couldn't stop herself. Her years of solitude, chasing her thoughts like a gerbil spinning its wheel, had created an overwhelming momentum.

"I was worried that all your creativity would be lost, diverted into things that require no talent," Serena said. "Things animals can do, probably better than humans. You could—"

"So now I'm subhuman? Where do you get off with that one?"

Oh boy.

Here we go again.

"I'm sorry," Serena said. "I was wrong to question your decision to have children. But if you'd followed the vision I had for you, to remain independent and follow your creativity, you probably wouldn't have had an iron thrown at your head yesterday."

"Whoa. Do you think we could keep those two topics separate? Children and abusive men are not the same thing." Morgan took a bite of her cannoli.

"True."

Mother of God.

She's handling this conversation better than I am, and I'm the one who offended her.

"So Morgan, I apologize to you from a very deep place for criticizing your choice to complete your pregnancy."

"Thank you."

"Really? After all these years, you can let it go?"

"Yeah. I better." Morgan laughed. "Have you noticed life is getting shorter? Feature this. I forgive you."

She felt herself shaking like a volcano about to erupt. In one long, shuddering breath, the tears came flooding. Morgan crossed the booth and held her.

I'm pathetic.

It's a good thing most of the patrons have left this shit-hole.

It was a long time before she could say anything.

"But I see you named your daughter after me," Serena finally said, grinning through her tears and blowing her nose with a loud, honking sound on the red bandana she pulled from her jeans.

Morgan laughed. "Now that is one nasty looking piece of fabric. Where in the world did you get that thing? On second thought, don't tell me. Would you believe it took me two years to figure out how much 'Sierra' sounds like 'Serena?'" Morgan slid back to her place across the table and returned to her cannoli. "Jane noticed right away, but had the sense to not tell me," Morgan looked into her eyes with affection. "Unlike you, Sierra's actually serene. And like the mountains she's named for, she lives big and she lives strong."

"I'm glad. I'd like to meet her. I've been wrong to be judgmental about having children. It's just that I got so sick of everyone judging me for not having them."

Don't go there.

"Be assured, some things about being a mother are not so great," Morgan said. "Giving birth is like pulling a dog through your nostril. Then you get to watch your daughter go through the same thing and your son turn into someone you don't know as soon as he figures out how to wax his monkey."

"Wax his monkey?"

"Never mind. I didn't completely lose it, Serena. I've always been aware of what my choice to be a mother cost me. I've missed that career you wanted me to have."

"Really?"

"Of course. But what I got from my kids, no career could ever provide. I learned things about myself, about ordinariness and its blessings. I became a better person so I could be a better mother for my children. Sierra and Ian kept me honest. They kept my heart open."

Is that why I've grown so bitchy?

I mean, angry?

Because I didn't keep Clarissa?

"I apologize," Morgan said, "for not going over all this with you a long time ago."

"I forgive you."

"Thank you." Morgan thought for a moment. "I dreamed about you the other night."

"Tell me."

Morgan told her about the underwater women and they both fell silent.

Suddenly the bad music stopped. Except for them, the restaurant was empty. The waiters were beginning to vacuum the carpets. "To be continued," Serena said. "Why don't you come to my mountain?"

Morgan said she had a vacation coming up in a week and hadn't made plans because she'd assumed she'd be with Adam.

"Why not come then?" Serena said. "We have so much to learn from each other."

"That's so soon."

"I don't have a phone, so it's difficult to make plans unless we pin something down tonight."

"Are we ready to spend that much time together?"

"Why not? I'm game. But if you'd rather wait… ."

"What the hell. I'll see you Friday, then. Before sundown."

She dropped Morgan off before she headed back to Jane's, where she was staying. She wanted to get an early start so she could be back by afternoon to tend the animals.

"Quite the little mother after all, aren't we?" Morgan said.

She cringed. "Don't jump in bed with the next man who yanks your chain."

Morgan laughed and stepped down from her truck.

"The last thing I want right now," Morgan said, slamming the stiff old door behind her, "is a man in my bed."

~ ~ ~

Morgan turned toward her house as Serena headed out. Life was good. The soft night air was wet and thick—she felt as if she were floating in a warm bath. A trickle of sweat moved down the small of her back as she moved up the stone sidewalk toward the familiar comfort of the darkened porch.

The trill of tree frogs, the rasp of cicadas—and, loudest of all, the comforting, rhythmic song of crickets—combined to bathe her in a sea of vibrant sound, the raucous music of Southern summer nights. Life was a gift, pregnant with possibility. Morgan's time of self-exploration was beginning and she would find her true path. Thousands of night creatures were inviting her to relax into that truth.

"Summertime, and the livin' is easy," she sang to herself, immersed in the feel of the old Gershwin tune. She ascended the porch steps, grabbing the post at the top of the banister with her good arm and twirling away from it a little with her sore arm outstretched.

"Fish are jumpin' and the cotton is high," whispered a male voice from the shadows of the porch.

Adam!

She jumped backward, losing her balance at the top of the stairway. Jake leaped out of the darkness and encircled her waist to catch her. He pulled her into his body at the same time that his words of apology tumbled over one another. He hadn't meant to frighten her. He thought she saw him there and was singing to him.

Jake continued to hold her and in her panic, she let him. Her heart was still pumping with a thunder that bombarded her ears.

Under the reassuring familiarity of Jake's touch, the determined queen who had sailed out of the house earlier that evening disappeared, yielding first to the quaking woman who'd been assaulted by her lover, then to the inner child who'd lived in fear all her life.

Jake's kindness, on which she'd always relied, became the tidal wave that swept away the wall of control she'd built to cope with the turmoil of the past thirty-six hours. She collapsed into the comfort of his warm flesh with the abandon of a lost child who'd finally found mother.

The heat of his body became one with the heat of the night. His woodsy scent, his solidity and comfort, were irresistible. Her face against the dampness of his shirt felt good and right as she pressed her whole body into the quickening rhythm of his heart.

Time stood still.

Before she saw it coming, he was kissing her mouth softly. She was kissing him back and he was telling her he loved her.

"Silver, my Silver," he whispered, and for a moment their hungry tongues spiraled like mating dolphins dancing in the waves.

But then she pulled away.

"Jake. Don't you think it's time for you to go home?"

CHAPTER 7

web

Now I blink, turtle eyed, a slow swoon.
Now I soar, swallow breasted, heart lilting.
Now I sink, silty, past clouds of algae
and rise again on the spiral flight
of two red dragonflies, yearning.

—Jessica Montgomery

I don't need that appointment with Dr. Forrester anymore.

I'll cancel in the morning.

Frankie and Martin were finally in bed and Clarissa was lying in the darkness of her steamy bedroom, staring at the ceiling.

When they returned from camp, the boys had been on a sugar high that was heightened by the pride they took in the manly accomplishment of having survived a night in the woods without their mother. They had boldly gestured and strutted when they shared the details of their adventure with Clarissa, interrupting each other to clarify the particulars.

Martin and Frankie had tolerated—in fact they had encouraged—mild exaggeration from each another. They had colluded to elaborate when one of them made something sound less spectacular than it truly had been or when, she surmised, the facts couldn't do justice to the thrill they had experienced. But when one of them went too far, they reined each other in.

Clarissa, who was exhausted from the emotionalism of her weekend, had amused herself by predicting when they would correct each other. Their shared standards were, it turned out, quite narrow, so her task had been simple.

The camp bus had been late by almost an hour. Between that and how long it had taken her children to run out of steam, she was ready for bed herself by the time she got the boys down.

While Frankie and Martin were gone, she'd come to terms with the fact that she wasn't going to be able to do anything about the nuclear dump.

The thought of nuclear waste being transported through town and stored near Hopewellen was, of course, sickening. It would poison the land, the groundwater—maybe even the roadways—for generations to come and could lead to another Chernobyl. That the dump was being pawned off on a rural black community infuriated her, re-igniting her desire to stop it, to demonstrate that people of color could be pushed only so far.

Slow down, girlfriend, or you'll never get to sleep.

She rolled on her side and stared into the patterns on the wallpaper beside her, trailing vines that were now mercifully gray in the light from the street instead of their daytime emerald and chartreuse on an orange trellis against a yellow background. She reminded herself, as she had over and over since she pulled herself out of the Back Street Bar, to be realistic and accept her limitations.

She needed the summer for herself and the boys after a grueling school year. And there were other compelling reasons why she needed to abandon the idea of fighting the dump. The summer break wasn't long enough to accomplish anything of significance, she didn't have the kind of community contacts it would take to get things moving, and her personality was too behind the scenes, too quiet, to take on such a daunting project.

It was sad, but what else could she do?

She tried to sleep, unhappy with her decision but convinced it was for the best. She couldn't continue to anguish over the dump. It had nearly cost her her sobriety.

Big Mom would be after her, of course, as soon as she drifted off, but Big Mom was simply going to have to understand she could do only so much.

~ ~ ~

Morgan's dream was a swirling tumble of water and women. She felt, rather than saw, the hideous way in which the peasant women among them had died, their dreams choked into silence by the stormy sea that drowned them.

Yet somehow these women were vital and intense, illumined from within by glowing fires that shimmered in their bellies and in their strange, staring eyes. For brief moments, they would come alive and swim with the bold strength of dolphins arcing in the waves.

There was the long and lovely caramel-skinned woman again with the ancient, round Indian at her side. The pair moved together through the water with the whimsical grace of a sleek tuna and her manatee companion.

Morgan saw herself and Serena playing in the currents like mermaid children. They were joined by the peasant woman who had gazed into her soul with such power the night before.

A sense of profound rightness filled her when the women swam. But when they went limp she panicked, tugging at their arms and fighting the sluggish water to rouse them.

She awakened with the dawn, rising slowly from the depths of sleep and floating into consciousness gradually. Before her eyes were open, she felt herself grinning. She pulsed with the most marvelous sensation of fulfillment throughout her vulva and deep inside her body where she was glowing, like the women in her dream.

But there was more. Every nerve in her body, every muscle, was relaxed in a way she hadn't experienced for a very long time. And there was the most wonderful scent, sweet and woodsy.

Jake.

Her eyes flew open. The first thing she saw was Grandmama's picture, which seemed to wink at her. She was lying on her side, with Jake tenderly spooning her from behind. His arms were around her, and the fingers of one of his hands were laced through her own. She could feel his breath, rhythmic on her shoulder.

Oh my God, we're naked.

Grandmama, what have I done?

When he stirred in his sleep, her body moved with his with the natural fluidity of water.

In the worst way, she wanted to laugh. The last forty-eight hours had tossed her life into the air like a schoolgirl's jacks.

Or, perhaps, set it right. Who would have thought she'd be lying in Jake's arms, as sated as a milk-drunk baby? Morgan studied his summer-colored forearm with its furry coat of blonde hair. His skin was so youthful, it reminded her of Ian.

Don't go there.

I'm here now and I'm not going to argue with myself about it.

Morgan gazed into Grandmama's exuberant face. She could almost hear her telling her that it's all right, you young people do things differently.

But this is how I get into trouble with men, Grandmama.

I use them as pacifiers.

Jake stirred and held her closer. "Sugar, are you sure you want to be doing that?" he half-whispered in her ear.

That sweet drawl.

Shit.

I'm going to have to deal with him.

"What?" she said, burrowing under the covers and not turning to face him.

"Thinking. You were thinking so loud it woke me up."

"Sorry."

"No problem. But I'd rather we think together."

~ ~ ~

Please, Goddess, don't let her regret this.

Don't let her see us as freaks.

Jake stroked Morgan's hair. He could feel her tension easing ever so slightly.

She's so soft.

Last night, the way she met me with her body—I never knew it could be like that.

He adjusted his torso slightly, so she wouldn't feel his renewed need for her rising against her hips.

"Good morning, Morgan."

"Hello, Jake."

He rose up on his elbow and leaned over her shoulder, careful to not put pressure on her sore arm.

"Are you ready to look at me?"

She was silent for a moment. "I'm not sure." She buried her head in the covers, then rolled into his chest and looked up into his eyes.

"You're still Jake!"

"You were expecting someone else?" he mimicked a pout.

"Do you know what I'm most afraid of?"

"Yes."

Her breath stopped. He chuckled and stroked her hair. "Don't forget I've had quite awhile to think about this," he said. "Fifteen years or so, on and off."

"You're kidding."

"I'm not. Your biggest fear is that we'll ruin our friendship."

She smiled, her eyes glistening. When he put a finger to the side of one lovely brown eye, he caught a tear as it spilled.

"That's what I'm second most afraid of," she said. "I'm most afraid I'll hurt you."

He drew a breath to speak, but she went on. "My life is a roller coaster. I don't even know who I am anymore. If I ever did."

He scowled.

"Which is a good thing," she said quickly. "I'm starting over. I won't be stupid with a man again. I'm not going to throw myself away for some childhood dream about a white picket fence."

"I wouldn't want you to—"

"I know, Jake. You're not the problem. This is about me. I need elbow room right now. And plenty of it. I have to find myself. No, that's not it." She bolted into a sitting position, her golden eyes crackling with brilliant flames, like sparklers. "I'm going to discover and create myself." Morgan gestured broadly with her arms, ignoring the obvious pain it caused her. "I want myself back—on my own terms—more than I want to breathe. And I will have that." She tossed her hair and set her jaw.

Her bite, her brains, her passion—I couldn't love her more.

"That's fabulous!"

"Taking a lover isn't a good idea. I can't—I won't—risk any competing priorities."

"Would you consider allowing time to be the measure of how that plays out?" he said. "I want you to do whatever you need to. But please don't ask me to go away."

This time it was Jake who wouldn't allow Morgan to respond. "I'm here with my eyes open, Sugar. I understand you were already reeling and now here you are, in bed with me. You can't possibly be feeling for me what I feel for you."

He brushed a long strand of silver and auburn hair away from her face and tucked it behind her ear.

"I wasn't fixing to rush us to bed," he said. "But now that we're here, I need to give us a chance. The only thing that could hurt me is if I didn't make a stand for us. About our friendship, we'll never lose it. That's a given."

"Good. Our friendship must survive. But yes, I'm reeling. Being with you is a shock." Morgan's eyes grew soft and unfocused. "Not only because my life is upside down and you're my friend, my *young* friend, but because I've—"

She crumpled under the covers again and buried her face in his chest. He let her be there for a time, then lifted her chin and asked her to look at him.

"What?" he said.

"I've never been with a man like you. One who—"

She was making herself continue to look at him, he could tell. But she couldn't say it.

"One who knows you?" he said, praying to sound as respectful as he felt. Her eyes were glistening and the muscles at the sides of her mouth were trembling. "A man who loves you completely? Someone you can count on?"

"Right."

"I know, Morgan. I know." He held her close—his desire replaced with an aching tenderness—for a long, long time.

~ ~ ~

Clarissa awakened at five and couldn't get back to sleep. The growing dawn illumined the ugly stain on the acoustic tile overhead. It was shaped like Louisiana. Louisiana in sepia outlined in rust. Whenever she found herself studying that stain, she knew she was awake for good. That tile was another thing she hadn't been able to bring herself to do anything about.

I'm too damned lazy.

She caught herself pacing in her small apartment with its dingy—but clean!—linoleum floors. She was barefoot so she wouldn't wake up her boys or the downstairs tenants.

To hell with this.

Clarissa showered and dressed carefully, choosing her black linen sheath and black heels. She hadn't canceled her appointment with Dr. Forrester. She'd thought about it—a lot—but she forgot to actually do it. Dr. Forrester had a twenty-four hour cancellation policy, so she was going to have to pay anyway. She might as well go.

Still, she wasn't happy about this therapy thing. These were problems she ought to be able to solve herself. So why should she be paying some *u-neg* to listen to her she thought, grinning tightly from her enjoyment in using the Cherokee equivalent of "honky."

Besides, I'm not crazy.

I just feel crazy.

She spent more time than usual arranging her short black ringlets. For once she didn't stop at a quick swipe across her mouth with lipstick. Instead, she meticulously applied her seldom-used make up and made herself eat.

Why did I put on lipstick before a meal?

She set out the boys' breakfast and left them a note. On her way to Morgan's office, she was extra cautious with her driving and arrived in the parking lot of the two-story brick building that housed Morgan's office fifteen minutes early.

"How can this be what you wanted me to do, Big Mom?" she said out loud.

~ ~ ~

Morgan was in her office preparing for her first client of the day—Clarissa Albright—reviewing her caseload, and going over her schedule. She still had a few minutes before Clarissa was due so, on a whim, she fumbled through the compact disks that came with her computer, popped in the one labeled, "Encyclopedia," and looked up "Inquisition."

Damn.

Serena was right.

A chill gripped her spine. She stared at the bright screen and saw reflected back at her the same numbers Serena spoke of. "Eighty percent of those accused were women." She felt numb, lost. Why did she feel so hurt about something that happened hundreds of years ago?

Yet somehow she could feel herself bound to a stake, fingers of flame lashing at her feet and finally engulfing her in searing pain. She felt her soul flee her body and seal itself in a wall of horror.

Wake up!

You're at work!

She jerked her attention back to the present. But not before noticing that her white picket fence—the one that was her birthright, if only Prince Charming would finally arrive and cram her foot into the glass slipper—had also been lost in the flames.

She slumped back in her chair.

No wonder I'm having a meltdown.

Half of me is an ancient goddess, guarding the harbor of love and sensuality like the Statue of Liberty.

The other half is June Alyson, propping up the white picket fence with one hand and with the other, baking a cherry pie for my founding father who, I try to convince myself, truly does know best.

The headline would read, *Man-Crazy Therapist Files Report on Missing Self.* The subhead would be, *Investigators Find No Evidence Self Ever Existed.*

Glancing out the window at the parking lot, Morgan noticed a tall, reed-thin woman unfolding herself from a decrepit monster of a car the color of dull steel. This must be Clarissa Albright.

What race was she? The woman was striking. She moved with unusual grace, yet had an air of stiffness and pain.

This one's holding it all in.

Big time.

She did a double-take. Clarissa looked exactly like one of the women in her underwater dream, the slender tuna who swam with the manatee Indian.

When she greeted her, Morgan noted Clarissa's drawn expression and the tremble in the fingers that reached toward hers to shake hands. Still, there was dignity in her bearing.

"Sit anywhere," Morgan said with a sweep of her arm that took in the whole room, then indicated the overstuffed couch she loved so much. She was always proud to introduce a new client to her office. It was a sunny room, decorated in lemon, rose, and lime tones, spacious yet cozy and filled with comforting, comfortable furnishings. Morgan wanted her clients to feel they were important enough to deserve a beautiful space in which to work.

❧ ❧ ❧

Clarissa glanced over the room and avoided the couch, where she would have her back to the door, in favor of a straight-backed chair. She surveyed the overly-spacious office with its opulent furnishings, tallied the cost, and wondered how much of her check would go toward such frills.

She's just u-neg.

She looked Dr. Forrester over. Why was she wearing long sleeves and a long skirt on a hot day? Apparently she didn't mind dishing it out for air conditioning. This woman was plump and soft. How hard did she have to work?

Yet at the same time that these thoughts generated an almost reassuring feeling of resentment, Clarissa experienced a tiny stab that told her she was judging this woman too harshly and too soon. There was kindness in Dr. Forrester's face and a solidity that doesn't come to the untested. The candid brown eyes challenged her as if to say, "Give me what you've got. I can take it."

She handed Dr. Forrester her check.

I don't want her to think I haven't got the money.

But Dr. Forrester looked at her check oddly.

"What's wrong with it?" Clarissa felt her hackles rise.

"I'm sorry. I guess I wasn't clear. I'm not a doctor. I'm a counselor. And please, call me Morgan."

~ ~ ~

Clarissa promptly expressed her reservations about trusting a stranger with her innermost thoughts.

I bet she isn't terribly comfortable about the fact that I'm white, either.

Morgan thanked her for her honesty and let her know it was natural to feel uncomfortable at first.

"I bet you say that to all your patients," Clarissa said.

She regarded Clarissa evenly. The eyes she was looking into were fierce. But beneath her facade was the unmistakably clear—if somewhat vulnerable—light of a soul who would make it.

She's closer than she realizes to conquering whatever brought her here.

The challenge will be in getting her to see that.

And getting her to trust me enough to show me what we're really dealing with.

"I hope you aren't *patient,* Clarissa. I hope you're *impatient* to get on with it."

Clarissa looked puzzled.

"You're not a patient," Morgan said. "You're not sick and I can't heal you. You're a client and I'm your consultant, your midwife as you give birth to yourself. My guess is you're simply trying to figure out how to be true to yourself in an extremely challenging environment.

"And like most of us," Morgan continued, "you didn't have anyone to teach you how to deal with the things that are troubling you. Our parents lived in a simpler time and were therefore unable to fully equip us for this one. So you hired me to help you.

"See this?" She waved Clarissa's check at her. "This check says I work for you. Now, what do you want me to do?"

"Just like that? You say your speech and I spill my guts?"

She forced herself to not grimace. This one had better drop the defenses soon and get down to business or she would have her hands full trying to prevent them from having a highly unproductive fifty-minute sparring session.

"What do you need from me to feel safe telling me why you're here?" Morgan finally said.

Clarissa looked at Morgan as if she were crazy. "I don't have a problem with being 'safe,' but I do have a question."

"Shoot."

"Do you have your life together?"

Morgan startled. For a split second she saw the iron sailing at her head as it had a mere three days ago. "No. Most things are good. Some things are better than others."

"Then how can you help me?" Clarissa even stuck her chin out.

She imagined the satisfaction she would take in ushering Ms. Clarissa Albright to the door and giving her a boot down the stairs.

The headline would read, *Defiant Client Buys It, Bouncer Counselor Trounced Her.*

"Because I work on myself," Morgan finally said. "Hard. Which means the obstacles that come up in my life, I deal with. And I can teach you how to do the same thing."

Clarissa looked unconvinced. Out of nowhere, Morgan remembered what Serena said about Chiron. But she didn't think Clarissa was ready for the wounded healer.

Or was she?

What the hell—things couldn't get any worse.

"My father raped me and my mother was an ice princess," Morgan said.

Clarissa's jaw dropped.

Good.

"Before I got therapy for myself," Morgan said, "I was lost in emotional pain. It was hell for breakfast, hell for lunch, and hell for dinner. And for a bedtime snack? Hell. But I learned I could heal from my past."

Clarissa appeared to be listening.

"No one's perfect, Clarissa. I'm certainly not. You don't have to be perfect either. In order to deal with what brought you here, all you have to do is listen to your heart, learn its language. Then follow the path your heart illumines for you. And when you fall down—which all of us do, quite frequently, too—forgive yourself immediately, dust yourself off, and take care of whatever tripped you up. I can help you learn to do all that."

She smoothed her skirt with the palms of her hands, then wrapped her fingers around the rainbow obsidian pendant at her chest.

"You don't need to have your life together, as you put it," Morgan said, "to be at peace with yourself most of the time and to do something about it when you're not."

I'm doing better than I realized.

Clarissa appeared to be looking inward. She relaxed her shoulders, surveyed the room, moved to the couch, and cleared her throat. She told Morgan she was being plagued by visitations from her Cherokee grandmother, Hattie Bigwitch, Big Mom, who was opening her ears to the cries of the earth. Clarissa was both disturbed and inspired by these visions and found herself wanting to do political work for the environment. She wanted to prevent a nuclear dump from being built in the area.

But she'd decided there were too many problems with that idea. So yesterday she made a final decision to abandon the project. It's just that she never got around to canceling her therapy appointment.

"Yet working to stop the dump is your dream," Morgan said.

"Yes, but I can't handle it."

Morgan gazed out the window into the willow oaks swaying gently across the street, their narrow leaves glistening in the sunlight like minnows in a stream.

"Maybe you aren't completely sure about that." Morgan turned her attention to Clarissa's eyes, which were nearly black. "Maybe that's why you didn't cancel your appointment, so you could get a different perspective on your situation."

"Most black people think white people fight for the environment instead of for people. It's like working for the environment is a sign of not caring about what really counts."

So she was raised Cherokee, identifies with African Americans, and has skin so light it could almost be a suntan.

"You're not most people, Clarissa. You're not answerable to anyone's standards but your own."

Clarissa was silent. Then she said, "Why don't other people care? The dump site is in a poor rural neighborhood where only blacks live. How can they stand for that?"

Clarissa's eyes, now that she was opening to Morgan, were luminous, deep.

"I don't know," Morgan said. "Maybe they don't feel powerful enough to change it. If so, they're right. Individually, they can do nothing. But if enough of them stand together, maybe they can stop the dump.

"Or maybe no one ever pointed out to them what they stand to lose personally, in their own lives." Morgan flicked her hair off her shoulders. She was beginning to enjoy herself. "If their concerns are more immediate, as you said, perhaps they don't realize the implications down the road. You might be able to help them with that. You could show them why you care."

Clarissa snorted. "That wouldn't get me very far. I care because I was raised by a full-blooded Cherokee elder who's making me crazy."

Morgan laughed. "You're not crazy. Far from it. You have a vision. And like most great visions, yours is terribly inconvenient. I'm not challenging you because I think you have to follow through on the dump. What I hope to do is help you examine your heart so whatever decision you make is one you can live with. Peacefully."

~ ~ ~

She's not bad.
She tells it like it is.
A u-neg *shrink who swears.*
I think I like her.
Maybe.

"Then there are my two kids," Clarissa said. "My teacher's salary barely keeps us afloat. On the other hand, Big Mom left me some money. Actually, it was my mother's money that she gave to Big Mom in case we needed it. I could use that, but I don't know if I should. It's for my boys' education."

"How long ago did Big Mom die?"

Clarissa glanced down quickly. The couch was soft under her hand, plush. For a moment she lost herself in the swirling yellows, pinks, and greens of the floral pattern.

"November." Clarissa chewed her lower lip. "Why is Big Mom trying to get me to stop this dump? She never would have. She was too shy, too quiet."

"Are you quiet and shy?"

"In a way. I definitely don't have the personality to head up a project like this."

"For someone who can handle a classroom, raise two kids by herself, and flip me off the way you did when you walked in here, stopping a nuclear dump would be a piece of cake."

"Flip you off?"

Morgan grinned. "It's a clinical term."

Clarissa hung her head, then apologized. "But I still can't stop this dump."

"Really? Tell me about it."

How can I?

She's white.

But then again, I paid my money.

I might as well go for it.

She looked at Morgan, really looked at her, for the first time. Morgan was so open. Her body seemed completely unguarded, like those Catholic paintings of Christ or Mary smiling softly even though their hearts were naked, raw, and bleeding from the thorns encircling them.

Morgan sat deep in her overstuffed chair, her legs slightly sprawled, her shoulders relaxed, her belly rounded and soft. Apparently no one ever convinced her to sit straight, square her shoulders, suck in her stomach, hold her knees together, and cross her feet at the ankles. Of course no one ever told Clarissa to do those things either, but she did them religiously, just the same.

"I look black to white people," Clarissa finally said. "Sometimes I even feel black, but I don't sound black, and I don't look black to African American people. Not completely, anyway. They know something's off."

"Go on."

"The only black thing about me is that my grandmother had a brief affair with an African American man and had a baby who turned out to be my father. Then my mother, who was white, had me and disappeared."

"Your mother abandoned you?"

Why does she have to put it that way?

Clarissa's eyes smarted with tears she refused to shed. She set her jaw. "Right. She sent money, but I never met her. She left me on the reservation with my father's mother. I was raised Cherokee, but I was shunned by the Indian kids. They called me 'nigger.' If I didn't have a lot of cousins who were halfway decent to me, I'd have been alone except for Big Mom. I was rejected by what I was."

"Hmm," Morgan said. She was running her fingers along her forearm as if there were something uncomfortable under her long sleeve.

"Hmm, what?" said Clarissa.

Sometimes this woman gets on my nerves.

"You said, 'I was rejected by what I was.'" Morgan's eyes were turned away, staring and unfocused. "Do you think that's how the earth feels at the nuclear dump site? Abandoned by her family. Abandoned by us."

Clarissa felt a howl coming up from deep in her belly, which was somehow the earth's belly. She could barely suppress the urge to scream. What she couldn't stop was a river of tears.

~ ~ ~

"Clarissa, may I tell you what I see?"

Morgan had been sitting silently, giving Clarissa the space to cry. Now that she had quieted, Morgan felt herself stepping out on a limb, saw in hand. She hoped they were safely on the tree side of where she was about to apply her blade. You could never know for sure.

But she sensed that if she didn't cut to the chase, her new client wouldn't be back. Clarissa looked up at her, her eyes raw and glistening. She took this as a go-ahead.

"You're glossing over Big Mom's death," Morgan said.

Clarissa blinked.

I hit a nerve.

"Big Mom was the only person you could count on. And now she's gone, except for these visitations that both comfort and trouble you. I sense you haven't mourned her yet."

She paused, giving her words a chance to settle. Clarissa was looking into her eyes squarely, tears slowly sliding down her cheeks.

"Then," Morgan said, "there's your mother's abandonment and the way you were rejected on the reservation. What about your father?"

Clarissa cut off her tears. "My father was a good man. But the older I got, the drunker he got. I never knew when he'd disappear. I'd get a postcard from Canada, Texas, L.A., wherever he happened to land."

"I'm not sure you've come to terms with all that. No wonder the thought of working to stop the dump is so overwhelming. It would be a huge project in any case, but for you it's tied in with all these unresolved feelings. Because of your history, you can't imagine standing up for what you believe in and being supported."

With a small stab of fear, Morgan wondered how much she held herself back with the same kinds of projections.

"So by fighting to stop the dump, I'd be fighting for myself?" Clarissa was saying.

"That's one way to look at it, sure. But there are other ways you can fight for yourself, gentler ways."

"Easier, softer ways," Clarissa said, as though reciting something from memory.

"What was that?"

"It comes from N.A."

"Narcotics Anonymous?"

"Yes. I go to N.A."

"I didn't know you had a drug problem."

"I don't. Alcohol is my drug of choice."

Morgan was puzzled.

"You didn't know? Around here, blacks go to N.A. and whites go to A.A."

"Great."

"Yeah, great."

Clarissa thought a moment. "You know," she said, "I like the idea of standing up for myself by fighting the dump."

Morgan sat up straight. "It's a very big goal. Bigger than what most people would be willing to take on."

Clarissa grinned. "Aren't you the one who pointed out I'm not most people?"

Morgan laughed. "That would be me."

"All right, then. It's my Cherokee heart that's crying out for the earth. And it's my black butt that's living where the dump is slated to be built."

Morgan smiled.

"I've always been afraid of black people," Clarissa said. "They assume I share an experience with them I've never had. Maybe it's time to put all that aside and take a stand as if those are my people. Which they are. And maybe my white aggressive side knows that this stupid dump can be defeated if we work at it."

"Did you hear what you just said?"

"What?"

"'We'. You said, 'if we work at it.'"

"So I did." Clarissa was smiling.

"You're a brave woman. Some part of you knows you won't have to do this alone." Morgan drew a deep breath. "There's just one thing... ."

"What?"

"Are you ready to do this in a loving way? One that doesn't cause you to drink? That gives you time with your boys and doesn't deplete you financially? Are you ready to set yourself a manageable task and call it good whether or not the dump is defeated?"

"I want to say yes. But the truth is, I'm not sure."

"Let me tell you a story I heard years ago." Morgan relaxed back into her chair. "Someone asked Mother Teresa if she was discouraged because she could reach only a small fraction of the people who were dying in the streets of Calcutta. Mother Teresa simply smiled. 'My Lord doesn't ask me to be successful,' she said, 'Only to be faithful.'"

"Turn it over, as they say in the program," Clarissa said. There were tears in her eyes.

"Exactly. Follow the laws of your own being and let go of the result."

Morgan examined the contours of Clarissa's strong face, her wide nose and full lips and the signs of Cherokee blood in her manner and in her high, broad cheekbones, speech patterns that were both easy and precise, and careful posture. She was radiant now, illumined from within by her own spirit and vision.

"I can't wait to get out there and do something," Clarissa said.

"Whoa, let's include some self-care in your plan. Otherwise you're swinging from one end of the pendulum to the other. 'I can't do a thing, I have to stop the dump.'"

"The alcoholic extremes."

"Perhaps. But let's not pathologize your dream. Ambitious visions are demanding. They evoke great passions. We, however, are only human. Success at any level is impossible without taking that into account. Examine your heart. What is it you most want to do? Let's start with the big picture first and make the necessary adjustments second."

"If nothing were in the way, I'd organize an event of some kind, something that brings the black community together with white environmental activists to stop the dump. I dream about it."

"Describe your dream."

Clarissa closed her eyes. "It's like some kind of big, theatrical, musical ceremony. The whole audience is participating. There's drumming, people are singing and shouting and dancing."

Clarissa was speaking in a reverent whisper. She was smiling, and her hands were outstretched as if she were lifting a newborn into the light. "People are grabbing hold of their power to make change. Not just with the dump, but in their lives. There's chanting, brilliant color, people in costumes." Her eyes and face were wide open now, her smile radiant.

"Amazing."

"Oh yeah. I get goose bumps when I think about it."

"Then do it. Try to be realistic about what's doable and what isn't, given your own needs for self-care. Certainly some kind of event, at some scale, is possible over the course of a summer. We can work with any obstacles that arise as you go along. Oh, and keep a journal of the emotions that come up as you move forward."

Clarissa didn't look convinced.

"I'm serious," Morgan said. "Keeping a journal could make or break your event. Write down your feelings. From what I've seen so far, you're going to have plenty of them and you may have a tendency to sweep them under the rug, which could make you want to drink again. It's better to be aware of your emotions, to get them down on paper so you can see and feel and acknowledge them. Then they can become part of what's going on instead of the force that's running you."

Morgan felt her excitement rising. She wanted to support Clarissa in living her dream.

"After you express what you're feeling, write down five qualities you want in your life," Morgan said. "The emotions you release will leave holes in your mind and spirit. Nature abhors a vacuum and will pull the released emotions back in unless you fill up those empty spaces with your desires. That will help you feel whole, affirming what you want instead of just feeling all that pain pouring out of you."

Morgan tapped her chin with her pen. "And while you're at it, write down five things you're grateful for each day. And five strengths you used to move toward your goal. Bring your journal in next time."

"It sounds like a lot of work.".

"It is. But you know what? You're worth it."

"Don't get me wrong, I want to do the work. But the thing is, I can't afford it. I can't come back."

CHAPTER 8

dreamers

By Moon Dark & Moon Bright
In Lightest Heart & Inner Night
We weave the Web
To set things right.

—Patricia Worth

"God. I mean goddess," Serena said out loud to Virginia Woof, who thumped her tail against the cabin floor. "No one's ever stayed here before!"

Serena paced in a tight circle, which was all her piles of books, papers, and junk would allow. She picked up one of the stacks of books from the floor and began shelving it.

"What's the matter with me, Woof? I criticize Morgan for her appetite for food and men. I claim the moral high ground, characterizing her as impulsive and weak. But damn it, all that sensuality keeps her in the game! She's alive. Even that, that, that..." She gestured with one of the books in rapid, tight circles. "Even that insane profession of hers connects her to the whole."

Woof let out a soft bark and bobbed her head.

Serena tossed various items from the floor into a box. An empty can, an old brush for Woof that was too worn to use, a bit of board.

"Morgan doesn't storm around her house with only animals to talk to." Her eyes fell on Hermie, who gave her a slow blink.

"But damn it!" She shook a shoe at Hermie. "This is how I am! Why did I ask her to stay here in the first place? She must know Jane always rents a room in town.

"Even so, I feel she must stay here.

"Why? This is insane. Maybe I can learn something from her, but is it worth it? I should have let it go as a pleasant reunion and gotten on with my life."

She finished clearing the junk from her floor, dusted the furniture with a damp rag, and swept and washed the floor. She hadn't cleaned in a hundred years. The place was filthy.

But I can't say I like it any better clean, knowing why I'm doing it.

I want to be close to Morgan, but not this close.

She'd better not criticize the inhouse.

And she'd better not bring a lot of stuff.

Serena's heart gave an unexpected little leap as she looked through the window and out over the layered blue ridges of the Smoky Mountains.

But this is what I need.

This is what I've longed for.

It's the beginning of something.

I know it.

~ ~ ~

"Oh? You feel you can't afford counseling?"

"Can't" was Morgan's least favorite word. Sometimes the same old tired lines from clients got on her nerves, especially since she knew their lives wouldn't change until they made the decision they were going to get the job done, no matter what it looked like.

"No," Clarissa said. "I don't feel I can't afford it. I can't afford it."

It's definitely time for a vacation.

Get ready, Serena.

"Try saying, 'I choose not to spend my money that way,' instead of 'I can't afford it.'"

What a brat, poking her chin out like that.

"But I can't afford it!"

"How much money did Big Mom leave you?"

"That's for my boys' education!"

"Bear with me. How much did she leave you?"

"A little over ten thousand dollars."

"So you can afford therapy, but you choose to use that money differently."

"How am I supposed to help my kids go to college if I spend that money?"

"I'm not trying to get you to come to therapy, Clarissa. That's your decision. I'm asking you to feel the power of your choice instead of using the words 'I can't,' words that put you in the victim role. Victim-thinking seems to be a recurring problem for you. It wound you up in a bar and it made you feel powerless to fight the nuclear dump."

"I'm thinking about spending some of that money to fight the dump, but I can't spend it on me. I just can't." Clarissa was studying the cushion on Morgan's couch, which she stroked methodically as if she were hypnotizing herself.

"Fine. But notice you're putting that limitation on yourself. Your boys might tell you there are more important things than saving for their education. They might prefer having a mother who teaches them, through the power of example, how to put self-care first, move beyond self-limiting beliefs, follow one's dreams, and stay clean and sober."

Clarissa said nothing.

"I invite you," Morgan said, "to think about the fact that you haven't asked me whether I might be willing to reduce my fee, consider a payment plan, or explore other options with you. We don't have time for all that now, so for the sake of expediency I'm going to make you a proposal. If you agree to come as regularly as we decide is optimal for you, I'll charge you half price. Under those terms, your check for today will cover this session and your next one. If you go through with the event, I'll make a donation equal to everything you've spent in therapy up to that point."

"You'd do that?"

"Yeah."

"Why?"

"Because I want to."

"There's one thing that keeps bothering me. Why can't I fight this dump myself? Why do I have to come here?"

"You don't have to come here. The real question is: could coming here help you? Big Mom gave you so much, but she couldn't teach you how to speak out for your beliefs. Unfortunately, the children on the reservation taught you that you were an outsider and your mother taught you that you were dispensable."

Clarissa was staring straight ahead, still stroking the couch, her eyes glistening with tears.

"Now," Morgan said, "you feel called upon to initiate something highly visible and you don't know how. That's okay. You can learn, overcoming the fears you've acquired along the way as you do. Most of us need help when we're learning developmental lessons that stretch us beyond our previous capabilities. Therapy is one place to get that kind of support. Personally, I'm glad therapy as we now know it exists, because when I needed help the most, I could find only a Freudian analyst who stared at me and never said a word."

"That's pretty creepy."

"No kidding. I felt as if I were trapped by a peeping tom."

"You may be right, but black people don't go to therapy. Indians don't either. My people don't ask for things from outsiders."

Clarissa looked directly at her with an expression that was both amused and challenging.

"So why did you come?"

"Because I forgot to cancel?"

"No. The real reason."

"Because no matter what it takes, I'm going to fight this dump."

"I see."

~ ~ ~

"Is there anything new you'd like to tell us about, Mom?" Sierra was grinning wickedly at Morgan, obviously struggling to contain herself. Rich choked in his efforts to stop his own laughter.

Morgan was as unprepared as she was unwilling for this to be happening. It better not be what she thought it was.

They were at Sierra and Rich's new house, in the baby's room. Sierra had somehow managed to fit into her old bib overalls and was hammering a shelf while Rich pondered paint samples. He was trying to choose between what he called a low calorie yellow and a buttery one.

She couldn't tell the difference between the two, really, but she assumed Rich preferred the buttery one because of the name he chose for it. But then again, Rich was overly fond of low-calorie cuisine, so who knew? Perhaps the low-calorie yellow was morally superior.

"What are you getting at?" Morgan said.

"Well, Mom, it has been a few days now, have you gotten *involved* with anyone?"

Oh boy.

They know.

Sierra was giggling too much to hammer and collapsed in a heap on the floor.

"Are you suggesting that your mother is on the *make?*" Rich was positively tittering. His voice sounded alarmingly like Aunt Lee's.

I have been altogether too lenient with my children.

Look how they treat me.

"With her *rake!*" Sierra spit the words out in an explosion of laughter.

Rich combed the air with an imaginary rake. "A rake and rambling boy. But delicious, like *cake.*"

"For whom women *ache.*" Sierra rolled her eyes and clasped her hands at her bosom. "Not at all hard to *take,*" she added, looking directly into her eyes.

The headline would read, *Shrink Awakes from Bad Mistake, Omits Jake from Next Retake.*

"To whom have you been talking?" Morgan said.

"Take," Rich paused, rolling his forefinger near his lips as though coaxing out the next word at the same time he helped his wife to her feet. Sierra drew close to him, making a "J" with her lips. Rich looked intently at her mouth, pretending he was struggling to make sense of it. "J. J. Jake!" he finally said. He turned brightly to Morgan.

"Take Jake!" he said. He and Sierra guffawed.

Sierra staggered over and put her arms around her.

"I'm sorry," Rich said. "But Jake was over here earlier and he was so serious, so sincere—"

"That we've been cracking up ever since," Sierra said.

"He wanted to be the first to tell us that the two of you were, how did he put it?" Rich said.

"*Involved.*" Sierra said. They were both helpless again. "He said he knew we'd be concerned."

"He asked us," Rich said, "not to get after you about getting—*involved*—so quickly, because that was his fault, not yours. He wanted us to know that his inten… ."

Sierra and Rich were clinging to each other, weak with laughter.

Sierra made herself come up for air. "His intentions were… ." But she was laughing too hard to finish her sentence.

"Honorable." Rich finally spit out the word and he and Sierra doubled over in hysteria.

Sierra tried to pull herself together and meet her eyes.

Why did Jake have to get the kids into the act five minutes after the curtain went up?

"After the talk we had the other night, I would think you'd be very disturbed by what Jake told you."

Sierra led them into the living room. "Actually, Mom, I was sort of relieved."

"Why?"

"Because you need a friend right now, and no one is a better friend than Jake. He loves you completely. Whatever's going on between the two of you, I know it's not the same old number that had me worried in the past."

"I would think you'd be shocked."

"Why? He's been in love with you ever since I can remember. Over the years, he's talked to all of us about it—me, Ian, Rich."

Ian?

"You're kidding."

"Good grief, Mom. I've even tried to talk to you about it."

"I don't remember that."

"I'm not surprised. Complete denial." Sierra drew the palm of her hand over the top of her head quickly and made a quiet whistling sound. "Right over your head."

Sierra and Rich put their arms around one another's waists. Sierra gave her a somewhat conciliatory, somewhat bemused look that was actually maternal.

❧ ❧ ❧

Clarissa created a makeshift office in her dining room. Frankie and Martin were fine with it because they preferred to eat in the kitchen anyway. No placemats and a shorter distance to cross while setting and clearing the table. She was actually making progress when the phone rang.

It was Auntie Lucy from the reservation. Auntie spoke of Big Mom, how kind she was and how she never got ahead of herself. When trouble came, Big Mom always turned the other cheek. Auntie actually used the word meek.

"Yes, Auntie," Clarissa heard herself say. She felt like a scolded child. At the same time, she was angry. When Auntie hung up, she felt herself sinking toward inaction and despair.

Her eyes fell on the journal she'd purchased as Dr. Forrester—Morgan—had instructed. It was sitting primly at the far corner of the dining room table, delicate splashes of brightly painted flowers on its unopened cover. She felt a slight tremble in her hand as she reached for it.

Wednesday, June 22nd

I was making a good start until Auntie Lucy called.

But when Auntie talked about Big Mom, I felt guilty and small. I don't want to turn the other cheek. It doesn't do anybody any good for me to sit still and allow that dump to be built.

I won't be quiet, Auntie Lucy. I can't allow ignorant people to ruin the land when I know there's a better way.

This is the earth we're talking about. I'm part of it. We are one.

That means I can, and I will, fight.

I Want:
to stop the dump.
to keep going when I feel criticized.
to stay balanced emotionally AND do this project.
to get Frankie and Martin involved, somehow.
to have a good family life this summer even though I'll be working hard.
Five Strengths:
I'm determined.
I'm methodical.
I'm organized.
I'm angry!
I can't think of number five.

I'm Grateful:
that the kids gave up the dining room.
that I care about stopping the dump.
that we have a roof over our heads and food in our bellies.
that I have a dream.
number five? that I can see that patch of sky outside the dining room window.

~ ~ ~

"Sug, what do you want? Really?" As concerned as Jake was about what Morgan's response might be, he had to know up front what he was dealing with. He was propped on his elbow in her bed, stroking her belly in gentle circles that skirted, but did not include, the furry place.

"What do you mean?" She drew up on her elbow to face him.

She looked like a wild woman. Her sex-tousled hair fell in lavish, swirling torrents across her shoulders and face. He was as enthralled as he was concerned.

"I mean now, if you could have anything you wanted, what would it be? Now that you're done with Adam, do you want to be alone?"

"No. I cried when I put my diaphragm away after I left him."

They laughed, heads thrown back, like whinnying horses. She sat up and wrestled him.

"Then how would you have it?" He captured her and held her tight. "If you could write the script exactly to your liking, what would it be?"

"I can and do write my own script, Buddy." She pinched his butt.

"That hurts!"

"I would have a lover." She was writhing against him in the most fabulous way.

"Yes?"

"Well, I might have waited a couple of months." She nipped his shoulder.

"Ouch. Okay, so you would have a lover."

"Yeah. But we wouldn't be in a 'relationship.' Not in the traditional sense." She pulled back to look at him and frowned.

"What's the matter?"

Morgan sat up on the bed, cross-legged, facing him. "I'm afraid I'll hurt you if I tell you what I really want."

"Impossible. I might feel pain, but pain isn't damage. You taught me that." He sat up to face her. "The only way you could hurt me is by not being completely honest with me."

"Smart ass." Her eyes grew serious, penetrating. "I don't know how to describe this to you. All my life, I wanted a partner, a husband, someone to share my kids with. The whole nine yards."

He nodded.

This could go either way.

"Now," she said, "I feel as if life was about to lasso me with my own dream, and I wasn't smart enough to run away. Hell, I was holding my neck straight so the rope could find me, sashaying my bum in front of the branding iron like a filly in heat."

His laughter didn't slow Morgan's tumble of words.

"But then, out of sheer dumb luck, Adam threw the iron and I ducked. In that moment, the lasso fell to the floor and lost its power. I don't want the same thing any more. In three years, Ian will be out of the house. What do I need with a white picket fence? But what else is there? Damned if I know. I still want love, and connection, and sex. But I won't trade myself in for them. Never again."

"Good!"

"Good?"

"Yes, Sugar. Good."

She thought for a long time. Then she looked up at him and said, very softly, "If I could have anything I wanted, I'd be with you, like this. Right now, it couldn't be anyone but you, because you're the only man with whom I've established enough trust to be who I am."

He felt his heart ramming against his rib cage. Her face was close to his and she was running one finger along his forearm. He wanted to take her in his arms and enter her softness again so much it sent a shudder through him. But it was time to listen.

"You're the only man with whom I share the kind of friendship I need for this… experiment. In my ideal, we would be lovers, we would be as close as two people can be. But we would be free. Each of us would be committed to our individual lives. We wouldn't worry about the future, orchestrate a social life together, or expect cooking and dishes from each other. We wouldn't be a 'couple' with all the expectations that go along with that. We would share our bodies as a way to find… ."

"What?"

"I don't know. God, I guess. We would make love and it would be worship. Our offering to creation, our prayer, our gift to life."

"Really?"

For the first time since they began to talk, she looked concerned. "Is that enough for you?"

"Is it enough?" He took her in his arms and kissed her forehead. "Darling, it couldn't be better. It's perfect."

"You mean we're on the same page?"

"Silver, my dearest love, we wrote the same page."

But Jake shuddered inwardly. Was Morgan simply on the rebound, clinging to him because she was scared and alone after what Adam did to her?

~ ~ ~

So what if I am self-righteous?

Serena tapped out the last few lines of an essay on her old portable typewriter, punching out the last three words with a flourish. She typed the final period with the reverence due the last note of a piano concerto played to a full house in Carnegie Hall. Then there was silence, the enraptured moment before the audience began its thunderous applause, its standing ovation.

Serena pulled her work from her typewriter with a loud zip, arranged the white sheets neatly, and placed them in a clean folder. She marched around the cabin straightening things, then headed out to the garden where she picked up a hoe and began weeding.

The world will never read my words.

Everyone thinks I'm nothing but an old crank, full of hate.

That's too damned bad, because civilization will die and never know how it extinguished itself, whereas if people would listen to me, the situation could be reversed.

But no, I'll die old and alone and no one will ever appreciate the truth I could bring them if only they'd let me.

Not Morgan.

And certainly not Clarissa.

She made her way to the barn to try to get ahead of some of the chores that would normally need doing during the time Morgan would be there. Virginia Woof, in an unusual burst of energy, trotted along beside her, grinning.

She nudged her out of the way.

~ ~ ~

As a way to create a relaxed atmosphere, Morgan began Clarissa's second therapy session by telling her about her upcoming trip to the mountains.

"So why are you going to see this old professor of yours after all these years?"

Clarissa had led with a personal question, as she had last time. Morgan studied her face. Her expression was friendly, but behind the black eyes was a flicker of fear.

She's so much more needy than she's ready to admit.

No wonder she's wide-open one minute, then slams the door shut when she feels threatened.

It had taken Clarissa less than a day to decide to continue with therapy. She even asked if she could squeeze in one more session before Morgan's vacation. Now she perched elegantly on the sofa wearing jeans, a tee shirt, brown lipstick and gold hoop earrings, her cloud of black curls framed by a long scarf that included the colors of denim and the orange of her shirt in its brilliant pattern.

Although it was only noon, Clarissa was her last client because she was hoping to reach Serena's place in the mountains before dark.

Jake had managed to get her Saturn fixed and detailed in two days. There wasn't a shard of glass or a dent anywhere to remind her of Adam.

She'd packed extravagantly for the trip, including plenty of food and her best casual wear in addition to three dresses with matching sandals for dining out. She knew she was over-packing as a defense. It would take awhile to trust Serena again.

In the meantime, she'd look good, eat well, and have plenty of reading material. She also brought her beach umbrella, two lounge chairs, and beach blankets and towels. She figured that if she and Serena didn't hit it off, she could always head east.

Jake had her little gold Saturn packed almost to the roof. Trying to be upbeat, he had given her a peck on the nose and cautioned "my Silver" to drive safely.

He probably thinks that once I'm by myself, I'll rethink being lovers with him.

And I could.

On the other hand, he makes Lilith happy.

Very, very happy.

Even though he is getting behind on the lawn.

The headline would read, *Moppet's Mowing Slows, Strumpet's Glowing Grows.* She stretched her whole body deliciously and almost laughed out loud, then caught herself and considered Clarissa's question. "You know, I don't really know why I'm taking this trip. It feels inevitable, somehow. So I'm doing it."

"Destiny?" Clarissa laughed.

Morgan wasn't smiling. She sensed she was embarking on a mythic odyssey. She felt, rather than saw, flashes of herself and Serena, like clips from a movie in which they were heroes fighting to awaken the underwater women she dreamed about each night. But who were these women? And what was the sea that had drowned them?

Then there was Jake's final word to her, which he delivered in a voice that was hushed and trembling with awe.

"Goddess." That's all he said.

She put these thoughts away quickly. What she needed now—and certainly deserved—was a rest, an opportunity to focus on herself and her path.

She brought her attention back to the moment and Clarissa's question. "Destiny? I don't know about that. A vacation? Definitely. So how are things going?"

"I set a date for the event and made a deposit on a hall."

"Congratulations."

"Don't congratulate me yet. The only date I could get at a decent price is in September, a month after school starts. That scares me."

She can't handle the acknowledgment.

"You committed boldly in just three days," Morgan said. I don't think you would have done that unless, deep inside, you knew you could pull it off."

"Maybe."

"Whatever blocks you might have, you're focused and determined."

"I don't know about that."

"Let's try something."

"What?" Clarissa looked uneasy.

"Let's start all over from the top. My line was, 'So tell me, how are things going?'"

"I set a date for the event and made a deposit on a hall." Clarissa's face was a question mark.

"'Congratulations' I say. Now you say, 'Thank you. I'm happy with myself.'"

Clarissa looked skeptical.

"Try it."

Clarissa did.

"Okay," Morgan said, "How did that feel?"

"Awkward."

"I bet. Do you tell yourself nice things when you talk to yourself inside?"

Clarissa looked shocked. "I thought I was supposed to become a better person by keeping track of the things I do wrong."

Morgan laughed. "Most people seem to think that. But is that what you do with your kids? At home, or in your classroom?"

"No. I encourage them."

"How?"

"I notice what they do well and I let them know. In the areas in which they need to improve, I encourage them. I tell them I know they can do it and I use examples of their successes to prove it."

"I see."

"I'd feel like an idiot talking to myself that way."

"At first. Do it anyway. Adults need encouragement as much as children do. And Clarissa, you need to know you're rooting for your own team. Especially now. If you're going to succeed at what you're planning, you're going to have to deal with skeptical people. Lots of them. Positive self-talk can help with that. Ask any team player. It's a very big deal. Sabotage yourself with your own negative projections and 'they' win, create your own positive reality and you win. Besides, you need to protect yourself out there. The best way to do that is to fill yourself with so much love for yourself you aren't bothered by what others think."

Morgan was leaning back to let Clarissa absorb their conversation.

I make mental health sound so easy.

But here I am, running up to Serena's—whom I no longer know—and jumping into bed with yet another guy when I could be taking this time to be alone, to focus.

Am I distracting myself with these people?

Or being guided?

Or both?

I don't know what I'm doing.

Or do I?

Am I wasting my time or am I having exactly the experiences I need to get clear?

Are Serena and Jake diverting me from my calling or are they allies on my quest for my true path?

All at once Chiron, the wounded healer, floated into her mind. The centaur, a lame yet dancing horse with the torso of a man, penetrated her heart with a wave of warm acceptance. It was appropriate that she, with all her vulnerabilities, was doing this work of psychotherapy. Who better?

Cut yourself some slack, kid.

You're telling a client what you need to hear yourself.

It's not the first time.

"How's the journal coming along?" Morgan said.

Clarissa hung her head. "I only did it once."

"Try, 'I did it! Once!'"

Clarissa smiled.

~ ~ ~

Daylight was beginning to fade, so Morgan should be arriving any minute. Serena surveyed the cabin with satisfaction. True, it wouldn't meet most people's standards, but then Serena wasn't most people now, was she? You could move around her place more freely and things were basically clean and organized.

Suddenly, Serena stopped dead in her tracks. Her eyes fell on Virginia Woof, whose tail was wagging. When Woof saw Serena's face, her tail stopped and dropped down between her legs.

"Holy shit. There's nowhere for her to sleep!"

~ ~ ~

On her way to Serena's, Morgan stopped for gas and found herself deferring to an enormous, red-faced man who butted ahead of her in the payment line.

He thinks I'm nothing but a fat old woman.

Worthless.

Back on the road, she chastised herself for being weak. She wished she'd stood her ground instead of allowing herself to be pushed aside. Shadow assumed the form of the man in the gas station and grinned at her from the passenger seat.

Leaving the interstate, Morgan began her journey along narrow roads that hairpinned deeper into the mountains. The sky was darkening and Shadow was growing more sinister. She kept her back straight and her shoulders erect, but inwardly she cowered away from him.

She'd told Jake about Shadow that first morning they were together. He'd asked her where Shadow was in the room. It seemed an odd question, but she pointed to the far corner. Before she knew it, he was on his feet, tilting with Shadow like Don Quixote leading a charge on a windmill.

She had tried not to laugh. He was naked and his privates, which looked vulnerable and silly under the circumstances, were wobbling as he moved to protect her. He muttered something about attacks on the goddess or some such foolishness.

He hadn't seemed to believe her when she explained that Shadow was in her mind, he wasn't real.

If only she could convince herself now of what she was certain of then. Just hours before she'd been so confident with Clarissa, as if showering oneself with self-love were as natural as breathing. If that were so, this would be what suffocation looked like.

She imagined Jake's arms around her, enfolding her. Shadow diminished considerably.

Maybe she should get a gun. The headline would read, *Shrink Shoots Shadow, Autopsy Reveals Nothing.*

Her insecurities increased with her fear as her low, sporty vehicle barely cleared the ruts in Serena's steep, two-track dirt driveway. Sometimes the nearly-full moon popped through the trees to illumine her way, but for the most part she bounced in slow motion through silent, eerie darkness.

She was furious. Serena hadn't warned her about the two mile driveway. What if she got stuck? Then she'd have to risk a sprained ankle to find Serena. Who had no phone, by the way, to call for help. Assuming there was such a thing as help that would come all the way up this treacherous mountain path.

Damn you, Serena.

Morgan set her jaw. How many more obstacles—distractions—must she face?

This much I can do, right here on this frigging mountain.

Universe, Spirit, I commit myself to honoring my calling.

I open to my true path and claim it as my number one priority.

Help me find it, please.

Guide me.

The forest abruptly gave way to meadows and she was pulling into Serena's yard. Serena flew out of her cabin.

"Your driveway is impossible! I barely made it!" It was supposed to be a joke, but she heard the edge in her voice and knew it didn't sound like one.

"What's *that?*" Serena indicated Morgan's Saturn with an imperial sweep of her arm.

Fuck you, bitch.

She thought of all the things she imagined Serena damned her for, and collected them quickly into a tense little bundle that she released in a controlled explosion.

"This is my midlife crisis car." Morgan's speech was clipped, mannered. "Last summer, Ian announced there would be no more family vacations, Boy Scout outings, or school field trips in the mini-van. It stung me in a way a childless woman would not understand."

She arched her brow at Serena. "I bought this sporty little number in retaliation. Since I'm soon to be a grandmother, I imagine I'll be trading it in soon. For a sports utility vehicle, I would think." She flashed a too-toothy, forced smile.

Serena retracted visibly.

Good.

I'm not going to cut you any slack, you creep.

You may be stuck here on this mountain, but I'm not.

One more crack and I'm outta here.

"I was referring to your things. There isn't room inside for all your things."

"Fine."

CHAPTER 9

standing behind her

The life of a dreamer is not easy.
The dreams keep you awake.

—Essie Parrish, Pomo healer

"Mama! I need you!"

Frankie.

Clarissa stumbled to her feet in the dark and woodenly moved her body toward the boys' room.

Martin stirred. "Mama," he said, smacking the roof of his mouth with his tongue as he used to after nursing. He gestured loosely toward his brother and said, "Frankie," then turned his back to the room and began to breathe deeply and rhythmically.

Easy for you.

Frankie was sitting up in bed, rubbing his eyes and fussing. Clarissa put her arms around him and found he was burning up. He whimpered, "My throat! It kills!"

Frankie's temperature was a hundred and one point two, not unusual for him. She got him to take some acetaminophen and cough syrup, then rubbed his back in lazy figure eights until he fell asleep.

As she massaged him, she thought about her work on the nuclear dump. She'd set up her office, borrowed a laptop and printer from the school, and made several mailing lists that included the churches closest to the proposed dump site, black churches in Hopewellen, environmental groups, newspapers, radio and television stations, state representatives, council members from Hopewellen and neighboring towns, student groups from the university and two colleges, and assorted liberal organizations throughout the community.

For almost every address, she had a phone number and a contact person. She had begun drafting mailings to drum up interest and attract volunteers. Soon, she was going to have to start pulling the event together. She needed to plan the evening and line up talent.

Then there was the matter of building community contacts. That meant getting herself out there, which she dreaded. It was so much easier to sit at home getting organized and preparing mailings. Worst of all, she was going to have to begin canvassing, intruding on people's privacy like a door-to-door salesman.

With the kids, don't forget.

Back in bed, Clarissa lay awake staring at those horrid vines that infested the wallpaper next to her. She felt like a cheerleader out of Prozac. She wanted her mother and she wanted to tell her mother off at the same time.

What mother?

She became more awake and more annoyed as the clock displayed one scarlet minute after another, like flash cards prompting her to calculate exactly how much sleep she was missing.

"*Shea*," she heard. It was Big Mom, saying hello in Cherokee.

Not this again.

She tossed onto her back. Hearing Big Mom frightened her the first time it happened. Now it peeled away her carefully constructed layers of denial and forced her to feel the depth of her longing for her grandmother.

"*Nunda!*" It was the Cherokee word that meant both sun and moon, the name Big Mom called her because her nature encompassed so many opposites. And because, Big Mom used to tell her, she lit up each moment of the day and night.

She felt two large tears slide down the sides of her face and lose themselves in her hair. Abruptly, she turned to the wall as Martin had. Some things were simply too much to bear.

Sleep came easily this time and with it, a dream about Big Mom sitting in front of the wood stove, weaving a basket. She was lit by the soft, yellow glow of a single kerosene lamp. In buckets at her feet, piles of river reed in varied earth tones lay soaking. She was a study in roundness from her cheeks to her hands, from her breasts to her feet. She was a brown, generous sphere—a warm, intense nugget—both comforting and awesome.

Big Mom was wearing her faded orange and green floral print dress. Her legs were separated by their girth, her feet in their black laced shoes were crossed at the ankles, knee-high nylons sagging just above them, and her now narrow single braid of white hair fell across one shoulder. It was a familiar scene.

Big Mom gazed into Clarissa. Her eyes were shining, lit from within, golden and silvery, bottomless and black. Then she smiled—a big, openmouthed grin that exposed two badly broken front teeth. Her eyes nearly disappeared behind a deeply furrowed garden of wrinkles.

"You are doing the right thing, Granddaughter." Big Mom spoke in the slow, careful speech the effort of speaking English often gave rise to, especially when she was working her hands in the ancestral rhythms of basket weaving. Her voice warmed Clarissa with the dry, penetrating heat of the wood stove.

"It is a time of great change," Big Mom counseled. "Be a carrier of that change, Clarissa. Don't let it carry you. Don't let it sweep you away."

In the air between them, an image began to form that was both finely etched and hazy as smoke. Clarissa saw herself in the vision. She was dancing barefoot around a fire and her arms, which became wings, were cutting the air. Then she was an eagle, not soaring on the thermals but beating her great wide wings, her eyes quiet and fierce. In her talons she was carrying a small, glowing bundle, the medicine of change.

The vision—which she knew Big Mom had conjured for her—slowly faded, leaving her eyes locked with Big Mom's.

"If you don't carry the changes, *Nunda,* the changes will carry you and you could lose all that you love. Your children are important. But do not trade in your grandchildren's grandchildren for them."

~ ~ ~

How did the mattress get so hard?

Morgan emerged from slumber with sunlight on her back instead of her face, where it should be. The wall was too close. It was made up of old barn boards. There was a flashlight next to her on an upended crate and a lovely black and white print of a standing, half-turned figure on the wall. It was a nicely rounded nude woman that, in a way, looked like her.

Serena was up already and apparently outside. They had shared her bed. Neither relished the idea, but it was a necessity given the lack of an alternative.

There had been an odd minuet while they decided who would sleep on which side of the bed. But then they settled in nicely.

Now she was going to have to get up and use that damned "inhouse" again.

Morgan stood. That wasn't a print, it was a drawing. Signed by Auguste Renoir! She shook her head as she padded to the inhouse, smiling at Serena's idiosyncrasies.

Serena's tiny log cabin had one room in addition to the bedroom, and the inhouse was a closet in the corner of the main room. Inside, it was like an old fashioned one-seater outhouse. You removed the round plywood lid by lifting its screwed-in handle. Then you sat on the bare wood over the round hole.

Afterwards, you threw your toilet paper in the paper bag at your feet. You tossed in one scoop of peat moss after yourself if you peed and two if you pooped. When the tub beneath the seat got full, Serena slid it through a hatch outside and hauled it to its own compost pile, where it sat for at least a year before adding it to the vegetables. When she heard that, she wasn't sure she wanted to eat the vegetables but hey, Serena probably knew what she was doing.

Last night, the inhouse had disgusted her. But this morning there was something pleasantly woodsy about it. The peat moss was cool and earthy at the same time that it was light, clean, and sweetsmelling. There was a small, high window through which she could see blue sky and treetops.

The window cast just enough light to make it easy to maneuver while at the same time creating the meditative quality of a forest. There was no odor, other than the earthiness of the peat moss. Serena had decorated the interior with postcards mixed with collages, most of which seemed to express obscure political views.

She left the inhouse and looked around the cabin. Last night, she and Serena had attempted to join forces by introducing her to Serena's world with all the care involved in acclimating a visiting alien. Besides the inhouse, there was an outhouse, to be used whenever it was daylight and it wasn't raining.

Oops.

I was supposed to use the outhouse.

There were so many things to keep track of. For example, you heated water for washing on the wood stove. When there was a fire, of course. Some of the water bottles were for drinking and some were for washing. It was important to be sparing with each.

Nuts to that.

I'm going to drink whenever I'm thirsty.

She didn't like that there wasn't a phone. What if one of her kids needed her? Serena had herself set up so she wasn't needed.

Then there was that stew last night. She thought it was delicious until Serena told her it was rabbit she raised and slaughtered herself. It was the cheapest way to get meat, Serena said.

Not if you puke it all up.

That's the last rabbit I'm ever *going to eat.*

She could swear the stew made her sick, but her upset could also have been because of the rising mix of anticipation and anxiety they both seemed to be feeling, though they didn't talk about it.

She perched on a stool in the main room.

I'm tired, that's all.

And in culture shock.

Morgan's eyes roamed the cabin. She was fascinated by the wildly incongruent luxuries scattered throughout the otherwise Third World dwelling. The cramped cabin was barely standing and many of its furnishings were courtesy of the local dump. These contrasted with items only the ultra-rich could afford, such as that fabulous Danish leather rocker.

Now that's *royal purple!*

Heavenly.

She was on her feet poking around. The leather felt like butter. A patchwork fur throw was draped across the back, brown and white. She loved the feel of it until she realized it was probably rabbit.

There were two more original Renoirs and a Degas, all set in thick, elaborate, gold frames. Assorted junk was stacked about, including broken furniture.

The walls were lined with sagging bookcases, three of which protruded into the room as they would in a library. Some of the books were falling apart and some were bound in rich leather. She was standing in the tee shirt she slept in, running her fingers over a row of embossed leather book bindings, when Serena strode into the cabin.

ಌ ಌ ಌ

Virginia Woof, whom Serena had taken outside so she wouldn't disturb Morgan while she did her morning chores, came loping through the screen door with more enthusiasm than she'd shown in months. Woof went directly to Morgan and slobbered all over her, which Morgan seemed to eat up. She was cooing at Woof.

That's no way to treat a dog!

And why is she snooping through my things?

She's been up for awhile, apparently.

I bet she used the inhouse.

She wouldn't have if she were the one who had to haul the crap.

Morgan threw her by flashing her a smile.

"Why is this called Mothers Mountain?" Morgan said. "Yesterday on the map, it looked like Founders Mountain. I couldn't find Mothers Mountain anywhere."

Take two.

"Let me show you something." She led Morgan out to the porch and pointed off into the distance. "What do those two mountains look like?"

Morgan gazed out over the mountain laurel and rhododendron blooming on the slopes of Mothers Mountain. "My god, they look like breasts! They even have nipples."

"That's what I thought. In Ireland there are two mountains that look exactly like that. They're called the Paps of Anu. Anu is one of their ancient goddesses. But guess what those mountains are called?"

"The Paps of Morgan? I know they couldn't be the Paps of Serena."

"Very funny. They're called the Spears."

"No. How phallic."

"Exactly. So to compensate, I named this Mothers Mountain." She thought of Clarissa with a little jab of guilt and longed to tell Morgan the real reason for the name.

"I see." The way Morgan studied her suggested she knew there was something she wasn't telling her. But she didn't ask, for which Serena was grateful.

She showed Morgan the dark bread, fruit, and nuts available for breakfast, telling her she was going to go back out and finish the morning chores. But Morgan wanted her to keep her company. Besides, Morgan said, she wanted to help with the chores as long as she was visiting a farm.

The animals were long since fed and watered and Serena had hauled the water up in the cool of the day. She wanted to finish the weeding before it got hot, but decided to accommodate her guest.

Outside, she handed Morgan a hoe. Morgan was trying to imitate her technique, but she spent most of her time prancing around trying to keep her spanking white athletic shoes from getting muddy. Her other priorities included preserving her manicure and keeping dirt off her matching teal shorts and shirt. She probably hired someone to do such things at home.

And Morgan kept stopping to pet Woof, Hermie, and the assorted other dogs and cats, who took advantage of the stranger's ignorance by coming into the vegetable beds when they knew they weren't supposed to. But at least she was trying. She was soft though, too soft. The amount of sweat she produced in the face of moderate effort was appalling.

"Spandex, Wynonna, get out of here!" Serena barked at two of the outside dogs. She gave Wynonna's fanny a little shove with her hoe when she scampered across the lettuce, knocking down three heads. Morgan looked stricken.

Later they went for a walk through mountain meadows and forest and began to catch up on the years they'd lost. They cooked together that night and Morgan was a good sport about the lack of amenities. Things were going well, Serena thought, except for the growing attachment between Woof and Morgan.

The next morning, Morgan rose with her and they did the chores together. Morgan even let her shoes get dirty. But she needed frequent breaks, which she spent sitting on the faded gray porch step, nuzzling Woof and watching a spider build her web. At one point, Serena joined her.

"See," Serena said, pointing to the spider, "She doesn't need a man." Morgan gave her a little shove with her foot and she nearly lost her balance.

Morgan was slowing down as the day heated up. She looked pale and finally said she felt sick and needed to go inside and lie down. Serena went on with her chores.

Thirty minutes hadn't gone by before Morgan flew out of the cabin so fast she could have been on fire. She bolted toward the bin used for the kitchen and garden compost, but didn't make it. She fell down on her hands and knees in the grass and vomited violently. It was as if gallons of dirty water were belching out of her.

Serena ran to her side but Morgan waved her off. She was spiraling on the ground, sobbing, and retching. When her stomach was empty of its contents and then some, she fell on her side on the grass, sweaty and weak.

"I'm going to get a damp towel," Serena told her. When she came back, Morgan was lying in the same position, staring, tears streaming from her eyes. She turned Morgan onto her back, away from the vomit, sponged her face and neck, and wiped her clean. Morgan responded with weak appreciation.

Woof, who had been barking fiercely at something Serena couldn't see, was quiet for the moment. She was looking at Morgan with great concern. Then she began guarding them. A low snarl rattled in her throat and she circled them with watchful eyes, her ears pricked and her hackles raised.

Suddenly Woof started barking again. When Morgan looked in the direction of Woof's gaze, her eyes grew wide and she huddled into Serena, burying her face in her lap and weeping.

Woof quieted. It was a long time before Morgan could talk. When she did, it was as if she were delirious.

"It was real!" she said, her eyes big with terror. She seemed frantic, looking up at Serena and searching her face for something.

"It's okay. You got sick and had a bad dream."

"No, no!" Morgan was shaking her head violently. "It was real!"

Serena stroked Morgan's brow. "What was real?"

"I was lying on your bed, trying to sleep. I thought I dozed off, but then I was drowning in the ocean. There was a violent storm. The waves hurled my body against rocks. I heard my bones breaking! I could feel myself being pulverized."

Morgan looked at her left arm, apparently marveling that it was whole. Then she touched her right arm and felt the bandage there. She looked at it in horror and her chin began to tremble.

"That's old," Serena reminded her. "That guy did it, remember? Adam."

Morgan squeezed her eyes shut. Tears were streaming down her face. "All of a sudden I was on my hands and knees, facing the foot of the bed. Another wave took me and I was pushed back hard, on my side, then tumbled around again on my other side. It was like something was throwing me from one part of the bed to another. My lungs and stomach were full of sand and salt water."

Morgan's sides began to heave again as though she could vomit up the sea. Serena held her, keeping her head on her lap but letting her turn her face to the ground. Nothing came out, but it was pathetic how hard she was gagging. Finally Morgan was spent. She turned back toward Serena. Her eyes were bulging, racing to find something that was gone.

"Take it easy, Morgan. You need to calm down."

"But I have to tell you."

"Okay, but try to relax."

"I was tossed like a rag doll. I kept trying to wake up. And I would, but only for a moment. Then I'd be slammed back under the water. The bodies of other women were being battered in the water all around me. Their bellies were glowing and there was horror in their… ."

"What?"

"Their eyes were dead, staring." These last words made her retch again.

"Easy, Morgan."

"I have to tell you this one last thing. It was the peasant women I've been dreaming about. Their mouths were screaming, but all I could hear was the sea. It was deafening."

~ ~ ~

Brigid rolled a little in her slumber. She could hear her name being called. It was most annoying. Since her death by drowning four hundred years ago, she had been allowed to relax undisturbed and had spent her time dreaming pleasantly in this place she knew to be her real home, the Other World, the Land of the Living.

She understood that for her good work in her last lifetime, she had been given a long rest she was beginning to assume would last forever. But here They were again, wanting more from her.

"Don't be daft!" she wanted to say, but couldn't.

As Brigid came around, she knew she didn't want to be disrespectful to Them. She would understand soon enough what They wanted from her.

They were telling her many things had changed on Earth. There was trouble there, and it was time to resolve it. She was being asked to help.

She wondered why she should. It was peaceful here, why must she leave?

They said that in helping, she would be helped. Besides, she hadn't completed her lessons. Fear had shadowed her in her last lifetime, but if she helped a living woman overcome her fear, she would learn how to work out her own. She would be free at last, to stay or go as she chose, and her beloved Earth would be saved.

"Earth?" Brigid mouthed silently.

Great Mother Goddess!

Earth is in peril?

A hard day has come, then.

Brigid felt an emptiness inside her as vast as any cavern.

She could feel Them lifting her the way a loving mother pulls a sleeping, reluctant child to its feet. They were beings of light more than form—tall, luminous, multi-pointed crystals, more beautiful and intense than anything she had ever experienced. They radiated shades of white light, silvers and golds streaked with the colors of the between times—dawn and dusk—radiant pinks, oranges, yellows, greens, blues, and purples. Even when she had been brought to this place, the entities who helped her were not so powerful as These.

Their voices weren't something she heard, exactly. Rather she understood them, like celestial music from within, powerful bells ringing inside and vibrating her whole being into alignment with the greater good.

The prospect of more work wasn't appealing. The world wasn't an easy place, she knew. But They told her it was time and she had a great deal to learn about this assignment. In spite of her resistance, Their words carried the resonance of undeniable truth.

Brigid knew she was reawakening to Earth because she felt a great stab of loss. Leaving her daughters behind when she died had tugged at her. But the loss of Earth Herself, with Her magic and beauty, had left a hole in her soul.

She attempted to look at what her guides were showing her. It was as if she were going from darkness into a light that was too bright. The ugliness was shocking, blinding. There were monstrous buildings unlike anything she'd ever seen, one after another, belching forth substances that make her feel sick.

Strange metallic carts were moving hideously fast over ugly black tracks that crisscrossed and divided the land. Even stranger were the huge and deafening metal birds that pierced the blue stillness of the sky.

The Earth had been invaded and Her beauty was now scarred beyond recognition. There were so many people. The trees were not as green as she remembered, nor the sky as blue. Compared to the way things were in Brigid's time, it was as if everything were covered by a pale brown fog.

But They showed her a place that was still beautiful, green and rolling, though not nearly so vivid as she remembered. She was being drawn gently down to the soft grass next to a rather large dwelling made of logs. Brigid hid around the corner from the two women who were in front of it.

There was a woman They were calling Morgan who was laid out on the grass and being tended by an older woman.

"She's a troubled soul, that Morgan," Brigid whispered, "and pale as a fish's belly."

"She's been through an ordeal, as you shall soon see," her guides said.

"And… Serena?"

"Yes," They said, in the tones of chimes and bells, "her name is Serena."

Serena was helping Morgan, who seemed to be terribly ill, to her feet. She held Morgan tightly as they slowly moved toward the structure. The cabin, They called it.

She followed them inside, careful to hide behind the—door, They said—so the two women wouldn't see her. Serena undressed Morgan and reverently sponged the sweat off her trembling body. She put her in a large bed that stood off the floor and brought her tea and crackers.

Brigid realized something that caused her to suck in her breath with such force she was sure she'd be heard.

This woman Morgan has been reliving my very own death!

As if it happened yesterday, which it did not.

But in the name of the Great Mother Goddess and all things holy—why?

Morgan rested for a long time while Serena concocted a thick soup. When Morgan finally awakened, Serena sat beside her on the bed while she ate.

Now will you look at how tender that Serena is with her, as though Morgan were the merest of babes.

Are they lovers then, like Grianne and Banba?

"Perhaps these dreams contain an opportunity, a message," Serena said.

"An opportunity? They're driving me nuts! I have to get past this."

"What can we do?"

"The only way out is through. Do you have any experience with guided meditation, trance work?"

"Actually, I do. From my attend-every-workshop-ever-invented days."

"Good. I need to create a state of conscious dreaming. Do you have the skills to guide me back out?"

Brigid shifted uneasily.

Doesn't everyone know how to do these things?

Not that I want them to invade my life.

'Tis some mighty strange doings indeed.

"I think so, but—"

"I'll teach you." Morgan was sitting up very straight on the bed. "The main thing is to help me get where I need to go, but don't let me go in too deep or be out of contact with you for too long. We'll develop signals—you can rub my feet, my arms, you can tell me to put my hand on my heart and remember how much I love my children and how much they love me, get me to describe what my body feels like—"

"I can get you to drink water—to feel where gravity is supporting your body."

"Exactly. Guide me in to retrieve whatever information I need to get resolution on these stupid dreams—at the same time that you keep me rooted in the present, in my body—and then get me out. You'll have to stay on top of it. Can you do that?"

"Yes."

"You're sure?"

"You bet. But are you positive you want to do this?"

"Absolutely. I refuse to let these dreams control me. They're coming for a reason. I'm going to find out why on my own terms. Tomorrow. I refuse any more dreams until tomorrow. Oh, and Serena? Thanks." Morgan wrapped her arms around Serena, which seemed to shock her.

Brigid moved out into the open in one swift step. "Are you daft as a brush? Barging into my life as if it were your very own?" She felt a great heaving in what was once her chest.

But Morgan and Serena didn't respond.

"Is it deaf you are? I'm talking to you, and sure as I'm standing here, I'll bloody well have you listen to me."

Still no response. Brigid lunged forward, insistent. Up to her thighs in bed, she suddenly understood. She had become one of the ancestors. Only the gifted could know she was there. She backed away.

And who is the dark one?

As mean a creature and as black a soul as ever I've set living eyes upon.

Brigid was gazing at a dark form, like herself without a body. He seemed to gain energy whenever Morgan was afraid. A mighty being, this one was. He lunged menacingly in Brigid's direction, but she intuited he was afraid of her in some way.

"Be off with you, then!" she told him, hoping to capitalize on his fear. She decided to try to work out why he was afraid of her.

Find out, and be done with him.

But though it was her voice speaking this thought to herself, it was Their words coming to her. Through Them, she surmised that this dark entity couldn't harm her. He was an agent, as she was, for a struggle that must be carried out at the human level.

Brigid watched the thing's focus on Morgan and Serena. She didn't like it one bit.

~ ~ ~

"Mama, my throat hurts!"

It was four in the morning and Clarissa was being awakened for the sixth time that night. Frankie was up and down with his cough, for one thing. But mostly she was fretting about whether or not she could actually pull off this antinuclear event. The weather wasn't helping. The air was hot, heavy, and still.

"Okay, Baby, Mama's coming. You can have some more syrup. It's time."

Stumbling to the bathroom for some water and Frankie's medicine, Clarissa felt her mind pick up where it left off a half hour ago, when a mosquito landed on her cheek and set the motor between her ears running one more time.

It was going to be easy enough getting the local environmental groups involved. Time consuming, but simple. The challenge was, how could she involve the black community?

She needed help from the urban black churches. She figured they were unlikely to respond unless she had the support of the rural black churches closest to the proposed dump site. But the minister of the largest church put her off when she called him today. Why? She suspected money was involved. Money or fear or both. Maybe she could get to him through his parishioners. But how?

These people were poor, working hard day to day just to make ends meet. A nuclear dump seemed so abstract. What did she need to do to make it real for them?

Besides, how often did poor rural blacks stop the fat cats from doing exactly what they wanted? For that matter, the whole damned world seemed to feel as if they couldn't change anything, it was all just rolling along the way it was, and if we make it, we make it, and if we don't, we don't. Find out on the six o'clock news. Sit back and watch it all happen. Or not happen. Pass the pretzels either way.

This was going to take a lot of talking, a lot of convincing. She would need to organize door-to-door canvassing. College students would be good for that. Could they get credit instead of getting paid? But it was summer.

Damn.

Speaking of which. That stupid shrink would be on vacation. Then again, what did Ms. Morgan Forrester know about these things anyway? Still, Clarissa needed someone to talk to, someone who cared. But if she didn't get the ball rolling on community support soon, when was she going to get around to preparing the event itself?

Frankie gulped the water she brought him and took the syrup-filled spoon in his mouth with a sleepy, innocent, righteous thoroughness that reminded her of when he was a baby. His forehead was hot.

So much for getting anything done tomorrow.

Feeling guilty for begrudging him his illness, she wiped his face with a cool cloth, kissed him, and padded off to bed where she finally fell asleep.

Too soon, she felt something shaking her awake.

"*Nunda! Nunda!* Wake up!"

She fought off the voice, clinging to her pillow and to sleep.

"The ancestors are stirring, *Nunda!*" Big Mom whispered. "Earth Mother is awakening the spirits of her daughters!"

Part of Clarissa slumbered on. Another part sat up straight—alert, awake, alive. She didn't hear Big Mom's voice with her outer ear. Instead she heard it within, from an inner place of knowing. Big Mom's voice was strong and sure.

"Listen to me, Granddaughter. Do this thing you dream of, stop this dump. There is help. But you must be brave and fight for your people, for the four-leggeds and the two-leggeds and the winged ones. Fight for the tree people and for your children. Do not think you're alone. You are never alone."

She could see Big Mom grinning, her face folding into a million creases. She could even see Big Mom's old potato nose and the gaps where her front teeth used to be. Her expression was sweet, sacred, urgent, and unrefusable.

"When the spirits of the land fill your heart with the longing to do a job for them, it is good for you to do it, my sleepy one. Stop this dump. It is your calling."

Great.

The ancestors are stirring, the spirits of the land have landed a great job for me—no pay, but hey!—and my shrink is on vacation.

This was the voice of the part of her that clung to sleep. Another part of her was moved to tears.

"*Nunda!*" Big Mom's voice continued. "Know this. It is as I have taught you. The only reason Earth Mother allows us to walk with Her is for the purpose of the soul's learning.

"Most people have forgotten this," Big Mom said. "But that does not excuse you from remembering what you already know, deep in your heart. Your spirit has tasks to accomplish in this life span, work that you yourself chose before you came here. You know this work because it lives inside you, in your dreams, in the whisperings, the stirrings, that call to your heart. This one you call shrink, this Morgan, will help you with this, and you will help her.

"And let your children help," Big Mom said. "Teach them that they, too, can walk a powerful path even though they are young and without experience. You must move forward with one foot in a moccasin and the other in a shoe. It won't be easy. But it will be good.

"Do you understand, *Nunda?*"

"I feel moved by your words. But I also feel small and afraid."

"Get up now and go to your window."

She pulled herself out of bed and stood by her bedroom window.

"Tell me what you see, child."

"I see the full moon setting, a gray light coming into the sky. I see the trees swaying."

"And what do you feel?"

"I feel sweat on my skin. But it's being gently cooled by the breeze."

"Good. And what do you hear?"

"I hear the songs of birds. So many different kinds of birds."

"What else do you hear?"

Clarissa listened. At first, all she could hear was the birds and an occasional car. But then she noticed another sound. "The wind."

"That's right. The Wind Spirits that Earth Mother sends forth each dawn to wake up Her children and bring them Her life force and Her messages for the new day. Breathe in this life force, Nunda, it will strengthen you." Big Mom paused for a moment.

"Now look again, Granddaughter. Notice the beauty of the Earth Mother as she spreads her dawn before you. Notice what you see and hear and feel and sense."

As she tuned in to the slowly brightening sky, the delicate rose and golden light, and the energizing force of the wind, she felt connected to her own body and to the land.

"Tell me," Big Mom said.

Clarissa sighed. "I feel quiet inside—comforted and full."

"Yes. This is the comfort She will bring each time you give Her your full attention. Remember this. She's a Woman Spirit, generous with us, as any mother is with her children. She wants only to give us her beauty and support. Thank her with your words, and your heart will be full. Thank her with your actions—by following your dreams, the laws of your deepest being—and your soul will be fulfilled. Thank her with your whole life, and you will be free. You will walk the beauty path. These words I have spoken."

Big Mom's voice faded. In her heart, Clarissa gave thanks.

For a long time, she stood by her window and watched the changes in the world outside. As the sky brightened, the gray shapes became defined and colors were painted on the flowers and the houses, the trees and the birds.

Gradually the part of her that had only wanted to sleep—the same part that had always run from Big Mom's words—came to life and joined with the part that quenched its thirst in Big Mom's loving wisdom.

Big Mom had named her *Nunda,* one word for two parts as different as the moon and the sun and for this moment, at least, the two were one.

She walked slowly to her bed and sat down. Many minutes passed. Finally she picked up her journal and wrote:

Monday, June 26th, the Dawn of a New Day

I Feel:
blessed.

I Want:
to fulfill my dream, my calling.

I Am Grateful For:
The voice of Big Mom.
That she tells me I'm not alone.
Frankie's round, soft, fat, little boy cheeks and the way Martin protects his little brother.
The wind.
My own willingness to take a chance on this damned amazing dream of mine.

Strengths I Have Used to Move Towards My Goal:
—Love for my children and all the generations to come.
—Love for this crazy, mixed up world, including all the fools who just make everything worse.
—Grit (and grits!). Determination. I am GOING to make this thing happen. Even if it kills me. (Which, at this rate, it probably will.)
—The sense to use part of Big Mom's money to take a stand.
—Right now I can't think of a number five. But that doesn't mean there isn't one!

❧ ❧ ❧

The next day, Morgan seemed to wake up refreshed and strong. She and Serena completed the day's chores quickly so they could have the afternoon for Morgan's trance. Brigid noted that the dog, Woof, showed unusual vigor for such an aged beast and never left Morgan's side, as though she were guarding Morgan from that horrible thing.

"The headline will read," Morgan said, "*Therapist Drowns on Mountain Summit.*"

They were setting up Serena's bedroom. They had to put Woof outside, because she was exhausting herself and distracting them.

"The subhead will be, *Meets the Deep while Steeped in Sleep.*"

Serena laughed sharply. It was more like a bark.

"How about," Serena said, looking up and to one side in her search for words, "*Mountain Mama Drenched by Delirium Deluge.*"

"That could work."

"I gather you're feeling somewhat apprehensive?"

"Try scared shitless. Wouldn't you be?"

"Probably."

"Okay, then."

"What are you afraid of?"

"It's not so much the drowning that scares me. I mean, you'll be here and I know enough about mental illness to know I'm not going to lose it at this point, since I haven't already."

"What then?"

Morgan was cross-legged on the bed, preparing to lie down for the trance. She told Serena about Shadow. She said she knew Shadow was only in her head, but she still wanted to feel safe from him.

Shadow looked at Brigid and snickered.

"Only in your mind, is it?" Brigid said. "I'm here to tell you that thing you call Shadow is real enough, and you had best protect yourself from him with everything you've got."

CHAPTER 10

the story again

... she leaned
her thick white braids into my face
to tell me
of the wise spirits she could see
behind me
"There are many Sabias, many, many,
They are in constant conference
standing behind you," she said.
"Las Sabias sing through our bodies."

—Sue Silvermarie

Brigid felt something spark in Serena.

"I have an idea." Serena called in the sister spirits of the four directions to protect them as she placed white candles in the east, south, west, and north, a short distance out from the bed.

When she lit the candles, she asked that what was about to happen be for the highest good of all and invited all the guides, angels, masters, and other friends in Spirit who were willing to help to join with and protect them.

"Smart woman, you are," Brigid murmured as spirit guides took up their posts at all four directions and in between. They drew her in and formed a ring, protecting the area inside Serena's circle of candles and forcing Shadow outside the periphery.

Using both hands, Brigid touched her forehead first, then her heart, then extended her hands, palms out, to the guides as she bowed her head a little. After a moment, she cupped her hands back into the center of her chest and turned toward Morgan and Serena.

"So you know the Old Ways, do you now?" she said softly. "A few of them, anyhow. The ways we feared would die. "'Tis a good thing you got rid of that dark one. Shadow. He's a rascal of a holy terror."

Morgan was lying down on her back on one side of the bed. "Thank you. I don't know why, but I feel better now."

Serena sat beside her, cross-legged. "Begin to notice your breath. With each inhalation, allow your body to relax more and more deeply, knowing that as you relax, you're safe and protected."

Serena kept her voice quiet and soothing, even, rhythmic. Under her guidance, Morgan slipped easily into a light trance. "Ask the guardians we have called in to help you understand the drowning experience you had yesterday."

Abruptly Morgan sat up. Staring straight ahead, she said she could see a woman waking up in a cave-like thatched hut that was so small it was nearly impossible to stand. She had a young girl and baby sleeping beside her.

Brigid had been pacing on the side of the bed opposite Serena, closest to Morgan. Her head was down and she was massaging her temples. With Morgan's words, she looked up.

"My babes!" Brigid gasped at the scene unfolding before her. "My wee, precious daughters!" There was a huge, shimmering ball on Morgan's lap. Inside the ball, She saw her hut, herself, and her children, glistening and clear, every detail exactly as it was nearly four hundred years ago.

The woman in the ball awakened with a stab of sadness because the man who was usually there would be gone for some time. Brigid felt the longing.

"He's off with the herds," Morgan said at the same time Brigid thought it.

"Aye, and faith, I shall see him no more," Brigid breathed to herself, an aching cavern in the space where her heart used to be. "My Seamus. What became of you then, my love? You and our sweet babes?"

Brigid let out a long sigh, then looked at Morgan. "You're a cool one, you are," she said. "And what else can you be seeing?"

Morgan reported to Serena, as Brigid relived, waking up before dawn, nursing the baby, Skatha, fixing stirabout for herself and her older daughter, Flidias, then setting out on foot with a large basket to gather herbs.

"Names?" Serena said. "You're getting names for the children?"

"Yes. It's unbelievably clear, like a movie. It's like I see this woman, and I am this woman, simultaneously."

"Incredible. I've never heard of a trance being so lucid."

"Me either."

"What's the woman's name?"

Morgan paused, her head to one side. "Brigid? Yes. It's Brigid."

Brigid paced. "Torture, it is!" she shouted, shaking her fist at some unseen authority. "I left this bloody world behind me. Can't you let it rest?"

"What does Brigid look like?"

"Bare feet, a rough dress that covers her body." Morgan fingered the light blanket covering her own thigh. "Like linen, maybe. She's lean, young but old at the same time."

Morgan went on, recounting all she saw. Brigid was drawn back to the ball. She stood transfixed, watching herself as she and her babies walked to the edge of the forest and played, picnicked, and napped in the sun.

It was a warm, fine day, and for once the sun was lighting up her children's faces and hair. She cuddled them both, tossing Skatha into the air as she squealed with laughter and playing hide and seek with Flidias amid the fallen trees and undergrowth in the forest. Together, they gathered blackberries from the edge of the wood and herbs from the forest—alder bark for incense, gorse for protection, and rowan for divination.

She held her mouth hard with her hand as she watched her children in the glowing ball on Morgan's lap. Flidias worked meticulously, gathering carefully so as to preserve the plants from which she picked leaves and bark, softly patting the earth and murmuring thanks as she went. Skatha's brow was furrowed. She paid strict attention to every move her sister made. She did her best to sort things out in her mind and was easily frustrated when she couldn't. Brigid cooed to comfort her, but Skatha pushed her away so she could see what Flidias was up to.

One of the guides gained her attention and sternly pointed at the floor near her feet. Brigid saw five big drops and realized they were her own tears. She struggled to make herself remain nonmaterial, to stop crying and look into the ball.

Now she and the children were skipping and playing, making their way back to the hut, where Brigid's best friend Madb was waiting.

Madb rushed to her side, frantic. She made her promise to come with her at nightfall to a meeting in the grove.

Brigid didn't want to risk the danger of a gathering of the wisewomen and healers, particularly in the grove. But Madb insisted and finally she agreed to come if Madb's eldest daughter would watch her babes.

"It's killing me, you are!" Brigid shouted again at some unseen power. "'Tis my last and worst day you're making me live all over again. Do you think I've two hearts to break and two bodies to batter?"

Voiceless this time, her guides answered her. As penetrating as a gentle spring rain, a profound stillness settled into the depths of her being, bringing with it clarity and focus. She sensed that no matter how painful it might be, what was happening was of an importance she couldn't understand but must respect. Trust sank into the center of her soul and locked into place. She squared her shoulders and returned her attention to Morgan and Serena.

"Morgan, come out of it a little," Serena said. "Morgan!"

Morgan, whose face was frozen with fear, began to move her head from side to side in response to Serena's voice.

"That's it," Serena said. Morgan looked toward Serena, her eyes blinking and unfocused. "Come out a little more."

"When I feel as if I'm that woman, Brigid, I'm terrified. She's risking her life and… ." Morgan cocked her head to one side. "And her children's lives in order to do what her friend is asking."

Brigid's newfound peace wavered and she began to pace, struggling to control what felt like muscles in her face and belly. The guides looked at her with a combination of compassion and reprimand. She forced herself to be still, inside and out.

"Okay," Serena said. "It looks as if this next part is going to be tough. So stay with me. If I call you, come out a little, as you just did."

"Okay."

"Are you ready to go back in?"

"Yes."

"All right. Just remember, this isn't happening to you."

"Right you are!" Brigid said. "'Tis happening to me, more's the pity of it. Sure, and once was enough. How shall I bear it a second time?"

She looked at the guides. They were gazing into the ball, their expressions serene yet intent. By ignoring her, they were saying, "Look. It's your job. Finish it." She straightened her spine, drew a deep breath, and fixed her eyes on the ball. Instantly, she was back in the scene.

She and Madb were walking in the full moonlight, staying near the edge of the forest to be less visible and doubling back now and again to confuse anyone who might attempt to follow them.

Now they were at the grove. She felt her heart sink to see the wisewomen had risked a fire. It was too dangerous. Much, much too dangerous. The others who were gathered around the fire nodded and made space for them in their circle.

Instinctively, Brigid relied on the wisdom of her mother and her mother's mother. She prayed to the Great Goddess, the Earth Mother, to give her the power of the willow, sacred tree to women, potent with the female powers of yielding, bending, and covering with protection.

In response to her invocation, she felt her feet growing energetic roots that penetrated deep into the Earth Mother. She brought the strength of the Earth up through her legs, into her opening place, and up to her womb. There she let it gather in force for a moment before she brought it up her spine and spread it throughout her whole body.

She imagined her body was the trunk of a mighty willow. Invisible branches shot out the crown of her head, up and out, dipping low and forming a canopy to shelter the circle of women. Energetically, she had created a powerful force field of invisibility and protection.

Rocking from one foot to the other next to Serena's bed, Brigid prayed to keep her distance, to let herself remain outside the ball, to not be overwhelmed. But it was no use, and she relived the scene as though it were happening in the present.

The wisewomen, the midwives and healers, the Circle of Thirteen, the Keepers of the Grove, had called this Council meeting. Cailin had left her father's deathbed to be present. The youngest, Erin, was there, next to the lovers, Grianne and Banba. Dana was missing. Why? Boan, the silent one, toothy Kele-de, and Macha, the eldest and Grianne's mother, were gathered around the fire, as were Deirdre and Cessair.

Mare, second eldest, took up Macha's normal task and circled between the women and the fire, carrying a shell containing alder bark and other burning herbs. With a sheaf of cormorant feathers, Mare swept the women with the herbal smoke while each woman inhaled deeply and used the vapors to cleanse her body and her aura.

From some other dimension, Brigid heard Morgan's voice.

"Serena!" Morgan was saying. "These women! These are the faces of the women in my dreams, the underwater women."

She felt nausea in the pit of her stomach as she remembered the rough and rolling sea. She forced herself to refocus her attention. The Council was about to cast the circle. Standing tall, the women joined hands for a moment and looked into one another, their faces both serious and sweet with love in the flickering light.

Turning as one, they faced east. They asked the Guardians of the East, the powers of air, to keep their minds and their communications clear as the windswept dawn. Turning to the right, they asked the Guardians of the South, keepers of fire, for passion and the drive to carry out their decisions.

Facing West, they asked the powers of water to bathe, soothe, and buoy them, allowing their emotions to flow like water.

They turned to the North and asked the ancient ones, the crystal beings, the powers of Earth, to lend them their groundedness and wisdom.

Facing the center, they asked the Great Triple Goddess to help them find the still point within, so each woman might contribute to the whole from her own center.

Looking down, they invoked the powers of Below, the unknown places within them and in the world, and asked them to reveal their wisdom.

Finally, they invited the powers of Above, the celestial beings, to enlighten them.

When everyone was satisfied that the needed guidance and protection had been called in, the women joined hands again and met each other's eyes around the circle, chanting together, "The circle is cast, we are between the worlds. And what happens between the worlds affects all the worlds."

They continued to look into one another for a long time, the golden blaze of the fire and the silver of the moon's glow illuminating each well-known and much-loved face.

Brigid knew now what she feared then. After all the countless centuries of women meeting in Council in this sacred grove, their grandmothers' grandmothers' grandmothers and back in time to the first woman, this would be the last time. There was a poignancy to the looks they gave one another, a sense of both rushing and lingering. They could risk little time out here in the night, and there was much to discuss and decide. Still they stretched this moment, knowing it must sustain them as they moved forward into an uncertain future.

At last Grianne broke the silence. "'Tis a cold moon that shines on us and a hard night we're under," she said. "We are called together for the bleakest of reasons, to consider news that affects all our people and aye, our children's children, should any be born."

Brigid was riveted on Grianne.

Should any be born?

"For those who haven't heard, I've news your ears will scarce believe. Coming straight to the point of it, Dana was seized this day by men from town. Aye, and named as a witch, her and two women from other tribes. She was accused by Airmid, who works as a maid in town. Taken into custody some days ago, Airmid was, and tortured long and hard, poor soul. In naming Dana, Airmid was only doing what she could to save herself and her two daughters. But now our Dana is gone and her fate is surely dire."

The women for whom this was news, including Brigid, gasped and cried out. Two began a shrill keen but were quickly silenced by the others. They had come to this, that they couldn't even mourn their losses according to their sacred traditions, protecting Dana's soul with the sounds of their wailing.

Those who knew of Dana's fate reacted each in her own way. Banba hung her head, Mare crackled with anger, and Macha spat into the fire. The others met the eyes of those hearing this news for the first time with compassion and confirmation.

"'Tis the bloody Scots," Macha hissed, spitting again into the flames and pounding her staff on the ground. She raised her wrinkled, bony face to the moon. "In droves they come, wave upon wave of them, relentless and steady as the sea herself. Wiping out the People and the Old Ways is what they've a mind to do, sure as the moon is full and this Grove is sacred. Destroy us they must, for by what other means can they can seize the Holy Land, destroy the Sacred Forests, build their castles, and cut our beloved Mother into pastures with their fences? I tell you, they'll put an end to life as we know it and us along with it."

"But perhaps we might share with them," Cailin said, her sweet face full of pain. "Surely there is room for us all."

"Share with them, is it?" Macha spat twice this time. "And pigs could have wings, dear, pigs could have wings. Stiff as cats' whiskers, the Scots are. Mean, penny-pinching creatures. But the love of the Land is what drives us. We do not harm Her with fences, nor crowd Her with sheep that turn the Land to scrub. We could no more cozy up with the Scots than a hen could lie down with a fox. Our men can bid a sad farewell to following the herds across our Beloved Land. And as for us, tending our gardens on the hillsides and teaching our daughters the mysteries of the Forest—'tis all from a day gone by. The sunlight of our people has faded and darkness has come. The Holy Ground will be taken and conquered, and there's an end to it. What's done is done and there's no use mooning over it."

There was a rustling and sighing as the women shifted their feet. A sharp gust of wind swirled around their legs and they gathered their shawls and blankets tighter. They were absorbing the harsh reality of Macha's words, a reality they had long feared might come but was now upon them like a sudden gale that stirred the sea into a fast-boiling cauldron.

The women were silent for some time, staring into the flames. Gradually they began to speak. They were afraid it was only a matter of time before they were all seized. If the witch trials sweeping Europe were coming to their island, they would be tortured and burned.

And it could happen fast.

Tonight, even.

It was only politics, they knew. The Scots could say the women were from the devil and kill them. All over Europe, the Church was taking the wise-women, the healers and midwives, the counselors and herbalists, and calling them witches so they could get rid of them. The loss of the Council would break the soul of the tribe and make it easy to conquer them. For what are a people without the love, wisdom, and guidance of their beloved holy women?

The Council discussed the children, what it would be like for them if their mothers were taken. In Europe, they knew, children had to watch their mothers shamed, stripped naked, tortured, and burned. Brigid felt a searing pain for Skatha and Flidias.

Boan, her simple face contorted with the fear, sadness, and anger they all felt, added wood to the fire while Banba repositioned the cauldron, nestling it once again next to the fire so it could continue to heat. The Council discussed the welfare of the rest of the women and men of their tribe. They asked themselves if there was any way to preserve their magic.

"Look to your hearts, women, and gather the powers of your wombs and your wisdom." It was Grianne who spoke. "Pierce your sadness, harness your anger, and still your fear, for the time has come to gather into our bodies the strength and ancient knowledge of our mothers' mothers. Know this! Beating the Scots in the game they have begun is our only hope. If we do nothing, 'tis dead we are and our power scattered like dust instead of seeds. We must find a way to preserve our magic, to leave something strong for our people and for our Great Mother, the Earth."

"'Tis removing ourselves, and in our own way, that brings us to that end." Madb said. "Or we'll be burned without a whisper. We must keep our magic and show our people we're not defeated. Were we born to be ground up for gruel? The Great Female did not bring our power into this world to see it burned like turf from the bog! We must do something, and do it with haste."

"We cannot go dandering off like children," said Deirdre. "'Tis a long trek over the drumlins, and to what? Lands long claimed by others, with ways as bad as the Scots, and well defended, too. Death would stalk us there, to be sure."

"But what are we to do then?" said Kele-de, "if we cannot stay and there's nowhere to go?"

The women were quiet as the inevitability of all that had been said worked its way into the core of their souls. The crackle and hiss of the fire grew loud. Finally, it was Brigid herself who broke the silence.

"The choice is clear. What I must tell you is a thing I know as well as I know the faces of my own wee babes." She blinked away tears. "'Tis a truth I feel in my heart." Brigid gently pounded her chest with her fist.

All eyes were upon her.

"I saw this in a dream," Brigid said, "a vision at the dark of the moon, and since that time it has cost me much thought, though I prayed we could escape it. It pains me to say this, but if there is no honorable way to keep the Old Ways and live on our Beloved Mother Earth in peace, then we must destroy our own bodies."

There was a sharp intake of breath around the fire.

"Aye," Brigid said, "and 'tis in the Otherworld we must find our refuge for the present time."

The women shifted their feet uneasily. Each was searching her soul, beseeching the Great Mother to help her find a truth rooted in a more profound reality than the swirl of emotion she was experiencing.

"Our task is great," Brigid said, "for we must find a means to do this thing that lifts the dignity of our tribe as high as the drumlins and keeps our magic whole for a time when it can be used for the greater good."

The mournful sound of an owl's call pierced the night air. It came from so close that Erin and Cailin both startled. But the elders nodded their heads and drew a deep breath, acknowledging a sign of agreement from the Goddess. The women became very grave.

"Take our own lives?" Erin said. "Have you gone daft? How can that help our people?"

"Sure, and what kind of a future would the people have without the wise-women passing on the Old Ways to our daughters?" said Cailin.

"Aye, and the soul of a people is their Council!" Banba said.

Banba lifted the cauldron, heavy with liquid, from its position next to the fire and placed it in the center of the flames. Cessair and Macha sprinkled herbs in the pot and Erin added a few sprigs of heather. Grianne stirred the brew with a length of rowan. Having been the one to state what Macha and Mare had obviously been thinking, Brigid didn't want to make the gesture of adding her herbs to the pot. It had to be a decision they each came to, not one they were persuaded to make. Still, she fingered the mugwort in her pouch and prayed that its essence enter the cauldron for clear vision.

The women took one another's hands and drew close around the fire. They knew how to work with the chaos of emotion churning within them as they contemplated death by their own hands. They would transform their emotions with the power of the Earth Herself. Open mouthed, they hummed a low sound together, creating a tone that formed one long note. They were raising great power with their voices.

One of the women spoke, her voice guttural and vibrant with energy. "We cannot in good heart bring more babes into a world where death hunts us down. A time of madness is upon us, like a cat on a mouse. Our fates could change in an instant. The Scots could take us all in one night, as they have in their own villages, leaving us powerless to act. Our only way through is to submit to the bad time and preserve what we can for the future."

The women commenced their humming, which grew louder until all mouths were round and there was a continuous "Maaaah," a tone resonant with mystical power. It began low and grew gradually higher in pitch.

Each woman was drawing strength up from the earth through her body and there was the tangible sense that the powers of the directions they had called were adding their energies to the moment.

The women's arms drew up into the air as if lifted by the sound they had raised, their hands and fingers outstretched, pointing up and to the center. The sound they made increased in intensity until it reached its natural end.

Grianne cried out, "Holy Mother of us all, grant us clarity of vision so we might see what to do. The life that courses through us is your own. Help us to know this one thing. Our time, is it come? Shall we return our bodies to you now? Grant us wisdom, and the strength to follow through."

"So mote it be," they said together. Then they dropped to their knees, hands and foreheads on the ground, absorbing into their bodies and auras the power they had raised and returning the excess to the Mother of Them All.

For a time they were silent. Then slowly, one by one, they rose and drew closer to the fire until all were seated in a circle on the ground, backs straight, staring into the whirling mist of steam rising from the cauldron. The moon was reflected in the surface of the liquid and a glowing sphere slowly formed in the center of the mist.

Finally Grianne said, her voice quiet yet vibrating with power, "We must hold the sacred fire of our magic deep in our bellies. There we must protect it with our intentions. And our love."

With the energy they had raised, her words held the power of sacred law. Not a law imposed on them, but one that grew out of who they were and the land they loved and were loved by. The golden sphere continued to glow in the center of the vapors rising from the cauldron, while outside the sphere, the mist curled and moved like waves on the ocean.

"Together, we will march to the sea," Madb said.

"Where for our leaving a great storm will gather itself," said Erin.

"We will join hands together and move into the waves," said Cailin.

"And deep in our bellies, the fire of our magic will be preserved," Kele-de said.

"Like the great, swirling, golden ball that appears before us now," said Cessair.

"The Great Mother, She will take us back into her womb," said Mare, "To the Land of the Living, the Otherworld."

Boan thumped her heart in agreement and looked into the eyes around the circle.

"For another time and place She will hold our magic, a time when the power of our love will be needed again, a place where our strength can take root," said Banba, "Then the spirit of the wisewomen will rise, as surely as the cormorant emerges from the depths of the sea with a giant fish in her beak."

"The Great Mother will come for us and take back our bodies," said Kele-de.

"And what of our children? Our people?" said Macha.

There was a pause. Then Banba spoke with the authority of the single-mindedness they had achieved. "Here is the way of it," she said. "'Tis for one of us to stay behind and tell our story. That our ways will always live on, preserved by the fire in our bellies. This is the message she will bring to our children and the People."

"She will say the wisewomen of the tribe received a vision," Kele-de said, "to let The Great Mother of Us All protect the power of the People for a later time."

Cailin added, "She will tell the men it is the will of the Council to not fight, for the honor of the tribe has been kept by holding the power of the People for future generations."

"Aye, she will say not to contend for the Holy Ground," said Deirdre. "To fight would be folly of the highest order. The message the Great Mother has given is to preserve power, not dissipate it in opposition."

"She will tell the men they must survive and protect the children," said Brigid, aching for her beloved Seamus and her children at the same time that she wholeheartedly supported the vision of the Council.

"Aye, take the babes and the elders and head far into the drumlins for a time," Madb said.

"Sure, until they can swallow their pride and go into town and work for the Scots," said Macha. There was laughter around the circle in spite of the circumstances, and Boan tapped at her chest and grinned. "Survive!" Macha went on. "Survive and sing to our children of the courage of their mothers. Our time will come again."

Those who had originally dissented had come around, their concerns put to rest by the power of the time, the inevitability of what must be done, and the strength of their shared vision. The protesters had spoken the pain all the women felt, and now all were equally firm in their joint resolve to act on behalf of the People and the Great Mother. They had become one mind.

It was time to choose the one who would stay behind and speak the Council's truth to the People. Cessair suggested they choose one of the younger women with many children. Erin, the youngest, felt it would be a stronger message to send one of the elders. All agreed. But Macha, the eldest, refused to stay behind.

"I will not live to see my daughter die before me," Macha said, looking into Grianne's glistening eyes. "And as the eldest, 'tis only right that I accompany the youngest to the sea." Macha turned to Erin.

So Mare, the second eldest, volunteered for the task they all knew to be the hardest. The Council bid tearful good byes to Mare and thanked her for her willingness to stay behind and face what was to come. They also honored Dana, and sent their farewells to her across the wind. Brigid slipped Mare her pouch and told her they would meet again in the Otherworld.

Erin left with Mare to see her safely home. While they awaited her return, the women huddled around the fire and sipped the liquid brewing in the cauldron from a large earthenware chalice they passed around the circle.

When Erin returned the group worked together, calling on the powers of the directions and the Goddess in her many forms to help them pull their power into their bellies. They cast a potent spell to protect the fire of their magic for a time when the power of woman could thrive again.

"That day will come," Macha said, "when women have the strength and numbers to restore our sacred womanly values to the land, when they're ready to make a stand for compassion and wholeness. Then once again women will bring the powers of connectedness, nurturing, and stewardship to the earth."

There was a hush after Macha's words. Then the Council called upon the Caillech, the mighty Goddess who stirred her cauldron of death and rebirth, to take them back to the place the people called *Tir-na-nog,* the Land of the Living, and the Land of Women.

While the winds rose and a great storm brewed, the Council women began their long march down to the sea. They walked easily at first. Though the sky was now overcast, the clouds were not yet black and the light of the full moon illuminated the women's path through the forest and then across open fields.

At the end, the sky was inky with churning clouds and they had to pick their way carefully down rocky cliffs while great rumbles of thunder vibrated through their bodies and flashes of lightning lit their path.

The women of the Council reached the edge of the surf-beaten shore just as great sheets of rain began to lash against them. They formed one last circle, holding each other's waists tightly while the wind tore at their hair and clothing. They leaned in for balance. Illumined by continuous flashes of lightning, their bodies streaked by rivers of rain, the women of the Council looked deeply into one another's eyes through their tears and the rain for one last time.

Brigid and Madb, who were next to each other in the circle, shared a kiss. Some of the women were crying hard but no one called out. Not that they would have been able to make themselves heard, for by now the surf, thunder, and wind were almost deafening.

Moving as one, they opened their final circle and struggled to form a line. They held each other close and the wind whipped them as it rose to a deafening scream. Their bodies pushed forward by a sudden gust, the women marched into the waves and added their voices to the fury of the night by shouting their prayers to the Great Mother to protect their children and hold sacred their power for the generations to come.

The storm rose up and brought a towering wave. The women of the Council were quickly pulled under.

❧ ❧ ❧

Brigid forced herself to come back to the present. Her sides heaved like bellows and her head felt as though it might spin off her body. She could taste the brine that was spewing up from her lungs and spilling from her mouth and nostrils in a rush of salty liquid. Still reeling, she hurled herself into a sitting position with her back against the bed.

This is mad. I haven't a body to drown, and there's the truth of it.

Time to come round to what's real.

She willed herself to experience her actual physical state, to feel her airiness, her lightness, how like the wind she was. Brigid reminded herself it's impossible for a spirit, an ancestor, to drown. There was no dark stain on the floor, no salt water coughed up. When she felt calmer, she made herself stand and turned her attention to the bed.

Morgan was coming out of her trance. She was panting hard. Her mouth was moving wordlessly, and she was pulling herself erratically across the bed on all fours. Her eyes were staring but unfocused, and she looked as if she were crying although her eyes were dry. Serena was crouching on the bed on her knees, moving to stay ahead of Morgan, guarding her from hurting herself or going off the side of the bed.

"Morgan, it's okay," Serena was saying. "Talk to me Morgan, it's over. You're all right. Morgan?"

Abruptly Morgan stopped moving and looked up at Serena. Their eyes locked and she burst into tears. Serena pulled her in close. Collapsed now, Morgan sobbed softly while Serena stroked her hair.

"Goddess love ya," Brigid heard herself say. "What a woman." Serena was sitting-cross legged and Morgan was sprawled across the bed with her head cradled in Serena's lap.

"'Tis a brave woman you are, Morgan of Mothers Mountain," Brigid said. "How you have strength for this journey, I cannot say. But this I do know, that often it comes, a miraculous power, to those who have survived much and need to endure still more. What I don't know is, why is this happening, child? Why now?"

As if in answer, the glowing ball in her belly caught her awareness. It was her power, the power of the Great Mother, preserved across the centuries just as the Council had willed. Something in that power linked Brigid to these women. She could feel it, crackling in the air between them. She wondered if she could somehow contact Morgan and Serena and if they could work together.

Without warning, Brigid felt a quick animal response take her over. She whirled around to find that just behind her—his long body jauntily poised against the wall, his arms crossed over his chest, and his weight on one leg with the other draped casually in front—Shadow was lurking.

He wore a perfectly tailored tuxedo and top hat, which only underscored the savage intensity beneath the restraint of his attire. There was deadly humor in his eyes and he had the look of a panther prepared to pounce.

"I won that round, didn't I, Luv?" Shadow whispered, his voice thick with the seductive, tender hatred of a demon lover.

"I think not! Besides, what would you know of it? You're all mouth and trousers." Brigid spat at him fiercely. But inside, she was shaken.

"Easy, Baby!" Shadow laughed. "Get this. The Scots never killed any women named as witches in Ireland." The words rolled off his tongue like honey. He paused to observe her response.

She tried not to react but inside, she felt herself freeze. Shadow took visible pleasure in this. With catlike precision, he propelled himself off the wall and began circling her with deliberate, menacing steps.

"You bitches did our work for us, my fine Irish rose," he said. "You killed yourselves." He veered in close for a moment, leering at her, his breath disgusting. "Your deaths broke the back of your people. We didn't have to do a thing."

Brigid felt herself stiffen.

"You killed yourselves with your own fear," he said, continuing to circle her. "'We must lift the dignity of our tribe as high as the drumlins and keep our magic whole!' Your tribe, as you put it, your clan, was pitiful. You women were their strength, which doesn't say much. And your 'magic?'" He spat the word. "Your magic was never whole."

Shadow laughed, then pulled in close and bore into her eyes with his own.

"If it were," he said, "you never would have done what you did, now, would you? Drowning yourselves like chickens! And you wouldn't be standing here in this cabin, a ghost with a job half done. Neither would these cunts," he gestured at Morgan and Serena with a long sweep of his arm.

"You know what you are?" he said. "You're frightened, simpering bitches. Little girls in women's bodies, good for one thing only."

He cocked his eyebrow at her and leaned in. "You do nothing. You stand for nothing. You are nothing."

Shadow grinned wickedly.

"Not bad to look at though," he said, stroking her cheek. "Want to get it on?"

CHAPTER 11

roots pulsing

My Body tells a story.
I look at my hands,
They are also the hands of my ancestors.
I turn them, palms facing me,
Like a book, I begin reading the
story again.

—Claire Serpell

Clarissa forced herself to keep a straight face.

In his hallmark expression of utmost concentration, Frankie flattened his tongue against his upper lip, forming a pale, glistening crescent. Using an iridescent orange marking pen, he was filling the spaces inside large letters that read "Dump the Dump." Martin was both more casual and more particular about his work, adding space ships, stars, and planets he told his mother were from another galaxy.

The boys had been bored and asked her what she was doing. She'd been putting the finishing touches on the flyer she'd use for canvassing. While the finished copies came out of the printer, forming a stack the boys somehow found fascinating, she explained to them about what nuclear waste was.

"Gross," Martin said.

"Scary," Frankie whispered.

"You're right," Clarissa said. "It's gross and scary."

What more did she want to say? She didn't want to frighten them. But she didn't believe in sugarcoating things to children. It insulted them. Besides, children knew when they weren't getting the whole story. That scared them more than the truth, in addition to subtly communicating they were incapable of dealing with reality.

"It isn't safe to transport nuclear waste because it could get into the atmosphere through different kinds of spills, leaks, and accidents."

"Or from terrorists!" Martin said.

"Right." She hugged them both. Nuclear waste is so concentrated even an invisible speck is deadly and remains active for thousands of years. That's why nuclear spills are impossible to clean up completely and why they threaten all life for miles around and for generations to come."

"But what else can they do with it?" Martin said, scowling.

"The very best thing would be to not make so much of it in the first place," Clarissa said. "For example, we can learn how to generate electricity from the sun and the wind instead of through nuclear power. But the safest thing to do with necessary nuclear waste, such as medical waste, is to never move it. Just leave it where it's made and store it above ground in sealed vaults that are constantly monitored for leaks."

"Can't the terrorists still get at it and blow it up and kill everybody?" Martin's eyes grew wide with fear.

She drew both boys in close. "Some nuclear waste is more dangerous than other kinds, because it's more concentrated. For example, the spent fuel rods used to generate electricity are very vulnerable when they're stored by the thousands—the way they usually are—in huge vats with only water to cool them. All you have to do then is to find a way to interfere with the cooling process or crash a plane into the storage facility and there could be an explosion that would be very dangerous." The boys huddled in closer. "But all we have to do is with spent fuel rods is change how they're stored."

"How?" Frankie and Martin said in unison.

"If they're stored above ground, a few at a time in dry casks made of steel-reinforced concrete with big gravel berms, or mounds, between them made of gravel," she said, drawing a picture to show them, "you wouldn't need water at all, it would be hard to crash a plane into more than one cask, and the explosion from one cask wouldn't be that dangerous."

"That's what they should do then," Martin said.

"Right!" said Frankie. "Mama, can I help?"

Clarissa showed them the flyer. She tried to figure out how they could contribute without slowing her down.

"Those letters would look better colored in," Martin said, sounding very manly.

"Yeah!" Frankie said, his eyes brightening. "That would be better advertising." He stuck out his chest.

So now all three of them were sitting at the kitchen table with markers and crayons, coloring in the letters and talking. Clarissa told them Big Mom loved the earth and would be proud of their work to stop the dump.

"She gave the best hugs!" Frankie said.

"Yeah," Martin said.

They reminisced about the bean bread and fry bread she would make them, the fried chicken and fatback and greens, and the old stories she would spin as they fished along the river or sat in a circle in the twinkling firelight with Big Mom's other great-grandchildren—tales about turtles and foxes and bears, timeless tribal lessons about how life worked. But mostly they remembered how she always seemed to know what to do.

She still does.

I wish she'd tell me why she led me to Morgan Forrester.

Do the ancestors speak to Morgan, too?

Do they ask her to do impossible things, as they do me?

Things she never imagined she could do?

~ ~ ~

"I asked you a question, bitch." Shadow's face was so close, Brigid couldn't breathe without inhaling his frigid breath. "Do you want to get it on? Or shall I take what I want and be done with it?"

Brigid squared her shoulders, tilted her head back, and made herself regard Shadow evenly from beneath lidded eyes. She was badly shaken, but a voice inside asked why he was so interested in them if they were, in fact, inconsequential. She forced her attention back to Morgan and Serena, and was relieved to find they had been oblivious to the exchange.

Morgan looked surprisingly refreshed and composed. A pleasant breeze wafted through the cabin.

"I'm going to open the circle and fix you something to eat," Serena said, "To ground you. To ground us both." She rose from the bed. "Sister spirits, guardians, masters, angels and other friends in spirit who have aided and protected us, thank you. The circle is open, but unbroken. Blessed be."

She blew out the candles. When Morgan emerged from the bedroom, Serena was putting away a loaf of heavy brown bread after slicing a thick slab for each of them.

"Wait! I want two pieces." Morgan opened the door for Virginia Woof, who jumped up on her chest. "And jam. And how about some of that stew from last night?" Morgan ruffled Woof's head, neck, and shoulders and received a face-full of wet kisses.

"Woof, get down," Serena barked. She handed Morgan an odd assortment of silverware, dishes, and two faded cloth napkins. "Sit down. You look wobbly."

"I need to do something normal. I want to eat and play with Woof. No more challenges today."

Serena brought bread, jam, and room-temperature lentil stew and twig tea to the table.

"That was Ireland, I know it!" Serena said while Morgan devoured her food. "Remember the way Brigid was dressed? You said it felt like rough linen. Had to be Ireland. Northern Ireland, four hundred years ago."

Brigid took a step backward.

I've been gone for four hundred years?

Of course she had known this, but suddenly it seemed incredible.

"Maybe we could put this discussion off until tomorrow," Morgan said.

"Around sixteen hundred, I'd say. Between sixteen hundred and sixteen ten. Not far from what is now Ulster."

"How could you know all that?"

"The Scots invaded during that period, ten thousand of them. They overwhelmed the local clans."

Ten thousand Scots?

When the Council had taken their magic back to the Great Mother, there'd been a few hundred Scots. Brigid sank to the floor, her head in her hands. She'd left Seamus and her girls alone to contend with a massive invasion, and for what? Was Shadow telling the truth when he said that no women were burned as witches in Ireland?

"Get out! Where is all this coming from?" Morgan said between ravenous mouthfuls.

"I'm Irish." Serena said. "My father used to spout Irish history, Northern Irish history, as if it were the only thing that mattered."

Brigid lifted her head. They'd been remembered. It wasn't all gone.

"Serena isn't an Irish name," Morgan said.

"No shit. I was born Caitlin Mary O'Neill."

Morgan stopped chewing. Her chin nearly hit her breastbone.

"You can close your mouth now, Morgan. That's disgusting. But yeah. Daily mass, Catholic school, the whole bit. And nuns. You should have seen me with the nuns. I had my knuckles rapped with a ruler and my ears boxed and my mouth taped shut more times than you can count."

"Geez."

"Imagine how my parents felt when I did my stint as a Zen Buddhist and changed my name to 'Serena,' just plain Serena, no 'O'Neill,' no nothing. No husband, no big Catholic family.... ."

"That explains a lot about you, Serena."

"Like what?"

I don't know exactly. It just does." Morgan paused for another big bite of bread. "That's why you wanted me to get an abortion, isn't it? Serena the recovering Catholic rebel. Why didn't you tell me this before?"

"I never talked about my parents. I hated everything they stood for. Money, power. And guilt. Don't forget the guilt." Serena was drumming both sets of fingers on either side of her plate.

"But Caitlin is such a fabulous name!" Morgan paused. "It sounds like a lightning strike." Morgan pushed back her chair and clapped her hands together once, hard. "That's more you, Serena. You're about as *serene* as a rattlesnake."

"Why thank you, Morgan."

"Sorry. I didn't mean that as a criticism. I meant it in a.... ." Morgan moved her arms up and out from her body, arcing in generous circles, "I meant it in a fierce, strong, good way. You're a force of nature, not a Buddha."

"And what about the reference to drumlins?" Serena said, her mouth a tight, white line. "Don't you remember? The council women used that word." Serena's eyes had a far off look.

"What are you talking about?"

"Mountains. Where Brigid lived, mountains were called drumlins."

Brigid felt tears welling up in the eyes she once had. This Serena was getting to her.

Serena bolted out of her chair, hauled out a decrepit stepladder, started pulling books off the top shelf of one of the more rickety bookcases, and tossed them to the floor. She scrambled down the ladder and brought a huge stack back to the table, moving her half-eaten bread aside with it. She thumbed through several books before settling on one.

"Yes! I was right. Sixteen hundred to sixteen ten." Serena looked up at Morgan. "Isn't that always the way? The invaders driving off the indigenous people. The odd thing is, Ireland simply absorbed all her previous invaders. The Irish can always add a little of this and a little of that, never needing to discard previous myths or beliefs, simply enriching the stew with the new ones. Makes a better story, and all… ."

"Speaking of stew," Morgan said, getting up to serve herself a second helping. "Do you want more?"

"But this invasion effectively overwhelmed the local people. It's the original source of the conflict in Northern Ireland today. The Scots did to the Emerald Isle what had always been unthinkable, forcing into parts what had always been one integrated whole.

"It was really like that, Morgan. There were regional differences, of course. Brigid, for example, lived in a remote area, isolated by the drumlins that separated her people from the fertile, more prosperous and up-to-date center of the island. Her people were living as they had for centuries until the Scottish invasion. But even with those regional differences, the Irish believed their island was the center of everything. It was the living, breathing, Goddess herself, mother, heart, and soul of the cosmos. Ireland—the land—was one. And the people were one with the land. Until finally the Scots split their world in two."

Serena's eyes traveled the contours of the mountains outside the cabin window. "Brigid gave up her life to preserve the power of that unity, that time when all was one."

Brigid shuddered convulsively, laughing and crying at Serena's words. The self-doubt Shadow had filled her with vanished. She bounded to her feet and twirled, her arms outstretched, spinning through the cabin like a girl.

"And you know what else?" Serena asked Morgan.

Brigid halted, leaning in for her next words.

"No, what?" Morgan said, between slurps of stew.

"I don't think they ever burned so-called witches in Ireland."

Brigid froze.

"Oh wait," Serena said, "I can look that up… ."

"Not now, Serena, I'm tired."

Serena looked hard at Morgan. "Brigid was right to do what she did. Even though they might not have burned women in Ireland, they were doing it all over Europe. In Brigid's corner of the world, the Scots were particularly brutal. They did unspeakable things to women accused of witchcraft. Had she lived, she could have faced mind-shattering torture, dividing her soul from her body—herself from herself—as surely as the Scots divided Ireland. Brigid was an amazing woman. She did the only thing she could to preserve the integrity of a magical oneness we yearn for but can only imagine. And now, four hundred years later, for some reason she's using her power to connect with you."

"Whoa. You believe all this? You don't think it was just a dream? You think what I experienced today is real, and we're supposed to do something about it?"

"Yes." Serena's eyes flashed brilliant blue. "Why else would I feel compelled to resolve things with you after so many years? Something bigger than either of us was bringing us together. I could feel it." She rubbed the goosebumps on her arms. "I think there's more to this than either of us can begin to imagine."

Brigid leaned against a bookcase and slowly lowered herself to the floor. She breathed fully, then crossed her legs and called her Guides to gather round for protection and counsel.

"That white-haired one," Brigid told them, "that Serena Caitlin Mary O'Neill, is several steps ahead of me, isn't she now? Help me! As sure as I'm sitting here before you, I don't know why I'm here. If you've got a plan, spell it out. For it's lost I am and not knowing what to do."

Brigid focused all her attention on the drawing in and releasing of her breath, breathing into the point of power in her womb center. No plan came to her, but her faith was restored as she inhaled the reassuring presence of her guides. She put herself in the hands of the Great Mother, knowing if she connected to the earth and the sky, to the seven directions, to the elements, it would become clear what possibilities were opening to her and she would be able to access her deepest center, her wise core, her power, the part of her that would naturally choose to act in alignment with her soul's intent and with the greater good.

From the profound silence she had entered with her breath, Brigid felt herself being pulled back to the present by the desperation in Morgan's voice.

"Please stop. That vision I had was terrifying. It was so real. The drowning, the whole thing.... I can't deal with any more today. I want to eat one last slab of bread and take it easy."

But Morgan didn't reach for the bread. She sat very still, her hands on her lap, her eyes unfocused.

"Sometimes I feel scared," she said in a voice so small Brigid could barely hear her. "It's as if my skin were too tight, ever since Adam threw that iron at me." Morgan blinked. "I have to tell you something weird, Serena. Really weird. Not that anything after today could be all that weird. On second thought… ."

"Good grief, Morgan, what is it?"

"Just don't laugh, okay? Or get on my case."

"I won't."

Morgan took a deep breath. "Remember just before we did the trance, I told you about this feeling I call Shadow? When I get scared, I feel this thing, I don't know, this presence. I always figured it was my imagination, something my fear made up. But after today, I don't know."

"Can you describe it?"

"Not really. It's like an evil presence that takes pleasure in my pain. It likes to frighten me. It likes to see me down. It's shadowy and unclear, but it reminds me of my father."

"I wonder how that fits with—"

"Serena, the thing is, I think I can feel it now. It started right after I got scared thinking about the drowning."

"See that one, Babe?" Shadow said to Brigid, gesturing toward Morgan with a white-gloved finger. "She's doing my job for me. Her and her kind. With them it's one step forward and two steps back. When they start to get power, all I have to do is spook them." Shadow leaped nimbly toward Brigid and splayed his fingers in front of her face, his eyes and mouth wide with mock surprise. "A little fright stops 'em dead." Shadow folded his lanky body in half, his shrill cackle piercing the air.

Brigid shrugged him off and turned away. But he scooped her up from behind with one hand around her waist and the other gently cradling one of her own. His lewd grin was hypnotic as he circled her with long, exaggerated steps, feigning the grace of a gentleman twirling a lady on the dance floor. He pirouetted her around to face Serena.

"How about this one? Completely daft, isn't she, to use your idiom. Doesn't even know what her name is. Duh." Shadow leaned disgustingly close. "Stuck on a mountain, too angry to move. Scared to do the only thing that would give her real power—getting involved with other people, getting 'connected,' as her fat friend would say." Shadow gestured briefly at Morgan, then focused on Serena again.

"But no," Shadow said, "she's holed up here on Lonesome Mountain running her own wild west show with her fool critters. All I have to do is keep her head in her books and there you have it. Nothing. She's one big zero. "I'll have an easy job taking these two out and all the rest like 'em, just as I did with you and your so-called wisewomen."

"Rubbish!" Brigid hissed. She ignited the fire in her belly with a sound like the firing of a furnace. Then she used her magic to root herself in the earth and to link with Morgan.

~ ~ ~

Morgan's skin twitched as if she were a horse trying to unsettle a fly. Attempting to rid herself of this fear was worse than trying to shake off a nightmare while she was still asleep.

Then suddenly the fear was gone, and she could feel her steadiness returning. It was as if the sturdy peasant woman from her trance had taken her shoulders in a strong grip, infusing her with strength.

Brigid.

Thank you, Brigid.

Serena's words were filtering through. She was going on about reincarnation and the women's holocaust.

Holocaust, schmolocaust.

Morgan rubbed her temples. She was trying to occupy her body, to be present on her own terms.

"You've really had it, haven't you?" Serena said.

You mean she finally gets it?

The headline would read, *Scholar Dusts Off Gold Card and Purchases Clue. Measurable Quakes Circle Globe.*

"I'm exhausted. Do you think we could do something normal, such as… feeding the animals?"

Serena frowned. She seemed to be having trouble making her mouth stop and was lurching in her chair.

Poor thing.

What a concept, Serena shutting up.

But then Serena looked at her, really looked. Her blue eyes, usually keen and piercing, became soft, and for once her shoulders relaxed ever so slightly. Morgan smiled inwardly. Serena was accustomed to bulling ahead. Could it be compassion was beginning to replace some of that drive? She had been almost tender when she was coming out of her trance. Tender and protective.

God, Serena, please stop.

No more heavy stuff.

As if on cue a faded red pickup, even more ancient than Serena's, rattled up the driveway. A short, wiry man with tufts of white hair protruding from his cap hopped out of the cab and strode toward the cabin. He was wearing overalls over long johns, and looked to have last shaved four or five days ago.

The man stopped outside the screen door and called out, "Hey, old woman! I figured I might could trade a half load of hay for some of that Sourwood honey."

"Who you calling old, Travis? You'd best get in here so you can sit down before you fall down!" Serena called back in her best mountain twang.

So that's how she fits in around here.

The little chameleon.

"Morgan, meet my neighbor Travis. Travis, this is my friend Morgan, visiting from Hopewellen."

"Pleased to meet you, Ma'am." Travis caught the screen door with his foot to keep it from slamming, removed his cap, crossed the room, and extended his hand, all in one seamless motion. "I ain't never figured you could fit three people in here, Serenity!" he said, pumping Morgan's hand. "What with your place being so small and all, not to mention the mess." He winked at Morgan. "Why, I imagine you must've dragged a goat in here and kept it a good long while to get it looking thataway."

"I can't fit three people in here. Not if one of them is you. That's why I have to go out to the barn and get you your honey."

"I reckon it'd kinda put a hitch in your getalong if I'd of brought my Elsie with me then, ain't that right? And we was fixing to come together, too."

"Naw, that would have been just fine. She's welcome here anytime. Me and Morgan and Elsie could have had us some sweet tea while you sat out there on the porch with the dogs."

"Well, that's all right. Probably wouldn't have been brewed tea anyhow. I'd be afeared it was that Yankee instant. Gives me the allovers just thinking about it." Lines extended from Travis's eyes like a child's drawing of the rays of the sun. "I reckon you put the sugar in after it's already cold, like they do in Indiana or Wisconsin or New York or wherever it is yu'uns hatched."

He grinned broadly at Morgan. "Course that's assuming it's cold. She don't always have ice." He pointed at Serena's cooler.

"Why look at all them books on the floor there!" He said before Serena could answer. "Same old same old. My mama would've tanned my hide if I'd of ever let a book touch the floor."

"Your mama doesn't live here, old man. I do." Serena tugged at the brim of Travis's cap. "Let me get that Sourwood." She headed for the screen door, which had closed only partially.

"You oughta get a new spring for that door," he said. "But then you always was tighter than the bark on a tree."

Serena shot him a look over her shoulder as she retreated to the barn.

"Except for all this foofoo." Travis beamed at Morgan through pale, watery eyes and patted the arm of the leather recliner. "She ain't right." He grinned, tapping his forehead. "Don't open any drawers. You might could find a big old copperhead. I looked inside that cupboard one time, and it looked as if someone stirred it with a stick." He rocked backwards and dug his fists into the small of his back, "Well, I guess I'd best go muscle up that hay into the barn."

He was gone before she had a chance to say a word. She followed him with the idea of helping. But by the time she got to the barn, Serena had opened the doors wide and Travis had backed in. The two worked together so seamlessly they were done before she could see what to do.

Travis climbed back in the truck and rolled slowly out of the barn. "Nice meeting you, Ma'am," he said to Morgan. "I hope you have a real nice stay. Y'all come on by before you head back to the city, hear? My Elsie put up three bushels of rhubarb, and now she's made so many pies I can't hardly keep up. I'd be mighty pleased if you'd help me out."

"Thank you, Travis."

"Glad to know you've got you such a real nice friend, Serenity. You be good to her, now! She's in a strange place. Yes Ma'am, she surely is."

Travis's truck creaked and banged its way down the long drive. "He has no idea how strange," Serena said. When their eyes met, they shook with laughter.

They dragged water up from the spring in big plastic jugs they hauled in the old wooden wagon, fed and watered the animals, had tea and and several of the never-ending Elberta peaches Aunt Lee insisted that Morgan bring with her, and went to bed as the sun was setting. While the room grew darker, they spoke of ordinary things and fell asleep with their backs pressed against each other.

~ ~ ~

Brigid imagined herself as a willow tree and threw up a force field of protection around Morgan and Serena, just as she had on her last day on earth. Now Shadow wouldn't be able to disturb them while they rested.

"There you go again. I'll let you get away with it this time." Shadow arched his brow. "But you can't keep that up, Sweet Cakes. You know they have to stand up to their tests on their own. You can only help if they ask you."

Shadow took up a position in the far corner of the room and stared at her. She glared at him, then turned to the two women, who were sleeping peacefully.

She stood over them all night long, watching the light of the full moon as it danced across their hair and faces and crept along the old quilt that blanketed them.

~ ~ ~

Clarissa thrashed beneath sticky sheets she finally threw to the floor. She was reviewing the events of the day. Or so she told herself. It felt as though they were reviewing her, and she was flunking the test.

In her long enumeration of the day's failures, she was reliving what it had been like to approach yet another ramshackle country home near the proposed nuclear dump site. She and the boys had finished coloring the flyers quickly and—wouldn't you know it—her kids just had to get out there and hand them out, which is what they had been doing for hours under the sweltering sun.

So there she was, in front of a sagging clapboard house, the paint long gone. It was a change from the more numerous trailers. First she knocked on the front door, then quickly stepped back so she was down two stairs from the entrance. She didn't want to frighten these people, or have them think she was imposing. Her arrival had already sent the chickens squawking and flapping across the yard. It seemed strangers were a rare sight in these parts.

She'd have taken her boys to the doors of these homes, which is what they wanted, but she was too timid. But Martin and Frankie could no longer be contained in the car even though they wanted to keep on going, as if an afternoon of canvassing would stop the dump. The two of them had fallen out of the car and plopped down on the dusty lawn, too hot and tired to play or even to complain.

Who could blame them? It had been as hot as when Big Mom used to fire up the wood stove in August and can vegetables from her garden. Clarissa felt tiny beads of sweat popping out across her brow. She reached for a tissue and was about to wipe them away, but the door swung open and a very large, very black, very old woman in a faded housedress boomed out from behind the screen door, "Who are you?"

She backed down another step and ached to melt into the dry wood beneath her feet. She was suddenly self-conscious about the color of her skin, which was several shades lighter than that of the woman at the door.

"Who's that, Grandma Mattie?" A teenage girl popped her head over the older woman's shoulder and disappeared before there was time for an answer.

"Mama? Sissy says we have company. Who is it?" A woman's voice from the back of the house was getting closer.

"That's what I was just fixing to find out." The older woman set her jaw and frowned. Clarissa tried to speak and failed. Her mouth was as dry as a ball of cotton. She had given the last soda from the cooler to the boys to split, and now every inch of her body was dripping wet but her mouth, which clicked its dryness when she parted her lips to talk.

She felt the older woman eying her all over, disapproving of her loose ringlets, her pale skin, the boys sprawled on the lawn, her dress, her lack of makeup, everything.

Then a younger, lighter, smaller version of the first woman opened the screen door and stepped out. "Car trouble?" she said, looking at the boys with concern.

Clarissa drew a full breath for the first time since stepping onto the property. "No, Ma'am," she heard herself say, "Car trouble is the only kind of trouble I don't have today. I'm trying to do something about this nuclear dump they're trying to build."

"Mm, mmm, mmmm," came Grandma Mattie's voice from behind the screen door. Clarissa felt, rather than saw, the deep scowl of disapproval.

"Oh, that," the younger woman said. She looked her up and down. "I've never seen you before. You new?"

"No, Ma'am, I live in Hopewellen. But I don't think this dump should happen. Do you? My name is Clarissa Albright, by the way."

"Rosa Brooks," the woman said, but didn't offer her hand. She paused, crossed her arms in front of her waist, and shifted her weight to one leg, which caused her hip to pop out a little. "Well, Miz Albright, if there's one thing I've learned, it's that what I think and a dollar six… ." Rosa Brooks looked her straight in the eye. "And you know the rest." She glanced at the boys, then back to her.

She thinks I'm a bad mother, dragging my boys through this.

And maybe I am.

"That's just the way things work around here," Rosa Brooks was saying, "I've heard it's not so different in Hopewellen." She arched her brow and shifted her hip. "Big money is behind that dump, which means it's gonna happen. Big money opens a factory and everybody eats, then shuts it down and nobody's working. Big money bypasses a town with a highway and the town goes dead, then puts hog waste in the river until the fish we used to catch for dinner turn belly up. It's just how it is."

"It doesn't have to be that way. We can do something. If we don't stop it, this dump is going to poison this land until the end of time."

"Listen, Miz Albright, I don't mean to be rude, but the end of time is what I face every morning when I wake up with a long day at work ahead of me followed by another eight-hour day when I get home. The end of time is when I'm gonna get caught up on my payments. And speaking of the end of time, I have to go. Got something on the stove. The end of time is when my family will eat whether or not I burn dinner." She stepped back behind the screen door.

"Wait, Ms. Brooks." She knew she was pathetic. "Please. Just take this flyer. Maybe you'll get a chance to read it sometime. My number is at the bottom. I sure hope you'll think about this and call me if you change your mind."

She had given up on sleep by now and was pacing, holding her throbbing head, and sweating. The whole day had been like that. One house after another. The ones who opened their doors, anyhow. And some of them were a lot worse.

She padded into the kitchen, her bare feet delighting in the small relief they received from the cool floor. The air was so thick she could slice a big slab of it and serve it up with the watermelon and cantaloupe she fixed herself before trying to go back to bed. It had been a tough, thankless day once they left the shelter of the apartment.

Finally she made it to bed, where her thoughts traveled to her mother. Was she, like Grandma Mattie, disapproving? But she couldn't be like Rosa Brooks' mother, because she had money. And she was white. She probably wore spotless white heels and white suits and carried a white briefcase. Upscale, professional, urbane. Or did she marry well and sneak money from her husband to send Big Mom for the child she was ashamed of? Either way, her mother was *u-neg* and didn't love her. But then again, why should she? Clarissa was a failure.

Not a single person behind the countless doors she had knocked on was the least bit interested in stopping the dump.

Hours later, she finally found sleep. She dreamed she was drifting underwater in a cool, sunlit sea. Women glided by—some dark-skinned in bright African clothing that moved with the currents in a swirling kaleidoscope of color. Some were Indians, while others were European women in some sort of peasant garb. All were smiling as they whirled and turned on the currents. They had fantastic balls of light glowing in their bellies that they tossed back and forth with the delight of children.

Morgan Forrester was there. She was swimming, her arms moving the water with strong strokes and her underwater laughter forming a rainbow of bubbles that drifted to the surface.

Big Mom swam by. She smiled at Clarissa, her round arms gliding with the slow dignity of ceremonial prayer.

They all seemed to be headed somewhere.

But where?

CHAPTER 12

infuse us

I want to watch you unfold
bend towards light
your translucent foliage pulsing
your hungry roots pushing into darkness.
Grow wild!
I will keep watch
marveling at each blossom.
And before the world
once more
curls under heavy frost
I want to harvest
fill baskets
jars
root cellars.
Move you into every room
so I can feast in candlelight
all winter.

—Lana Mareé

Brigid continued her watch over Morgan and Serena throughout the long night and into the next morning. Though the sun was already high in the sky, Morgan was still sleeping, damp curls pressed against her round cheeks.

Like a wee babe lost in slumber.

Something about how Morgan was both soft and brave got to Brigid. But the growing bond between them went beyond emotional attachment. It was as though she would never be free until Morgan was.

And won't you just look at that Serena, Goddess love her.

Serena had been up and feeding the animals long ago, when the sky was barely light. She had brought an old, unused door and two saw horses up from the barn and created a table that took up most of what little free space there was in the main room of the two-room cabin.

Strewn all over the makeshift table were books, pencils, and legal pads in which she'd been scribbling all morning in between bouts of feverish reading, involuntary pacing, and frequent trips to the bedroom to see if Morgan was awake.

The screen door was propped open with a rusting cast iron pot. Serena was striding back and forth between the remaining available space in the cabin and the front porch, her brow scored with deep lines and her stringy, uncombed hair tied to itself in a careless knot from which three pencils now protruded. Well out of her way, assorted dogs and cats sat in a prim, self-consciously well-behaved row, heads cocked, and followed her with their eyes.

"Careful, woman," Brigid whispered. "You'll worry yourself half to death."

"That's where you're wrong, Darling." Shadow laughed. It was an ugly sound. "This one will worry herself all the way to death. Cancer, I'd say." He pulled at his chin. "Yes. My money is on cancer of those tiny, unused, useless breasts." He emphasized each word and watched Brigid carefully.

Holy Mother Goddess, how I hate him.

But her response only seemed to please him. He grinned at her wickedly.

Suddenly Serena stopped pacing. It was as if Morgan's eyes had made a sound when they opened and she heard it. She rushed first to the wood stove and then to the bed, where she plunked down a steaming mug of strong coffee on the upended crate beside Morgan.

"Good god, Serena, what's gotten into you?" Morgan, yawned deliciously as she stretched her toes as far as she could under the covers, bringing the stretch up her legs and spine and into her arms and fingers. "You're looking a little crazed this morning, if you don't mind my saying so. What's going on?"

Serena brushed off her comment and launched into a harangue about the evolution of women and their oppression. She talked about how Brigid's fear was like the fear of all women, and what a force women would be if they acted with power and in unison in spite of that fear. She was beside herself with anger at the men who drove Brigid to her death. Simultaneously, she was frustrated with Brigid's choice.

"It's *deadly* for women to let their emotions run them," Serena said. Look at us! I'm stuck up here on a frigging mountain. You're stuck in your grandmother's house with your damned men. We could change the world if we got off our asses! We have the numbers. After all, we are the majority. But no, here we stay, frozen in place."

Frozen?

Luvie, you are far from frozen.

You're a woman on fire, and there's the truth of it.

Brigid raised an eyebrow at Shadow, who stopped smiling and became a little smaller and less dense.

~ ~ ~

"Are you listening to me?" Although Serena was racing on the gerbil wheel of her own thoughts, she was hypnotized into a slower pace by the easy grace with which Morgan lavished her body with self-massage, as though greeting the morning was a royal ritual into which her body must be initiated each day anew.

Morgan rose languorously from the bed. Soon she was standing outside in the large enamel bowl in which Serena bathed, sponging her naked body with sunlit streams of warm water from the wood stove.

A peasant woman's bath.

Marvelous.

Serena thought Morgan could be one of the Renoirs.

Except Renoir didn't paint women with graying hair and sagging bodies.

The son-of-a-bitch.

I mean bastard.

I mean asshole.

A woman's aging body is a thing of beauty.

Immortal.

Sublime.

"I feel fabulous." Morgan stretched again in the sunlight. "I'm, I don't know, so here, so *awake.* And you know what else? Brigid is here with us. I sense her presence."

She draped herself with an enormous, plush, peach-colored towel she had brought with her and looked out over the mountains that stretched across the horizon in soft blue layers, like waves on the ocean.

"I felt her all through the night," Morgan said, "as if she were watching over us. I think she's real and good and will help us with whatever this is about."

She tossed her bath water onto the vegetable garden, came back inside, and pulled on jeans and a shirt, smoothing the fabric with her hands and relishing the textures beneath her fingertips as if they were velvet.

"I see you've been busy while I slept." Morgan picked up a hairbrush, which she began working through her long red and silver waves.

"Do you know what Mary Daly says?" Serena said.

"No. What does Mary Daly say?"

"She says women are indigenous to the earth. You can tell because we nest easily and happily here. She thinks men are aliens."

"No kidding. That's pretty funny. Why?"

This wasn't supposed to be a joke.

Lighten up.

Don't run her over.

"Because men aren't capable of generating their own energy on this planet, so they have to rape the environment to get the energy they don't have."

"Rape? That's not a word to use lightly."

Get on with it!

No, be patient.

She drew a deep breath and made herself slow down. "Okay. The point is, men have to conquer everything—land, people, money, each other—to get whatever it is they think they lack. They aren't content here, they can't find what they need inside themselves. They always want more, more, more."

"I could use a little more myself right now. Is this the last of the bread?"

She pulled another loaf of multigrain bread off a high shelf and handed it to Morgan along with a bowl of fruit.

"In their mad drive for power," Serena said, "men are going to destroy this planet. It doesn't matter how—genetic engineering gone awry, the foolish nuclear experiment finally poisoning everything everywhere, or hacking away at the rain forests until we run out of air. You'd think they'd finally get it—now that their precious sperm counts are dwindling—that people are animals too, and one day our number will come up in the great extinction lottery. Do you know what they say about this country in Australia?"

"Good grief. Who wound you up this morning?"

"They say Americans are in so much denial, we're in denial of denial. Stay with me on this. Please. Can you deny that men compete aggressively for whatever they want?"

"Some do, yes." Morgan was drizzling honey over a big slab of brown bread. They were sitting at the small table by the window. "You've been holding out on me. This Sourwood is fabulous."

"Most do. They don't feel they're enough inside. Instead of dealing with that, they steal from the environment."

"Now you sound like a shrink. Kind of demented though."

I'm finally getting somewhere, though she'd never admit it.

"Well, get this. Daly says men also require the use of their own private battery pack. A wife."

Morgan laughed so hard a piece of the apple she was eating flew out of her mouth, slapped against Serena's forehead, and paused there for a moment before sliding down her nose.

"You think that's funny?"

"It's over the top." She was laughing so hard she could hardly speak. "I bet you wish that apple went over the top," she said, spitting again. Morgan had been attempting to dab Serena's face with a napkin, but now she was doubled over and helpless with laughter. Finally she was able to draw a breath. "That part about the wife being a private battery pack is pretty good, though. I like that." She surrendered to laughter again.

Serena frowned.

Why isn't she taking this seriously?

Morgan regarded her with what looked like compassion. "Sit still."

Morgan positioned herself behind her and pulled the pencils and knots out of her hair before she began moving her brush carefully through the tangled whiteness.

Serena wanted to bolt out of the chair, grab her by the shoulders, and make her listen. Instead, she forced herself to sit still. "Damn, this feels good," she thought as Morgan began to pull the brush through her hair with long strokes.

"I can see some of what you're saying, Serena."

"Please don't be condescending."

"I'm not. I was Rex's battery pack. He never lifted a finger around the house unless I begged him to. And then he acted as if he were doing me a favor, instead of contributing like an equal adult to the environment we were mutually responsible for creating and maintaining. I basically raised those two kids alone, even when I was married. And I felt used. I wanted a partner and I got another baby. So yeah, I was Rex's battery pack. I've probably been a lot of men's battery pack, but that doesn't mean—"

At last!

She gets it.

"Right! You're either a housewifized, domesticated battery pack or an outcast like me! Do you have any idea how often I've had to defend my decision to remain childless? And it never occurs to people that I actually chose to not marry. They skirt the issue, not wanting to embarrass me, obviously assuming I remained single because no one ever asked me to marry them. People treat me like a freak."

Of course I am *a freak.*

I have a daughter and I'm too cowardly to meet her.

But never mind.

"It makes me so angry," Serena said, "I want to build a shoe factory up the rear end of every asshole who treats me that way. Listen to me. For five thousand years, men have been subjugating women. Did you know the most physically dangerous thing a woman can do is to get married? That's what the statistics show. A huge percentage of married women are abused by their partners. Between twenty-five and forty percent of all girls are sexually abused. Not to mention adult rape, sexual harassment, pornography, unequal pay, the glass ceiling."

"You told me all this before in the restaurant, remember? You have to stop going over and over the same points. You'll make yourself nuts."

"And what about prostitution? A mere hundred years ago, unless you were born rich, if you were a woman you could be either a wife or a prostitute. Period. Anyone who tried to be anything else—like a governess, for example—ran the risk of displeasing her employer and ending up without references, thereby being forced into prostitution anyway. So an unscrupulous employer could force a female employee to do anything he wanted. Calamity Jane said the way she had it figured, most women made their living by either washing a man's drawers or pulling them down."

"Stop."

No way am I going to stop.

You should know these things!

"Those were the days when they invented the term 'rule of thumb.' Do you know what that means? It was a legal term. It meant a man could legally beat his wife with a stick, as long as the stick was no thicker than his thumb."

"Serena, I said stop! I mean it!" Morgan quit brushing her hair and pulled up a chair directly in front of her, so when she sat down, their knees were touching.

"And 'third degree' comes from the witch trials." Serena wasn't about to quit. "The third level of torture, the one that killed untold thousands of women, the one that was so bad everyone confessed to being a witch by the time third degree of torture was applied. Don't get me started on the witch trials... ."

❧ ❧ ❧

"Great Mother Goddess," breathed Brigid. She was looking at Shadow. "He's just like those cursed invaders, those Scots, and there's the truth of it."

She felt her guides nudging her in the ribs. She realized she'd been getting caught up in Serena's anger and fueling her own. When Brigid looked where her guides were pointing, she saw Shadow growing larger, more distinct, and more pleased with himself.

"Hi Toots." Shadow winked at her.

She felt a gentle pressure coming from her guides on all sides. She saw what they wanted her to see. Resentment and blaming didn't diminish Shadow. It strengthened him.

Better to feed the power of what's good, her guides seemed to say, even when the good is so small as to be barely visible, than to waste your vital, nourishing energy on the feeding of negativity.

"Serena, I said stop."

Brigid's attention flashed back to Morgan, who looked as if she were listening for something.

"Why? Can't you take this? Are you so hung up on men, so dependent, you can't stand a little truth about what they've done?"

"You're so angry. But it's not current anger, as when someone steps on your toe or slights you. It's old and seething and rehearsed."

"So?"

"So I'm feeling that presence I was telling you about. Shadow. When you got angry, he showed up. The angrier you got, the stronger I felt him."

"Do you think he's real, too?"

"Suppose they're both real, Brigid and Shadow." Morgan, suddenly pale, stopped. "He scares me, Serena. He frightened me before, when I thought I only imagined him. But when I think he might be real, he terrifies me."

Shadow was leaning forward, panting with excitement. But when he saw Brigid glance at him, he leaned jauntily against the wall and shot her a wicked, self-satisfied smirk. He set his eyes into narrow glints of red, brilliant as flame.

Serena drew her friend's face closer to her own. "I know he scares you. But I think we're stronger than he is."

Morgan pulled back. Serena took her hands, keeping the contact.

"How do you get that? We're both stuck, as you said, you with your anger and me with my fear. What if he has us in checkmate?"

"What just happened? Your hands turned to ice."

"My god, Serena."

"What?"

"As soon as I said—"

"Tell me."

Morgan was quivering, her voice had become shrill, and her nose was bubbling with mucous mixed with tears. Brigid's hand went to her heart. Morgan leaned forward and whispered, "'Checkmate.' As soon as I said that, I felt him stronger. He's there, in the corner, leering at me. So ugly. Do you see him?"

Virginia Woof was pacing, positioning herself between the two women and the corner. Her hackles were up, and she was growling.

"No. But Woof does." Serena grabbed Morgan's shoulders. "Listen to me, Morgan. Get a grip on yourself. You said he only shows up when you're afraid. What can you do right now to stop being afraid?"

Morgan wiped the tears from her eyes with her arm and searched the room. Her chin was trembling. "I could pet Woof. And you, Serena, have to let go of your anger."

"I can do that for the moment. Come here Woof."

Woof hesitated to leave her post, but she obeyed. As soon as she looked into Morgan's face, her brown eyes became soft with love. The fur along her back began to lie flat, her tail wagged, and she jumped up, swinging her front paws and much of her weight onto Morgan's lap. Morgan rubbed her all over while Woof licked tears and mucous off Morgan's face.

"In the name of the Mother and all that's holy, help me," Brigid said. Her guides placed hands of light along her spine, healing and strengthening her, and her own fears diminished. In spite of Shadow, she sensed how this could work, if she supported Morgan and her guides supported her. Her heart reached toward Morgan.

For an instant, Brigid glanced in Shadow's direction. He had condensed to a frantic pinpoint of evil, staring into her with his remaining eye.

"So you're not so high and mighty after all," she said to him.

He hissed and grew larger.

Her lesson learned, Brigid turned her back on him and focused on the two women.

"How are you doing?" Serena asked.

"Better."

"Is he still here?"

"No. I don't think so."

"Remember that. What did you do to get rid of him?"

Morgan looked lovingly into into Serena's eyes, her own eyes still bright with tears. She stroked Serena's hand with one hand. With the other, she rubbed Woof's ears. Woof looked up at her with an adoring doggy grin, her head cocked so she could lean into Morgan's massage, her tongue flopping out of her mouth and her tail wagging.

"I know exactly what I did to get rid of him. I loved. I loved, and I let myself be loved."

~ ~ ~

"There's something wrong with all this anger at men, Serena."

Morgan was admiring Serena's strength as she brought her ax down on the log she'd stood on end beneath her. They'd gone outside to release the tensions of the past two days, Serena by splitting wood and Morgan by digging in the dirt with her bare toes. The sky was a blazing blue, there was a steady breeze from the north, and she felt the vitality with which she'd greeted the day rise in her body, up through the earth, into her feet, and out to her extremities.

"Really? That sounds old, dusty, and rather conventional. What's right about my anger?" Serena made a particularly neat split that had the sharp, hollow ring of a bowling ball executing a strike.

"I don't want to go there." Morgan was chewing on a piece of grass and circling the periphery of Serena's work area. The grass gave in her mouth, the insides sweet.

"Great. I walk you through a lifetime from four hundred years ago, we experience eleven women essentially bullied to death by men, you bring this

Shadow guy in here, now we're in a dance between good and evil that spans at least four centuries, and you won't hear me out? What if I can help us break through on this?"

"How can you when you demonize half the human race? There are plenty of good men out there."

"Perhaps," She brought the ax down with a resounding crack. "But they must be wimps, because they sure as shit aren't doing anything about the ones who aren't 'good,' as you put it. They come up with a pill costing ten dollars a pop that makes a man hard and it's the fastest selling drug in history. That's what men want, a perpetual woody."

Serena tossed the log she'd split into a pile to give herself more room to work. "Why haven't they come up with a pill for men's heads, instead of prescribing eighty percent of the mood altering drugs to women, pumping us with so-called 'antidepressants' so we can accommodate to what's making us miserable instead of doing something to change it. Men are the ones who need the hormone therapy. Turn down the aggression and turn up the compassion! Betcha no one's breaking a sweat coming up with that one!"

"Maybe Viagra helps men open their hearts," Morgan said. "Men open their hearts in bed."

"Give me a break! We're in a crisis of epic proportions and all you can think about is sex?"

"You brought it up! All I know is: if we keep going around in circles, feeding your anger and my fear, we won't get anywhere. Besides, maybe you're not really angry."

"Oh, I'm angry all right." She was pounding a wedge into a huge log.

"Think about it. There's rarely anything of any real consequence out there, outside ourselves, to make us angry, frightened, or hurt. We get triggered into old, unresolved childhood wounds—old patterns of feeling and thinking—by things that in and of themselves are harmless. We react the way we did to our parents, our siblings, our teachers. We take the old emotional pathways that protected us once but no longer serve us because they aren't about now. They're about then. We project our shadows instead of integrating them, creating enemies where there needn't be any."

"What's all this 'we' stuff? Speak for yourself. Besides, the things I'm angry about are real—and are going on right now—rape, battering, female genital mutilation."

"Bear with me. I don't agree that all men are scum, but you've taught me some things I didn't know. So let me show you what I know. Allow me to employ my skills as a psychobabologist to our present situation." Morgan made with a low dip with her torso, one arm extended, as in the introduction of a noted performer.

Maybe if I lighten this up, she'll listen to me.

Serena laughed. "Do I have to? What you just said is a crock. Sounds like a shrink I had long ago."

"You had a shrink?"

"Never mind." Whack, whack, whack went the ax.

"Okay. Then hear me out."

"Not if you're going to tell me anger isn't healthy. Anger isn't healthy in men, because anger and lust are about the only emotions they allow themselves—"

"Here we go again."

"Whereas women get stuck in fear, and don't let themselves get angry. Maybe if more women got angry, we'd get somewhere. Anger is a powerful fuel."

"I agree. But your anger hasn't exactly launched you off this mountain. Or gotten your manuscript out there."

Serena paused in her work. She rested the head of her ax on one of the log piles, crossing her arms over the end of the handle and resting her chin on them. "Touché. I'm listening."

"Okay." Morgan perched on one of the fatter logs scattered on the ground. "In my work, I've found that when someone is stuck in anger, there's a deeper emotion they're avoiding, something more painful and difficult to experience. They use the energy of that deeper emotion to feed their anger. Then they don't have to experience the pain and vulnerability of their true feeling. They become walled off from themselves, because they're denying what they really feel."

"Hey, I really feel anger."

"That's your experience. But what's underneath the anger?"

Serena was silent.

"Usually anger is covering fear," Morgan said. "Essentially there are only two emotions, love and fear. Any troublesome emotion boils down to fear." She could see Serena getting defensive. She held Serena's gaze, making her expression both gentle and firm, as she often did at work. She wasn't going to let her off the hook.

"That's bull crap, but I'll play along. I think my anger is covering something a lot worse than fear." Serena picked another log to split and positioned it in front of her. "My anger is covering powerlessness." She brought the ax down hard.

"Which is frightening," Morgan said softly.

"Very."

Serena is terrified of admitting she's afraid.

"So what's the antidote to powerlessness?" Morgan said.

"Power!"

"And what makes you feel powerful?"

"Anger!"

Annoyance flamed up Morgan's spine and engulfed her head.

"Gotcha!" Serena's eyes were twinkling turquoise. "I think I see what you're getting at. Give me a minute." She looked out over the ridge and into the blue gray of the far mountains, her eyes contemplative and softer, like the landscape into which she gazed.

Yes!

She's going to work this one.

Morgan took a long breath of fresh mountain air and drank in the enchantment of sunlight dancing through leaves still young enough to be lush with green. The trees waved at her and in her heart she waved back, not wanting to distract Serena with a gesture. Instead, she wriggled her toes, massaging the grasses beneath her feet and, as if in acknowledgment, the trees waved more enthusiastically.

Serena rested on a nearby log. When she spoke, for once she was slow and quiet. "My road to power begins with allowing myself a vision, something I deeply desire. When I commit to that vision and follow through, then I feel powerful."

"How do you commit and follow through?"

Serena thought for a very long time. "I can't do it from my ego, my personality, or I get caught up in inner conflict and self-doubt."

"What do you do instead?"

Serena closed her eyes and tilted her head back. "I have to transcend my personality and do it from my soul. I connect with the still place within, the Serena place. Then I'm an eagle, I can soar. I serve the goddess because I am the goddess."

"The goddess?"

"Mary Daly says as long as god is a man, men will think they're god."

Will you get off it!

"Never mind," Serena said. "The point is, I connect with my own sacred essence, the same holiness that suffuses all that is. Then I can do anything."

"That's beautiful. How do you do that?"

"It's not always easy. Yoga generally works. And connecting with nature—watching the sunset, gazing at the moon, lying on the earth, leaning against a tree. Or I sit still and bring my attention to my breath as it goes in and out, letting go of other thoughts. Then I can go to the Serena place, to my core. Sometimes, anyway."

They looked out on the distant roll of mountains, and Serena pointed to a hawk riding the thermals. A soft breeze lifted Morgan's hair and gently wafted it across her face.

"So the antidote to fear is love. And the antidote to powerlessness is the power of living your vision," Morgan said.

"Okay, so… ."

"So that's important. Think about this, Serena. Maybe it isn't about men. Maybe it's about us. Maybe we're the ones who have to change."

"Come on. Men have been the problem for thousands of years."

"I mean it. Men controlled us at one time." She caught Serena gathering herself for another tirade, which she was determined to head off. "And they still do, to a certain degree. But we have a lot of power now, much of which we don't use. Besides, we can't do anything about men, so let's work on what we can do something about. It's time for us to quit focusing on other people, in my case with dependency and in yours with anger. Instead, lets focus on our love and the power of living our dreams."

"Hmm… ." Serena said.

"And I'll go you one better."

"Now what?"

"What if all women did that? What if we all stopped, even if only for five minutes a day at first, and took time for ourselves in which we weren't taking care of others or reacting to them? What if we put the focus on us? On what we love and what we want. What if following through on our own visions becomes our first priority? Maybe Brigid and her Council wouldn't have drowned if they'd done that. And perhaps Shadow would be a mere shadow of himself. I'm beginning to think that's what real integrity is, living in alignment with who we really are, the soul and personality moving as one."

Morgan drew a deep breath.

"You're very pleased with yourself, aren't you?" Serena said.

"Yes. I am."

~ ~ ~

Clarissa awakened before dawn, having been visited by Big Mom throughout the night. She felt rested and confident, even with the fuzzy outline of Louisiana staring at her from the stain on the ceiling and a heat wave coming on.

As a rosy glow penetrated the night sky, Clarissa drew a full breath, relaxed, and closed her eyes. Deep within, a fresh vision of her event was forming, a kaleidoscope of brilliant color, stirring music, and smiling faces. The rhythm of the drums was so compelling she sprang to her feet and danced. And as she whirled and stomped, her vision grew more vivid, more compelling.

People of all races were joining forces to stop the dump—and they were ecstatic. Their hearts were wide open. The event was experiential, spiritual, and emotional more than it was political, touching something so vital to the human heart that everyone had to respond.

Big Mom was right, the ancestors were stirring, because she saw people—mostly women—from every period in history coming together to celebrate their power to make the changes that honor and protect life.

When she had exhausted herself dancing and was streaming with sweat, she stretched her whole body like a cat. Forget yesterday. Today was going to be a good day, beginning with a shower.

That night, she wrote in her journal.

Thursday, June 29th

I Feel
FABULOUS!

I Want
I'm on a roll and I want to keep moving toward the event I envision.

I Am Grateful For
The boys helped me collate a mailing today.
Frankie even said he was doing it for his children's children. I'm glad I didn't laugh. I felt like laughing and crying, both.
I guess I'm really not alone. Doris, that wacky downstairs neighbor of mine, actually helped us out for awhile. I do believe she was

standing a little taller when she left. Good thing, too. She needs it. Bad. She even said she'd help with the canvassing. Joshua called to see how I was doing and said he had a lot of time to give.

Whether or not I make it with this dump thing, my kids are learning so much. They feel strong and proud. I can see it.

I have a vision. I believe in what I'm doing. And that belief is changing my life and my kids' lives.

Strengths I Have Used to Move Toward My Goal

Love for my children, again.

I did a really good job of explaining to them about Big Mom and the dump yesterday. It helped them feel like they're part of a family that stands for something, even though it's just the three of us. They're even proud about not having so much money to spend this summer and are trying to think of ways to earn their own money and give some of it to help stop the dump. Best of all, they felt really good about themselves and we had fun.

Okay, fun. I know how to have fun with my kids Even when all we're doing is collating a mailing.

I took the time to be in nature today. I even Talked Frankie into coming with me to the park. We fed the ducks. Martin was feeling too cool to take this whole family thing that far, but he did seem more than a little envious when he found out we saw a turtle come up under one of the ducklings, pull it under, and eat it. Boys.

I always have trouble with number five. Okay. I didn't worry. I just did what I had to do.

She put down her journal and turned off the lamp next to her bed. As she relaxed into slumber, she thought about how Morgan was going to be reading what she wrote and how close to her she was beginning to feel.

She doesn't just talk the talk.

She walks the walk.
So I can trust her.
I have a feeling that wherever she is, she's pulling as hard as I am.
We're both doing the best we can.
And that's enough.
I think we're gonna make it.

~ ~ ~

"So. Keeping the focus on us, what makes women wonderful?" Morgan said. They were sitting on the porch steps. She looked out over the pale pink of the mountain laurels and the fuchsia of the rhododendrons, bathing her heart in the balm of abundant color.

"That's easy! Our strength."

"How about our love? We bring life into the world. We nest and we nurture. We're concerned for the welfare of others. We're sensitive."

"Yes?"

"With those qualities, what would the world be like if women made the fulfillment of our dreams our first priority? What if we started acting as if the things we love are so valuable, they should be foremost in the world? Nurturing ahead of political greed, children's welfare over the bottom line, a clean, healthy planet ahead of economic gain, beauty combined with efficiency instead of sacrificed to it, a decent life for everyone instead of power and wealth for a few. We could do that. As you said: we've got the numbers, we're the majority. We've toted our briefcases for the last several decades and learned how to be seen and heard. What if we put our newfound 'masculine' skills to work in support of our feminine values?"

"Hell, if you pull that off, I'll come down off this mountain and join y'all."

"You could start with that, Serena. Come down off this mountain, roll up your sleeves, and join in the fracas.

"Well, I don't know about—"

"Hush!"

"What is it?"

"Stand here beside me." Morgan sprang to her feet and sank her heels and the balls of her feet into the earth, wriggling her toes in the grass.

"Have you lost it? I'll do no such thing."

"It's Brigid. I've been sensing her all day, opening my heart to her, asking for her help. I think she wants to show us something. Are you game?"

"Why didn't you say so in the first place? Of course."

Earlier, when Morgan began to realize how persevering Brigid's presence was and how good it felt, she had instinctively run a check to be sure it was all right to get involved with her.

She'd prayed to the Spirit of Divine Wholeness that Brigid be allowed to stay only if she loved Morgan and was working for her highest good and the highest good of all. When Brigid withstood the test, she opened her heart to her. For the first time since Grandmama died, she had a true ally.

Serena was on her feet.

"Now," Morgan said, tuning in to Brigid. "Position your feet shoulder width apart and release your knees—don't lock them. Let the energy flow."

Show me, Brigid.

She followed the guidance she felt coming in. "Let yourself feel tiny, tough roots growing down from your feet and giving you a broad base in the earth. Allow those roots to grow stronger, longer—send them deeper and wider, let them be touched and embraced by the roots of the trees around you, steadying you."

She could sense Serena doing as she asked. "Good. Now send a long tap root down into the earth, through the bedrock, deeper and deeper until you reach the earth's fiery core. Bring up a ball of that source of all life from the center of the earth, up through your roots and into your legs, healing you. Bring it up into your womb. Let it glow there, like the bellies of the underwater women, like the power of the women in Brigid's tribe, and let it energize your body and your spirit."

She breathed fully, allowing herself to feel the healing warmth of the glowing ball in her belly. "Then let that ball of healing energy come up your spine and spread throughout your whole body, finally moving out your head and arms—your branches, and experience the sensation of the breezes blowing through your leaves as you draw in the healing forces of the sun, the moon, and the stars."

"I'm not sure I'm doing this correctly. I don't feel it in my body."

"Brigid says that's okay. Don't be attached to the intensity or clarity of your experience. It's enough to simply intend that what I'm describing is real. Take what you get and trust something is happening. Brigid says with practice, we'll both become more skilled at this.

"Now," Morgan said, "let your body be the vehicle for heaven and earth to communicate with each other. Then, after they're finished exchanging energy, give yourself the gift of playing with this life force any way you choose, for your own benefit and enjoyment."

When they felt complete, they dipped low to the ground, instinctively grounding themselves by placing their palms on the grass and returning the excess energy they had gathered to the earth. Then they stood and stretched, breathed deeply, laughed out loud, and hugged each other. They gazed up into the trees and felt a sudden rush of cool, green energy grounding and strengthening them. The trees waved and Morgan waved back.

She scanned the area around them, feeling with her senses, and found that, for the moment at least, Shadow had completely disappeared. The gift of Brigid's teaching had strengthened both her body and her spirit, bringing her focus all the way back to herself.

~ ~ ~

"So why is Brigid coming to us now?" Serena asked quietly.

Brigid listened intently.

It was evening. Morgan and Serena had eaten salmon steaks Morgan had brought frozen from Hopewellen—they'd concluded it was the last day before they'd go bad—along with lightly sautéed broccoli leaves from the garden, Vidalia onions from Jake, and a salad made with assorted baby greens Serena had grown. Now, they were finished with their meal and were sitting at the table enjoying the warm, flickering light of lanterns and candles, sipping chamomile tea and chewing on crystallized ginger.

Morgan was quiet for some time. "I get the sense that the women of the past need the women of the present to break the shackles of our emotions and move forward with our dreams."

"They need us to clear emotional baggage not only for ourselves, but also for them?"

"I don't know. Maybe... for all of creation. All the multiverses." Morgan was thoughtful. "Yeah. I think that might be it."

"That's huge,".

"No kidding." Morgan glanced toward the ceiling and wagged her forefinger in all directions. "You better help us with this if we have to deal with your baggage, too! Do you hear me?"

At first, Brigid felt stunned. Then she experienced a leap of giddy joy, as when she felt her first babe turn in her womb, brushing her insides like a butterfly, promising new life.

"What did it feel like to be inside Brigid's experience?"

"Amazing. Connected. She was alive with love—for the land, for her man and her children, for the other women, for their magic,"

Morgan paused. "Remember how you said Brigid gave her life to preserve the power of a time when all was one? I tasted the experience of that oneness when we did that tree meditation today. I was a tree. I bet if everyone on earth had that experience and felt it, really felt it, even one time, they would become incapable of harming nature. Including their own nature. Because they would know, in their bodies, that we're one with all of life, that we can draw from the strength of all life at the same time that we need to protect it."

Now there's the truth of it.

Morgan was fanning herself with her napkin, hard. Her face was red and streaming with sweat.

"Oh my Goddess, Morgan."

"What?"

"Are you hot all over, or just your head?"

She cocked her head to one side. "It started in my head. Now it's moving into my chest."

"You're having a power surge!"

"A what?"

"A hot flash! Has this ever happened before?"

"No."

"Fabulous. You're starting menopause right here on Mothers Mountain."

"Great." She dabbed at her temples with her now soggy napkin and fanned herself with her hand.

"It is great. They used to say that at menopause, women hold their blood inside to make wisdom."

'Tis true.

And 'tis a fine crone you'll be, Morgan Forrester, with the wisdom of the earth in your bones and a great healing counsel to share.

Serena popped up and brought Morgan a glass of lemon water, a damp washcloth, and a section of the New York Times to fan herself. She pulled her chair up to her and grabbed her forearms.

"Think about this. What if what's happening to us has the potential to impact all of human consciousness." Serena grinned and sank back in her chair, leaning back on its rear legs and rocking.

You've got my attention now, Duckie.

"Whoa. How did you get from my first hot flash to global implications for our recent escapades? Did I miss a few reels or something?"

"I brought you the paper, right? And for no apparent reason, my eyes were pulled to the page number."

"One hundred. So what?"

"So then I looked up, and here's the book I was quoting from at dinner. Look what page it's open to."

"One hundred."

"Right. The hundredth monkey popped into my head."

"Huh?"

Serena told Morgan how scientists had been dropping off bushels of potatoes to feed monkeys that lived on a group of islands. On one island, one of the young monkeys began washing the grit off her potatoes before eating them. The other young monkeys joined in, and soon all the hundred or so monkeys on that island were washing their potatoes. Soon afterwards, on the other islands, monkeys started washing their potatoes without ever being exposed to the monkeys on the island that started it.

"Do you get it?" Serena said. "If a small percentage of a population makes a conceptual leap, the whole population follows automatically. Initiating an evolutionary shift in consciousness doesn't require a genetic relationship, a majority, or even contact."

"Wasn't the hundredth monkey theory refuted?" Morgan said

Serena glinted at her. "By some. But I don't believe them. Besides, there are countless examples of the same phenomenon. Rats could barely find their way through a maze years ago when scientists first started testing them. But now rats anywhere in the world can easily get through a maze, whether or not they're from the same gene pool. It's the same with pigeons. Scientists thought they were too dumb to push a red light to get food. It took forever to teach them. Now any pigeon can push a button to get something to eat. A bird in England, the blue tit—"

"The blue tit?" Morgan couldn't help giggling.

"Listen to me. The blue tit started pulling the tops off milk bottles that had been delivered to people's doors—you know, to get at the cream. The blue tit is a homebody. It doesn't fly more than fifteen miles. But the habit spread throughout all of Britain, and then went on to Holland, Sweden, and Denmark."

"Creamy blue tits all over Europe."

"Be serious." She paused and gazed at her. "Morgan, what if you're the hundredth woman?"

Shadow, who had been shuffling listlessly around the periphery of the room, winced.

"Do I look like the type to waste my manicure scrubbing potatoes? Besides, everyone already knows how to do that."

"But how many people have the heart and imagination to enter the world of the ancestors and retrieve the message that it's time to break the shackles of centuries of emotional patterning, step into our dreams, and thereby create a better life for everyone?"

"I'm sure I'm not the only one," Morgan said.

"Exactly." Serena said. "You're part of a small but critical mass. Highlight the word 'critical.' It's the most important job on earth. Talk about a purpose. Wrap yourself around that one and you'll never feel empty again."

Brigid grinned at Shadow, who slithered out of the cabin and skulked down Serena's driveway. As he receded from view, Virginia Woof barked insistently in his direction.

Before he disappeared, he shouted, "You haven't seen the last of me!"

CHAPTER 13

unbound

For the sacrament of the body,
claim and consecrate us now.... .
May we who would
penetrate your mysteries
dare dissolve in you.... .
Infuse us with your fever heat.
With your revels, Great One,
charge the body of creation!

—Sue Silvermarie

Inner resolve straightened Morgan's spine as she drove back to Hopewellen. The amazing discoveries she and Serena had made were only the beginning of... what? Greater tests were coming. Her certain sense of that raised the hair on her forearms.

But there was nothing she could do about the future except summon her courage and clarify her intentions. She formed a vision of herself meeting life with courage, an open heart, and gratitude for the lessons each day brought. She'd longed to find her path in life and now, perhaps, it was beginning to open to her. Her challenge would be to stick with it.

Morgan turned into her driveway. As she'd anticipated, Jake was on her veranda before she reached the house. He was dressed from head to toe in white, his golden hair lifting off his shoulders in the warm breezes of twilight.

He was at her side before she opened her door. When he helped her from the car, he accorded her the formal grace reserved for royalty. In that instant, she saw he already knew that in the nine days she'd been gone, a transformation had occurred.

She ascended the stairs to her veranda with the dignity of an initiate entering a temple of sacred mysteries. As she turned to survey the trees and plantings in front of her home Morgan realized that—in some subtle way—everything felt different.

Colors vibrated and she could see the energies in the air shimmering with life, seamless and unified. Everything was part of her and she was part of it in a way she'd never experienced. Returning to the familiarity of her home heightened her awareness of the metamorphosis she'd achieved on Mothers Mountain.

After her time with Serena, her home was deliciously spacious and clean. But the comfortable house created a barrier between her and the natural world from which she now drew so much support.

She went to the kitchen for a drink of water. Gazing through the window, she anchored herself in the wildness of the trees beyond the gardens. The brambles on the edge of the woods must be offering their summer harvest because a bowl of perfect blackberries rested near the sink, placed precisely at the point Jake knew she would visit first.

She savored one, rolling it on her tongue before releasing the intense, tart juices into her mouth, then slowly emptied her glass and returned to the foyer, where the contents of her car were already stacked in a neat row. Jake was standing beside them as though awaiting instructions.

A flash of irritation mingled with guilt ruffled her composure when she saw how lovesick he appeared. She quickly moved her consciousness into her feet and belly, where she found a deeper truth. They each had lessons to learn. As long as they were honest and mindful, they'd be all right.

"Jake," she said, making her voice as gentle as she could, "you know I'm not in love with you."

"Yes."

"And that's all right?"

"I'm hoping," he said in his quiet drawl, "it's a temporary situation."

"It may not be. And I can't bear the weight of expectations."

He crossed the hall and brushed the hair from her face. "Sugar, I don't mean to pressure you. I'm fine with how things are."

She searched his eyes. "Are you sure?"

"Yes."

"I need a lot of space."

"It's yours. Do you want me to go?"

She led him upstairs to her bed, where she left him and her clothes while she showered briefly, relishing the ease and abundance of running water as she never had.

She returned naked and dripping, glided across the room to her bed, and nuzzled her face in the large display of lavender, periwinkle, and pink hydrangeas Jake had arranged on her night table. She pulled out one of the long stems and ran the blooms along her body, circling her breasts and lingering on her vulva and thighs.

He drew back the covers. She lay back on the bed, already in a sensual trance. He shed his clothes and stretched out on the far side of the bed, careful to give her room, approaching the moment like a novitiate waiting to be trained.

She closed her eyes and reached for his hand, weaving her fingers though his large, gentle, calloused ones while she ran her free hand lightly down her body from her shoulders to her hips, across her pelvic bone, and over to the damp hair in her center. She didn't move to pleasure herself, but breathed deeply instead and prayed for guidance.

She sank into the bed, feeling the power of the earth below and the sky above, relaxing and breathing in the erotic power of her connection to herself, to the earth, and to the powers that brought Brigid and sparked all of creation, the forces that made her the hundredth woman.

She had been unable to savor her sensuality in Serena's crowded cabin and cerebral company. But Jake's sweet, animal warmth invited her to relax into this vital part of herself, her sacred sexual core. She wanted him close to her, she wanted the warmth of his naked flesh beside her.

But the love she was feeling, the lust, was for that which was far greater than either of them. It was for all of creation.

Lying beside her, both hands reverently cradling her one, he was her ally in the passion, the prayer, she needed to express. Somehow he knew to let her be, to not engage her as she felt a powerful force gathering within.

Blissful and hot, wanting and full, she felt her vulva swell. She found herself cradled in a steamy, vibrant jungle of her own creation. Each cell in her body was alive. Every muscle was poised, both taut and receptive.

She was on her back, sweat streaming over her belly and breasts as she closed her eyes and pulled into herself the force of universal love from the powers behind Brigid. She moved closer to Jake.

"Go ahead," he murmured, his voice cracking. "Go with it, Sugar. Do what you want to do." She glanced at him through flickering lids and saw he was trembling with feeling. Her fingers closed on his erection for a brief moment, causing them both to gasp, then released him and sought her own wetness.

She was throbbing with the power of the magic that was now her life. The force was building in her clitoris, her cunt, and her womb.

She cried out for Brigid and the powers behind her, praying silently that they guide her in the most positive use of the energy vibrating through her body.

In that instant something happened she had never before experienced.

At the very moment when she would have surrendered to the orgasm she was trembling on the verge of, she intuitively switched gears. She gathered up the power of her impending orgasm and began to breathe into it, sending her breath to her vulva and using the force of her breath to generate a fiery sphere of liquid energy between her legs.

She rolled the energy with her breath, building and expanding it until her entire lower torso was pulsing with a power that was intensely sexual in a way she had never before experienced at the same time that it was beyond sexuality—it was in the realm of pure creative energy, the life force behind everything.

Breathing fully, she played with this energy until she began to lose the sense of it a little, at which point she focused her breath and her attention back into her vulva until she was able to regain the intensity of the swirling ball of fiery energy.

This time she was able to expand the ball beyond her lower torso to include first her solar plexus and then her heart before it lost some of its strength and she had to go back into her vulva to begin rebuilding.

Her body was heaving with the force of her breath. When she caught Jake's eye, they threw their arms around each other, tossed their heads back, and laughed.

He urged her to continue. She gathered the force in her vulva again and pulsed the whirling sphere of sexual power throughout first her torso, then her throat and head, then her entire body, sending one stream of the force she was building into the earth and another into the heart of the cosmos.

She felt as if she were making love with all of creation. After a time she pulled her energy back into her body, asked it to circulate through each cell for healing, then gave in to a full body orgasm unlike anything she'd ever experienced. It wasn't centered in her genitals and there were no shuddering convulsions, yet every cell in her body released and she felt whole and complete.

She lay on her back panting and laughing, then rolled into Jake's arms and buried her face in his chest. Soon they were both shaking with laughter. She pulled back so she could see his face.

"That was fantastic!" she said.

"No kidding. Can anybody do it?"

"I'll teach you." They held each other and she began to breathe into her vulva again. She found she didn't need to begin by stimulating herself this time, but could simply use her breath. Once she felt her vital sexual energy building between her legs, she began coaching him.

It took him several attempts. But she was patient and finally he, too, could move a ball of sexual energy up his body. She taught him to return his focus to his perineum, the point between his penis and his anus, whenever the energy began to dissipate.

When her energy left through her crown, she felt as if she were making love first with the trees, which tossed her about in ecstasy, then with the wind, which blew through her entire body and soul, then with a fountain of fire, which lapped at her delightfully before consuming her, then with a huge waterfall that tumbled through her being, then with the earth herself, which took her into delicious, dark, muddy places before plunging her deep into mineral caverns where she became one with towering crystals filled with light.

Finally she was flying through the air with Jake, looking down at the beautiful darkness of earth and up into the endless stars, which seemed close enough to touch and within which there seemed to be gateways leading out to other dimensions of reality.

He was unable to go out his crown as she had and didn't travel to the elements, but when they finally released their breath and their laughter in unison, he was completely satisfied.

"Morgan, how did we do that? How did you do that?"

"I was led."

"I didn't know it was possible to have an orgasm in my whole body like that, and without being hard, without ejaculating."

"I know. It's a whole different thing. It's incredible." She breathed fully. "Hold me," she said, encircling him with her arms and rubbing his back. She silently prayed her gratitude to the forces leading her on this journey. Within moments, she was sleeping soundly in Jake's arms.

~ ~ ~

"She's remarkable, isn't she."

Brigid startled. Beside her, the spirit of a very old woman stooped over a cane. A cameo nestled in the lace at her throat. Her speech was lilting and soft, like Jake's.

The old woman smiled. "Morgan is my granddaughter."

Jake was watching Morgan as she slept. The diaphanous curtains behind them framed a waning moon.

"She is, is she?"

"Yes." Grandmama searched Brigid's face. "Welcome to my home. I've been expecting you."

"And why would that be?"

"We are in need of your aid. The time has come for the ancestors to gather. We must do our part to clean up a terrible mess."

"Tell me your meaning."

Brigid shifted her weight to one foot and relaxed. The only other spirit she had met since coming to Morgan was Shadow. It would be good to have an ally. She smiled down at the smaller woman.

But Grandmama's eyes were grave. "Morgan is a perfect example. Look what she's inherited. Her father raped her. Her father, my son."

"Great Mother of us all." Brigid drew in her breath sharply. Jake was softly stroking Morgan's sleeping face, as if he knew what had been said and was comforting her.

"How your poor heart must have ached," Brigid said. "Where did you find the strength to withstand it—knowing your granddaughter was raped by your very own son?"

"I didn't know until she was a grown woman. She had left her husband. She already had one child and her belly was full with another. I helped her the only way I knew how. I took her in and loved her—with all my heart. I cared for her children while she worked and gave her this house. I took a stand against my son, Brigid. I cut him from my will, left everything to her and her children, and protected them from contact with him. It was all I could do. I felt helpless."

"Aye, and what strength you had to summon."

"I did. The reward is that now she's several steps ahead of me. Miles, in fact."

They stood together quietly. It was Grandmama who finally broke their silence. "Hers is the first generation in thousands of years for whom it's common for a woman to leave her mate and raise children on her own. She's paid a price for her courage. But what does she do with her pain? She won't be defeated by it. Instead, she helps others with theirs. She's very good at it."

"Aye," Brigid said, "her heart is great. But tell me, why is it you were waiting for me?"

"Things are in an appalling state, Brigid. I couldn't see it clearly until I left my body behind. But now it's unmistakable."

"What do you see, then?"

"The environment is being decimated, the sexes are dangerously out of balance, war and hunger ravage the world. People aren't getting along—with themselves, with each other, with their world. Something must be done. Yet how can Morgan and her kind change things when they're still dragging us around, with all our fears and unfinished business?"

"You sound like Morgan's friend, Serena."

"No one listens to this Serena. Am I right?"

Brigid startled. "So she says."

"There's a veil around the truth for most of the living. We must lighten their load. We must change. I don't know what we have to do, I only know we have to do it. We need greater numbers, and we need to act. Now."

"Get real, Granny!"

It was Shadow.

He grinned at them lewdly. "You nailed it. People are sleepwalking and you're part of the reason. You and your lot are an albatross around the neck of yonder slut. But that's been part of the plan all along. You can't do a damned thing about it, so get over yourself."

Morgan awakened before dawn in Jake's arms. Though his woodsy scent was comforting and his presence sweet, she felt restless. She'd had enough togetherness in the last ten days and wanted to be alone. So she eased herself from under his arm, wrapped a silvery silken robe around her body, and padded down the hall in the dark.

She peeked into the room near Grandmama's bedroom where Jake had lived periodically over the years. As she figured, he had been sleeping there. She could make out his open duffel bag against the wall. He'd wanted to create a presence in case Adam showed up.

She felt trapped and annoyed. She loved her dear friend and yes, the sex was beautiful, but she needed to be by herself to integrate the changes she sensed were only beginning. What had made her think taking a lover could work?

So much for spiritual elevation.

The headline would read, *Grouchy Goddess Grounded, Brave New Hopes Unfounded.*

Avoiding the squeak on the third and fifth steps, she crept quietly down the stairs, moved through her kitchen, and stepped into the garden in her bare feet. The air was humid but, with dawn's light breeze, not unbearable. Bird songs subdued what might have been silence.

She seated herself on the low stone bench Jake had erected for her beneath the willow tree, leaned back against the trunk, and enjoyed the protective canopy of branches sweeping low all around her, a dark shelter in the growing light.

By having a lover, am I betraying the strengths I built in my time with Serena?

Yet if I don't make love when it feels right, am I not betraying myself?

She felt her stomach turn. There was an unpleasant clamminess in the air—as if something were trying to pull her down—so she chose a more positive tack.

Sex had been a gateway last night. She'd traveled beyond the limits of her individuality and touched all of creation.

Isn't that being one with God?

Perhaps sex truly was her religion.

Could she be with Jake in a loving way without giving herself up to him? He didn't want her to do that—he'd said as much. Maybe this was one of her lessons, to learn how to be with a man without being subsumed by him. It was a worthy experiment.

Goddess Takes Consort, World Awaits Report. She spoke the headline to herself in a backwoods accent that made the words rhyme, then laughed out loud. The clamminess was gone.

Shadow?

Had Shadow been there?

All at once she knew why she'd been so vulnerable to men. When she was happy in a relationship, Shadow never bothered her. So unconsciously she'd always been desperate for a lover. When she didn't have a man to define her, she doubted herself and Shadow came in.

The resolution wasn't to have a man, it was to learn how to trust herself and create her own experience of satisfaction. When she was positive and engaged—an attitude she could choose for herself instead of waiting for a man to provide it—Shadow couldn't get to her.

This dawning realization—that she had power over her experience in an area previously ruled by her unconscious fears—rose in her chest with the airy freedom of a balloon taking flight. She leaped to her feet and danced around the garden, swirling her robe out around her and dancing like a fairy. The moist morning air caressed her naked flesh and she twirled until her whole body was as wet as the dew on her toes. Finally, she came to rest and brought her palms together between her breasts.

"Thank you," she said out loud. Under Brigid's guidance, she breathed infinite love into her heart, suffusing her body with its healing essence. On her exhalation, she sent out into all of creation what she didn't need for herself.

She returned to the stone bench beneath the willow, wrapped her robe close to her body, and seated herself with the slow dignity of high ceremony. Responding to a pull from within, she drew a deep breath and closed her eyes, then focused on the feel of the ground beneath her feet and the energetic roots connecting her to the heart of the earth.

Morgan allowed herself to appreciate the gift of gravity supporting her body, the sweetness of the air, the brilliance of the orange sun beginning to pierce through the trees, the gurgling of the water garden across from her, and the fecund smell of the earth.

"Brigid," she whispered.

"Aye, I'm here, Luv," she seemed to hear Brigid say. The words came from Brigid but she heard them deep in the quiet of her own mind. "But reach beyond me, seek the greater truth. Go to the field of pure consciousness, pure spirit, pure light. Summon all the highest of the guides, angels, and masters who work for your highest good."

Go straight to the heart of God.

A great stillness enveloped her. As her breath deepened and slowed, she received the message that she was, indeed, the hundredth woman, one of many drawn to a magnificent calling.

A small but critical mass of souls was forming, people who were committed to bring in the balance of the feminine energies of…

Love.

Beauty.

The words resonated within, like a stones dropped into a pool and creating ripples that permeated her entire being.

Nurturance, nesting, stewardship.

Harmony.

Compassion, connectedness, gratitude.

Cooperation, sharing.

Intuition.

Productive creativity.

Reverence for all life.

Her eyes flew open. This was beyond anything she could have imagined. As her eyes gently closed again, Morgan received the message that most of the souls called to this task this were female but some men, like Jake, were also doing the work or supporting it. That was why she was attracted to him. Their connection was part of the seeding of a new consciousness.

The women who were carrying the momentum would lead the way for all of humanity to experience an evolutionary leap in consciousness.

But there was a problem. Too many women were controlled by fear. They had buried their dreams and conformed to what they thought was expected of them for so long that they didn't even realize they were holding themselves back out of fear. They couldn't see that fear was running them, buried in their unconscious minds so deeply they couldn't yet make the change. Morgan's job was to transcend her own fears. She was to begin by embracing herself with the fullness of sacred love. Then she'd be able to lead others.

The words she heard came in the form of her own thoughts, yet there was something far greater illuminating them. Not exactly the sound of bells or the colors of white, rose, and golden light, but the sense of those things.

She was told to learn how to receive instead of always giving. To practice compassion for herself, to appreciate her own value, to know she deserved the gifts she received. It was time to treat herself as well as she had always treated others, and to teach others to do the same.

She took a series of full breaths and slowly opened her eyes. The colors around her were vivid and the energy pulsing through everything she saw was almost palpable.

She closed her eyes again. Knowing she was being led by unseen, loving forces, she followed her breath, observing and releasing the thoughts that came to distract her and settling more deeply into what she discovered was a vast and rich silence. Her entire being slowed. It was as if she had found the rhythm of the eternal heartbeat, the eternal breath. The sun was high in the sky before she opened her eyes again.

I must have a calling—even if I don't know exactly what it is—for these extraordinary things to be happening.

It's not being the hundredth woman—that's a job, not a path, right?

Still, chances are I'm already on my path.

But what is it?

I have to know what it is.

~ ~ ~

"Look, there's another one!"

Brigid moved closer to the window to see what Grandmama was pointing at. In the parking lot, a caramel-skinned woman was walking toward Morgan's office. There was a spirit moving beside her, a short, straight-backed, stout woman with skin like pine bark and a long white braid.

~ ~ ~

Morgan looked refreshed. Refreshed and something else, too. Stronger. Her eyes were clear and steady. Clarissa hoped she was ready for what she had to say. She handed her her journal and her check and plopped down on the couch, releasing a long sigh.

Morgan looked at her with concern while she briefly leafed through her journal. "You've been keeping up with this. Great! I'll read it later. You look like you have something more pressing to talk about."

Clarissa was slouched back into the couch. "I give up."

"On what?"

"Everything."

~ ~ ~

"Who's that old booger?" Big Mom said.

"That's Shadow," Brigid said, smiling. It was good to have another woman spirit on the team.

"I've seen him before," Big Mom said. "He tries to make Clarissa feel bad. I don't want him around her."

"He's been terrifying Morgan all her life, every chance he gets," Grandmama said.

"Ignore him, then," Brigid told them. "'Tis the only thing that works. In my tribe, the way we dealt with his lot was to preserve our own power rather than waste our energy in opposition. I've tried the other. And I'm here to tell you, it doesn't work."

Shadow was wearing an up-to-the-minute tuxedo with a black on black silk shirt and a black satin tie. He was draped casually across the back of the couch and was pretending to stroke Clarissa's cheek. When he heard the ancestors speaking about him, he moved sluggishly to his feet.

"Look at him," Big Mom said. "He's as slow as a copperhead in April."

A loud hissing startled them and Shadow's head was suddenly in the middle of their tight cluster. His head was larger than their bodies with three evil faces, one to stare at each of them. His breath was foul and his eyes were leering.

"Ah, but there's where you're wrong," he said, his words echoing from each of his three mouths. "And as for you, you little twat," he said to Brigid, "tell me exactly what good it has done *you* to ignore me."

Shadow shifted back to his customary form and began to promenade around the room with exaggerated grace.

"I'm here, my pretty," he said, bowing to Brigid, "playing a little game of cat and mouse with you fine ladies." He gestured to include the three of them and Morgan and Clarissa. "Until, of course, I become bored." He flashed a smile that exposed his canines.

"The best you can hope for," Shadow said, "is that I do not become bored too quickly."

~ ~ ~

"You've given up on everything?" Morgan was grinning. "That's a lot to give up on."

She's not taking me seriously.

Now watch her try to convince me to give up on giving up.

"You don't understand," Clarissa said. "I'm accustomed to order, organization. I like things to fall into place, you know? I got my M.A. at twenty-four, I got a job, got married—to a professional, of course—bought a house, and had two kids. Boom, boom, boom, boom, boom." With her hand, she chopped the air in front of her at regular intervals.

"That's how I stopped being the nigger on the reservation."

Morgan recoiled at the “n” word.

“You heard me. I watched television and copied how the white people did things. I had it all, for a few years anyhow. I actually had a white picket fence. Do you understand what I’m saying? Then Ray and I both started drinking too much and he started sleeping around. I said quit or get out, and he didn’t quit. But even then I had it all figured out. I got rid of him, quit drinking, and organized my life so I could raise my kids in peace. I never got the white picket fence back but at least I knew, more or less, what to expect. Until I started working to stop that damned dump. Now everything’s up in the air. I’m not used to that.”

“What’s up in the air?”

She straightened her spine, slowed down, and looked straight into Morgan’s eyes. “Here I am, trying to organize this event. I’ve got it all planned. I even have some of the talent lined up. I’m supposed to be the M.C.”

“Great!”

“Hold on. I want this event to be entertaining and educational, spiritual and emotional, but I can’t seem to wrap myself around a way to focus it that would engage the various segments of the community I’m trying to bring together. I can’t find a unifying principle. The thing is, I’m so frustrated right now all I can imagine doing is yelling at the audience if it’s white or folding over if it’s black. If, that is, there is an audience.”

“Why are you so frustrated?”

Are you listening to me?

Or are you just dense?

I’d like to see you haul your privileged white butt to some of the places I’ve been to in the last two weeks.

She reminded herself to be patient. At least Morgan cared. “It’s not just frustration. Sometimes I get frightened. The kind of exposure I’m creating for myself could be dangerous. I feel haunted, as if an assassin is waiting for me in the shadows.”

“Tell me about the assassin.”

Now there’s a standard shrinko line.

Right out of the movies.

“Besides, I’ve been out there canvassing like crazy in the area where the dump is planned.”

“Great!”

If she says “great” one more time, I’m going to lose it.

"Not so great. The people I've been meeting don't even want to think about a dump. Last time I was here, you told me to love myself. That's a cop-out. What about the poverty and oppression I'm facing out there? I can't break through to those people by loving myself."

"Don't be so sure."

Morgan Forrester, you are wearing down my last nerve.

"Anyway, how am I supposed to love myself when all I'm getting is doors slammed in my face?"

She's just so u-neg.

What made me think a fat, privileged white shrink could have any idea what I'm talking about?

"I would suggest a lot of compassion and forgiveness toward the part of yourself having those feelings," Morgan said.

"Here we go with the 'love yourself' stuff again."

"You're angry, Clarissa."

"No shit! Excuse me."

"I don't have a problem with swearing. I think it's good for you. So what's underneath the anger?"

She looked Morgan straight in the eye. She wanted, in the worst way, to keep sparring with her but something in that question and her clear, brown eyes made her stop. "Fear," she said, suddenly overwhelmed by emotion. "I'm afraid." She felt her chin trembling.

"I understand. Stay with that feeling, Clarissa. You're doing great. Close your eyes and let yourself feel the fear. And keep breathing. That's it. Long, deep breaths. Keep them coming. Breathing keeps the emotions flowing."

She felt two big tears slide down her cheeks and her nostrils began to fill. She heard Morgan pulling tissues from a box. Very gently, she placed them in her hand.

"Stay with the emotion and follow it back in time. What is the youngest age you remember having this fear?"

She traced the fear back, past the numerous scrapes and illnesses of her kids, past smelling another woman's scent on her husband's shirt, past the racial taunts, past her fears she would never leave the reservation. Suddenly she cried out and began to sob.

"What is it, Clarissa?" Morgan's voice was kind.

She opened her eyes a little and looked through her tears into Morgan's compassionate face.

"What's going on?" Morgan said. "How old are you?"

"I was six."

"Use the present tense and tell me what happened. It will make it more real."

"I'm with Big Mom. We have to go to town to get some things. We're walking out of a store." She felt her chin trembling hard. Tears and mucous were sliding down her face.

"This white man is there." She struggled for air. "He's drunk. And he's really, really big. I guess he's trying to come in the store. He runs right into Big Mom. He says she's a dirty redskin pig and to get out of his way." She let out a jagged sob. "She just looks at him."

Clarissa paused, remembering how she gazed up at Big Mom in that moment with such admiration and love. The drunk man was scary, but Big Mom wasn't moved.

"That was Big Mom," she said quietly, blinking at Morgan and finally wiping her face with the tissues. "I guess she was clearing his words from her world. Or else she was doing medicine on his soul or something, you know, trying to help him.

"The drunk man, he socked Big Mom in the mouth and broke off her two front teeth." She felt the sting of acid at the back of her throat from the vivid childhood memory. "At first she was choking on them, staggering and choking. She reached out to the man. I think she was trying to get her balance. The man joined his hands together to make one huge, ugly fist. He came down on her hard, on the back of her head. Big Mom fell. There was blood everywhere. I thought she was dead."

"Nobody did anything." Her breath caught and her eyes flooded with tears. She felt her mouth involuntarily form into a silent scream of childhood horror. Her next word was a whisper.

"Nobody."

CHAPTER 14

becoming

unbound from memory
I could gather seashells
and start all over again.

—Ila Suzanne

"Stay with it, Clarissa."

Clarissa felt herself responding to Morgan's coaching. But then Morgan went too far. "Let yourself cry," Morgan said. You're safe now to mourn this."

Easy for you to say.

But her body shook until she was sick with sobbing.

When she finally quieted, Morgan said, "And in that moment, what did you decide?"

Clarissa was silent. "Oh my god," she finally said. Her stomach lurched.

"Breathe, Clarissa. Good. Now, what did you decide?"

"I decided it wasn't safe to be… me."

"Exactly. And?"

"And the best way to get along is to be invisible, go along with whatever the stronger people want and keep my… ." She couldn't finish.

"Keep your what?"

I won't say it.

"This is important, Clarissa. Get it out."

You're as sick as your secrets.

At least that's what they say in N.A.

But what do those junkies know?

Clarissa was silent for a very long time.

"The best way to get by is to be invisible and keep my place." She raised her chin.

"And how do you like keeping your place?"

She faced her. "I hate it." She felt the muscles in her jaw rippling.

"Good." Morgan brought out an enormous pillow, a two foot length of rubber hosing, and a pair or work gloves that she placed on the ottoman in front of Clarissa. "Say that again, louder, and put on those gloves."

"I can't," she said, and did it anyway.

"Good. Now pick up that rubber hose and beat the pillow and yell, 'I hate it!'"

She knew for an absolute fact she couldn't do that and said as much, but Morgan refused to take no for an answer. Clarissa found herself on her feet beating the shit out of the pillow and yelling "I hate it!" Once she got going, she kept yelling and pounding until something deep inside broke free and she was totally spent.

She felt clean and exhausted. She was about to sink back into the couch, but Morgan asked her to stand tall.

"I am going to ask you a question," Morgan said. "I'd like you to take all the strength and energy you put into beating the pillow and concentrate it into a golden ball of power in your belly. Good. Now, with the dignity of freedom and invincibility, answer the question I'm about to ask. All right?"

"I'll try."

"Good. The question is, from this moment on, are you willing to be invisible, go along with what other people want, and keep your place?"

"Hell, no." Another kind of mist dampened her eyes, her reaction to the power in her own voice.

Clarissa let Morgan lock eyes with her. "Clarissa, it's time to free that frozen little girl who thought Big Mom was dead. Rise out of that hellhole and fly. Let your anger be your wings." Morgan's voice was like steel and velvet, both.

"I can do that."

"Good. What are you going to do?"

"I'm going to stop this damned dump if it kills me."

Morgan laughed. It was a free, easy sound. "Say, 'I'm going to stop this dump because I feel like it and it's fun. And no matter what happens, I'll love myself passionately.'"

Clarissa chuckled, squared her shoulders, and proclaimed her vow. Then she sat down and grinned.

"What are you feeling?" Morgan said.

"Relief. Strength. Love." She ducked her head for a second then looked up at Morgan with a big smile and fresh tears in her eyes. "I feel loved. I feel Big Mom here with me."

"Great."

That word again.

But this time, she smiled. "Yeah, it's pretty great all right."

Morgan got up from her chair, sat down on the floor at her feet, took one of her hands firmly in both of her own, and looked deeply into her eyes. "All the things that hurt you in the past are just that—in the past. The rest of your life begins now."

Morgan returned to her overstuffed chair. "You say you can't change things by loving yourself. I disagree. When you canvass to stop the dump, people are watching you. At some level, they're picking up on the self-respect and courage it takes for you to speak up for what you want. You're a role model."

Clarissa snorted. "I don't know about that."

"Did you think they'd invite you in for sweet tea and ask if they could sign a petition your first time out?"

"A girl can dream."

"Dream this. They're thinking about you. They may not be ready to show you, a stranger, that you got to them. But you did. Count on it. And keep showing up. They need to see you coming back to them again and again. We human beings are animals." Morgan tossed her hair behind her shoulders. "We need repetition in order to feel something is real. Give these people a chance to come around. Believe that they can, that they want to. Do you think they want to be powerless? Do you think they want their children to be poisoned? Keep the dream alive, Clarissa."

Morgan leaned back in her chair and stretched. "I think loving yourself is a fine place to start when you want things to change. The fear will come up again, and the frustration and anger. Beat up your bed with it, or scream at the top of your lungs when you're driving down the freeway, or sing out the sweetest tone you can find within you, or buy a bag of ice cubes and smash them against an outdoor wall, a handful at a time, or write about it in your journal. Continue to feel and release your emotions.

"Yeah, right. If only they could see me on the reservation, doing these crazy, weird things you want me to do."

They both grinned.

"It's nothing but a bunch of crazy *u-neg* bullshit," Clarissa said.

"*U-neg?*"

"That's Cherokee for honky."

Morgan's laugh was like the yelp of a dog. "Okay. Try it anyway."

"All right, all right."

"Remember this—you're not alone, Clarissa. Your fear isn't only about racial oppression. It's also about being a woman and speaking up, being visible, claiming your vision. Most women who choose to follow their passion go through what you do. It's in our cells.

"This is a new learning for me," Morgan continued, "one that's given me insight into my own struggles. Next time you question your courage, think about this. It's only in the last hundred years that women could be anything but wives or prostitutes."

"Or servants or slaves."

"Exactly. Except in the case of independently wealthy women, there were few alternatives. We didn't even have the right to vote!"

"Not with the Cherokee. Strong, independent women were the norm until we were conquered by white people. But women are still central in many ways."

"Wonderful. I didn't know that. So you can draw on your reserves of Cherokee strength. Which is good, because—though you'd never guess it from seeing powerful females on TV and in the movies—practically every woman out there who seems to have her shit together is just like you, a bird cutting the wind with no safety net, precious few role models, and less to fall back on than she'd like." Morgan let out a burst of air.

"That's a lot to take in."

"For me, too."

Clarissa withdrew into her own thoughts.

"What is it?" Morgan said.

"Sometimes I think about how badly hurt African women have been. Did you know millions of girls and women there and in the Middle East have been forced to have clitoridectomies?" She wanted to grab her own crotch in protection.

"Female genital mutilation. I can hardly imagine women being robbed of sexual feeling."

"It's so they won't be unfaithful to their husbands. They believe if you die from the procedure—as many do—you're a witch."

"The women's holocaust. It's still happening.".

"The what?"

"Clarissa, let's stand up and move around a little, take a deep breath."

Morgan stood.

"Why?"

"To stay in our bodies, in the present. These things aren't easy to take in."

"No shit."

Following Morgan's lead, Clarissa took a series of deep breaths, shook out her body like a wet dog, and stretched. They moved to the window.

"What's the most wonderful thing you see out there?" Morgan said.

"The puppies playing in the yard a cross the street."

Morgan chuckled. "And who do you love the most?"

"My kids."

"Good. Keep all that with you—along with your sense of your own body—as we talk about these things."

"So what's the women's holocaust?"

Morgan led them back to their seats. "Somewhere between hundreds of thousands and nine million people were killed as "witches" during the Inquisition, eighty percent of them women."

"My god." Clarissa's mind fell through a door she always kept shut, bolted, and tightly locked. A tear slid down her cheek.

"What is it?" Morgan's voice was soft.

"I haven't let a man near me since my marriage."

"Why?"

"I felt… demeaned. Dehumanized."

"How?"

"Ray expected me to wait on him. I felt like his servant."

"Tell me more."

"At first I felt insulted, then hurt."

"Did you talk to him about it?"

"Yes. But nothing changed." The injury was fresh, as if it happened yesterday. "Over time, the pain built—it became so big, it was a wound to my soul." Twin tears fell to her lap.

Damn.

All I do in here is bawl.

"Stay with it."

"When he started fooling around with other women, it was almost a relief. I had an excuse to get rid of him. Even with two babies and the loss of my home, life was so much easier without him."

Morgan drew a ragged breath and faced her. "Clarissa, your pain is both personal and universal." She rose and returned with an ivory-colored candle, which she placed on the small table between the couch and her chair. As she lit it, she said, "I light this candle to honor and restore the wounded feminine in all of us."

Clarissa wanted to ask Morgan what she meant. Instead, she drew a deep breath, contemplated the flame, and settled into the part of herself that already knew.

"Please," Morgan said, "give yourself some time to heal your sacred feminine soul. Light a candle each day, give yourself baths, go to the health food store and find special oils to anoint yourself with, massage your whole body while you reclaim your womanly essence. Build an altar and dedicate it to your sacred feminine soul. Add items that have meaning to you and spend some time at your altar each day. Create your own rituals to affirm your commitment to the sacred feminine, both your own and the universal."

"Wow." Her tears were still flowing, but she didn't mind. "That sounds wonderful. I'll do it."

"Good. The next step is to not take it personally when you get overwhelmed, Clarissa. We have to clear all that history from our cells, history that has been accumulating for thousands of years. Cut yourself some slack."

"I'll try."

"Please don't try, Clarissa. Do it. Hold compassion in your heart for yourself. Turn off the self-critical part of your mind. I'll never forget the day I discovered I might not be able to control my emotions, but I can certainly, with practice, control my thoughts. Every time you put yourself down, say, 'Cancel, clear,' and create a compassionate, supportive thought about yourself."

Morgan went on. "Emotions, on the other hand can be overwhelming. When I get terrified," Morgan said, "I create a time-out. Then I approach myself with kindness. I trace the disturbing feeling back and find the decisions I made and the resulting patterns in my life, as you did today. I say encouraging things to myself like, 'Of course you feel that way, who wouldn't, given what you've been through?'

"I have to talk to myself like that, Clarissa. I'm a wounded healer. I got this job because I had lemons and decided to make them into lemonade. I require of myself that I be tender toward my wounded parts. I nourish them, listen to them, and see what they need. At the same time, I refuse to let them run me. Those parts of me are like little children. They need for me to be the responsible grownup, to take charge and not let them make decisions that children aren't equipped to make. I'm the adult here."

Morgan looked at her, hard. "And if I can't clear myself, there's no amount of money I won't spend to get help. There is no material thing worth more than my peace of mind. Including a roof over my head."

A roof over her head?

But then again, it made sense. What could be more valuable than feeling free? She looked into Morgan's eyes, which glowed like amber nuggets, for a long time.

She's an amazing woman.

But so am I.

If she can do it, I can too.

She's changed somehow—she's like Big Mom, piercing through all the dimensions to the purest truth.

As if in response to her thought, Morgan said, "What if the challenges you confront as you pursue your vision aren't merely personal? What if your work on yourself is a service to all life? What if only a small, critical number of people is needed to generate a change in the whole?

"What if *every single thing you do matters,* Clarissa?"

Morgan leaned forward in her chair, her eyes bottomless, intense. "Listen to me. What if the combination of dreaming your dream and taking action matters in and of itself, even if no one comes to your event? What if the energy of your intention and action is reverberating throughout the planet?" Her eyes fluttered. "I know this sounds weird, but I've been getting messages from worlds beyond ours."

I knew it.

"I think one's coming in now," Morgan said. "That's where these messages are coming from. Are you interested in taking this further?"

"Oh yeah."

Morgan's eyes were nearly closed and her hands were on her knees, palms facing skyward. She drew a series of long, round breaths. When she spoke again, her voice was both quieter and more powerful.

"We're not simply healing ourselves, Clarissa. We're restoring womanly consciousness so it can balance the excesses of masculine energy and create global healing. Only if we accept this responsibility can earth and all her creatures thrive. Our task involves nothing less than a great awakening into love, vision, and creativity, first by a critical mass of women, then by greater numbers who will teach men how to move into their hearts—their compassion, nurturing, and intuition.

"When our task is complete, humanity will be able to create abundant, sustainable life for all creatures. Then the Earth Mother can relax into the grandmotherly pleasures of the crone, having raised children who can finally act like grown-ups and assume collective responsibility for supporting and maintaining life."

Now Morgan had gone beyond anything she'd heard even Big Mom say. Her eyes had grown prophetic and otherworldly at the same time that they were loving, kind, and filled with an unmistakable integrity. Her words raised goosebumps on her arms. Big Mom, she remembered, used to get goosebumps when great wisdom was being spoken or when the ancestors were near.

"What happened just now?" Clarissa said. "Where did you go?"

"I'm not sure." Morgan smiled. "But somewhere I plan to build my home." She shook out her body and drew a deep breath. "I have no idea where this stuff is coming from, but I love it."

Morgan closed her eyes again. More was about to come through. "As you work on your event, you're learning to act from your highest self and to let go of all those old beliefs, those judgments and worries, through choices you're making in your daily life, moment by moment. Each of these choices—especially the choice to believe in yourself and your dream and to act on that belief—is critically important because it not only determines the quality of your life, but also radiates out into the world. You're seeding a new consciousness at the same time that you're actualizing your soul's mission.

"Basically, Clarissa, it amounts to this. Do you want to experience fulfillment? Do you want to experience purpose? If the answer to these is yes, then your task is to turn away from self-limitation and move into self-love. Let go of your judgments of yourself and everyone else, including all the people you want to influence to stop the dump. Accept other people where they are, make your own choices, and move forward.

"Simply formulate your desire. Give it your attention, but work effortlessly. Enjoy yourself. Don't worry about what anyone else thinks. Instead, be your own yardstick.

"And always remember you aren't required to be perfect. You're human. So when you stumble, simply forgive yourself and move on. Don't dwell on it. The mistakes we all make are opportunities to learn and nothing more.

"And whenever you have even a small success, congratulate yourself right away. That moves your energy into alignment with self-love, which gives birth to the truest form of love for all beings and creates a change in the energetic grid that supports the greater collective process. All of creation will thank you."

~ ~ ~

"That woman is on fire." Big Mom grinned.

"That's my baby!" Grandmama was beaming.

"Great Mother of us all!" Brigid said.

"What is it, child?" Grandmama said.

Brigid gestured toward Big Mom. "When you came in here, your two front teeth were broken."

"Why so they were," Grandmama said. "And now your teeth are as perfect and even as a row of corn on a cob of Silver Queen."

"The magic," Brigid said, "it's coming back. Your granddaughter's work has healed you."

"Something big happened while you were away, didn't it?" Clarissa said.

The ancestors turned their attention to her.

"You seem different," Clarissa said, "wiser, more of the earth yet speaking from a far-off place."

"Yes. Now I too have heard Spirit speak."

"I knew it. When you were gone, I felt it."

"Good. All the more reason to trust it."

"I have a hard time with trust."

"So do I. But we will learn to trust now, won't we?"

Clarissa grinned at her. "Yes."

"Just follow the guidance and stay in your heart."

"Do you think the ancestors are here with us now?"

Morgan closed her eyes for a moment, then looked around the room. "Was Big Mom short and round, with a long braid?"

"Yes!"

"She's here, with an ancestor named Brigid. There's a third one. It's my Grandmama." Morgan's eyes filled with tears and she smiled. "Hey, Grandmama," she said softly.

"Will they speak to us?"

Morgan closed her eyes. "They're very pleased with us. They want us to learn from their mistakes. Don't let fear stop you, they're saying. Don't let any emotion stand in the way of your dreams. Don't make excuses. Don't justify keeping your life on the same old familiar path. Step into your vision."

Brigid nudged Big Mom and Grandmama and pointed at Shadow. He was small and faint, wavering in and out of view. Suddenly Brigid thought of something.

"What's the date of your event again, Clarissa?".

"September twenty-second."

Morgan cocked her head. "Brigid wants you to know the timing is fortuitous. It's the fall equinox—the harvest of your hard work this summer in the form of the people who come to your event, the ideas they generate, and the commitments they make. Then the earth moves into the darkness of winter, the quiet time from which your dreams will germinate, like seeds, into reality."

Their eyes met, burning with love and the clean passion of their vision and their connection with the ancestors.

"That was amazing," Clarissa said.

"Yeah. But it seems awfully easy. Too easy, maybe."

"Is that self-doubt I hear?" Clarissa chuckled.

"A little. This is all so new."

"Not to me. I'm used to words from Spirit coming through Big Mom."

"That's reassuring. "What's happening with your event?"

Clarissa smiled. "I've researched how much money I'm going to need. What Big Mom left me is enough, but I want to save most of it for my kids' education. So I got a part-time staffer and some funding, both donated through the local branch of a national environmental group. I've set up meetings with the leaders of a number of local activist organizations, which are white, and with several local black leaders. I'm looking into getting college students to help with canvassing. My boys are actually enjoying helping me, which I never dreamed would happen. It's wonderful. My downstairs neighbor is giving me a hand and so is a fellow teacher, Joshua."

"That's great," Morgan said. "Look at what you achieved, even with all that fear on board. One thing, though. Something in your eyes made me wonder, is there a little something going on between you and Joshua?"

"No, he's just a friend."

"After your feminine soul has time to absorb your commitment to healing, maybe you won't have to be so quick to answer a question like that in the negative."

"That would be good."

"Yes. Because something in your voice tells me part of you isn't sure Joshua is just a friend."

"No." She couldn't help grinning.

"Yes." Morgan laughed. "Our time is up. Deepest thanks to all who helped us today." Morgan made a broad sweep of her arm that included the room, the earth below, and the heavens above.

She looked at Clarissa. "Do you get the feeling your people and my people did lunch?"

❧ ❧ ❧

"Do you think they'd like it? I know the wife just loves unicorns."

Morgan and Aunt Lee were seated on the glider on Morgan's veranda. Aunt Lee had dropped by, supposedly to ask her advice about a wedding gift for her great-nephew, Buddy.

"You have exquisite taste," Aunt Lee had said. "So modern. Of course I had to bring my Peach Blossom in on such a big decision!"

She had settled in beside her, her back ramrod straight, pointing to the gift she'd selected. Now she was smacking her dentures gleefully, apparently confident of Morgan's endorsement.

The item in question was a "Bath-i-corn" from a well-worn and seriously dog-eared catalog. It was a unicorn made of gold marbleized plastic swirled with ivory.

The description said it had flecks of iridescent mauve, pink, and blue and had space to store three rolls of toilet paper on the horn. There was a holder for the roll currently in use at the end of the curved tail.

The mane had three slots in which to store rolled-up spare washcloths (coordinating colors available), and spare towels could be draped across the back like a saddle blanket, over which you could sit an adjustable saddle (three clicks, fits any size) with a fairy in it (included).

The fairy was iridescent green and looked like a leprechaun with chaps.

What am I going to say?

"They could coordinate their bathroom using the colors in their Bath-i-corn as a basis," Aunt Lee said, smacking and clicking.

"I thought most people worked with the colors in their porcelain fixtures, floors, and tile."

"What I like most about it is it's so practical."

"That it is. And unusual. You just know that no one else will give them a Bath-i-corn."

"Precisely!" Aunt Lee patted Morgan's cheek. "It's settled then."

"Do you know how big their bathroom will be?"

"Why, I'm not sure. I know it's a small house, and they just have the one."

"You might want to find out, because it says here the Bath-i-corn is three and a half feet by three and a half feet by eighteen inches."

"Is that too big?"

Morgan made a box with her hands to illustrate the approximate dimensions.

"Still and all, when the babies come, it would make a wonderful toy horse."

"Did I misunderstand? I thought you said they were planning to remain childless."

"Oh they're probably just saying that. The family will talk some sense into them. It might take awhile, but... ."

Aunt Lee popped up from the glider, snatched the catalog, stuck it in her purse, and reached for her rhinestone-studded maroon cane.

"Thank you so much, Peaches. I knew you'd help me make the right decision—you are my wise girl!"

She patted her cheek again. "Bath-i-corn it is, then. I'm going to specify the pink polka dot gift wrap and the silver bow."

~ ~ ~

Morgan threw down the mail and her keys on the pale pickled table in the foyer of her old Victorian and pulled the pins out of her hair, giving it an emphatic shake. Jake wasn't home. Good. She was incredibly angry.

I am sick to death of watching people get plowed under by misery.

That day, Morgan had listened as one client after another listed the things—the people—that had broken their spirits. She had encouraged each of them to name their dream and follow it. But by the end of the day, she was furious with all the perpetrators who had damaged her clients. She was defiant, energized, determined. Even though it might be giving Shadow something to feed on, Morgan was enjoying her anger.

"To hell with all you perps," she said out loud. The headline would read, *Raging Counselor Throws a Hissy—Challenges Shadow, Things Get Pissy.*

Suddenly the phone rang.

"Good lord, woman, what are you doing on a telephone?" Morgan said.

"It's mine!" Serena said. "It's new."

"Oh sure, they got the poles up on two miles of driveway in the time since I've been there."

"Actually, I had telephone and electrical cable buried along the drive when I first moved in, and then thought better of it," Serena said. "All I had to do was hook them up. Travis installed three outlets for me. Next, I'm getting electric heat and plumbing. I had some lamps and a computer overnighted, and I've been reveling in the wonders of the Internet."

"Things are happening fast for you, too."

"Oh yeah. I'm working on an outline for a new book and I'm thinking about building a stone house on the crest of the ridge."

She'd forgotten how rich Serena was. That was easy to do after repeated trips to the outhouse. She began to fan herself furiously with one of the catalogs that had arrived with the mail.

"I'd ream you out about getting off that mountain, but I seem to be in the middle of a hot flash."

"A power surge?"

"That too. Oh, and I'm forgetting everything. I guess that's part of it."

"Maybe it's time for some hormones to even things out," Serena said.

"Hey, I'd buzz my hair off if that's what it took to stay cool, but I'm afraid I'd look as if I stepped off the cab of a diesel."

Serena laughed. "Not you. You would look trés chic. It would start a trend."

"How's Woof?"

"Lazier than ever. She barely moves."

"Is she all right?"

"Oh yeah. I'm sure she is. What's new with you?."

"Brigid's been around a lot."

"Yeah?"

"And I'm pissed as hell."

"Good! Why?"

"I don't know exactly. But whatever it is that has kept people down, it had better look out, because I'm becoming a force to be reckoned with."

Of course Serena hopped on the bandwagon. They fed off each other's anger. When they finally hung up, Morgan felt Shadow was gaining strength, but she didn't care. She turned up the air conditioning and stuffed down first one fat-free microwaved frozen dinner, then another.

Two hundred eighty calories?

That's not a meal.

She wanted to do something with the energy building in her body. Standing in front of the living room window, she focused on the greenery before her and the dazzling light filtering through the trees, then pulled energy up from the earth and into her belly.

"Brigid! All those who work for the highest good! Take me to the heart of evil. Show me Shadow's greatest cruelty. Teach me what I'm up against and what to do about it."

Some part of her knew that what she was doing was dangerous. Could it ever work to call in evil? Wasn't suffusing oneself with love the only way to prevail against darkness? Didn't evil feed on the negativity confrontation produced? Didn't it grow stronger with any attention it was given? And at the very least, shouldn't she be praying for protection for herself before she began?

But her impatience to know overcame all caution.

As though in flight, she was taken from point to point around the world, images of death and destruction flashing rapidly in front of her, everything from war and famine to the suffering of animals and plants as the environment collapsed. Worse was the blind cruelty people inflicted on each other in private. As she traveled, she was blasted by negative energies that chilled her soul, then assaulted by flashbacks of her mother's frigid eyes and her father's probing hands.

But none of these turned her from her course. She knew she was being reckless, but all she cared about was getting to the bottom of the pain Shadow caused and doing something about it. She wasn't going to let him continue to dominate her or anyone else.

The scenes of horror continued to flash. When she saw a group of naked children shivering on the fringes of a cult ritual, everything slowed down. More than anything else, she wanted to do something for them. She asked that her spirit appear before them and teach them how to ground themselves in the earth and pray for help from the light.

The children's souls were open. The wanted help, so they learned quickly.

Holding her left hand high above her head to receive the power of the light and facing the palm of her right hand toward the children, Morgan channeled spiritual power for them.

Simultaneously, she was receiving messages about how to proceed.

She was told it would be inappropriate to use her newfound powers—which weren't hers anyway, but came from the light—to do anything to the children. But she could offer assistance, making it clear it was up to them to choose whether or not to accept it.

Her guides told her to show the children how to move a rainbow of light through their bodies to cleanse them of the toxins they had absorbed from the cult—first red light, then orange, then yellow, green, blue, indigo, and violet.

Acting on guidance, Morgan instructed all negative energies released by this process that they couldn't replicate themselves or harm or return to anyone ever again. But they could enter into the sacred light to advance to the next level of learning about love, and they could take any other negativities with them who wanted to come.

Next, she taught the children how to pray to be infused with divine love, then wrapped in a force field of white light so their bodies and their divine essences could be protected with all the power and might of Infinity.

The children seemed to feel more whole. She knew they now had a powerful tool to protect them from absorbing the full impact of the horrors they were exposed to.

The abuse planned for them might still occur, but she sensed they wouldn't be as terribly scarred by it and might feel less alone.

Something had shifted in the energy. Before her arrival, the children had been victims, both in fact and within their own hearts. But since working with the light, inwardly the children were now the ones with real power, for they were now firmly connected with the light—no matter what occurred on the outer level. The day would come when they could move from victim to survivor to thriver.

With Clarissa, she had received the knowledge that positive intentions and actions created an energetic shift. And that was enough. She could do small things and that would make all the difference. She smiled her love to the children one last time and prepared to return to her living room.

Just as she was bringing her soul back to her body, grounding herself in the comfort of the familiar and pleased with the good use to which she had put her anger, she felt something.

It wasn't good.

I'm not alone.

Evil eyes were on her, she could feel it. Somehow she knew helping the children had violated certain malevolent laws. The dark forces that held the cult in place knew immediately their innocent prey had been shielded from the soul harm they intended. Someone was interfering with their plan.

They chose immediate retaliation.

She could tell they were scanning her physical, emotional, mental, and spiritual fields for weaknesses. Dark, evil entities surrounded her. They were trying to bore into her, grind her down, penetrate her. The largest came at her from behind and parted the energy shield she had created as if it were a flimsy veil. She felt a paralyzing chill, as if icy fingers were wrapped around her backbone, strangling her nerves.

Shadow.

Morgan fought him hard, using everything she had to force him out. Instinctively, she filled herself with herself, attempting to become so full of her own essence there was no room for him.

But he was like a python. Each time she exhaled, he tightened his grip, leaving less and less space for her to breathe, to fight him, to know what to do.

Even in the midst of battle, she knew that what she'd done for the children must have been powerful to inspire this level of attack. If they had sent out the big boys, she must be a very big girl. This knowledge helped her hold the other entities at bay, though it took all she had to keep them away from her energy field.

She could sense them—they were eager to come in for the kill once their leader overcame her ability to resist.

Shadow was wearing her down. She was flailing, he was steady. By now, he was wrapped around and around her inner essence, his head out in front of her, penetrating her with orange, serpentine eyes.

The stench of his breath almost suffocated her.

Her spine was colder than death.

All he had to do now was wait.

Her breathing became more and more difficult. Shadow was no longer tightening his grip with her exhalations. He seemed to prefer a slow demise, one he could savor. Morgan gasped for air. She knew he wanted her to regret what she had done for the children, to second-guess her decision to free them, to doubt herself.

That I will not do.

I will not bow to you.

Summoning all her energy, Morgan screamed out. "Brigid! Help me! Grandmama! All the forces that work for the highest good, come to me now!"

~ ~ ~

Shadow bore down on Brigid. With a mighty shout, she summoned her guides and ignited a blazing ball of energy in her belly that she transferred to

Morgan. The pain Shadow inflicted on her was horrendous. She was gasping and heaving, trying to ride the waves of energy, to stay on top of them.

Grandmama and Big Mom showed up and took Brigid's hands. Their contact gave her the strength she needed to help Morgan. Using the force of her magic, the strength of her guides, and the intensity of will Big Mom and Grandmama exerted on her behalf, she imparted to Morgan's mind the image of a whirling vortex of white light, a vacuum that pulled everything dark into it and drew it up to the Source for cleansing and purification.

Morgan created a vortex and set it in motion, counterclockwise. The entities surrounding her were whipped by the wind it created. They struggled to hold their ground as the vortex began to draw them toward it.

"Focus, Morgan!" Brigid shouted. She could feel Morgan increasing her attention on the vortex. Some of the dark entities fled while gradually the whirlwind of pure white light pulled the remaining others to its center. Occasionally one broke free and struggled to make its way back toward her, but eventually the vortex whirled all the dark entities away except the one that continued to hold her firmly in his grasp.

❧ ❧ ❧

The horrible thing strangling her spine seemed unaffected by the vortex. Morgan was terrified. In some ways it would be easier, more familiar to give up—to freeze in fear and let him have his way. But she refused to yield to that. If she were going to go down, it wouldn't be without the best fight she could muster.

Stop that.

You're not going down.

She focused her attention on the vortex, asking it to become more potent and compelling. And so it was.

She shifted the roaring, blindingly brilliant vortex with the force of her mind, willing it to come closer and closer. She could feel her own negative energies, her fear and self-doubt, being swept up into it, which left her greater room to breathe and focus.

She was surprised Shadow didn't take advantage of her now deeper exhalations and tighten his grip, but he all he did was continue to gaze hypnotically into her depths.

Ignoring him, she willed the vortex to enter her body, removing all that was not for her highest good and returning it to the light.

Eventually, she was able to align the core of the vortex with her spine. She was exactly in the center of what was now total silence and blazing light.

She closed her eyes and gave herself completely to the light, surrendering the struggle and her very soul to the highest good. When she opened her inner eye, Shadow was still there. They looked into each other for a long time. This time she didn't resist, she simply held his gaze while the light swirled around and within them. They were together that way for what seemed like an eternity.

Abruptly, everything she had been experiencing with such intensity was gone. The vortex and the entity had disappeared and she was sitting on her living room couch with her feet on the ottoman, wrinkling the cover of some women's magazine.

She blinked hard and looked around in disbelief. Then she saw the faintest outline of Shadow. He came in more clearly for an instant, dressed in white coattails. In a sweeping gesture, he removed his white high hat and bowed low. Then he straightened, looked into her eyes with a combination of humor and malevolence, and disappeared.

Morgan had moved to the edge of the couch when she saw Shadow. Now that he was gone, she leaned back and put her feet up again. She took a very long, very deep breath and released it slowly.

It was the first time in her life she had ever been completely without Shadow.

~ ~ ~

"Damned Internet," Serena said to Virginia Woof.

But Woof didn't stir.

The more she read, the more out of date she felt. "www, dot, whatever," she muttered.

In the two weeks since Morgan left, she had made several stabs at an outline for her book. Each time she only became angry at men. So she had decided to warm up by writing essays about the merits of women. But then she felt restricted and got even angrier. Sometimes, she sensed Shadow nearby.

Wasn't I perfectly happy being angry on my mountain before Morgan Forrester came along?

Did I have to contend with any stupid apparitions back then?

I most certainly did not.

Then there was the matter of Clarissa. Now that she was online and had a phone, she could probably find her. If she didn't want to fool with it herself, she could hire a detective. How tough could it be? She could face Clarissa and tell her the truth. Then she'd have finally cleaned up everything.

But she wasn't handling that mess, either. In fact, she wasn't doing much of anything. Day after day, she kicked about the place, doing a half-assed job of her chores and feeling as if she were going around in circles.

I'm as useless as Clarissa's father.

Serena stopped herself. It hurt to put Lloyd down. Before the alcohol got him, he was a kind man. They had loved each other. But neither of them had done much for her little Pearl, her Clarissa.

She couldn't stand the way her mind was working. At least Woof wasn't following her around, grinning at her all the time. It seemed Woof was was sleeping all day and all night. And she wasn't eating much.

Is it the heat?

She'd better not be sick.

That's the last thing I need.

Serena went round and round about these things. This morning, however, she woke up feeling as if she could finally make some kind of fresh start. She had a few ideas about her book and was conducting research on the Internet.

But everything that excited her was at least a decade old, which was a bad sign and she knew it. When she read a post about how dated one of her favorite authors was, she jumped out of her chair and ripped the cords to her computer out of the wall.

She finished her fit and was ready to get back to work, but then she realized she'd permanently damaged the end of the cord she needed to get back online. So she plowed through her piles of unresolved mail to find the catalog she had used to order her computer and accessories. She'd gone through everything twice before she noticed the catalog was in the pile of papers next to the wood stove, already partially shredded for burning.

Serena wanted to throw her computer on the floor. Instead, she made a space for it in a corner and covered it with a rag, then got out her old manual typewriter and started typing what she wanted to write. It was all about how angry she was at men.

~ ~ ~

Morgan was lying on her back under the willow tree, enjoying the twilight. The pink of the mimosa blossoms and the fuchsia of the crape myrtle still glowed in the fading light. Canna lilies and hollyhocks were backlit by the last rays of the sun, creating brilliant bursts of color that danced in the breeze like sunlight on the ripples of a lake.

The mesmerizing song of tree frogs, cicadas and crickets was punctuated by a Carolina wren calling, "Get here! Get here, get here, get here, get here." Its tail and head were flipped up, sassy.

"Why are all these dark entities showing up?" Morgan asked Brigid.

CHAPTER 15

the sanctioning dark

Imitate your dreams
until you become them.

—Ann Megisikwe

"Brigid? Are you here?" Morgan raised up on her elbows and waited until she felt the warmth of Brigid's presence, then flopped back down on her back and gazed into the swaying willow branches. "Why are all these dark ones gathering around us?"

They'd been besieged for days. Shadow hadn't launched another direct attack. Instead, he stood to the side in his annoyingly jaunty manner and watched while first dozens, then hundreds of dark beings came to Morgan.

They began by menacing her, which was terrifying at first. But before long she and Brigid had noticed the majority of the dark ones threatened Morgan only to get her attention. If she activated the vortex immediately, they simply stepped into the light. They wanted to go up.

Sometimes other entities showed up who wouldn't go into the vortex. They'd circle the periphery and intimidate them. But when she and Brigid kept themselves in the center of the whirling light, the menacing ones would eventually leave.

It had been so intense Morgan put everyone on a schedule. She told the dark ones they could show up in the garden only every other evening after dinner. She asked for domes of golden white light to protect her body and her home, office, and car so they couldn't interrupt her at other times.

On alternate evenings Morgan would work with dark entities for thirty minutes in the garden, and that was it. Hundreds, if not thousands, of dark ones had returned to the light in this way. Tonight was a night off, and they had the garden to themselves.

"Root with me, child," Brigid said. Together they connected to the Earth Mother. "To answer your question about the purpose of these visits from the dark ones, we must seek the highest of the high, the deepest of the deep, the center of the center."

Answers began to come, ringing within and resonating with profound wisdom. They were told earth had been involved in an experiment in duality for thousands of years. The great light beings who set up the experiment had agreed to create an environment in which souls could learn about the polarities of good and evil, joy and sorrow, love and fear, pleasure and pain.

Souls could choose to come here and create lives with certain obstacles so they could learn. Half the light beings who agreed to create this experiment held down the light and the other half held down the darkness.

Because so many species had disappeared from the earth and thousands more were threatened, the great light beings knew the darkness was becoming too dense for earth to continue to sustain life.

So earth was in the process of being shifted from an experiment in duality to an experiment in balance.

Those who held down the darkness had agreed that when the appropriate time came for the experiment to shift, someone would tap them on the shoulder and they would return to the light. That time had come and Morgan was helping them go back to the Source of All for purification, re-calibration, and learning.

The problem was that some of the dark entities had learned to enjoy their roles too much and were now unwilling to return to the light. They had become invested in dominance, control, and power over others and the environment.

"Shadow," Morgan said.

"Yes, child. They're talking about Shadow and his kind."

~ ~ ~

Brigid smiled inwardly.

This is why I've been called here.

It wasn't enough to preserve the magic of the Old Ways in our bellies.

Now we must deliver it, with all the quiet power of the Great Mother of Us All, to usher in a new era.

Morgan was frowning.

"What is it, Child?" Brigid caught herself feeling maternal toward Morgan, though she herself would have been the younger woman.

"It's a beautiful learning we've been given tonight. But for me, it's incomplete."

"Why is that?"

"I went down the wrong road, Brigid. I feel it in my gut."

"Tell me more."

"The other night I called in evil, I acted out of anger. And I went to the children with my own limited ideas about what needed to happen, instead of praying for the highest good. Worst of all, when I got into trouble I sought help from my guides only, instead of going to the Earth Mother and to Divine Wholeness, to the Limitless Source of All That Is."

"Aren't you being, as you would say, hard on yourself?"

"Hey, I'm paying for the choices I made that night. Look at all the freaks showing up in my back yard. I played small and consequently got assigned the role of cosmic janitor in a halfway house for negative energies, when what I really want is to create the alternative, the balance of the feminine."

Brigid's laugh was sudden and deep. "I take your meaning."

"I'll do my cleanup shift for awhile. But soon I'm moving on. I'll pray for sacred light and the mineral strength of the Earth Mother to become available to all who'll use it for the highest good. But I want no part in a battle between good and evil."

"But will that work, Luv?"

"I hope so." Morgan thought for a moment. "And another thing."

"What?"

"I've been trying to corral dark entities into the vortex."

"So?"

"So don't they need compassion and respect as much as anyone else? Don't they have free will?" If they've been separated from the light for so long, wouldn't they be afraid of it?"

"I'd not thought of that."

"Neither did I. But I'll never get where I need to go unless I can open my heart to everything. Even darkness. I need to learn how to be open and protected at the same time. I've never achieved that, not once in my life. It's always been one or the other."

❧ ❧ ❧

"How did I ever get by without this therapy stuff?" Clarissa asked herself out loud as she thumped Morgan on her back on her way to the couch. The plush fabric felt comfortingly familiar under her fingers.

"What's up?" Morgan said.

"I feel as if I'm on a roller coaster. Even more than when I first came here."

"Ah, but there's a difference," Morgan was wearing a teal and gold floral print that highlighted the ruddiness of her complexion and the fire in her eyes. "Before, you were going around in circles, stuck in your emotional reactions to things. Now something new is happening. You're clearing the repressed, pent up emotions of the past. Imagine a log jam in a river."

Morgan was clearly enjoying herself. "The logs are your feelings you hadn't been allowing to flow because it didn't feel safe. They've been accumulating for a lifetime in what has become a huge pileup. Now you're breaking up the log jam, and so many logs are racing down the river at the same time, sometimes you can barely see the water. Right now some of those logs, or emotions, are from the present. Most of them, however, are from the past. But guess what?"

"Do I have to?"

"Once you get most of the old emotions unjammed, you won't feel as if you're on a roller coaster. Your consciousness will be cooled by the removal of all those toxins. Won't that be wonderful?"

Clarissa felt herself smiling weakly. "Sometimes I feel as if I'm nuts."

Morgan laughed. "You're not nuts. Far from it. You're simply clearing away debris, both for yourself and for the collective. If you examine your process carefully, aren't things different now? Don't you see light at the end of the tunnel?"

Clarissa gave herself a moment to look inside. "Yes, I guess I do." It was true. She no longer felt hopeless. Even when she was in pain, she had a sense of purpose that hadn't been there before.

"Your context has changed." Morgan leaned forward, squaring her shoulders and facing Clarissa head on. Her eyes became clear and piercing, almost hawklike. "Listen to me. We no longer have the luxury of thinking of ourselves as crazy, inadequate, fucked up little women. It's time to claim our magnificence."

"Fucked up?"

"It's a clinical term."

"But I thought I got through all that in our last session," Clarissa said.

Morgan's burst of laughter seemed to resound off the walls. "No darling. Wouldn't we all love it if it were that simple? What we've done so far is to clear enough emotional debris for your soul to begin to realize and manifest its calling. Now everything that's always been in the way of answering that call is coming up for you to deal with. It's like peeling an onion. We clear one layer, and the deeper one appears."

"I hate peeling onions," Clarissa said.

"Yet it's the secret to a good stew, isn't it!" Morgan said. "The more pain, sadness, fear, grief, and anger we release, the more capable we become of sustaining love, creativity, and joy. It's natural law. If you want to enjoy the baby, you have to get rid of the old diaper and clean up the shit."

Clarissa snorted. She knew Morgan was just getting started.

"Here's another way of looking at it. Before we start clearing, we're going around in tiny circles, going over the same stuck thoughts and emotions again and again. But once we start clearing, the circle starts to expand open and move up, so now we're orbiting out on a spiral." Morgan used her forefinger to describe a spiral, creating expanding circles in the air that moved up as they got bigger.

"Notice that when I'm am back here in the small circle," she said, going back down to her lap to draw tiny, rapid circle in the air with her right forefinger, "If my left forefinger represents my shit," she said, causing her left forefinger to intrude into the circle her opposite finger was making just enough to snag it and disturb its revolution, "then when I'm down here in these tiny circles, I'm spending a lot of time reacting to my history, my shit.

"But when I begin to clear," she said, raising both hands and expanding the circle up and out, "There's a longer orbit before I run into my shit again. I'm spending less time with my shit and more time expanding, more time doing what I want to do."

"I didn't realize you shrinks get paid to talk about shit," Clarissa said, laughing.

"Oh yes," Morgan said. "It's another clinical term. The headline would read, *Cleaning Up the Excremental Creates Joy Exponential.*"

"Eeeuew."

Morgan raised one eyebrow and grinned.

Morgan was sitting in front of the mirror in her bedroom. She was brushing her hair when Adam's fierce eyes and the image of the iron sailing toward her flashed through her mind.

Her first impulse was to tuck her head. Instead she pulled her attention to her belly, relaxed her spine, and imagined herself immersed in the earth, sitting with loose soil surrounding her naked body up to her arms. She felt herself leaning back into the dirt, infusing her body with the mineral essence of the earth, and allowing all tension to be drawn off.

Testifying against Adam had been easier than she'd thought. This simple meditation would be enough to release the strain of a day in court.

She'd learned that Adam had been arrested three times previously for domestic violence—in Miami, Atlanta, and Richmond. He'd broken parole in Richmond when he moved to Hopewellen, which was a federal offense.

Officer Briggs, the woman who originally took her statement, had been at the trial. "They're going to throw away the key in Richmond," she'd said. "He won't be out for at least twenty-two years, seven on his sentence and fifteen on the federal. But he won't ever come back here. I think you can count on that. His M.O. is to move on when he gets busted."

Morgan drew a deep breath. With a mix of curiosity and admiration, she looked—really looked—at the changed Morgan in the mirror. It had been barely a month since Adam hit her, but she'd changed so much since then that the incident felt as if it were part of some strange and distant past.

Morgan raced to unpack the groceries, jumped in her car, and headed for the veterinary hospital at the university. Since her numerous encounters with Shadow, she'd learned to center, to root herself in the earth when facing a difficult situation. Which this one promised to be.

Virginia Woof was terribly ill.

Serena had been calling several times a day, trying to figure out what to do. First Woof was sleeping more and more. Then she lost her appetite. Today she was listless and unresponsive and hadn't had anything to eat or drink for nearly two days.

Serena didn't want to take her to a country doctor, as she put it, so she had a helicopter pick them up and fly them to the hospital at the veterinary school in Hopewellen.

Morgan arrived at the old brick hospital well before Serena who, she learned from the receptionist, would be landing at the airport and arriving by limousine. The dark-eyed receptionist flashed her a conspiratorial look that combined compassion with lighthearted disapproval of the excesses of the rich.

The woman directed her to the emergency area, where she found a chair against the wall not far from the door Serena and Woof would come through when they arrived.

She leaned her head against the wall, took a long breath, and stretched her whole body, extending her legs and thereby causing a technician she hadn't seen coming to suddenly veer from her path. She was rushing toward the outside entrance to the emergency area.

The technician shot Morgan a look that said, "don't get in the way," and flew out the door.

The roar of a chopper drew closer. Woof must be in bad shape for Serena to ignore protocol and land at the hospital. White-coated staff rushed to the door, looking both annoyed and curious. Perhaps they thought some celebrity pet was about to arrive, celebrity in tow.

The doors burst open and aides rushed in. They were carrying a blanket they were making taut, like a stretcher. She glimpsed a patch of still fur. Had she not identified Woof, she wouldn't have recognized Serena, who was running alongside Woof, shouting details. She was wearing makeup and had on a black Armani pants suit, black heels, and a strand of expensive looking pearls with matching earrings. Her hair was in a tiny bun from which a few white tendrils had escaped. A rich black leather duffel bag hung from her shoulder.

Serena's eyes met hers just before the stretcher disappeared behind a set of swinging doors. It was the first time she'd ever seen Serena look desperate.

An assistant tried to make her leave, but she insisted she was family and took her place next to Serena, brushing Serena's fingers with her own as they stood side by side. She breathed deeply and rooted herself.

Serena gave a complete history to a man with a stethoscope around his neck, a Dr. Hind. Woof seemed barely conscious while Dr. Hind and two interns examined her. Her breathing was labored.

Woof, although she was an old dog, had exuded vitality when Morgan was with her on the mountain. Something about her danced even when she felt stiff and disinclined to move. But now her eyes were dull. Morgan hurt to see her this way.

She put her face down next to Woof. Woof grinned just a little and thumped her tail once. Morgan managed to tell her to hang in there, she was in good hands, before one of the interns whisked her out of the way.

"We'll have to keep her here, at least overnight, to try to stabilize her and to run some x-rays and tests," Dr. Hind said.

"What's wrong with her?" Serena asked. Her voice was thin.

"We won't know for sure until tomorrow, Ms.—" Dr. Hind searched Woof's chart.

"Serena. No last name, just Serena."

Dr. Hind looked perplexed.

"Please tell me what you think is happening," Serena said.

"Based on my examination, which, of course, is inconclusive without x-rays, an EKG, and an echocardiogram, I would say she has congestive heart failure. She has edema and on examination I hear a slurring of the heart valve."

"Is she going to die?"

"Eventually. We'll know a lot more tomorrow but I think you caught it fairly quickly. We may be able to stabilize her on medication and she might have a few good years left. She's an old dog, Mrs. Serena. You need to remember that."

"So you think she'll make it through the night."

"I don't know. I hope so."

~ ~ ~

Serena did her best to settle into the passenger seat of Morgan's Saturn. She always did think the color gold was ostentatious for a vehicle.

If you're going to spend the money on a new car, go with black.

Besides, this car is undersized.

To say the very least.

She hated that Woof was sick. She hated being off her mountain. She hated being driven. First the helicopter pilot, now Morgan. She had to tip the pilot an extra three hundred dollars—cash—to get him to land at the hospital instead of the airport, This left her with a mere forty-seven hundred dollars. On top of it all, the landing had been sloppy.

She herself was, of course, an excellent driver.

Morgan's driving seemed careful enough, though her habit of setting her cruise control for five miles over the speed limit and hovering in the far left lane was most annoying.

She took a good long look at Morgan.

She was different—more focused, powerful, wise. And disturbingly sensual. At the hospital, Morgan had stood next to her like some ancient priestess. Her bottomless eyes were wells of compassion.

It makes me want to puke.

But instead here I am, forcing myself to accept her hospitality.

Morgan's sprawling Victorian turned out to be as lavishly lusty as its owner, tarted up with bold colors in every room. Take the front hall, for instance. Gold-flecked wallpaper with gold trim. Metallic gold trim.

What's with this gold thing she has going on?

True, the entry was done with a certain flair. But it was, nonetheless, nouveau riche. Unmistakably. Of course those floozie white gladiolas overpowered one. To think Morgan actually bragged about some Jake person having them flown in twice a week—ridiculous.

The foyer was comfortably large but the gladiolas, with their harsh, up-lit, decadent sprawl, created the sense of too little space. Yet the huge rooms on either side offered no comfortable alternative.

The forest green of the living room, which was to the right of the foyer, could have been all right had it been handled correctly. But of course it wasn't. The floral print swirling on the overstuffed furniture combined with the overblown decor created a jungle-like effect. Tarzan could come swinging across on a vine at any moment. It was actually quite frightening.

The library to the left of the foyer was worse. It had magenta walls, burgundy trim, and red leather furniture. It could have been a brothel but for the dart board, exercise bike, entertainment center, and assorted joysticks and musical instruments.

What are those, bongo drums?

Chaos.

Complete and utter chaos.

And then of course Jane arrived before Serena had time to put down her bag.

"Serena!" Jane threw her arms around her, nearly toppling her. "I'm so sorry about Woof. How is she?"

Great.

She hadn't realized how accustomed she was to being alone. She relied on it.

Morgan led her upstairs to what she jokingly referred to as the west wing. There were five bedrooms. She was afraid of what hers would look like, but Morgan took her to a large, old-fashioned bedroom, perfectly made up.

"This was Grandmama's bedroom," she said as she helped her settle in. "There's someone else staying here. Jake. His room is on the other side of the bathroom the two of you share."

Yuck.

She shuddered, but Morgan didn't notice. She was relieved to find the bathroom was as clean as Grandmama's room. The toilet seat was even down.

Is Jake one of Morgan's men?

She carefully wiped the seat of the commode and lined it with a double layer of paper before sitting, took a quick shower, and threw on some jeans and a tee shirt before joining Morgan and Jane.

One never knew when that Jake creature might appear.

Wait!

Isn't Jake Gladiola Man?

I bet he borrows Morgan's clothes.

He's probably the driving force behind the decor in this dump.

To think I left my haven of sustainability only to wind up in this monument to self-indulgence.

If this were going to be a long stay, she'd have Saks overnight her some proper robes. Conservative, with good coverage. But of course that wouldn't be necessary.

It better not be.

Get well, Woof.

I haven't been here thirty minutes, and already I can't stand it.

She found Morgan and Jane on the front porch—the huge front porch, which reminded Serena of an old plantation even though it was too new by several decades. The sun was slowly setting, relieving the air of its burden of heat.

Morgan was gently rocking herself on an antique double glider with Jane sitting opposite her.

"Hey, Serena!" Jane was nauseatingly perky. "Sit by me."

A power surge apparently hit Morgan hard, because she reached for the fan tucked in the waistband of her flowing, multicolored, diaphanous skirt.

Serena seated herself next to Jane.

Not that it's easy to choose between the basic double negatives.

"You're a real Southern belle now with your fan," Serena said.

Jane recoiled and looked at her. Serena hadn't intended for the sarcasm of her thoughts to spill into her tone but evidently it had.

Morgan regarded her evenly.

Oh boy—she's onto me.

She's been taking off like a spiritual rocket while I've been wallowing on my mountain.

"You must be very worried about Woof," Morgan said.

Morgan's compassion sailed straight through her anger and landed in the center of her heart. Simultaneously, it infuriated her. It was one more reminder that Morgan was now the serene one, so at peace with herself that she extended yet greater kindness when she jabbed at her.

She felt so stuck she could choke.

Why didn't I stay in a hotel?

The impersonal familiarity would have been a balm. Instead, she was compounding her anxiety about Woof by forcing herself to experience how someone else lived, someone who actually had a life. Morgan had been a gracious guest by comparison, even with the lack of amenities on Mothers Mountain.

She was jealous of her.

"I don't relish leaving Virginia Woof in the hands of all those men. Why didn't we at least get a female veterinarian?" Serena said.

Jane simply sniggered, but Morgan gave her a penetrating look. She was getting ready to take her on.

Christ Jesus, why am I baiting her?

"Serena, I've experienced your love in many ways."

Love?

We're talking love now?

"It's in your desire to change the things that don't work. It's in the care you gave me when I was sick and when you guided me through Brigid's last day. It's in how you rushed Woof to the hospital."

Man oh man, look at her.

She's just getting started.

"You know what it is to love, Serena. So why spend so much energy fighting with life? What we resist persists. Why don't you let go and let yourself be nurtured by the help that comes your way? Take Woof's vet. He really cares."

"Come on. I've had a rough day. Can't we just leave it alone?"

"What if you were to consider the possibility that whatever you're branding as evil is there for a purpose?"

Great.

Free therapy with the accommodations.

"Yeah right," Serena said. "You mean like Shadow?"

"Like Shadow," Morgan said. "What a wonderful way to look at him."

"What's up with Shadow?" Jane said.

Oh god.

I mean, goddess.

Why did I bring him up?

Serena didn't have the energy to deal with that one, but she soon wished she had.

Morgan stared at her own gaudy toenails, her feet splayed across the white wooden slats that formed the floor of the glider. "Why did you leave teaching, Serena? You were so good at it."

"I beg your pardon?"

"You heard me."

"I always wondered about that myself," Jane said.

"The publish or perish thing got under my skin."

Jane let out a long whoosh of air and faced Serena directly. "What's the real reason?"

"I wrote one treatise after another, but none of the male-dominated academic presses had the balls to print them. I got passed over for honors and promotions and I couldn't get a position of power on an academic committee, all because I'm a woman. An independent, freethinking woman who speaks up and doesn't kiss ass.

You asked for it!

"I didn't go into academia resenting men," Serena said. "My experiences brought me to that. Of course the students loved my classes, but watching them give it all up for their boyfriends was depressing as hell."

Here we go.

I might as well give them what they really want.

Maybe they'll shut up.

"Let's face it, women. I've turned into an old crank. I can get along with animals, sort of, but not people."

Jane reached for her hand but Serena pulled away.

I don't want sympathy, damn it.

"That's a choice," Morgan said, "and like all choices, you can change it. Why not try getting closer to us? Why not let us support you tonight, when you're so worried about Woof? Besides, how can you work for a better world without embracing your own goodness and that of others?"

Morgan's eyes began to flutter, then closed. She drew a series of deep breaths, her spine straight and her palms up.

Shit.

She's going into one of those trance thingies she was telling me about on the phone.

Jane leaned forward, her elbows on her knees, and rested her chin on her hands.

Holy crap.

Jane's already a trance freak.

It's a Morganfest.

Hail to the queen!

Where's my rosary?

The glider stopped. The air was still, no bird called, and the sounds of far-off traffic faded to silence. In spite of herself, Serena held her breath and leaned forward as if her life depended on what Morgan would say.

"When you engage your hopes and your ideals to work for the greater good—as you do, Serena—your focus brings the whole force of nature to work behind you. But to be effective, you must gain control of your thoughts and honor the importance of every single decision you make."

Serena drew a ragged breath.

That pretty much counts me out.

"In each life, there are opportunities, challenges, and decisions to be made." Morgan's voice seemed to come from a faraway place. "Each choice is a chance to affirm what one believes. Like a strong yet peaceful river, all lives have a ribbon of light running through them, flowing through each of these points of decision."

As if by magic, Serena felt her anger dissipate. Morgan's words resonated with a truth that pierced through the emotions of the day to the raw hunger in her soul. She allowed herself to open.

"We're talking about choices we would stand up for," Morgan said, "to the point of risking everything. In human terms, what would you die for? But that's a crude example because anyone who is consciously aware of being on such a path is beyond the point of being frightened of leaving the human realm."

Serena was breathing fully, evenly, for the first time in a long time. It was as if her breath had been released from bondage.

"What you need to come to terms with," Morgan said, "what we all need to be looking at, is the deeper nature of the choices that are now available on this planet. It used to be that each choice had little significance on its own. But taken all together, a lifetime of choices became one or two big choices about beliefs. These big choices defined what stars or lights got added to that soul's energy field. At this time on earth, each choice carries more weight. More can be accomplished with a single decision than was true twenty years ago and certainly two hundred years ago, so there's a bigger responsibility attached to every single choice. There's also the opportunity to understand how all the choices on this planet are woven together, forming the fabric of a living, breathing belief system. Each individual belief system is like a square in a patchwork quilt, contributing to the whole of consciousness on the planet."

In the deepening twilight, Morgan's eyes were as vast as galaxies. A full moon was rising behind her. What Morgan said next both thrilled and terrified Serena because she couldn't question that her words were coming from the heart of the cosmos.

"Choose well, for every single thing you do matters. Use your power for the highest good. This is not a request, Serena. It's a reminder of the commitments you made before you were born. We're counting on you. All of creation is counting on you."

Serena was entranced. Until, that is, Morgan stopped talking and fluttered her eyes open.

You're the hundredth woman, not I—you fat, far-out floozie.

Haven't I got enough problems without trying to be perfect so I can save the world?

In a flash, Serena found her voice.

"What a load of crap!"

CHAPTER 16

in excess of that expected

There is a brokenness
out of which comes the unbroken,
a shatteredness out of which blooms the
unshatterable.

There is a sorrow
beyond all grief which leads to joy
and a fragility
out of whose depths emerges strength.

There is a hollow space
too vast for words
through which we pass with each loss,
out of whose darkness we are sanctioned into
being.

There is a cry deeper than all sound
whose serrated edges cut the heart
as we break open
to the place inside which is unbreakable

and whole,
while learning to sing.

—Rashani

Clarissa was up late working on a mailing, feeling overwhelmed by the magnitude of the task she'd set for herself and unspeakably lonely.

She was longing for the mother she'd never known. Big Mom had been as loving as any mother and her blood mother was white and therefore of another world. But Clarissa felt she and her mother were somehow the same. So without being close to her mother, how could she truly embrace herself?

She bowed her head and tears blurred the page in front of her. Even knowing she was working for an important cause couldn't comfort her tonight. What she needed was her mother.

❧ ❧ ❧

It was unclear how long Woof would be in the hospital, so Serena and Morgan moved Morgan's home computer into Grandmama's room. Now Serena could pop online and do some writing while she waited. Of course she would simply order another computer if she were going to be here more than a few days, but having Morgan's made her feel more at home.

Serena settled in for her first night. In spite of her concerns about Woof, she was beginning to enjoy the benefits of staying in a real home.

Until, that is, she walked in on Jake in the bathroom.

❧ ❧ ❧

"I went to the town council meeting in Macon, the community where the dump is slated to be built." Clarissa caught Morgan watching her twist a ringlet of hair on her forefinger. She might as well be sucking her thumb, too. She straightened. "You'd think they'd have their own concerns about it, but when I raised important issues they put me off. What's worse, one of the councilmen pulled me aside and told me he'd heard about the canvassing I've been doing. He implied I might be in some kind of danger if I continued."

The early morning sunlight glared outside the windows of the therapy office. Morgan was wearing a long, flowing, forest green and aqua dress. Her round, comforting body was draped casually across the overstuffed chair she seemed to prefer and her brown eyes were soft with concern.

"What do you want to do?"

At their last session, Morgan had told her about Shadow, whom Clarissa recognized from her own experience of fear mixed with pain that was so overwhelming, it seemed to come from both within and without.

"I thought about approaching the situation as if it were a lesson," Clarissa said, "a test with Shadow. But I have to remember I have two kids to raise."

"I understand."

"I'm not going to give up because I've been threatened. I'm going to see if I can work through the women in the churches."

"Build a broad base of community support before you take on the big boys."

"Exactly."

"Brave woman. Creative and brave."

"But I'm afraid."

"That's okay. Fill yourself with love and take reasonable precautions. You already know that most of your fear comes from seeing Big Mom get hit, stepping outside your comfort zone and taking risks, and being a visible, outspoken woman. And, of course, from feeling motherless."

She cringed. Hearing Morgan describe her as motherless made it more real.

"Love, connection, and living your dreams—these are your pathways out of that pain. You can use all these tools as you move toward your event."

"I'm afraid I won't get everything done. I'm working myself around the clock, but what if it's not enough?"

"Of course you can't do it all. Only together can we create change. Try looking at yourself not as the person who makes the event happen, but as the midwife who's easing the birth of the event. Bring others in to help you. Daily."

Tears that refused to spill blurred Clarissa's vision.

"What is it?"

"My mother. How can I miss her when I don't even know her?" For several moments she couldn't speak. "I wonder how she'd feel about me."

"My guess is, very proud."

"When this event is over, I'm going to find her."

"Oh?"

"I need to know why she left. Big Mom said it was for the best, but she didn't say why."

"You don't have to wait until you find your mother to heal, Clarissa. What if your soul chose this condition of motherlessness as a way to learn? Your soul's agenda is deeper than the mere pursuit of comfort. It wants strength, wisdom.

I once felt motherless. I used that feeling as an opportunity to learn how to mother myself, to love myself unconditionally."

"I'm trying."

"And succeeding. You're learning to mother yourself and simultaneously mother your kids and the earth. Pretty impressive."

"It's hard to love myself fully when I see how much there is to do and I'm not getting it all done."

Morgan's eyes fluttered shut and she drew a long breath, becoming very still. As if speaking simultaneously from somewhere deep within the earth and from a far-off galaxy she said, "The only way we can fail is by making an effort." Her eyes sprang open and she laughed. "Keep track of this one for me, will you? I have no idea where all this is coming from, but I think I need to hear it."

Clarissa nodded, laughing softly. Morgan's eyes closed again. Her back was very straight and she had her palms on her knees, facing skyward.

"You've heard the story of the lilies of the field, whose every need is met because they're dearly loved. And you, Clarissa, every hair on your head is counted."

A rush of tears spilled from Clarissa's eyes.

"Remember, the Great Spirit lives in you, as it does in all things." Morgan's eyes fluttered open momentarily, mysterious as the moon, then closed for what seemed to be a very long time. At last she spoke. "Your job then, as God, is to desire, to intend, so the Limitless Source of All That Is can manifest."

"As God?"

"Yes. You are God, as we all are. You're a wave on the ocean of Infinite Potential. The power of that ocean is there for you. Its whole reason for being is to support you. All it desires is to manifest your dreams. Your only job is to create your intention, give easy, unconditional attention to your part of the task, let go, and trust."

There's that word again.

Trust.

"Two things get in the way of manifesting your desires. The first is old patterns in the mind saying things like, 'what I want is impossible,' or, 'I don't deserve that.'

"Thoughts are like prayers, and if the Spirit of Creation hears you making negative statements, even at the unconscious level, It assumes you don't want what you said you wanted and—out of Its profound love for you and Its eagerness to manifest your desires—It doesn't give it to you."

They opened their eyes and smiled at each other, trying to assimilate what they were hearing.

Morgan's eyes fluttered shut. "Continue to let go of these old weights and judgments, then manifesting what you want will become easy.

"The second thing that gets in the way of manifestation is making an effort." Morgan peeked at Clarissa and raised an eyebrow, then closed her eyes. "You're a mother, Clarissa. Do you pace back and forth in front of your boys, wringing you hands and saying affirmations so their feet will grow? Do you stay up all night, watching their feet? No. You simply provide good nourishment and before you know it you're at the shoe store buying the next size up."

"Ain't that the truth," Clarissa said.

Morgan's eyes popped open and they both laughed hard.

"Wait 'til you hit the teenage years!" Morgan closed her eyes again. "It's the same with all things. Follow the example of nature. Plant the seed, weed and water it, throw on a little compost and don't worry. Have faith that the Creator Spirit is taking care of how a seed becomes a plant that bears corn, beans, or squash.

"Simply focus on each small choice as an opportunity to be happy with yourself and your world. Trust that the Creative Energy that gave you life—and sees to the perfect functioning of your body—is available to fulfill your desires.

"You simply need to have the idea of what you want, the willingness to bring your love and attention to the process, and the ability to let go, trusting that the universe wants to create what you requested.

"You're thinking, 'What if the universe doesn't want what I want?'"

Clarissa's laughter bubbled. "Got me!"

"It's simple. When you don't get what you ask for—provided you're not blocking your desires by negative thinking or by efforting—you can trust that for now, in the larger context, what you desire isn't in the flow that serves the greater good. You and the larger collective are being served in ways that are even better than what you wished for.

"The Creator Spirit isn't your mother, Clarissa, it didn't give you life and then disappear."

Clarissa felt her throat catch at the mention of her mother and she had to force herself to listen to what Morgan said next.

"You can tell because the world still surrounds you. Look around for the small miracles, the wonderful coincidences, that happen every day. Allow yourself to feel that support."

Her mind traveled back to a month ago when the boys were at camp and she had set the weekend aside to figure out how to stop the dump. She had been so angry with herself for not getting anything done, she ended up in a bar.

Yet in spite of her weakness, her intention to stop the dump must have gone out into the universe.

What had come back was a series of apparent coincidences that led her to Morgan and a spiritual path that was bringing her—one step at a time—closer to the manifestation of her dreams.

Is that how it works?

By following your dreams, you find your spirit?

"When you're canvassing and you knock on someone's door," Morgan was saying when Clarissa's attention returned again to the present, "it's God who answers. Honor that God. In India, when people great each other they say, "*namasté,*" which means, 'the God in me greets the God in you.' See the Creator in each moment, loving you. Trust."

Trust.

"When you encounter an obstacle, don't get upset. Instead, allow it to become your teacher. Find out how it's benefiting you.

"We bless you, little one. If you knew how much we love you, you'd never stop smiling."

Morgan drew a deep breath, opened her eyes, and gazed out the window, apparently not yet all the way back.

"Who was the 'we' who spoke at the end?" Clarissa said.

"It was a group giving the message throughout. It was as if they were singing and dancing, inside and all around me. I can't tell you who they are, but their presence is wonderful—reassuring, uplifting."

Morgan's eyes traveled around the room. "Do you see that spider web?" She pointed to the window frame. "What if it's really that simple? Look how she moves, creating her world step by step, weaving the dream inside her as if there's no other way."

They locked eyes for a moment.

"So," Morgan said, bobbing her head and smiling up at her, "how's Joshua?"

Clarissa's face grew hot.

~ ~ ~

Virginia Woof was stretched out on an area rug in Morgan's living room. Serena was comforting herself and Woof by brushing her coat gently. She had congestive heart failure but, as Dr. Hind had hoped, she was stable on medication.

"We'll be able to head back to the mountains in a few days."

Morgan left the couch to join them. "Virginia Woof is a very loving dog. She risked her life to get you off that mountain."

Woof dipped her head and wagged her tail. "Woof," she said.

Morgan grinned and so did Woof but Serena wasn't having any. She lowered her head to avoid Morgan's eyes and brushed Woof's fur with more than her usual diligence.

"Don't allow her sacrifice to be for nothing," Morgan said. "Stay here."

Morgan moved in close and gently placed her hand on Serena's. "I know you better now," she said. "You're a very precious woman. But you don't know you're precious. That's your problem."

Serena withdrew her hand.

"Precious" is strictly a Hallmark sort of word.

These shrinks make me puke.

Morgan's losing it.

She tried to make her voice even, non-offensive. "I'm not up for this right now."

"You told me about your parents. They meant well, but they didn't raise you with the quality of attention you needed. They didn't convey to you that you were loved and accepted and connected to them."

Serena began to tear up.

I hate it when I do that.

She hid her eyes from Morgan.

Morgan went on. And on. And on. "You lacked the modeling for how to get along with others, so naturally your opinionated approach has alienated people all your life."

Did I contract for your services, Morgan?

I don't think so.

We'd better increase your client-load, a little something to occupy your mind.

"People think you're rude. You're already very sensitive and then, when you're rejected, you keep spiraling inward until you end up talking to yourself instead of to others.

She does have a point.

"Try an experiment, Serena. Move into this house. Come out of your shell, meet new people. Take some chances with me, Jane, and Jake."

Jake?

That'll be the day.

Morgan's boy-toy was as annoying a human being as she had ever encountered. It wasn't that there was anything wrong with him. But he was so nice, he was disgusting.

Morgan stood and slowly walked toward the stairs.

At least she has the good sense to leave after delivering a line of bull like that.

What am I, a sociology experiment?

Morgan was already upstairs when the doorbell rang.

"I'll get it!" Serena yelled. She didn't want Morgan to come back down and see her face. She would notice the splotches.

She peered through the peephole and found a very short old woman who's wig shaded her eyes like a baseball cap. Serena opened the door.

Who is this?

Oh yeah, Morgan's Aunt Lee.

Aunt Lee pushed past her, tap-tapping with her cane on her way to the living room. "Just the one I want to see," she said.

Oh god.

I mean, goddess.

"Oh, and here is our precious little patient now."

It was that word again.

Precious.

Aunt Lee indicated Woof with her cane, having seated herself in a straight-backed chair Serena found to be particularly uncomfortable. "Serenity, I brought you this card."

At least she didn't call me Calamity.

I feel more like Calamity.

Aunt Lee began to pray over Woof.

It seemed to be the beginning of a particularly long prayer—judging by Aunt Lee's sighing and the energetic, driving journey her voice took, sailing to the stratosphere, then dipping to the depths—so Serena turned over the envelope.

On the front, the name 'Serenity' was scrawled beside a crude drawing of praying hands with gold rays emanating from them like exclamation points.
Inside was a card with an image of Jesus holding a lamb.
But Aunt Lee had pasted the head of a cocker spaniel over that of the sheep.

~ ~ ~

Serena awakened early and miffed. She was exhausted. Who could sleep with those two carrying on half the night? It was one thing to know they were doing it, but quite another when you could make out every word.

Well, I couldn't hear Morgan.

But that Jake, my god.

I mean, goddess.

The Southern drawl was bad enough under the best of circumstances, but last night was beyond belief.

The hayseed sounded like an evangelist at a tent revival. Shouting out to Morgan to accept his love, the love of the sun and the moon, the stars and the earth.

Holy crap.

I was waiting for him to get her to accept Jesus.

What kind of a nutcase is he, anyway?

Worse, he looks exactly like Troy Donahue.

Troy Donahue with a platinum Little Richard wig.

Serena strode out into the yard, which was vast by urban standards but nothing like her very own mountain. She paced back and forth across the width of it, frustrated at the aimlessness of her efforts and longing to sink a hoe into something. But that beast Morgan slept with had all claims to the garden.

How could a place be more humid than a jungle and parched at the same time?

Damned Piedmont.

She hated that the grass was crackling and dusty under her feet.

Of course Fuck Boy would have the place as lush as a rain forest, but Morgan wants to conserve ground water.

Hunkus Neanderthalus Derangus is only allowed to water the flowers.

The mimosa blossoms were drab and faded, the crape myrtle looked dreary, and the leaves on the trees looked as if they were being pulled in by their veins. Even the willow appeared to be attending a wake.

Now in the mountains, of course, all would be green and lush.

And I wouldn't have to worry about Pec Man.

Why did I let Morgan talk me into staying here?

Two huge case of books she'd ordered on the Internet had arrived yesterday afternoon. Nobody bothered taking them up to her room, least of all Troy Boy, so they were still in the foyer. She opened the box and took the top dozen books into the living room, where she settled on the couch.

It was hours before Morgan finally traipsed down the stairs. Her gray hair was tousled and wild and her black silk robe gaped, exposing deep cleavage. Her breasts rolled as she moved and she was smiling. Serena imagined she tantalized herself with the feel of the silk against her skin and that was why her nipples were stiff.

Unless, of course, they've been at it again.

She couldn't bear the thought.

Look at her.

She's nothing but a fat, aging slut.

"It's cold enough in here to hang meat." Serena rubbed her arms.

"Good morning, Serena."

It could have been a jab, but it wasn't. It was a light reminder to be positive and—what was that word she used? Connected. The sweetness in Morgan's tone pissed Serena off even more. It was all she could do not to leap off the couch and belt her.

"Where's Penis Man?"

"Why are you attempting to draw me into conflict?"

"Shrinked again! Are you going to send me a bill? What I want to know is, why can't you find anything better to do with your time than fucking men?"

"Why are *you* wasting *your* time attacking me?"

"Maybe it's because I *care* about you, Morgan. What with your screwed up childhood and all."

"I'm serious. What's wrong?"

"Hey, your boy toy is what's wrong. That ape is young enough to be your child."

Whoa, that got her.

Morgan stuck her chin out and drew her robe in closer around her body. "I have made the choice to take all of who I am—including the part of me that likes to, as you put it, 'fuck men'—and move forward in my life. Jake, I will have you know, is an excellent example of a nontoxic, supportive male. If you would open your mind a little and get to know him, you might learn something."

Oh man.

She actually believes all that psychobabble.

"I think I'll stick to my books, thank you very much."

"This is a perfect example of you alienating people so you can feel like shit instead of being part of."

"'Connected,' you mean? Isn't that the word you shrinks use?" Serena swooped her books into her arms, marched upstairs, and headed for her room.

Jake was standing in the hall. He had on jeans and a crisp white shirt that was still unbuttoned, exposing his deeply tanned and well-muscled chest. His summer-whitened hair fell in curls across his shoulders.

What an empty-headed piece of fluff.

Move over, Fabio.

She glared at him.

"And what, exactly, do you know of the value of pleasure, Serena?" he said softly.

"Listening at the top of the stairs, were we? Good. I'll have you know I've had many lovers. Men *and* women. But I don't throw myself away the way Morgan does."

"Oh really? Might I inquire when the last time was that any of that happened?"

She recoiled.

"I thought so," he said.

He was doing that overblown, deeply mannered, Southern gentleman thing. His tongue rolled his words, the honey only adding to the sting.

Piercing her with his eyes, he said evenly, "Morgan is in possession of a rare gift, Serena. She gives herself completely to her experience of life. She loves. And it all comes back to her. How unfortunate it is that you can't see that."

Please.

Spare me the homemade homilies.

"Morgan educated me about the Eve/Lilith mythology you're so fond of, and I've given it my careful consideration. You are not Lilith, Serena. Where is your freedom, your imagination, your desire, your sense of humor? Morgan has all those virtues. And so many more."

Serena showed him her back and slammed the door to her room. Kicking her jeans and tee shirt across the floor, she pulled on her Armani suit, tore her hair into submission with mad strokes of her brush, and put it up in a twist, which she secured with a heavy pounded-sterling barrette. She pushed sterling earrings—by the same artist, of course—through her ears, one of which she had to pull off again so she could use the telephone.

She spoke to the first detective in the yellow pages who picked up the phone.

"Drop everything," she told him. "I'll double what you're making now. All right, I'll triple it then."

She grabbed her new cell phone, stomped out of the house, and roared off in her rented black Mercedes.

I'm going to find Clarissa if it's the last damned thing I do.

❧ ❧ ❧

What am I, Serena's piñata?

She's a walking spewfest.

Like I need to be reamed out in my own home.

"Cut it off, Randy." Morgan said. "And I mean cut it all off. I want style and texture. Something sassy, contemporary."

She was fanning herself furiously with a magazine. "And dye it red. Not some subtle, tasteful auburn, either. I want my hair so red everyone knows it came out of a bottle. And give it highlights the color of scarlet cellophane."

Randy looked as horrified as if she'd jammed her tongue in his mouth.

"You seem a little upset today, Morgie. Let's wait a month and see how you feel."

He pranced around her salon chair. "You've had your hair long ever since I've known you." He was actually wringing his hands.

"Relax, Randy, it's only hair. My hair, I might add."

"I don't think you understand the consequences of what you want me to do. It'll take years to grow back. Besides, it's easy to go from gray to color, but don't ask me to go back from color to gray. It's impossible. Besides, I thought you were proud of your gray." He was actually pouting.

"I appreciate your concern. Really, I do. And I don't want to be rude, but please do as I ask. Get rid of this mess."

Randy was frozen in place.

In the mirror, Morgan could see beads of sweat forming on her brow and upper lip. She lunged forward, grabbed his scissors, and lopped off a handful of hair close to her crown.

"Okay. I think I see where you're going with this." He took the scissors gently from her hand.

"Nice save." She fanned herself harder while he went to work.

When Morgan left, she blasted the air conditioner and opened the sun roof. She wanted the sunlight to catch her new color so she could pretend to admire it at every traffic light while she got over her shock.

There was something deliciously wicked about it, she decided.

She took herself on a shopping spree and started back to the house with an outlandish pair of magenta sunglasses, the most vibrant, low-cut orange sundress she could find, a scarlet thong, a pair of gold sandals—all of which she wore—a new lime-colored vibrator that was supposed to work underwater, and a CD of salsa music.

There's just one thing.

How am I supposed to be the hundredth woman with an abusive grouch like Serena in the house?

Morgan heard a sort of rasping, scraping sound.

It was Shadow, laughing.

❧ ❧ ❧

"I'm sorry, Ms. Albright. I know you were counting on us. But our own grant money has fallen through so we won't be able to supply you with the funding we promised."

Clarissa hung up the phone. Martin and Frankie were on the living room floor, sorting a mailing by zip code. There was no way she could produce her event with only the money she had from Big Mom, and it was too late to seek alternative funding.

Besides, she didn't have the energy.

I'll have to pay off the debts I've incurred and cancel.

The idea hit her in the chest with a numbing thud.

She picked up the phone, dialed Morgan, and spoke quietly so her boys, who were watching television while they worked, wouldn't hear.

"You were wrong to have such faith in my project," Clarissa told Morgan's voice mail primly. "So was I. My money has fallen through, which means I have to cancel all future sessions. Sorry."

It was only a couple of hours before Morgan returned her call. Clarissa let the machine take it even though she was standing right there.

"Clarissa," Morgan said. "I'm so sorry to hear about your funding. You must be terribly upset."

Clarissa's chin trembled.

"But please come in for at least one more session. This situation, tough as it is, is an opportunity to discover what doors might open for you as this one closes.

"It's a time to trust.

"Part of that trust is honoring yourself, the work we've done together, and me by sitting down to talk about what's going on and feeling it through together.

"I believe that in your heart you don't want to amputate our connection."

~ ~ ~

Morgan climbed the steps to the veranda slowly. She was crushed. She loved Clarissa and hated what was happening to her as much as she hated how Clarissa pulled away from her in response. She knew this wasn't supposed to be the way she felt, at least according to what she'd learned in her psychotherapy training.

To hell with what I'm supposed to feel.

What I do *feel is hurt.*

A tear slid down her face. Inside, an abandoned child struggled alongside the grieving woman who loved Clarissa. Morgan's legs felt suddenly weak so she seated herself on the top step of the veranda. She put her hand on her heart and spoke to the child who trembled within.

"Why does this hurt so much?"

"It's Serena *and* Clarissa," said the young girl, smoothing her flowered bodice with the palms of her hands, "Love switches fast. It never stays."

"That's not true. I love you *all* the time." Morgan embraced the troubled child and placed her in a transparent bubble of protection where she could be safe, be a child, and play. She placed herself inside her own safe bubble, and created an enormous bubble of protection that contained them both.

She remembered an old psychology mentor describing how he woke up one morning and said to his wife, "Why do I have so many crazy people in my life?"

His wife replied, "Because you're a therapist!"

She'd been taught to accept with equanimity that her clients were going to behave erratically. She was supposed to think of their swings as information, grist for the mill. Taking it personally meant she had issues of her own to deal with.

I hate that word, "issues."

It trivializes everything.

With Clarissa, the situation was compounded because she recognized in Clarissa, as she did in Serena, another potential hundredth woman.

It hadn't been a good day for hundredth women.

Was Shadow winning?

Were Clarissa, Serena, and Morgan all going to fail?

Jake was in the living room, repairing an antique chair whose legs weren't cooperating. When he saw her, he jumped to his feet, let out a low whistle, and looked her slowly up and down from her toes to her hair and back again.

"You look right pretty, Ma'am," he said, removing an imaginary cowboy hat.

He moved to kiss her, but she turned away. She did let him remove her magenta sunglasses. When he registered the pain in her eyes, he picked up his guitar, hopped on the back of the love seat, gave her a long sideways look, and strummed to the refrain,

Silver has gone copper now,
Copper with a silver glow—

She couldn't help laughing. Jake was adorable.

Is enlightenment simply being here, in the moment, instead of holding on to what belongs to some other time?

"That's a red glow. I paid a hundred and five dollars specifically for a scarlet cellophane glow."

She hugged him from behind, falling across the back of the love seat. He deftly moved his guitar out of their way as he broke her fall. They tumbled over each other onto the floor, laughed, kissed, and made up verses about Randy the copper chopper, Morgan the copper shopper, and Jake, the copper head.

CHAPTER 17

the most called for thing

As the kindness of verbena
expresses in excess
of that expected
As the clemency
of pansy utters far beyond
demands of fairness
May my mouth make the round
sound of mercy
Enough of pursed lips, the straight
line of judgment.

May dianthus and alyssum
be the syllables I chant
Let my mouth now sing
compassion in the shape
of a perfect peony
Like lilacs awaited
for years of spring,
unfolding finally this season,

may mercy from my mouth
ring into the world.

—Sue Silvermarie

Serena eased her rented black Mercedes into the driveway and parked between Morgan's car and Jake's truck. She drew a jagged breath and gave herself a moment in the low purr of the air conditioning before going in. The flutter in her chest reflected her fear that she might not be able to make good on her spanking new commitment to connect with Morgan and Jake.

Morgan's word again.

"Connect."

She'd decided over lunch that "connect" was a good word. She needed to learn how to hang in there with people if she were going to stand a chance with Clarissa and maintain Morgan's friendship.

Will Morgan and Jake forgive me?

I'm too damned old to lose anyone else because of my own stupidity.

Sometimes being right just isn't worth it.

She hadn't let them be who they were, just as she hadn't let herself be who she was—a lonely, frightened woman who wanted to change her life. A woman who wanted to make a difference in the world but didn't know how.

And then there was the message she had received—through Morgan that first night on the front porch—that all of creation was counting on her and that every single choice she made mattered. Serena felt daunted by that concept, but she couldn't turn away from it.

Yet toying with a new idea and being able to act on it were two different things. She was afraid she would turn into Jekyll and Hyde and Morgan would throw her out for "connecting" one minute and being an old crank the next.

All I can do is try.

She opened the front door to find Morgan sprawled on top of Jake in the living room. They were helpless with laughter and Morgan's skirt was flipped up over head, exposing her buttocks and the scantiest underwear she had ever seen—in scarlet. They heard the door close and Morgan's head popped up. Her hair was ultra-short, choppy, ruffled, and vibrant red.

It looks—

Churning in her belly, ready to spew, was a keen desire to criticize. But she stopped it before it passed her heart and flew out her mouth.

Take two.

It looks fabulous.

Morgan's got guts.

She had promised herself she would go with the flow.

And what would that look like right now?

Tentatively, an olive branch in her heart, she approached the puppy pile.

Jake's expression was that of a wolf prepared to protect the pack. Morgan's eyes fluttered, then froze. Two quick tears escaped Serena's eyes, leaving them clear. Instinctively, she ducked her head, grinning like a submissive canine, before she fell on top of them, laughing and tickling. They pulled her in. The three of them tumbled over one another, giggling, wrestling, and tickling. They hurled at each other first the throw pillows from the furniture, then the cushions, then grapes from the bowl on the coffee table.

Later, alone in her room, Serena shed her black Armani suit, inspected it, and found that except for some dust and the remains of one smashed grape, it had survived wrestling just fine.

A good end to what had turned out to be a good day.

Earlier, in the detective's office, she'd sat for what seemed like forever watching him search for Clarissa on the Internet. He was pretending to have tools she didn't for the so-called "investigation."

Where's John Wayne when you really need him?

While waiting, she'd engaged in a long battle with her evil inner twin—who, of course, wanted to hightail it back to the farm.

But it had become clear that there was no satisfaction at the end of that road. If she were going to take Morgan up on the true spirit of her offer to stay in Hopewellen and "connect," she needed to stay. She didn't know if she could succeed but she had to try.

What did she have to lose, really? Besides her sanity, of course, which she would lose anyway if she returned to Mothers Mountain with a chip on her shoulder and her tail between her legs.

Over lunch at a wonderful little cafe she'd found, Chez Nous, she'd used her cell phone to get things settled on the farm so she didn't have to be back there for months. Of course she might have Travis's grandson bring Hermaphrodite down eventually. But other than that, everything was in place.

So what if I don't have a garden this year?

Lunch had consisted of smoked trout salad, the most marvelous sourdough rolls, unsweetened iced tea, and a small lemon bar. Serena was celebrating because the detective had found Clarissa.

What was even more amazing was that Clarissa still lived in Hopewellen, as she had years ago. She had her phone number and the detective had even located Clarissa's street on a map he gave her.

Now all she had to do was call her daughter.

My little Pearl.

Of course actually placing the call would be another matter altogether. But Serena didn't want to think about that right now. She wanted to take a page from Morgan's book and try to be positive.

Who knows?

Maybe Clarissa actually wants to see me.

~ ~ ~

The lightning, which flashed brightly enough to startle Morgan, was followed by a clap of thunder so loud she nearly dropped the glass she was returning to the kitchen sink.

Serena was at a department meeting and Jake was at the movies. She'd enjoyed watching the boiling clouds rolling in before sunset. Anticipating a good thunderstorm, she'd curled up in the living room with a sexy novel and a cup of tea. But when the storm got wild, she decided to head for her bedroom with a candle in case she lost her lights.

The power went out before she had a chance to follow through on her plan.

What a night to be alone in the house.

She was unsuccessfully fumbling for candles and matches when the phone rang.

It was Rex.

Nothing like a call from the ex-husband when the shit hits the fan.

He began the conversation by meandering through a litany of trivialities the way he always did when he had bad news.

"Rex, I'm standing here in the dark in the middle of an electrical storm. Please. Cut to the chase."

"Don't you have any candles?"

"Rex, please." She was trembling.

Has something happened to Ian?

"Okay. Well, Ian—"

There was a loud crackling on the line as another bolt of lightning hit.

"I didn't hear you. What's wrong with Ian?"

"Morgan, don't be so impatient."

"Just tell me."

There was more static on the line.

"Rex!"

"Okay, okay. Ian needs surgery."

"My god! What happened? Has he been hurt?"

The line went dead.

She panicked, trying again and again to get a dial tone. Finally, she placed the handset back in its cradle and placed both hands on top of it, willing Rex to call.

She stared into the blackness of the night, dimly aware of trees tossing wildly.

But what she saw most vividly was a kaleidoscope of images of her baby. Ian as a newborn, pink in her arms, his scent the sweetest perfume she'd ever known. Ian taking his first steps, giddy triumph in his eyes. Tears filling those eyes years later when the playground bully called him a wimp. Ian pitching a no-hitter against that same playground bully. Her baby bent over a school project, squeezing his pencil tightly the way he had since the first time he held one, in spite of her constant reminders.

Don't let him be hurt.

Please, please don't let him be hurt.

For the first time since before Sierra was born, Morgan fervently longed for a cigarette.

Is a hurricane coming?

She hadn't seen the news in days, but she knew from experience—that horrific Fran disaster—this storm could be trouble.

The phone rang so loudly Morgan jumped. It crashed to the floor and she groped for the receiver.

"That must be quite a storm you're having."

"Tell me about Ian."

"He needs surgery."

"You told me that. Was he in an accident?"

"No, nothing like that. Remember the hydrocele the doctors warned us to keep an eye on? He has a hernia. They have to go in and fix it. It's no big deal, really."

"Any surgery is a big deal, Rex. Will he need anesthesia?"

"Of course."

"When is it?"

"Tomorrow."

"Tomorrow! I'll be on the first plane."

"It doesn't sound as if the planes are flying, Morgan."

"I'll get to the airport somehow and wait, then. Tell my baby I'll be there as soon as I can."

"That's just it. He doesn't want you to come."

She felt as if someone had uprooted a tree, picked it up, and swung it into her chest like a baseball bat.

"What do you mean, he doesn't want me to come? I'm his mother! You might not want me to come, but I'm sure Ian does."

"Morgan, relax. The doctor assured us this surgery is very simple."

"Doctors always say that. They figure if you're not dead, you're fine. Did you talk to any nurses?"

She could barely hear him. "The point is, I think Ian's clinging to what the doctor said."

"I'm his mother. I have a right—and an obligation—to be there."

"Morgan, he can barely tolerate my being there. It's his age, you know? He doesn't want to feel like a little boy. He'll be more frightened if we're both there hovering over him. I think—"

The line went dead. This time there was no reviving it.

Was Rex's tone condescending, or was she making that up? In some subtle way, was he telling her she was a bad mother? Was he saying she had doted on Ian too much and now he was afraid of surgery because of her?

Her psyche exploded and scattered across the kitchen floor like shards of glass. Every cell in her body wanted to hold her baby, to stroke him, to mop and kiss his brow. But she was trapped in Hopewellen by this hideous storm and Ian's adolescent need to enact his superhero fantasy of manhood.

An intense ripping sound—painful to hear—tore through her consciousness. The uprooting tree crashed into something, branches snapping. It hit the earth with a force that shook the floor and shivered up her legs.

The grandmother oak, the one nearest the willow, had come down.

She couldn't drive in this.

Given how hard the rain had been falling—on top of all the rain the previous week—the ground was saturated. There would be flooding on every road between her and the airport.

If only she'd been able to speak with Ian herself, so she could read in his voice what he was feeling.

Was he in pain?

Why was the surgery tomorrow?

Was it an emergency?

Or had they known before but not told her?

But that couldn't be. She'd talked to him on the phone a few days ago and he hadn't mentioned a thing.

It was very dark, with no lights on in the neighborhood and the storm still raging. Nonetheless she could see the sinister, glowing outline of an all too familiar figure.

Shadow.

This time he hadn't bothered to disguise himself as the dandy. He had reptilian legs, a dozen flailing arms, a cockroach's torso, and a throbbing, pimpled head.

He'd set this up and was assaulting her in the one place she was vulnerable.

My children.

Shadow's grin exposed a roladex of shark's teeth. He lumbered slowly behind her and stepped into an energetic doorway to her spine, her center, as easily as if he were entering a revolving door at the bank.

This time, she couldn't get him out.

~ ~ ~

"I'm sorry I couldn't get back last night. I was trapped by flooding. I tried to call you, but the lines were dead. Were you all right?" Jake said.

It was early morning and Morgan was cleaning the kitchen cabinets, which seemed odd. She didn't turn to face him, but he could tell something wasn't right. Her body radiated tension.

"Fine. What's that?"

"A bearded collie." He glanced down at the wriggling, shaggy, gray and white bundle in his arms. "I thought—"

"How old?"

"Six weeks."

"That's nice. It'll be a good companion for you. I don't mind, as long as I don't have to take care of it and it doesn't wreck the place."

"What's wrong, Sugar?" He moved close and put his hand on her shoulder.

"It's Ian. He's having surgery today."

I should have been here.

"I finally got through to him this morning. Everyone's saying it's no big deal. He sprouted a hernia yesterday. The surgeon had a last-minute opening for this morning and offered to get him out of his pain."

Morgan's eyes filled with tears. "He doesn't want to be fussed over, so he doesn't want me to come."

Jake put his free arm around her. "It's a guy thing. He wants to go off to his cave and lick his wounds until he's all better."

"That's not how I raised him."

"I know. But it's a phase he has to go through. Think about all that surging testosterone he's learning to cope with."

She smiled weakly through her tears. "Sometimes testosterone has its good points." She gave him a little pat in the crotch.

But he could tell she didn't want to be fussed with either, so he left her alone and took the puppy upstairs. It was supposed to be a surprise gift for her. But he should have asked her first if she wanted it.

Now what am I going to do?

Serena's door was open. She was at her computer, clicking away on the Internet. Her hair was a knot of pencils and she had on a pair of outrageously short cutoffs and a tee shirt.

What if this pup was actually meant for Serena?

He leaned his head in the door, keeping the puppy out of sight, though Virginia Woof was onto him. She was sniffing the air and grinning.

"Busy?" he said.

"Yes." She spoke without looking up, then caught herself and grinned. "I mean, come in."

He seated himself on the edge of Grandmama's canopy bed, next to her chair.

"Cute puppy." She took the wriggling ball from Jake and ruffled its fur while Woof sniffed and licked it. "Where are your eyes?" she said, drawing back the fluff until she found its bright baby blues. The pup licked her hand.

"Good boy!" he said.

"Boy? Don't you know females of any species make better pets?"

"Why is that?" He laughed.

Serena paused, apparently trying to remember.

"I'll help you," he said. "Females are easier to *control.*"

She pretended to wince.

"What are you up to?" he said.

"Research. It's fascinating. You know how Morgan is always talking about how people need to get into their hearts and go for the love, the connection, the dreams, and all that?"

Jake chuckled. "Sure."

"It turns out she's right. I'm finding studies and clinical documentation supporting her theories. You can generate thoughts, feelings, and meditative states that actually change your own physiology and even those of the people around you. It's amazing! You can cure yourself of disease, increase your physical abilities, raise your intelligence, and change your future. You can affect all kinds of physical, mental, and emotional problems by creating—get this!—*new physical pathways in your brain* through any number of techniques. It's all been proven! It's like Shoots and Ladders, or Parcheesi."

She was sawing the air with her forefingers. "You know. The games, how you can make these shortcuts. Morgan says it can be a bit of a slog job to actually reroute the brain, but it works."

Serena tossed the puppy on the floor, jumped up, and shook Jake's shoulders. "Are you getting this? You can change *yourself* by changing your thoughts. I can be whoever I want! So can you! Isn't that fabulous? Did you know that love—"

"Hang on. Can you keep the puppy for a minute?"

"Sure."

He was back with his second load in no time. Serena was on the floor wrestling with the puppy. Woof was wagging her tail and licking both of them.

He had brought two bowls for water and food, a bag of puppy kibble, chew toys, dog biscuits, a crate, paper towels, a stack of newspapers, and a book on housebreaking and training.

"He's for you," Jake put down his load and set up the crate.

"No."

"Yes. He'll help you with your research."

~ ~ ~

"Ooshi," Clarissa said, giving Morgan a sheepish hug and taking her usual seat on the couch.

"What does that mean?" Morgan settled herself uneasily in her chair.

Am I a human yo-yo?

She felt like one sometimes, with these clients turning her on and off like a television. Actually it was more degrading, like prostitution. She put out her best, the finest her human heart had to offer, and they picked her up and dumped her at their whim.

Back in the days when she worked for other people, several supervisors told her she put too much heart in her work. It was dangerous, they told her. It was why so many therapists committed suicide. But no way would she listen to people's most intimate vulnerabilities and not bring her heart to the encounter.

Maybe it was her fault. What if she had her clients sign contracts committing themselves to talk about it first when they wanted to go? But she doubted that would make any difference. She always discussed the best way to end therapy in the beginning of the work. But when clients went into crisis, they managed to forget these things.

They love their drama more than they love themselves.

She was sick of it. She wondered why she kept this job. She had invested her inheritance from Grandmama well and could conceivably quit, if she were willing to pull in her belt. But then there was Ian's college.

Ian.

His surgery would be over by now.

He was in recovery.

She'd decided to maintain her schedule to keep herself from focusing on him. But she didn't want to let her helplessness over Ian's surgery affect her feelings about Clarissa.

"I'm sorry. *'Ooshi'* means 'brrrrr' in Cherokee. But I have no right to complain. I'm just glad you agreed to see me after that awful message I left you last week. I apologize. I got so caught up in my feelings, I panicked."

"Everyone seems to think I run the A.C. too high."

"Are you mad at me?"

"Not mad. Irritated. I felt sad your funding fell through. And hurt and a little used because you dropped our work over the phone instead of coming in to talk about it as we'd agreed. Then as soon as you needed help, you called me. You took me for granted and I don't like that. But if my face looks somber, it's because my son had surgery this morning.

"I'm sorry. Is he okay?"

"As far as I know. What's up?"

"I wish I could tell you I'm here because I thought better of the way I left. I was getting there, but then I got a call about something I need your help with."

"Clarissa, I don't want to work with you on whatever you came here for unless you agree to schedule a session for closure after this one."

"I understand. Is it all right if I reaffirm my commitment that when I want to stop seeing you, I'll talk to you about it in a session? I don't want to stop right now. Not after the phone call I got."

"Okay."

"Really?"

"Really."

Who cares? is more like it.

I have problems of my own, and I won't let you be one of them.

She was shocked by her reaction. Ian's surgery was coloring her emotions red, black, and gray. And there was something else, something sinister she was pushing away from her consciousness.

You're at work now.

You love this woman.

So put your little girl in her safe bubble, yourself in yours, the larger one around both of you, and get with it.

This is not about you.

Clarissa's up to her eyeballs in her own stuff, that's all.

"Thanks," Clarissa said. "Out of the blue, I got a call from a friend of my mother's. She wants to see me. The friend, I mean. The friend wants to see me."

"Geez. Why didn't your mother call you herself?"

"I don't know."

"How do you feel about it?"

"Mixed. Very, very mixed."

"I bet you do." Morgan's felt her heart beginning to warm. This was a big step for Clarissa. "What do you want to do?"

"I know this is a lot to ask after what I pulled, but I want to meet with my mother's friend in a session with you."

"That would be fine. When?"

"Soon. My mother must be loaded. Loaded and wacko. Get this—her friend told me to ask you if she can 'purchase,' as she put it, an entire day of your time so we can talk, then break and get back together if we need to. What do you think?"

Weird.

Why does Clarissa's mother want someone else to spend a day telling Clarissa something she can't tell her herself?

"I think it's strange," Morgan said. "But it could be very effective. I'm game. What else is on your mind?"

"I can't bring myself to call off the event. You know, 'Dump the Dump.'"

"That's what you're calling it?"

"Yeah. 'Dump the Dump: Mothers and Others for a Living Earth.'"

"I like it."

"Thanks. Anyhow, I keep moving forward—going back to the neighborhood over and over, rehearsing acts, drumming up community interest in so many ways. Why am I doing all this, even though I know it's impossible to proceed?"

"I wouldn't be too quick to judge what is and isn't possible."

What's the matter with me?

This is an opportunity to punch home the points we've discussed about manifesting and trust.

But I don't have it in me.

Morgan felt Shadow tighten his grip on her spine ever so slightly but she was too emotionally exhausted to care. He'd been inside her all night.

She'd done all the right things anyway. Most of them, at least. Following Brigid's suggestions, she'd visualized Ian's guides and angels going to the hospital ahead of him, first to arrange for the best in staffing and conditions and then to meet with the surgeon's and anesthesiologist's guides and angels to coordinate the surgery.

She'd asked for protection for Ian, visualized the surgery and recovery going easily and well, and prayed that all these things come to pass provided they were for Ian's highest good and the highest good of all. And to her credit, she hadn't tried to get Jake to rescue her when he found her cleaning cupboards this morning.

But what she hadn't done, in spite of Brigid's insistent urgings, was to get Shadow out of her spine.

I'm tired of clearing myself.

I don't have the energy or the heart.

This was a day when all she could do was show up, recite the party line, and intend for the best.

"What do you mean about not being too quick to judge what is and isn't possible?" Clarissa said.

Morgan forced herself back to the present.

"Anything is possible. You manifested your mother, didn't you?"

~ ~ ~

Serena never tired of watching the dynamic between her dogs.

Beacon, her puppy, was growling at Woof. His rear end was poised high in the air, tail wagging, and his front legs were on the floor in the universal canine challenge to play. Fortunately, Beacon was so small he was able to amuse himself by running over and around the older dog, so Woof didn't have to do much to keep him happy. Woof was lying down with her head on the floor, peering up at Serena, wagging her tail, and grinning.

She was piling books into the two floor-to-ceiling oak bookcases that had arrived this morning along with a computer desk and chair, a fabulous high-speed computer she discovered on the Internet, and two large lamps. The room was becoming a pleasant combination of her and Grandmama.

Jane had stopped by earlier. A professor at the university who was scheduled to teach two fall courses in women's studies had to leave town indefinitely on a family matter. It was too late to conduct a search to replace her. Jane wanted to know if she'd be willing to take over the courses. With her experience, she was guaranteed the position if she wanted it.

She had accepted. In her mind, she was already delivering her first lecture.

It had been a good day. A very, very good day.

Suddenly she heard a sound in Morgan's room.

But isn't Morgan at work?

She crept quietly down the hall, peered into Morgan's room and saw something unbelievable.

Jake was twirling in front of the mirror.

In a dress!

He had on one of Morgan's longer, looser garments—a crepey, broomstick style. The sleeves hit Morgan at the elbow, but on Jake the dress was short-sleeved.

"What are you doing?" Serena felt as if she were shrieking. But she must not have been because he turned calmly to face her.

"I'm exploring my feminine side," he said.

"Oh my goddess."

"Are you into the goddess too?" He was grinning. "I should have known, with that Eve/Lilith thing." He winked. "Happy Lammas. Hey, do you want to go to the feast tonight? We could bake some goddess loaves this afternoon. Or maybe we should stay home and make sure Morgan is okay."

"She wouldn't want that. I already spoke to her about doing something together but she said she needs some space. What's Lammas? You're not inviting me to some frat boy thing, are you?"

He laughed hard. "Lammas, Lughnasadh, you know. The pagan harvest festival halfway between the summer solstice and the fall equinox.

Pagan festival?

Is Jake down to his last marble?

Oh well.

"Sure, I'll go."

What the heck.

These are the "try-anything" days.

Serena stared at Jake in Morgan's dress, allowing the sight to wash through her, rearranging her cells.

"What's the matter?" he said.

"I'm believe I'm having an epiphany."

"Describe it."

"That's just it. I can't."

"You? Speechless?"

"Yeah."

❧ ❧ ❧

"Come on, Clarissa," Joshua said. "Everybody has to take a break sometime." His grin spread over his whole face before spilling into a warm, rolling laugh that rippled through Clarissa's muscles, bringing the pleasurable sensation of sweating to the rhythms of an outdoor dance band in the dark thickness of night.

Joshua had the easy confidence, gentle insistence, and sensual humor that had always attracted her to black men.

They'd been poring over potential funding sources and he'd agreed to make the contacts himself. Before that, they spent some time choreographing the event. Joshua had been organizing their fellow teachers and his other contacts into work teams. It was exactly what she needed, someone in the number two position to bring the details together.

"Dump the Dump" was beginning to seem doable.

After hours of work, Joshua surprised the boys with a ride for each of them on a bicycle for two he had rented. Now he wanted Clarissa to try.

"Let's go for a ride," he said. "Frankie and Martin can take care of themselves for a little while, can't you boys?"

"I don't think that's a good—"

"Don't do me that way! Let's go."

"Can we watch a video, Mom?"

"Oh, all right," Clarissa said, then whispered to him, "you get to buy me a strawberry cream soda."

"That's good!" He grinned at her. "That's real good."

~ ~ ~

Half her clients were on vacation, so Morgan didn't have any late afternoon appointments. She stretched back on her bed with a cool washcloth over her forehead and eyes.

Her temples were throbbing. The blinds were shut tight and the ceiling fan was whirling quietly.

Jake and Serena were in the kitchen making goddess bread, whatever that was. She'd told them she wanted to rest. Jake shot her a concerned look, then wisely pulled back and immersed himself in their project.

Good boy.

Before she left her office, she had managed to speak to Ian. He was still groggy from the anesthesia but was waking up to the reality that there was more to surgery than he'd anticipated.

He was going back to Rex's that evening. She and Rex decided Ian would call her the next day, Saturday, when he was awake. She gave Rex a lecture about the importance of good nutrition after surgery—which she was sure he didn't appreciate. She wanted to do something for Ian so much it hurt.

"Brigid, where are you?" Morgan whispered.

"Here, Luv."

"I don't understand what's going on."

"That's just it, isn't it?" Brigid said. "The worry. I've been as lost in that mist-laden bog as you have, and there's the truth of it. With your troubles with Ian, all I can think of is my own wee babes. Poor Flidias and Skatha, adrift and alone when I died. Motherless, they were, like your Clarissa. Today I tried to lift the veil between the worlds to find out what happened to them. When I did, I saw my girls taken into servitude by the Scots. Then I saw my beloved Seamus and the other men of our tribe tossing the daughters of the Council over the high cliffs and into the sea to break the curse of our drowning. Next I saw the whole tribe slaughtered, and my wee ones in the thick of it. It took all that to see that none of it was real and Shadow was simply having his own good time tormenting me."

Morgan wished she hadn't heard Brigid. It only made her head hurt more. They fell silent.

Suddenly Morgan sat bolt upright and threw off her washcloth, which hit the floor with a soft plop.

"Don't you see, Brigid? This is how he manipulates us. We have children to protect, so we don't stand up to him the way we would if we were alone." Morgan was up and pacing now. "And when we're not worrying about our children, we're fretting about whether our mothering is good enough. Being mothers keeps us small."

Her headache had miraculously disappeared. "Brigid, somehow we have to let go."

"But we're responsible," Brigid said. "How can we let go of their wee hands?"

"Maybe we have to loosen our stranglehold on their little hands enough to open up to the big picture. Maybe it's more about respect for their destinies and our own."

Morgan was crisscrossing the huge bedroom with long strides. "Our children have lessons too, even when they're small. I know I did. Our children's souls are as ancient and immortal as our own. I'm not saying we don't protect them."

"No. You're saying we can't let our motherhood hold us hostage."

"Exactly. We have to play big in spite of our kids. Because of our kids."

She thought of Clarissa, how she took her children canvassing to protect their future. "We have to look beyond our babies' sweet heads until we can see the impact of what we do on our grandchildren's grandchildren. Our actions shape the world." Morgan stopped and raised her arms as if supporting an enormous globe, then continued to pace. "I used to think being a mother to my children was the most important job there is," Morgan said. "I no longer think that. There's a much bigger job of mothering to do, one that begins with the self and reaches out to heal our species and embrace all of creation."

She checked her spine. Shadow was no longer there. She missed him, not because she wanted him back but because she almost wanted to thank him. She'd learned something from this round, as she had from all the others.

Just then Beacon pushed the door open and scampered into the room. He was running full-tilt, his little torso on the bias, his tail wagging furiously. He went straight for the washcloth she had thrown on the floor and shook it furiously, growling happily. Then he plopped down on the floor, held one end of the washcloth between his paws, and began to tear at it. She took the washcloth from him and scooped him up.

Serena and Jake poked their heads in the door of her room. She accepted puppy kisses from Beacon while they proudly displayed funny little loaves of bread shaped like great, fat, laughing women. Morgan and Beacon followed them downstairs, where Sierra and Aunt Lee showed up practically at the same time.

"Give me some sugar." Aunt Lee patted Morgan's face and leaned in for a kiss.

She was there to borrow a light bulb from her Peach Blossom, drop off pimento cheese sandwiches left over from some church function, and praise the Lord. Her rhinestone pin twinkled, "Jesus Saves."

Morgan thanked Aunt Lee for the sandwiches. She didn't tell her she thought it might be prudent to discard mayonnaise sandwiches that had been left out in August.

Sierra rubbed her belly and whispered to her mother, "At this point, I need saving. Don't tell Aunt Lee."

"What's the matter, Honey? You're not loving this last trimester?"

"It's rough."

"Are the body pillows I got helping you sleep?"

"They make it easier, Mom. Thanks. But they're not enough."

"I'm sorry. Get as much rest as you can, any way you can."

"I'm trying."

After everyone else left, Morgan and Sierra decided to override Rex's suggestion to wait until tomorrow to call Ian, who was high on pain pills and revealed more to his sister and mother than he normally would have about how the sight of the new girl in Rex's neighborhood affected his teenage male anatomy.

Morgan felt enormously comforted. If he could think those thoughts—the day of surgery so close to the area in question—he was going to be just fine.

That night, Morgan slept like a baby. She dreamed she was an enormous grandmother whale—giving birth to her species and filling her life with purpose, sensuality, and joy—her eye firmly on the big picture while she rolled easily on the waves that were her life.

Her dream was peaceful except when Clarissa splashed by, frantically searching the sea for her mother.

CHAPTER 18

reflection

Sometimes to be alone
is the most natural
called for,
difficult place to be.

Sometimes to be wise
is to follow the most natural
called for,
difficult thing to do.

To be alone and wise
is a gift that comes
from the most natural
called for
difficult birthing of Self.

—Marguerite Estanalehi Bartley

"How are you?" Morgan invited Clarissa to sit by gesturing toward her normal spot on the couch.

But Clarissa couldn't sit.

Not yet.

It was The Day.

In fifteen minutes, her mother's friend was supposed to show up.

"I feel like throwing up. I could melt between the cracks in the floor. If it weren't so *ooshi* in here."

"Do you want me to make it warmer?"

"No. Then I *would* throw up. And sweat. I don't want to embarrass myself in front of my mother's friend." She paced, avoiding the windows.

She didn't want to be caught scanning the parking lot like an orphan at Christmas with her nose pressed against the glass. Even though she felt like one.

"Take some long, deep breaths. You're going to be fine. Pull energy up from the earth and into your belly through your feet."

Clarissa smiled, comforted by how much Morgan reminded her of Big Mom. As she breathed, she felt herself gently restored to balance.

"What are you feeling now?" Morgan said. She was wearing a calf-length dress, more close-fitting than her usual, with swirling patterns of gold, rust, lemon, and orange with highlights of fuchsia and accents of brown. With her new red hair, she looked vibrant and contemporary.

Clarissa glanced down at her own hands. She was wearing a silver bracelet that she'd had made to feature a large piece of turquoise her father had given her long ago. It was one of two pieces he'd had since childhood. Twins, he called them. He'd given the other piece to her mother the summer they were together. She wore her turquoise today to feel supported by of the one parent she'd known, however briefly, before alcohol claimed him.

She fingered the stone, reassured that her hands were neat and manicured and her simple black shift flattered her slim figure. Now that she was ready to move toward the woman who left her, it was important she look her best.

"I feel less nervous. Still, something's churning," Clarissa said.

"Excitement?"

She felt around inside herself, then laughed. "Yes, I feel excited."

"That's wonderful. How's the rest of your life?"

She felt herself deflating, like a balloon with a slow leak that was losing its sheen and becoming flaccid and rubbery. "Don't ask."

"Why?"

"Because wouldn't you think I'd have given up on this stupid event by now? I can't proceed without jeopardizing my children's education, yet I won't stop. I'm too stubborn to give up and too hopeless to continue."

"You? Hopeless? I don't think so. I asked you because it might help to remember you have a life to go back to that's yours—a bold, vivid life—no matter what happens here today."

Clarissa smiled from the inside, a smile that grew deeper and broader until it suddenly died when there was a sharp knock on the door. She jumped up and Morgan rose slowly to her feet, stepping ahead of her to answer the door.

~ ~ ~

"You'll be okay," Morgan said quietly. She embraced Clarissa, then pulled back and looked her in the eye. "Stay in your feet and breathe. Remember who you are."

Morgan cautioned herself to do the same thing. For days she'd been increasingly tired and frail. She'd thought she got him out, but Shadow had been subtly working on her spine in the week since Ian's surgery, entering and leaving her body at will.

Though she worked hard to get rid of him, the effort was exhausting and tedious. Sometimes she ignored him so she could enjoy some semblance of normal life, but he only used those times to strengthen his grip on her. He'd worn her down so much she had to budget her energy. It was as if she were allotted only a handful of vitality each day and had to plan how and when to parcel it out.

She reminded herself to let Clarissa and her mother's friend do the work. All she needed to do was remain calm, relaxed, and at the helm, expending only the energy necessary to keep the ship on course. She envisioned a sleek yacht—one that could be efficiently navigated through the choppiest waters with one finger on the wheel—and opened the door.

Morgan's stomach did a full turn, as when a nearly ripe baby flips over in utero.

The woman on the other side of her threshold was Serena.

Serena clapped her hand over her mouth. "Oh my god, Morgan, I didn't know it was you, I swear I didn't!" She was clutching a piece of paper. "All I had is the address!"

"You two know each other?"

She heard Clarissa speaking from far off in the distance, her words barely distinguishable.

How can I conduct a session between my client and my friend?

Impossible!

How was she going to maintain therapeutic boundaries with Clarissa, run this session in an appropriately detached, professional manner, and honor her friendship with Serena?

No matter what happened from this moment on, her professional relationship with Clarissa was compromised.

It was a double bind and very, very messy.

At least Serena isn't the mother.

This might work if it's only one session.

Morgan's breath caught in her throat.

Holy shit.

She'd better not be the mother.

Naw, she can't be.

Can't, can't, can't.

Can't be.

"Morgan?" Clarissa said again.

Rein it in.

This isn't about me.

"I'm sorry. Yes, Clarissa, this is Serena, an old friend who's living in my home. She's the one I visited in the mountains. Come in, Serena. We need to decide where to go from here."

It was confusing at first, but they opted to go ahead with the session. Clarissa needed to proceed as planned. They all agreed it was better to carry on than to find another therapist and postpone.

Serena looked emotional, yet strong.

Clarissa's eyes were brimming.

Morgan was rattled. Still, it was better to get on with it.

Serena plunked a stack of bills on Morgan's desk and threw herself on the couch.

~ ~ ~

This Serena wears more turquoise than a Wannabe Indian at a powwow.

I don't understand u-neg.

Clarissa settled herself on the couch—as far as she could from Serena—in a manner she intended to be prim and collected.

So why all the jewelry?

She sure is a skinny little thing.

And why is she wearing jeans?

So inappropriate.

So disrespectful.

Is that yet another way of dissing me?

I can't imagine my mother having a friend who's such a slob.

At least she ironed that stupid denim shirt.

"Where shall we begin?" Morgan said.

"I want to ask some questions." Clarissa turned to Serena. "Why did my mother send you, instead of coming herself?"

Serena looked startled.

She thinks I'm too abrupt.

Why is she staring at me like that?

She probably figures I'm an Indian, so I'll be as passive as I was on the phone.

Guess again.

You're on my turf now, Baby.

And I'm ready for you.

Serena took a long breath before speaking. "One reason your mother sent me is so you don't have to deal with her unless you want to. You can ask about her and take whatever time you need to decide if you want to meet her."

Serena's eyes were clear, a blue both brilliant and silvery. It seemed odd to see such vibrant color in the face of an older woman. There was strength there, but she was holding something back.

"You said one reason," Clarissa said. "Tell me another."

"Your mother is a very wealthy woman."

Morgan dropped her note pad and excused herself for interrupting while she picked it up.

Serena glanced at Morgan almost sternly. "Years ago, she set up a substantial trust in your name that would become available to you when Big Mom died."

"You know Big Mom?"

Serena shifted. "Your mother does. She kept in touch with her until her death and sent money from the trust when either of you needed anything. Now that Big Mom is gone, your mother wants you to have control of that money."

This was incredible. Was she to remain motherless—and grandmotherless—and have some kind of meaningless fortune to contend with?

I don't need a trust fund.

I need a mother.

"Is there any other reason she didn't come herself?" Clarissa said.

"Frankly, she was… ." Serena paused. "She was afraid."

"Of little old me?" Clarissa batted her eyes.

Serena recoiled, obviously registering the racial overtones in her question. "She's an emotional woman, Clarissa. She didn't want to overwhelm you with her own feelings when you're bound to have so many of your own."

Serena's mouth twitched. "Your mother knows you have every right to reject her. But that doesn't make it easy for her to face the possibility. She's afraid of her own cowardice, which has kept you apart needlessly in the years of your adulthood."

My adulthood?

How about my childhood?

"She's afraid you might have needed her and she wasn't there," Serena's eyes fluttered and her breathing was rapid and shallow.

My mother is emotional?

Big whoop.

This "Serena" is pretty emotional herself.

"When we spoke on the phone, you told me my mother refers to me as 'her pearl.' Why does she call me that? Does she know my skin is so light?"

She was good and angry now.

Being with this Serena person was much more difficult than she thought it would be. She tried to remember what Morgan had taught her, that there was hurt beneath her anger. Maybe so, but this time she couldn't stave off the anger. She was staring straight into all the layers of her mother's rejection.

The fact that her mother had discussed her with Serena and that Serena knew all about her mother made her feel even more peripheral, more alone.

"She calls you her Pearl," Serena said, drawing a jagged breath, "because to her, you're rare and beautiful and apart from her, like a gem locked in a shell she can't open."

Clarissa looked down at her hands so Serena wouldn't see the tears she was fighting. She tried to breathe, to be in her feet. Morgan wasn't coaching her.

She's letting me handle it.

Good.

I don't want to show this Serena anything.

She'll tell my mother.

And if my mother wants to know me, she can damn well find the guts to get here, as I did.

But on the other hand, what the fuck?

Clarissa raised her head, squared her shoulders, and looked Serena straight in the eye.

"Does my mother want to see me?"

That was it, the question beneath the questions. Was the real reason her mother sent Serena because she didn't want to come herself?

"She wants to see you more than she wants to breathe." Serena's eyes were shimmering. "She doesn't want to push you, that's all."

"There is no reason for you and I to pursue this, then. I want to see my mother."

"When?" Serena said.

"The sooner the better. Yesterday. Now."

"Now would be good." Serena's whole body was shaking with emotion. She sobbed briefly then caught herself, reached for a tissue, and blew her nose loudly. It was a honking sound.

Disgusting.

Serena wiped her eyes and faced Clarissa.

"I'm your mother, Clarissa. And I am so very, very sorry for all the pain I've caused you."

~ ~ ~

"Great balls of fire!" Grandmama said, then clapped her hand over her mouth.

"Did you know Clarissa's mum was Morgan's friend?" Brigid asked Big Mom. She could scarcely believe what she was hearing.

"I felt it, but it was hidden," Big Mom said. "This meeting could change a lot for my *Nunda.*"

"Or it could break her." Shadow appeared from nowhere, his breath even more foul than usual.

He was playing the dandy again, sliding his fingers lightly along the brim of his top hat. "Can you see the little bitch going forward with her stupid 'event' now that she has this crisis to get oh-so-dramatic about?"

Shadow rolled his eyes and hypnotically compelled Brigid into a slow waltz. "And of course her Mountain Mama might as well commit suicide here and now and get it over with. She's her own train wreck."

"He thinks he's Fred Astaire," Grandmama said, her nose in the air.

Shadow released Brigid, grinned wickedly, produced a cane, and broke into a tap dance.

"You unholy bastard!" Brigid said. "We'll show you what strong women can do."

"Set your sights low," Shadow said. We wouldn't want you girls to be disappointed now, would we?" He shot a flame from his mouth that singed her nose.

~ ~ ~

Clarissa wanted to slap this woman across the face as hard as she could—to beat her, to pummel her into the couch, to make her disappear. Her desire to run out the door of Morgan Forrester's office and never come back was overwhelming.

Through her tears, her mother was a shimmering sliver of blue beside her on the couch.

She lied to me about who she is.

Then she has the gall to tell me she's my mother.

No preamble.

Nothing.

Clarissa blinked hard and looked at Morgan.

"It's all right," Morgan said. "Breathe, Clarissa." Morgan touched Clarissa's hand.

The contact was too much. Clarissa jumped up and ran toward the door.

I'm getting out of here before I deck both of them.

She hated herself for every step she took but she couldn't stop herself. She couldn't breathe. She had to get away.

"Take a break," her mother called after her. "I'll be here for you. Come back when you're ready. I'll wait!"

~ ~ ~

"Ta da!" With great flourish, Shadow swept his cane toward the still-open door. He tap danced toward the window with tiny, mincing steps and mimicked Clarissa's run toward her car, prancing across the back of the couch with his white-gloved fingers. Then he tucked his cane under one arm, bowed, and gestured with both hands toward Serena, who remained on the couch, her head buried in her hands.

"Such a pity," he said, grinning at Big Mom, Grandmama, and Brigid. "I believe the term is, 'major meltdown.' Ba da bing, ba da boom." He danced swiftly around the room on tiptoe and disappeared.

~ ~ ~

Morgan was on the veranda sipping sweet tea and absently swinging on the glider. The air was still and hot but the humidity had let up some so—if she exerted no energy whatsoever—she didn't sweat and it was tolerable to be outside.

She and Serena had waited all afternoon, but Clarissa never returned. They agreed to not discuss what happened until they could—hopefully—set another appointment.

Her heart ached for Clarissa, alone in her pain, and for Serena, who'd finally reached out only to experience the rejection she most feared. And Morgan wasn't sure that in her weakened state she'd been a great buffer between nitro and glycerin.

But when she'd discovered Serena on the other side of her door that morning, her handful of vitality—the one she'd needed to parcel out in careful measures over the course of the day—had scattered like a flock of startled birds. Every thought, emotion, and movement since then had drained reserves she couldn't spare, as if each ticking second robbed her of a thimbleful of herself.

Now it was evening, and all she wanted was to be alone. She was more exhausted than ever and Shadow had taken up what felt like permanent residence in more than half her body.

Eventually, Clarissa and Serena would be fine. They were both survivors. But was she, now that Shadow had her in his grasp? Restlessness brewed in her belly and nausea gripped her throat.

Morgan's eyes filled but didn't spill. The scene before her—the trees, the flowers, the well-manicured lawn—shimmered behind the pool in her eyes. A great sadness exploded in her head, then crashed down her torso like a rock slide of boulders that bruised her heart before landing hard in her belly.

Her task was too great. How could she, in her inexperience and ignorance, take on Shadow and his endless armies? And what was her true path, anyway? She felt farther away than ever from the answer to that question. Worse, she'd used her one opportunity to find her calling—a summer alone—to fill her house and heart with everyone else's crises.

What have I got to show for six weeks of what was supposed to be a retreat, a time of soul-searching and solitude?

> *—a rehabilitation center for lost academic mountaineers*

—*a sex camp for adolescent lovers*
—*a zoo startup project*
—*a ghostbuster's boot camp and halfway house for wayward entities*
—*a staging area for the mother/daughter estrangement society.*

Others might think these were significant accomplishments. But were they what she wanted?

What am I doing for myself?

Abso-fucking-lutely zip.

It had all been very theatrical—discovering Brigid, becoming the hundredth woman, battling Shadow, being lovers with Jake, and bringing Jake, Serena, Woof—and now Beacon—into her household. She had traded the drama of searching for her one great love for the drama of being the hundredth woman.

But where was she in all this? Except when she was helping someone else, it was as difficult for her to hear her inner promptings as it had been when she was in love with a man.

She was taking better care of herself, true. She'd been able to act fearlessly—even boldly—with Shadow. And she was learning how to tap into profound spiritual truths she could share with others in a way that seemed to help them.

Yet she didn't know who she was.

Besides if she was, indeed, the hundredth woman, hadn't she better find out what that meant? But wasn't it even more important to feel her own path underfoot—instead of constantly responding to calls from outside herself?

Morgan sensed a quiet, reassuring hand on her shoulder. It was Brigid. The touch reminded her to shift out of her restlessness and seek a deeper truth. She drew a full breath, closed her eyes, connected with the earth and the heavens, and opened her heart to Spirit.

It came to her that if it was the task of women to lead humanity into greater harmony, then the buildup to that shift would surely be one of increased polarity, broader swings of the pendulum, and greater emotional extremes. Her turmoil was natural. She was falling apart, like the caterpillar in the cocoon before it emerges as a butterfly.

And she was, after all, like Chiron—a wounded healer. It was her gift and her challenge.

But does Chiron know what to do with himself when the wounds heal?

The emotional weights that had pulled her down for a lifetime had eased, the tasks of motherhood were diminishing, her career was rolling along, and she was no longer hungry for a man to fill her up.

She had space.

The question is, what am I going to do with it?

She didn't know who she was because she had always waited for something outside herself—a baby, a man, a responsibility—to define her. Now she needed to discover who she was *for herself.*

The headline would read, *Wounded Healer Seeks the Real Her so that Shadow Cannot Steal Her.*

She sensed Brigid again, waiting for her to get something. Simultaneously, a mourning dove landed on the veranda railing and looked straight at her.

That's it!

I don't need to find out who I am and what I "should" be doing, as if I'm someone else's creation and my only job is to unveil some faceless master's work.

No.

I need to listen to my heart—with everything I have—and create my life.

It's up to me.

I get to decide, through my choices, who I am and what my life is about.

And when my choices don't work, I'll know it in my gut—because I'll be listening to myself—and I'll back up and choose differently.

I can do that over and over until I know, as truly as I know my breath, the solid feel of my path underfoot.

Morgan drew a deep breath, took a long sip of tea and kicked off her sandals. She pressed her bare feet flat into the floor of the glider and felt the power of the earth rise into her body. She allowed the strength of that groundedness to flow throughout her torso, up her spine and head, and out to her arms, until her palms and forehead tingled with the energy.

What do I want to do?

Her burgeoning household was about to get bigger with Ian returning in less than two weeks. And Sierra's baby was on the way. It would be easy to lose herself in her children.

I need to make things simpler.

I need more time with myself.

She stretched her body, digging the sore spots in her shoulders into the upper slat of the glider, luxuriating in her solitude and intuiting her next step. She grinned. She would go upstairs right now, curl up in her bed, and drift, allowing her dream—her path—to take shape in her mind out of the swirling mists between sleeping and waking.

The pull of that between-times world was so tantalizing she could smell it—a mingling of sage and jasmine, earth and split-pea soup, wet leaves from the forest floor and the smoke of ancient bonfires, sea mist, horse sweat, and roses.

She was about to stand when she saw Aunt Lee making her way up the driveway, tap-tapping with her cane. She raised her free arm in a wave and cackled, "Hey, Peach Blossom!"

Just then, Jake's truck rattled up the street followed by Serena's Mercedes and Sierra and Rich in the S.U.V. they had bought in anticipation of family outings. It was parade of loved ones, but also a parade of distractions. The three vehicles pulled in next to one another just as Aunt Lee approached the steps. Soon everyone was talking at once and laughing, their rising volume piercing the stillness.

I forgot an item on my list of summer accomplishments

—a lost souls' reunion center and tent revival.

She hated being being mean-spirited, but she needed time alone so badly.

The whole gang ended up on the veranda. She moved to a rocker, as they all did, fanning out in a circle and sipping sweet tea Jake brought out along with cheeses and grapes and a bucket of ice. Sierra was due in five weeks and nothing could burst the bubble she and Rich shared. Their joy was infectious.

Jake had swiftly claimed a chair next to hers. He got out his guitar and everyone started playing with lyrics from old tunes Morgan recognized and new ones she didn't. Even Aunt Lee had something to add.

Morgan tried to stop herself from being annoyed about being annoyed. Jake was being too perfect again. Recently she'd noticed how he was always a little too available, a little too right there—like Serena's puppy, Beacon.

He'd been so attentive—as if he were constantly monitoring her emotional temperature—that she never felt she could be the one to close the emotional space between them. Even when she felt a genuine impulse to reach out to him, he always sensed it and moved on her. It began to frustrate, then anger her.

She had to force her mind back to the present, where she noticed that Serena—in spite of the strain she must have been feeling after waiting for Clarissa all afternoon—was making herself open to the experience of warmth and laughter that flowed between the members of the little sextet. She followed Serena's lead and made herself join in. She needed time for herself, but that didn't mean it had to come this second.

And she was enjoying the company of her daughter, who had launched herself from her rocker and was seated on a cushion on the floor of the veranda, her back pressed against Morgan's legs so she could receive a shoulder massage. Sierra didn't realize that this easy time, free of the responsibilities of children, wouldn't return for decades.

She tried not to feed her concerns about Sierra's choice to have a home birth. She knew how precariously her daughter's I've-got-it-all-together facade covered the insecurities of one too young to have the life experience to see where her choices might lead. And Sierra was going through a trough on her cycle of hills and valleys that determined whether she would be receptive to her mother's input. So Morgan, apart from secretly researching the midwife's credentials and learning she had a great reputation, had stayed out of it.

Sierra returned to her rocker next to Rich. Morgan was actually beginning to enjoy herself until Jake turned serious and sang her a love song.

It was subtle.

Neither Aunt Lee nor Serena seemed to realize he was singing to her. But after a few verses she saw Sierra squeeze Rich's hand. Rich chuckled to himself and Sierra winked at her mother.

Morgan felt something snap. Before the song was finished, she excused herself to take a shower and get out of her work clothes.

Jake looked as if he'd been shot, a fact Morgan chose to ignore.

Let him take care of himself.

He knows better than to make more of what we have than there is, especially in front of my kids.

Morgan kissed Aunt Lee on the cheek and embraced Sierra and Rich.

"We can't wait to see you," she whispered to her grandchild, giving Sierra's belly a little pat before climbing the stairs to her room.

She showered, hoping the tepid water would wash away the thoughts in her head. It wasn't working. She threw on her white terry cloth robe and lay back on the bed. When she heard Jake climbing the stairs, she invited him in.

~ ~ ~

Jake closed and locked Morgan's bedroom door and sprawled across her bed, hoping her mood had shifted. Raising one eyebrow invitingly, he extended his hand to her.

When she sat up instead of taking his hand, he felt foolish. He lifted himself up on his elbow and tucked his legs into a more formal position.

What's wrong?

She was frowning and her skin was pale beneath the golden tan that popped out against the white of her robe. With her trendy haircut, she looked younger and more sophisticated. At the same time, the summer's experiences had conferred upon her a deepening wisdom that accentuated her power. Even though she hadn't been feeling well, her presence had become stately, commanding. Invincible.

She was awesome.

He regarded her carefully. Whatever was coming, it wasn't good.

"Jake, I've been thinking. Summer is nearly over, Ian will be home soon, and—"

Jake bolted upright.

"Oh God, this is it," he said, knowing exactly where this was going. "The *conversation.*"

He didn't want to hear the words.

Why did I have to sing her that song?

Why did I push her?

And in front of Sierra and Rich!

"Don't you know how many times I've seen you go through this?" he said. "Summer begins, Ian goes to visit his Dad, and you get involved with someone. Summer winds down and you have to evaluate: is this relationship viable, can I expose my son to it?"

"Jake—"

"Let me finish. I can see it in your face. You've decided telling Ian you're shacking up with his former baby sitter doesn't cut it."

"Can you argue with that? Put yourself in Ian's shoes. But that's not the point, Jake."

Morgan's face grew gentler and she looked at him with soft eyes. "If I thought we could be good for each other over time, I'd work it out with Ian. I think you know that."

He felt his face go slack. He knew what he looked like. His cheeks and neck were getting blotchy as his eyes filled. He gathered Morgan in his arms, tenderly laid her back on her bed, and mounted her.

Her body yielded to him and he kissed her very softly through trembling lips. Two big tears splashed down and landed on Morgan's cheeks.

"I thought if I loved you enough, you'd stay," he said. An overwhelming sadness rose up from his belly, spread through his heart, and captured his throat. He lowered his head into Morgan's neck and wept.

"We love in the same language," he said.

She rolled over on top of him and let him sob between her breasts while she caressed his hair and his neck.

He held her tight. This might be the last time and he wanted the moment to last. He felt Morgan loving him with all she had to give. Simultaneously, he sensed her moving into the future she envisioned without him.

Suddenly she pulled away and made him meet her eyes. "I love you, more than you know. But we live in separate worlds."

"Yet we're good for each other."

"Yes. We always have been. But we can't go on as lovers. It doesn't work for me. I wanted that wonderful coupling you want, too, when—"

"Please don't say, 'when I was your age.' You wanted that only a few months ago, with Adam. How many men have I seen you want that with? They were all jerks. Isn't it time for you to try a relationship with someone who loves you? Someone who treats you the way you deserve to be treated?"

"Jake, I don't know if you can get this. You've treated me better than any man ever has and I love your friendship and our lovemaking. But all those relationships you saw me in were because I thought I needed a man to be whole. Now I need to take all that energy I've put into men and build a relationship with myself."

"I think you're running away from real love because you don't know you deserve it and can handle it."

"You don't get where I am or you wouldn't say that. I need me."

"If you want both, you can have both. I'm not sure you're using your best judgment right now. I still think a healthy working relationship scares you—there's not enough drama and angst."

"Thanks a lot."

"I'm going to stick around and see what shakes down."

"I've had those issues in the past and maybe I still do. But that's not the page I'm on. I'm on a quest and until I get where I need to go, a relationship isn't on my agenda."

"But then it will be?"

"How should I know? Ian's coming back and I have enough trouble knowing who I am in the face of his wants and needs. Sometimes I can barely hear myself."

They were sitting up, facing each other cross-legged. He lowered his head. She lifted his chin ever so gently and made him look at her. "It's not you," she said, stroking his cheek and his hair. "It's me."

"Do you want me to move out?"

"I want you to do what works for you. You know you're always welcome here."

"I guess I always knew this was too good to be true."

"But it *was* true. It will always be true. Invisible cords will link our hearts forever." She motioned back and forth, touching his heart and hers again and again. He gently took her hand and held it to his chest.

"We'll always be in each other's lives," she said. "But now I need to be on my own. I have to know I can give myself the same focus and attention I give others."

"All right, my love. If that's what you need, you've got it."

"Thank you."

Jake stood and kissed Morgan lightly on the forehead. He looked into her eyes one more time, then backed soundlessly out of the room.

❧ ❧ ❧

Clarissa was experiencing the oddest sensation. It was as if Big Mom were there, stitching cords of light between her mother's heart and her own, binding them to each other so they wouldn't lose this new opportunity for love.

It was a good thing she'd been getting help. Since she met her mother a week ago, her emotions had run the gamut from fear, anger, and defensiveness to longing, relief, and curiosity.

Now she and her mother were back on Morgan's sofa. It had taken less than a day for her to realize she wanted to know her mother more than she wanted to run from her. But Morgan's schedule had been too full to accommodate an extended session until today.

She'd done a lot of thinking. If her mother were living in Morgan's house, she must be a good soul. Clarissa and the boys had been on their own for too long. If a relationship was possible with her mother, she was going to do everything she could to make it happen.

She was dressed simply in a tan cotton geometric print. Her only adornment was the turquoise bracelet from her father.

Her mother was elegant in a muted aqua linen dress that grazed the top of her espadrilles. She wore a single piece of turquoise at her throat.

Only Morgan was lavishly adorned. She was wearing layers of teal and gold chiffon with multiple strands of beads.

The air outside was still, as it often was in August, making the scene beyond the windows look like a photograph. But inside Clarissa a tropical storm threatened. How do you form a relationship with a mother you don't know, half want to hate, yet long to share everything with?

She asked her mother that question.

"I don't know. We'll learn."

"You'll work it out," Morgan said. "There's an advantage to my knowing each of you. I can tell you you're both tenacious. When you want something, you go for it."

Clarissa felt tears brimming. She turned to her mother and found that her eyes, too, were ready to spill.

"I don't know what to feel," Clarissa said. "I've wanted to be with you all my life. But now we're together, and I don't know what to say."

"I know what you mean."

"I've been angry with you for leaving me. Then I got angry because you showed up. You lied to get me here. It's hard to trust you after that."

"I'm sorry I couldn't find a better way."

"I'm trying to let go of that. I'm glad you're here now." She looked down at her hands.

I won't cry.

I won't.

She squared her shoulders and faced her mother. "I've thought about it all week, and I decided getting to know you isn't such a bad thing. But it's going to take time.

"I know. We've got time."

Clarissa's chin trembled. "But there's something that really bothers me, something I must know. It's tearing me up."

"What is it?" Her mother's eyes were soft with concern. She reached out to touch Clarissa's face but withdrew her hand awkwardly before she got there.

"Why did you leave me?"

CHAPTER 19

more like wings, less like harpoons

She looked at herself, at her
reflection on the moving waves
of the enormous river and saw
that she was a strange new angel
that she had never seen before.

—Sophia West

Clarissa's eyes gushed like the springtime brook that splashed down the mountain behind Big Mom's cabin. All her life, she had imagined collapsing into the ample breasts of a mother twice her weight, like Big Mom. Yet here she was on Morgan's sofa with a twig of a woman who was barely as tall as her chin.

Still, she was able to be open enough to allow Serena to see her need.

Her mother gripped her hand so hard it hurt and her piercing blue eyes nearly disappeared behind the contortions of her face. She released a soft sob, bowed her head, and held Clarissa's hand to her brow. Then she sat up and worked to compose herself while she traced the outline of Clarissa's fingers with her own.

Clarissa gently withdrew her hand.

Morgan reached for the tissues and put them on the ottoman in front of them. "You're doing fine. Just breath deeply and give yourselves and each other plenty of time. Serena, Clarissa wants to know why you left her."

Her mother took a long drink from the glass Morgan offered. "Why did I leave you? I was so young, Clarissa. I didn't see any other way." She frowned. "That must sound unbelievable to you. I know that on the reservation, girls much younger than I was keep their babies."

"True. But you didn't grow up there."

"Are you sure that's where you want to start?"

"Yes. I feel as if I won't be able to hear anything else until I know. I want to get past it."

So much had changed. Morgan was as warm and serene as ever, but now the balance between them had shifted. She hadn't realized how much she'd drawn on Morgan for maternal support. But now that her mother was here beside her, she sensed the possibility of support from her.

More importantly, the work she had done on herself and on Dump the Dump—combined with meeting her mother—had helped her become more self-reliant.

Dealing in truth was healing her.

"I was young and very immature," her mother began, "a rich, sheltered, twenty-one-year-old girl. I became pregnant on my summer vacation and went back to college in the fall. It was inconceivable at the time that I would do otherwise." She drew a ragged breath. "Though leaving your father and Big Mom amounted to ripping my heart out and leaving it behind in those mountains."

Through tears and mucous, Clarissa gasped.

"What is it?"

"I was conceived in love?"

"Oh, Baby." Her mother reached out to cradle her face. "I thought you knew. I thought your father would tell you, or Big Mom."

Clarissa pulled away gently. "They did. But I couldn't believe them. If you loved my dad, why didn't you stay?"

"I couldn't, Pearl. I mean, Clarissa. I'm sorry."

"I like it when you call me Pearl."

They smiled at each other through their tears.

"I thought I was doing what was right for you," her mother said. "I couldn't leave everything I'd ever known and I couldn't take you with me. Back then, in my world, single mothers were unheard of. Besides, you'd have been miserable because I was too ambitious to be a good mother. I had to be a scholar, Clarissa. It's what I was born for. That dream had kept me going throughout my entire miserable childhood, though few women at the time were doing what I wanted to do. But for me, there was no other way."

Clarissa barked a laugh.

Her mother startled.

"It sounds like me," Clarissa said. "That's exactly how I escaped the reservation. I schemed from the time I was a little girl. I used television to train myself to speak without a hillbilly accent, I made sure I was always at the top of my class, I worked as many jobs as I could find, and I took advantage of every scholarship I could dig up to get out of that place. And your money, of course."

"Why?"

"It wasn't home. I was the black kid on the reservation. But no other place ever felt like home, either. Now I'm the honky Indian in the ghetto. Not that they call it a ghetto. It's called *East* Hopewellen, a place no one goes unless they live there. It's a racial thing."

"I'm sorry. No place ever felt like home to me, either. It's a Serena thing."

"Like mother, like daughter," Morgan said softly. They fell silent, digesting.

These two old u-negs *are crazy if they think their white alienation thing compares to dealing with racism.*

"Did you and my father discuss marriage?"

"Never. What we had was too special to tie it down like that. I don't know if you can understand."

Too special to tie yourselves down with a kid, either.

Her mother glanced away for a moment, then faced her. "My mother had a beautiful voice and had been studying opera before she got married. She told me she would have been a great singer if I hadn't come along. I felt I'd ruined her life simply by being. She was cold to my father—probably so he wouldn't give her any more children. So I thought it was my fault he was unhappy, too. I knew if I kept you, I would do the same thing to you. And I wanted something different for you, Clarissa."

"I got something different, all right. The kids called me nigger.'"

Her mother flinched. "I'm so sorry."

"It was bad. But Big Mom wanted me. She loved me and never once gave me reason to doubt that."

She thought she saw her mother recoil again and hated to admit she'd enjoyed it. "I was able to have the career I wanted and to be a mother. I've done well."

"I'm glad. You have children?"

Cut her some slack.

"You have grandchildren. Martin is twelve and Frankie is nine."

Her mother's eyes were glistening. Clarissa gave her a moment and glanced at Morgan, who gave her a small smile and nod.

"Please, go on," she said, "Mother."

Clarissa and Serena looked at each other solemnly.

"I thought it would confuse you to know me," her mother said. "And I didn't want either of us to be torn between two worlds. So I did the only thing I could. I sent you money. Not so much it would call attention to you, but enough to make sure you were always all right."

"Why did you give me to Big Mom?"

"I don't know if I can answer that without telling you the whole story."

"Tell me, then."

She was in sync with her mother in a way she couldn't quite put her finger on—and more comfortable with her than she'd imagined she could be. Her mother seemed to feel it too because before she began speaking again, she slipped off her espadrilles, arranged a pillow against the arm of the couch, and turned to face her.

"I was on my summer vacation from college. My parents were in Europe, so I was staying with Nancy, my roommate from college. Her family had a huge summer home in the mountains, not far from the reservation. It was the first time I'd been anywhere without my parents or a chaperone.

"Her parents were gone a lot and didn't seem to care what we did. They had a whole fleet of cars, so we would take one out every day, usually the little red M.G. We headed for the reservation because it was, frankly, exotic. And we sensed something there we didn't have. This was back when the reservation was mostly dirt roads and small farms, before tourism hit."

"And long before that damned casino."

"Right."

"The only time I'd ever been outside New York was to visit another big city like Philadelphia or D.C. It was an adventure to be unchaperoned in the wild greenery of the Smokies. I might as well have been on my own in a South American rain forest. It was romantic and I was impressionable. I felt as if being in a different place meant I could be a different person."

Clarissa never understood why white people were so fascinated by the reservation. They came in search of the old Cherokee spirituality, but what remained of that was deeply hidden. Most Cherokees had been fundamentalist

Christians for a very long time. The ways in which the culture was still strong were either invisible to white people or misunderstood and criticized by them.

Like how people joked about Cherokees always being late because they ran on Indian time. They didn't appreciate that her people didn't try to own time and measure it into quantifiable, bite-sized spoonfuls. The fluidity of time was understood. Signs in each moment were clues from Spirit that guided her people where they needed to be, when they needed to be there. Time was a sacred river—everchanging—and they swam with it.

There were still a few scattered elders, like Big Mom, hidden deep in the woods. In these souls, many of the old ways lived on in all their layered richness. Of course these elders were increasingly rare, but Big Mom was one of the truest.

Clarissa's gaze traveled to the window, the distant trees, and the sky beyond until her vision went soft and she could see the reservation through her mother's eyes.

"There was a little greasy spoon in the bus depot back then," her mother said. "It provided us with an opportunity to get out of the car and get something to eat. Your dad and the waitress were the only ones in the place, so naturally he overheard us talking. I was being a smart-ass."

Her mother smiled at the memory and Clarissa found her warmth infectious.

"About what?"

"I probably shouldn't tell you this, but I was boasting to Nancy about my sexual exploits. Of which, by the way, there had been none. But I was bragging as if I knew all about it.

"Suddenly I realized this guy was giggling. I shot him a look, assuming he was being crass. But he wasn't. The way I looked at him only made him laugh more.

"I couldn't understand his reaction. The way he was acting—he was unlike any man I'd ever met. He wasn't put off by my big mouth the way other guys were. In fact, he seemed to like it. He didn't appear to think less of me because I was talking about sex, yet he wasn't coming on to me.

"He was just looking at me with those slow, sweet, mischievous black eyes. He was laughing at me, yet I didn't feel ridiculed. Later, when I got to know him, I found out he admired all the things about me that I'd always been told were unladylike. He liked it when I spoke my mind and went after what I wanted."

"That's very Cherokee," Clarissa said. "The women are strong. I was told growing up that a woman doesn't really need a man, you just take up with them when you feel like it because a woman can take care of herself and her kids just fine."

"Seriously?" Morgan said.

Serena smiled. "Yes. I saw that on the reservation, between Big Mom and your various aunties and cousins. It was wonderful.

"Lloyd was so exotic looking. He was beautiful, Clarissa, before the alcohol took him over. He was a giant of a man. Physically, I should have been intimidated by him. But he had that baby face. I'd never met a man who was both solid and soft. He reminded me of a big black bear with a Buddha belly. He was vulnerable yet strong, a combination that was inconceivable.

"I knew I could hurt him, but never overpower him. I had force, he had patience. He had the strength of water, which flows around obstacles without stopping, eventually wearing down everything in its path. And I was a rock—a jagged rock from a long line of rocks—who longed for the smoothing effect of water.

"His hair was black and glistening, like his eyes. Later, of course, I learned he got his long, thick hair from Big Mom and the tight ringlets in which it fell from the black man with whom Big Mom had been involved for a time.

"But all I was aware of then was how warmly he accepted me and the comforting bulk of his body. He was so steady, so present.

"In contrast, I was self-conscious and nervous. I didn't know what to do but talk louder. It's a good thing the waitress was in the kitchen, especially since I found out later she was Lloyd's aunt. Would you believe I said, 'You haven't lived until you've tried oral sex.'"

Clarissa and Morgan exploded in a loud burst of laughter. Her mother joined in with a chuckle that managed to be both low and tinkling. Something about the ease of her own laugh, combined with the comfortable familiarity between Morgan and her mother, reassured her. She folded her feet beneath her and sank deep into the couch.

"Lloyd laughed, too. In fact, he almost choked on his sandwich. But you know what? It was as if he knew I was really saying, 'Look, I'm a virgin with her foot in her big mouth and I don't know why, but I really like you.' Because what Lloyd said to me was, 'You haven't lived until you've picked *so-chan.*'"

Clarissa drew a sharp breath and tears filled her eyes. She remembered that when she was very little and her daddy was still around, he would go out with Big Mom and her aunties in the springtime and pick wild greens. He would bend down, the crack of his butt showing above his belt, and and gather the plants gently, with the same devotion as the women.

"He dared me to go with him," her mother said. "Which of course was the best strategy with me. Nancy wanted no part of it, but I couldn't turn down the dare. Or so I told myself.

"The truth was, I immediately felt safe with Lloyd and wanted to be with him. He was introverted, but that didn't stop him from showing me what he wanted. This was all new to me. The young men who'd shown an interest in me before were aggressive and in control, which I hated. Shy boys, on the other hand, were wimps. But Lloyd was both quiet and clear. He was someone to contend with.

"We devised an elaborate excuse to give Nancy's parents, one of many I used that summer. Not that I needed one. They didn't pay much attention to me and I basically spent the summer on the reservation, living with Big Mom and Lloyd and whoever else happened to be at Big Mom's tiny cabin.

"Clarissa, I believe you were conceived that very afternoon. I have so many memories of those first few days with Lloyd, but they're all woven together by now. We spent many long hours picking greens high in the mountains. But that day, we picked *so-chan* in the valley, close to the river and near an old spring."

"I know exactly where you mean." All three women smiled at each other.

"I remember the trillium with its firm, white petals and the delicacy of buttercups in bloom. Everything was new and lush. And wild. Quietly, easily, wild. I'd never seen anything like it. My own untamed spirit was being mirrored back to me by nature and by your father and for the first time, it was okay to be me. I was in heaven.

"There was a huge sycamore leaning out over the Oconaluftee River with so many trunks and twists and turns, it looked like some strange and ancient beast. The roots, which sprawled above ground, were as thick as large trees. Lloyd and I spent hours sitting on the roots, dangling our feet over the river, holding hands, and talking."

"The dragon tree, I called it," Clarissa said. "Oh my god, I remember something. Daddy said he once knew a beautiful spirit who loved that tree. A spirit with a heart like thunder, skin as white as sycamore bark, and eyes like turquoise. He meant you."

Suddenly her eyes went to the large piece of turquoise at Serena's throat, so much like the one at her wrist. Serena followed Clarissa's eyes, removed the stone, and offered it to Clarissa.

"No," Clarissa said. "You keep it. I have one. See?"

❧ ❧ ❧

Moving slowly and ever so gently, Serena touched the turquoise Lloyd had given her to the one in Clarissa's bracelet. Then she held it on her lap for a few moments before putting it back on. She remembered the day he gave it to her.

They were saying good bye. He brought out a deerskin pouch in which he kept the twin pieces of turquoise carefully wrapped in a piece of old red kerchief.

"This one is for you," he told her, placing the large blue-green and black nugget in her palm. "The other I will keep for for our child. Bring our baby back here and I will make her this gift."

Somehow, they had both known their love had created a baby, a girl-child.

Overwhelmed to be in the presence of her daughter and to be relieving herself of the truth she had kept secret for so long, Serena was flooded with images of those early days with Lloyd.

When the session began, Serena had felt prickly and critical. Clarissa was too tall, too present. Her need was too great and her skin was too dark.

But she hadn't let these feelings show. Instead, she told herself she was simply in an old pattern, reacting negatively because she was afraid and because she cared so much.

Before the session, Morgan had told her to "fake it 'til you make it," to act as if she were already the mother she wanted to be.

Clarissa's vulnerability had helped her drop her defenses and now she was in a state of grace, blessed to be with her daughter, to be received. It was what she had dreamed of. She felt that she, Clarissa, and Morgan were cradled in the loving arms of the goddess and she was being favored with a new beginning.

She was reborn.

A born again mother.

Even the busy pastels in Morgan's office looked marvelous.

Before her was her magnificent daughter, with her hair, nose and mouth so like Lloyd's, her bearing straight and dignified like Big Mom's, and a body that was a taller version of her own. Her hands were Serena's and the black depths of her eyes were pure Lloyd.

Serena's thoughts drifted back to that first day with him. She could almost see the blooming yellow poplar down by the river with its strange tulips of green and orange. Later the petals drifted down on them where they lay naked on a soft blanket Lloyd had in his truck—for times, he said, when he wanted to sleep under the stars with only this blanket between him and the earth and sky. Sometimes he slept in a tree, he told her, and awakened in the middle of the night to witness the dance of rabbits mating in the moonlight and the hunt of the screech owl.

She recalled how the softness of the Smoky Mountain air had complemented his gentle touch, the round contours of the mountains, and the new greenery, which was more prolific than any she'd ever seen.

They found shelter from the frequent rain beneath thick forest growth and in the same mountain caves his people had hidden in to avoid the white soldiers who rounded up the Cherokees and forced them to march to Oklahoma.

Serena remembered waterfalls and bittercress, smooth river rocks, huge insects, and the evening sound of peepers. There were flowers, dogwood and azaleas, later to be followed by mountain laurel and rhododendron.

But more than anything, she remembered Big Mom. Lloyd brought her to Big Mom's cabin that first day, after they picked armfuls of *so-chan* and made love by the river.

He'd been gentle with her. His touch was reverent and wise, as if he knew what it was to be a young woman in bloom. She'd never known what home felt like until he touched her, and she never found it again after they parted.

It was she who decided to go further in their exploration of each other's bodies. He let her take the initiative, which made her feel all the more safe. She relaxed with him and for the first time found out what her body was capable of.

There was a tender piercing when he slowly entered her, watching her eyes for any sign of distress. He tried to withdraw when she hurt, but she pulled him back to her. He moved slowly, cradling her face in his hands with such gentleness that her body opened to him, ripples of pleasure flowing through her unlike anything she'd ever known.

Afterwards, he took her to meet Big Mom. She felt like a princess being led to meet the queen as they rattled down country roads in his truck.

Her body and mind were one for the first time. She was aware of everything—the warm air wafting across her face through the open windows of the truck, her hair lifting in the breeze, the feel of the truck's connection with the road, the slippery heat and raw fullness inside her, the nuances of green in the foliage and in the brush, the little log cabins along the road, and the reassuring animal presence of his body.

He shifted the truck through its gears without ever altering the gentle pressure with which he held her small hand in his larger one. But when they left the dirt road to bounce over a deeply rutted track for two tires with grass growing in the middle, she felt a little stab of fear at the wildness she was entering. Simultaneously, she realized the honor she was about to receive was far greater than what she had imagined.

They came at last to Big Mom's home, a small log cabin nestled in a curve of one of the branches that fed into the Oconaluftee River. The cabin had a rusty tin roof and was chinked with whitewashed river rocks and covered in roses and wisteria vines that would flower later. The air was even gentler here, like the curving stems of the Bleeding Hearts that grew along the side of the cabin and the warm soul of the woman who greeted them.

Preceded by a half dozen barking dogs, Big Mom stepped off the porch before they were out of the truck. She looked slowly from Serena to her son and back again with a welcoming, wise expression that told Serena she was completely accepted. At the same time, it communicated that Big Mom already knew the story of Serena and Lloyd and how it would end.

Big Mom wore a necklace of corn beads—large gray seeds in the shape of teardrops—which she removed and placed gently around her neck. It reminded her of the time she had traveled first class to Honolulu with her parents and they were greeted with leis. But the quality of Big Mom's gesture was unique—both deeply personal and casual, light.

She soon learned that Big Mom gave something to everyone who visited her. Still, she felt moved because—as had been the case with Lloyd—when Big Mom touched her, she made real contact. Lloyd and Big Mom provided her first experience of true giving.

Lloyd's mother was short and round with thick black braids that were wound in fabric and swayed against her broad behind when she walked. She wore a frayed and faded patterned dress and heavy shoes. Even then, she had plenty of years on her, but she moved with an easy grace. She led them onto the back porch, which faced the river and was lined with mismatched chairs in various states of disrepair—including one rocker, which you could tell she had been sitting in because it had basket-making supplies circled around it. Big Mom made her take the rocker.

Big Mom began to gather up the splints that were soaking in washtubs but Lloyd stopped her. He pulled a solid-looking oak chair closer to the rocker for her and put away her supplies himself.

Serena fell in love with him then, watching him take care of his mother. Big Mom started to go inside to boil water. She asked him to pick some comfrey for tea, but he told her to sit while he did both. While they drank their tea, he sharpened the knives she used for scraping her splints.

After their tea, they went inside so Big Mom could cook up the *so-chan.* What Serena didn't realize until later that summer was that she was the first white person to ever set foot in Big Mom's home.

Even though it was still daylight, the little cabin was like a cave because the windows were small and low and the porches cut down the light. The wood stove was already going but Lloyd added several more logs for cooking in spite of the heat. She wanted to help, so Big Mom sent her outside to pump water.

This gave her an opportunity to take in where she was. There was a clearing with a newly planted vegetable garden, three tire planters with bright splashes of color in their centers, and several whirligigs amidst the patches of daffodils. What appeared to be herbs were growing in a smaller garden where foxglove was about to bloom. Down a dirt trail, there were several rusted cars with the seats spread out around them. A tethered brown horse grazed between the junk cars and the gardens.

Before long, gaggles of family arrived, aunties and cousins and their children, plus one of Lloyd's sisters, Betsy—pregnant out to here and with two small children in tow.

With so many hands, the preparation of the feast they ate that night went quickly. Big Mom washed and picked through the so-chan in a laundry tub, inspecting each cluster of leaves and slapping it against the side of the tub to get the water out. She boiled the greens in a large pot. When they had cooked down to a fraction of their original volume, she fried them and added a little vinegar.

They made stewed potatoes, boiled cabbage, fatback, and bean bread, which was like cornmeal dumplings made from corn and beans. She and Betsy were wrapping the bean bread mixture in corn blades when Betsy told her something she never forgot.

"The day I got pregnant with each of my children, Big Mom knew right away there was a baby coming." Serena glanced up and caught Big Mom looking at her intently. Although Big Mom averted her eyes immediately, Serena knew in that moment that her life would never be the same, though at the time she wasn't sure why.

Later, she realized both Betsy and Big Mom knew she was pregnant and were telling her as much in their quiet Indian way. It proved to be the first of many times she experienced the incredible intuition of the Cherokee people—the uncanny ability to see through the surface to the multilayered and subtle levels of reality.

That night, she and Lloyd spooned together on a single cot next to Big Mom's bed. His huge arms around her protected her from falling out. While she listened to the soft snoring of Big Mom, Betsy and her children—all in the double bed—and the three cousins who spent the night on the floor, she experienced for the first and only time in her life how it felt when human beings were actually connected with one another.

Under the comfort of Morgan's silent witness, Serena shared her story with Clarissa, reserving some of the more private moments.

"He took me tracking in the woods in the daytime. Or we helped Big Mom in her garden. And then of course we must have visited every cousin Lloyd had that summer. You know how that goes—he had at least a hundred of them."

Clarissa laughed.

"At night, we went skinny-dipping in the river under the stars. I loved the life he taught me so much, I spent the last ten years trying to recreate it all by myself in the mountains. Which didn't work, of course, because what made Big Mom's place so special was the people. That's why I had to come to Hopewellen, to find my people. To find you."

She and her daughter gazed at each other, their eyes shimmering.

Morgan gasped. She and Clarissa whipped around.

"Big Mom's place sounds so much like your cabin."

Serena's eyes filled with tears. She turned to Clarissa. "It was my way of being close to you, even though I got my cabin long after you left the reservation. My place is covered with wisteria and roses, with no running water and no electricity. I farmed there and raised animals, and even named it Mothers Mountain to honor my love for you. Pretty lame, huh, to build a shrine to your life on the reservation instead of finding you."

"Yeah, that's pretty lame."

Serena couldn't help smiling. Her daughter was beautiful.

"I'm sorry I put it off. I wanted to see you, but I couldn't bring myself to make contact. Until this summer, I was too stuck to do much of anything that makes any sense."

"You're here now."

"Thanks. How are you feeling about the saga of your beginnings?"

"Mixed. This is going to take some getting used to. But I want to know."

"However you want to do this is fine with me."

They broke for a moment to stretch and move around.

This is going well.

We've got a shot.

The view outside Morgan's window—homes with tidy yards looking out on the generous willow oaks that lined the street, interweaving their branches with the trees beside them and those across the way—seemed to confirm Serena's dawning realization that there could be something good and right about family.

"Are we ready to reconvene?" Morgan said.

When they sat down again, Clarissa said, "I want to hear the rest."

"By Christmas break, I was showing so much my parents realized I was pregnant. Nice Catholic girls from wealthy New York families don't have babies until they're firmly wed, mind you, so my parents got me out of town as fast as they could.

"I didn't have Christmas with my family because they were afraid someone would see me and I'd be 'ruined.' I felt ostracized, frightened, and alone—a thing to be managed instead of a young woman in need of love and help. But that's how I always felt around my parents.

"They made some excuse to the school so I could take the semester off and graduate the following year, then sent me to Switzerland to have my baby in what used to be called a home for unwed mothers. I never told anyone you weren't going to be white.

"When you were born, it caused quite a stir at the hospital. I hadn't realized my parents were planning to have my baby put up for adoption. I don't know what I was thinking.

"But I had made up my mind about one thing. I knew I couldn't raise you, so I took you back to the best place I'd ever known, the only place where people seemed to actually care about one another, a place where people were more important than property. Or propriety.

"I had to steal you from the hospital. I had enough of my own cash to do what I had to do to get you back to Big Mom. It wasn't an easy journey in those days, especially for a young woman traveling alone with a dark-skinned baby, but we made it."

"You protected me."

"I loved you. I always have and still do."

~ ~ ~

Morgan had kept herself out of the conversation between Serena and Clarissa as much as possible. It was to both of their credit and a very good sign that they didn't need her intervention, only her presence, while they got used to each other. She was grateful that the session went easily because lately she'd felt increasingly ill. If it weren't for this appointment, she'd have spent the day in bed.

Once Clarissa had her history straight, she and Serena began to ask about each other's lives. When the flow of words between them began to sound like a normal conversation, Morgan suggested that they were ready to take it from there on their own.

But the three of them needed to discuss their situation because Morgan would no longer be able to provide therapy for Clarissa now that they knew Clarissa was the daughter of her housemate.

It was a highly unusual situation. Professional ethics decreed that a therapist-client relationship precluded any social contact once therapy was finished. But professional ethics didn't take into account unusual circumstances such as this. The trick was to create the outcome that would best serve Clarissa.

Clarissa seemed stung by the news she would have to end her therapy relationship with Morgan, but she understood. They recognized that if Serena and Clarissa built a relationship, which they were committed to doing, Clarissa would be spending time in Morgan's home.

"I don't have a problem with that if you don't," Morgan said. "It's not as if we've been meeting weekly for years. You've never been heavily dependent on me, so I think after a short break we can make the transition to my being a sort of friend of your family. But we need to decide if you're going to continue getting help. If you do, I'll help you find someone."

Clarissa felt she didn't need a new therapist, but Morgan said she'd feel better if they discussed that subject in depth later. They agreed to meet in a few days to acknowledge the profound changes Clarissa had made and to formally end their therapeutic relationship.

"There's something you need to think about, Clarissa. Therapy has undergone tremendous change in the last decade. Legally and ethically, it's increasingly defined as the diagnosis and treatment of mental illness, under the umbrella of traditional medicine and insurance companies."

Morgan worked her jaw hard. "I don't define my mission that way, but I'm a dying breed and practitioners who operate the way I do are taking a risk.

"I would recommend you continue your work. You're in a period of major transition and you don't have to go through it alone. Guidance helps.

"But you certainly aren't mentally ill. You need someone who understands your calling in life and the spiritual and political nature of your path. You might do better with one of the people who advertise as life coaches, spiritual mentors, something like that. They post their services in alternative newspapers and in metaphysical and health food stores.

"Shop around and don't settle for someone unless you have a good gut feeling about them and they seem to both understand your situation and possess the skills to help you.

"If you do use a therapist, I recommend you don't use your health insurance. You don't need a diagnosis of mental illness on your permanent health record for future employers to see."

"I can't think about any of that right now."

"I understand. But I wanted to give you some things to consider for our final meeting."

Morgan, who had given up a much-needed day of rest to meet with Clarissa and Serena, didn't go home immediately after they left. She was delighted they'd made such a good connection. But beyond the exhaustion that had become her way of life, something was off with her.

"That went well!" Grandmama said.

"It did. But I want to know what happened to that old booger, that Shadow." Big Mom said.

"Last time," Brigid said, "the bloody scoundrel behaved as if Serena and Clarissa were going to be hurt. Nothing came of his ramblings, and there's the truth of it."

"I think he acts that way whenever something upsets us," Morgan said, hearing them so clearly she could enter their conversation. "He tries to make us think hard times lead to disaster. But only we can make that happen, by giving up on ourselves.

"Aye," Brigid said. "Bright Goddess, I think you've got it."

But Morgan realized there was something she didn't get.

The awareness brought with it a fresh wave of exhaustion.

She was tired of this dance—tired of feeling sick, tired of knowing there was always some next move Shadow would make, tired of wondering what it meant to be the hundredth woman, tired of the responsibility of trying to act not only on her own behalf, but also for the highest good of all.

And tired of not knowing what my path is.

Tired.

Tired.

Tired.

Tired of everything.

CHAPTER 20

juicy ground

yes she lives her dream like, like drawing
without looking at the paper, she lives her
life without looking down at the pencil of
her feet, where she is scribbling with her
body. she is not a pencil looking down at
the page of the ground. she is not a ball-
point pen. she is the sunset minstrel lyre
and harp, many brushes painted without
looking down. she doesn't speak the language
but she is eloquent. many brushes
passionately moving without looking down.
that is why she is like flying, more like
wings. less like harpoons.

—Marna

Serena sank into the love seat, closed her eyes, and savored the blend of ricotta, Greek olives, sun-dried tomatoes, and garlic on her second piece of pizza. New York style, yet. Who'd have guessed such a treat could be had in Hopewellen? Jake knew where to find the best food.

"Beautiful," Serena said. "Like my daughter."

Jake and Morgan laughed. They knew she couldn't stop talking about Clarissa.

I'm on a maternal high.

"Why not bottle all that positive energy?" Morgan said. "Better yet, use it to get an outline done."

"A book outline?"

"Why not? Haven't you been reading enough to complete the research for ten books? I can hear your wheels turning all the way in my room."

"Yeah," Jake said. "I have to wear earplugs."

"But—"

"Your birthday is in two weeks, right? Have an outline done by then, as a present to yourself."

"No way."

"Way."

"Let's talk about something else."

"Not until you promise."

"Okay. I'll *try*."

"Trying is lying!" Jake was laughing.

"All right! I'll have an outline done by my birthday. Now, that's enough of that."

Oh my god.

I mean, goddess.

Help me find a way to do this.

"Hey," Morgan said. "The house looks great, you guys. Thank you. It means a lot to know Ian's coming home to a clean house."

Morgan's head was rolled against the back of the couch, as if her neck were too weak to hold her head up. She hadn't touched her pizza.

Serena and Jake exchanged concerned looks.

"I wish you'd go to the doctor," Serena said. "It's been weeks since you've had any energy."

Jake slid forward in his chair and grabbed Morgan's feet, which were propped on the ottoman. "Please make an appointment. I've never seen you like this. You're not eating, your skin is so pale it's nearly gray, you have to use the railing when you climb the stairs. And you haven't cracked a joke in ages."

A tear slid down Morgan's cheek.

"I don't need a doctor. It's not medical."

"I know you think it's Shadow," Serena said, trying to keep her voice from sounding frantic. "But what if you're wrong? Why not rule out a medical problem?"

It better be a medical problem.

What can any of us do about Shadow?

Jake shot her a look that said, "Ease up."

Morgan sat up and buried her head in her hands. Her words were barely audible. "I'm so scared."

Moving as one, Serena and Jake slid onto the couch on either side of her. He put a hand between her shoulder blades and she melted into his shoulder, sobbing, then straightened and blew her nose. "I'm sorry. I don't mean to give you mixed messages."

"You're not." He continued to rub her back. "We've been friends too long for you to think that way. Don't be alone with this. Talk to us."

"I'll go to the doctor if it means that much to you."

"Please," Jake and Serena said together.

"I'm afraid going to a doctor will make things worse. Besides, I know what it is and it's not medical."

"Shadow," he said.

"Right."

"If it's Shadow, how could seeing a doctor make things worse?" Serena said.

"What if Shadow is trying to distract me, to worry me so I don't pay attention to what I really need?" She was crying so hard it was difficult to make out her words. "What if he can manipulate reality, so I get some scary diagnosis and start focusing on that instead of on my path, my soul?"

"If it's Shadow," Serena said, "why not just get rid of him, as you did before?"

"I would, if I could. But even when I think I've gotten him out of my spine, I'm still sick. I don't know what to do. Exorcism wasn't covered in graduate school."

"That's not funny," Jake said.

"It wasn't meant to be. I'm so confused. This could be any one of so many different things."

"Like what?" Jake continued to gently stroke her back.

"What if I can't get rid of him because he's here to teach me something?"

"That son-of-a-bitch?" Serena felt herself screeching.

Rein it in.

"I mean, creep."

"What if there is no Shadow out there? What if he's really part of me, and I just think he's out there because I've been a victim all my life? Then it's me making myself sick, and I'm the only one who can make myself better. Or maybe it's not for my highest good to get better. Maybe this is my lesson."

"That's ridiculous," Serena said.

"Sugar, I don't see how—"

Fresh tears seized Morgan.

"What is it?" Jake was holding her and rubbing circles on her back.

"What if he's trying to kill me—or worse, to cross out my soul so I can't be the hundredth woman, in this world or the next. What if I can't win? He's getting more and more of me every day. He's sucking the breath from my body."

"We have to do something!" Serena heard herself shouting.

"But I'm not sure taking action is the way. How about a little faith, here? That's what I'm struggling for—faith. Let things unfold. Give it time."

But Serena didn't feel they had time. One thing ten years on a farm had taught her was to notice when death had its eye on a living thing.

~ ~ ~

Clarissa and Joshua found a place to sit on a stone bench next to a fountain near the mall's arcade. He gave Frankie and Martin eight quarters each and the boys sped off.

"You're so kind to them," she said.

"They're good boys. They deserve it."

She stared into the fountain.

"You're very quiet," Joshua said.

"I keep thinking about how to fund the event. I could ask my mother for the money from the trust she set up for me. But I don't want her to bail me out. I need to know I made Dump the Dump happen myself."

He pulled a penny from his pocket. "Make a wish."

Clarissa smiled, held the penny tight in her hand, and closed her eyes.

Bring me money to fund Dump the Dump.

She tossed the penny into the fountain, where it spiraled down to join mounds of pennies, nickels, dimes and quarters.

I wonder what they do with all those coins?

~ ~ ~

"Brigid, I'm so tired."

It was one in the morning, and Morgan had yet to sleep. Her body ached everywhere and though she was bone tired, her mind jangled with an artificial buzz.

Shadow was lurking in the corner, grinning at her. All she could see was the yellow glow of his eyes and teeth, like some sickly fluorescence penetrating dense fog.

"I know, Luvie. I know. Don't lose heart."

"Why does it have to be like this?"

Brigid put a firm hand on her shoulder.

Steady, woman, don't give in to him.

Was it Brigid's words, or her own? It didn't matter.

She was tired of feeling sick. It was hard to resist the anger Shadow was nudging her toward. He wanted her to fight him. And though she had no interest in conflict and knew it would drain her scant reserves, giving him the upper hand, she was so frustrated she was close to taking his bait.

The only thing she'd been able to do that day was meet Ian's plane. On the way back from the airport, she had eased the window down to allow the warm, spicy scent of ripening tobacco to roll over him. She was helping him come back to the South.

Ian looked splendid. He'd come to the conclusion that girls like a clean-cut look. His hair was a moderate length, which it hadn't been in years unless he was growing it out. He wore a new pair of khaki pants and a white cotton shirt.

She'd wanted to prepare his favorite foods, have a cookout, and invite his friends. She had to take him to dinner instead, which he didn't seem to mind. He had a lot to talk about before taking off for the evening with his buddies.

He'd several new theories, for instance, about what it took to be a songwriter, the best ways to keep a band going, how to cope with wayward drummers, and why girls sometimes responded to him and sometimes didn't.

He'd seemed satisfied with her listening, but Morgan was frustrated because she didn't feel strong enough to be completely present. She was used to being there for her kids.

Shadow had done something to her body that she didn't know how to undo. She prayed continually to Mother Father God to heal her, to fill her with love, and she'd asked her body to be healthy and well. Yet her energy drained from her body a little more each day, like sand leaking from a hole in a burlap bag. Her doctor was concerned, but could find nothing wrong. The lab results would be back Monday.

Her frustrations kept her from sleeping. She had to find a way to release her emotions without engaging in conflict with Shadow.

Help me!

From within, gentle guides urged her to activate the now-familiar vortex to whirl away all negative energies. This time, they suggested she call in the forces of the Archangel Michael to help.

Her heart opened in compassion for the dark ones who were being pulled into the vortex, swept along by the gentle wings of Archangel Michael's helpers. She could sense the fear that gripped the hearts of the dark entities. They'd always been told there was no light.

"You don't need to be afraid," she told them, showing them the light. "You'll simply be taken the next step up, where you'll be able to learn and evolve."

Some of the entities threw off negatives, blueprints, to replicate themselves.

Morgan chuckled. "You can't leave those behind," she said as Archangel Michael's forces swept them into the vortex. "You won't be coming back. But you don't have to be alone. Bring your families, your friends, and your communities with you. And you don't *have* to go into the light if you don't want to. But you can't return to—or harm—me or anyone else ever again."

More and more dark ones entered the light. Mentally, Morgan asked that a permanent vortex of healing light be activated in the woods behind her home, so entities could go up at any time without having to get her attention first.

Her guides prompted her to jerk her body once to activate flashes of blue lightning to break up, loosen, and release stuck energies so they could go up.

She was told to mentally visit every room in her home, from the basement to the attic, and to think "crash" as she sent blue lightning into every corner and closet, every junk pile and piece of furniture, every floor, wall, and ceiling and through all the electrical, telephone, and plumbing systems, pipes, and ductwork.

She was to cleanse her land and car—everything except for Jake and Serena, because it wasn't appropriate to clear them without their permission. But Ian was another story. She could wash her baby and the animals. She was also to ask for everything to be cleared ten miles up, down, and in all directions—but only insofar as she and Ian were concerned.

Finally, she cleared her own body. She felt the blue lightning releasing negative energy while the vortex cleansed her, surrounding her with the highest vibration of light, circling her with love, cradling her. She asked for a force field of of divine light to infuse and surround her, Ian, and their home, protecting their bodies and divine essences with all the power and might of infinity.

And she let go.

She sobbed out all her frustration and her fear. The will power and discipline she'd used to buck up—to maintain a positive attitude and carry on—melted into the vortex and was gently whirled up and away.

She let it all go.

Thank you.

Thank you, thank you, thank you.

Pastel light glowed throughout her being, her home, and her land, infusing all with protection.

In her cleansed and peaceful state, messages from realms beyond began to flood her awareness.

She'd been besieged by entities, she was told, because enlightened beings beam out a light the dark ones are attracted to—some because they want to go to the light, and some because they want to put it out. She was going to need to clear her home, office, car, and body—at least weekly.

But how could she be an enlightened being? Wasn't enlightenment some unemotional, beatific state?

Release the old masculine ideas of enlightenment, she heard within, those austere images of motionless meditators, grim-mouthed and detached.

Embrace feminine enlightenment. The open, nurturing heart. The simple dignity of being alive to your essential nature—the pleasure and the pain. The spirit of love and creativity. The heartfelt honoring involved in every form of stewardship. Celebrate the integrity, wholesome and true, of being the life-giver.

Embody the joy of the flower.

Budding.

Blooming.

Opening.

Fading.

Falling.

Blooming again.

Morgan breathed deeply, cherishing the support with which she was being blessed.

Everything she had been through had led her to this place.

She had even benefited from being sick. It had forced her to be quiet, to be close to Spirit.

She felt loved in a way she never had.

Cherished.

Why can I send so many dark ones to the light, but not Shadow?

The answer came inside—why indeed?

It didn't matter.

What she had, even with Shadow, was glorious.

No matter what he did, everything was going to be all right. Being ill was helping her learn how to entrust her spirit to the hands of the Most Loving.

Shadow could never defeat her there. He might take her body, but her spirit was ever more securely on the path of love. And being on that path, she knew, was more life-giving than anything she'd ever known.

Shadow wanted to lure her into conflict, a fight with a winner and a loser.

But she was being taught a more elegant and satisfying way of prevailing, the way of love. She was setting her own agenda. Because she was loving herself—even in her sick and weakened condition—she was putting an energy into the universe that made Shadow obsolete.

After all, without victims there could be no persecutors. And Morgan was beyond being Shadow's victim or anyone else's. Even if he took her body, she would go on and on, expanding the energy of love. In so doing, she would be helping all life, everywhere.

She was making a difference at the subtlest and therefore the most powerful levels. So what if she hadn't had the energy to pay the bills this month? What did it matter if she'd had to cancel a few clients? And if she couldn't explain what her path was to herself or anyone else—did that mean she wasn't on it? She was doing the work she was made to do. Her worst fears were dissolving into love and she was learning the way of the hundredth woman.

She didn't need to be physically healthy to do this work. All she needed was her intention.

Intention.

She set her intention to live in this conscious space of love and to contribute that power to the world. She released her prayer into the universe in complete trust that whatever would come was for the best. Even if she became more ill and never learned how to be free of Shadow.

It was nearly three and the light of the full moon slanted across her bed. She threw off the covers and bathed herself in moonlight, breathing in the grandmotherly essence of the moon through her skin at the same time that she connected with the strength of the earth from below.

The next morning, Morgan awakened to Beacon tugging at her sheets and growling. Ian's head appeared in the door.

"It's ten, Mom."

"Come in, Sweetie."

Ian ambled across Morgan's room and tossed himself on the bed beside her. They cuddled for the few seconds Ian would allow while Morgan drank in his baby man smell and rubbed circles on his chest. Then Ian sprang up from the bed and jogged in place and slightly backwards toward the door.

"Come on downstairs," he said. "Jake went for croissants."

"How do you feel about all these people and dogs in the house?"

"It's kinda cool. Especially Beacon and Jake."

The two puppies.

Beacon heard his name and barked and the young males trotted off. Morgan stretched and said a quick prayer, her palms together to increase the energy. She made herself throw on a pair of denim shorts and a tank top—instead of simply pulling her robe around her—and went downstairs.

Ian, Serena, and Jake were sprawled on the overstuffed furniture, indulging in a spread of maple yogurt, cantaloupe slices, fresh croissants, and iced herbal tea. Ian waved her into the room, his mouth full.

Virginia Woof was lying near the food, her head on the floor. Her eyes followed every bite with a pitiful look that invited someone to relieve her misery with just one bite or, preferably, an entire croissant.

Serena was laughing, her legs sprawled over the arm of her favorite overstuffed chair. She wore faded denim jeans that were shot through in the knees, among other places. New turquoise-rimmed reading glasses dangled around her neck from a turquoise, coral, and silver beaded chain. Several pencils protruded from the knot in her hair.

She was going to Clarissa's that afternoon for the first time to meet the boys. Between that and looking forward to teaching at the university—effective tomorrow—she seemed truly happy.

Apparently Beacon heard her laugh because he bounded around the corner from the dining room where, judging by the dust on his nose, he'd been trolling for dirt again. He loped across the living room on the bias, tongue dangling from his grinning mouth, and catapulted himself onto Serena's lap. She was licking croissant crumbs off her fingers, a task Beacon was thrilled to help with. She ruffled Beacon's fur all over, then put him on the floor so she could dive into the cantaloupe as Ian left to get himself another glass of milk.

Serena rose to close the open books around her chair, apparently hoping to protect them from Beacon. As she did, she exposed the open split across the seat of her jeans. She wasn't wearing underwear.

"Nice jeans," Jake said. "Nice bum, too."

Serena winked at him, grabbed two slices of cantaloupe, and resumed her sprawl in the chair.

"I've got a teenager here," Morgan said.

"He's fifteen, Morgan." Serena said. "He'll be seeing women's flesh soon enough."

"Not on my friends, he won't!"

"Okay, okay. I won't let him see." She whizzed through the cantaloupe and took two more slices.

Morgan had never seen Serena so relaxed. She was radiant. Ian came back with a full glass of milk and the carton, just in case.

"As I was saying," Serena said between bites, "it's all about how we think, and about love. The power of thought is so strong that if a society thinks its future is bright, it will be, and vice versa. It's all been documented." Serena dropped her cantaloupe rinds on the tray and took another croissant.

"Really? That's cool." Ian washed down his fourth croissant and poured himself another glass of milk.

Morgan couldn't take her eyes off her beautiful baby. It was heaven having him back.

"What it boils down to," Serena said, "is that love is the answer to everything. Scientists are discovering it actually heals people."

So I'm on the right track, then.

And with Serena's most beneficent blessing.

How about that?

The headline would read, *Therapist Fills Herself with Love, Receives Approval from Above.*

Serena turned to her. "Did you know people with dogs actually live longer? It's because of the love they feel toward their pets." Serena took a huge mouthful of croissant and talked right through it.

"I've been practicing with Beacon. I pick him up and love him. I mean I really, really love him. Then I put him down and give myself exactly the same quality of love I gave him. I do this three times a day. It may sound weird but I'm telling you, it's changing my life."

"Actually, that sounds very effective." Morgan decided to begin with a slice of melon. It was perfectly ripe, she knew, but she couldn't exactly taste it and the texture was strangely unappealing.

"Oh yes. Try it with your clients. Except it might put you out of a job."

Serena polished off the rest of her croissant in two quick bites. "Would you believe I used to think men should be abolished?" she said to Jake and Ian. "But I know better now. Men can't help it that they're stupid."

"What?" Morgan almost lost her mouthful of cantaloupe.

Jake raised his eyebrow and Ian guffawed, spitting some of his croissant on his jeans.

"Not you two, of course," Serena said to Jake and Ian. "You're different."

Morgan and Jake exchanged grins. He wiped his brow in mock relief. Ian looked to Morgan for a cue, as if to say, "Who is this woman?"

"I'm not putting men down," Serena said. "It's just that their brains aren't as well developed as ours."

"Actually, I think I heard that on the news," Jake said, grinning.

"Dude, you mean you actually understood what they were saying?" Ian said.

"That was good, Ian." Morgan chuckled. "Really good." She decided to try another slice of cantaloupe.

"It's true," Serena said. "Research shows men's brains are more compartmentalized, while women's are more free-flowing. The various parts of our brains talk to one another much more easily, and we use more of our brains. We can be emotional and intuitive and rational and communicative all at the same time." Serena took a long sip of tea.

"Men are simply more emotionally and functionally primitive," Serena said. "They can't help it. We're a step ahead of them on the evolutionary scale, that's all. They rely on a primitive part of the brain more frequently than we do, whereas we have advanced to a newer part of the brain.

"I've learned to be compassionate about their condition," Serena said beatifically, gesturing with her glass.

Ian dove to the floor and crawled around on his belly, lizard-like.

Morgan smiled to herself about the concept of Serena being compassionate toward men while Ian got to his feet and took up an imaginary collection for the males.

"I saw that," Serena said.

"I can't help it," Morgan said. "Gotta love ya, kiddo. But I don't think it's a male/female thing so much as a masculine energy/feminine energy one. Look how compassionate, open, and loving Ian and Jake are. Whereas so many women are men with boobs."

"Like me, you mean."

"I didn't say that."

"You don't have to. I how how I've acted in the past. It's what I'm trying to change."

"You're succeeding. You've transformed your life. My point is, it's not about women over men. Women have developed our masculine side since the sixties. We're out there in the world in our careers. We're individualized and visible to ourselves and others more than ever before. Now we need to use that masculine strength to make a stand for our core feminine values of compassion, connectedness, stewardship, and nurturing. We're the life-givers. It's time for us to get out there and use our power to bring what we believe into the world."

"Awoman," Serena said. "More and more, feminine consciousness pervades everything. It opened the way for the Internet, which is about connection, community, the web of life. Like cable television, the Internet nurtures intimate knowledge of other people and cultures. And feminine consciousness spawned the environmental movement."

"But that's led mostly by men," Jake said. "And it's way too hierarchal."

"Yes," Serena said. But look what it's about—housekeeping. Global housekeeping. I'm talking about the power of feminine consciousness, not feminine rule. This is subtle."

"And men like Jake and Ian," Morgan said, "make the job so much easier."

"Right! It's not about dissing men," Serena said, "but about bringing in the Divine Feminine energy. The shift is coming and the only way to support it is through faith and love."

"The shift?" Ian looked puzzled. He'd been providing a running commentary on their conversation by mimicking everything they said, beginning with men with boobs and ending with global housekeeping, which apparently entailed dusting the globe with a leaf he plucked from a plant on the end table.

"Oh, yes. An evolutionary leap in human consciousness. We're in the middle of it. It will come to completion in 2012 according to the Mayans, the Hopis, and various prophets. That's when we'll vibrate into higher dimensions. It's all in the books." Serena reached her toe across to a pile of books and tapped it. "Beacon taught me, too. You just have to go with the flow."

Morgan smiled. Serena was discovering her own quirky version of what Morgan had been trying to teach her all summer.

"What's this?" Morgan shook her head so hard her tongue was wagging. No one could guess her riddle. "Can't you tell? I'm vibrating into a higher dimension."

"Very funny. Remember how angry I was at men?" Serena looked at Morgan and Jake, who looked at each other and laughed. "Okay, okay, I was a bitch. I mean jerk. But listen. My anger was for a reason, the same reason women need to get their history straight. Women's history of oppression is important because we carry the memory of it in our cells. It's entwined with our D.N.A and our job is to get it out of there."

Beacon pounced on a cave cricket as savagely as if it were the oppression-infested archetype for female D.N.A. Jake got up and took it away and then scratched Woof, who looked as if she were about to take the training of Beacon into her own paws.

"The way to release all that negativity is to feel it," Serena said, "to be compassionate toward the negative emotions. We acknowledge the feelings, experience them, validate the reasons for them, create new beliefs to support the way we want to behave, and let the old feelings go. The process unleashes our power because it frees us of our limitations so we can create whatever we want."

"Or," Morgan said, "you can work more directly. You can change your behavior as you choose and heal yourself that way, by charting a new course and confronting negative emotions only when they trip you up."

"Right," Serena said. "I've done my share of that lately."

"You have."

"First we shed our shackles, then we fly."

~ ~ ~

Morgan pulled Ian's sheets off his bed, laundered them, and hung them out to dry. The ground was dusty in the late August drought and the brown lawn rustled underfoot. Leaves the color of fall slowly drifted down, too dry to complete their season in spite of the humidity. The dust-covered trees were like straws, sucking the ground hard and coming up empty. She could almost hear the jagged sound of suction at the bottom of a glass.

While she waited the short time it would take the sun to dry Ian's sheets, Morgan ate her breakfast and intentionally filled herself with love.

The now-familiar process had become easy.

In trying to feel out who she was and in becoming more aware of her choices day by day, she was beginning to realize she'd been a woman of purpose—on her path—all along. Her problem had been that she hadn't honored—or even claimed—her essence and its power.

She'd always had something to give, some way to celebrate life, whether it was the care she put into arranging flowers she picked from her garden or the encouragement she offered a friend, a child, or a client. With its ongoing cycles of acknowledgment and thanksgiving, her life was a spiraling circle of offerings to the endless altars to life that seemed to dance in front of her each day.

But before, she'd made the mistake of thinking that her giving was about others and had judged herself based on their reaction or the result. Now, she shifted her focus to the desire she felt in her own heart and found that what she wanted was to give—to others and to herself. Now her satisfaction grew out of the alignment between her deepest desires and her actions.

In the past, she'd looked to others instead of herself and to the results rather than the process. In so doing, she'd lost the center she was now regaining by focusing on the promptings of her own heart.

When Serena wrote and when Clarissa created her event, they were moving toward a kind of success the world recognized. They would have a product to show for what they were doing. So theirs was a more concrete, socially sanctioned form of accomplishment—the kind of success the professional, male-driven world utilized to chart and measure a person's worth.

Morgan's work was less quantifiable—to herself as well as to others—so it had seemed less significant to her. She knew now, thanks to Serena, that this response was understandable, since women have a long history of feeling they don't make a difference. Yet her self-judgement was, she realized, an injustice. She needed to develop her own yardstick to measure her life by.

When she observed what she did day to day, she saw she was a weaver, moving life along with small, rhythmic passes of the shuttle. People's lives changed because she saw their inner light and found ways to help them see and build on it. She was a spider, weaving the light she gathered into the greater web that cradled all of creation.

As she pulled Ian's sheets from the clothesline and made his bed, she saw how this gesture supported him in the same way she supported her clients. Ian loved fresh sheets in summer. He said they smelled like sunshine. Tonight, he'd pull his sheets up around his face, inhale their fragrance, and drift off to sleep feeling loved because she'd remembered him with this small gift.

And now, Morgan reminded herself to give herself a gift. She was learning that when she balanced giving to others with giving to herself, she kept her sense of wonder alive, as if her inner children were playing happily and she was filling herself with Spirit's love. As she stretched her body from her toes to her arched back and extended arms, all the way through to her fingers, she inhaled the boy smells of Ian's exuberantly chaotic room and gave herself a long moment to sense exactly what she wanted.

She chose to savor a long bath with essential oils, candles, and music.

As she immersed herself in the fragrant, steaming tub, something began to come to her.

Out of this gift she'd given herself, another gift was blooming, an offering that, as it slowly took shape, was both mysterious and as familiar in its buoyancy as the water in which she floated.

It was her calling.

Clear.

Strong.

This is what it is—for me—to be the hundredth woman.

My path isn't about outward accomplishments.

Or perfection.

Being the hundredth woman—with all my frailties—begins with taking responsibility for myself.

I'm the only one who can change my life.

I'm the chick breaking out of the shell, the cage I was taught to see as my prison, the cell from which I searched for someone else to fulfill me and worried about everyone else's needs but my own.

I'm shaking that off, stretching my wings, and taking flight.

On my own terms.

We must achieve critical mass if we're to survive.

And we will.

I can taste it.

To support that, my job is to live fully in the present and honor my ever-deepening awareness of my truest self.

Then I'm a catalyst.

Every single thing I do matters.

But that's not a burden—It's an opportunity.

By facing my fears and committing to my essence, I'm doing my part to create the matrix that frees women to lead the world toward a more humane future.

The change will come as women acknowledge that the love we give—whether through bold action or through the silent swelling of our hearts—is a power second to none.

In becoming visible and important to ourselves, in loving ourselves and making that love primary, we will create a shift—from power over to power from within, from having to loving, from doing to being.

We won't adhere to the old polite invisibility.

We won't cloak ourselves or defer to our opposite.

Rather, we'll make a stand for our feminine values, make noise, and take up space.

All those skills we've honed to achieve equality with men in the workplace and in the world will become our tools for forging a compassion-based ground of being for our species. Combining the hard-won powers of women with an insistence that our basic nurturing values become fully manifested at all levels of society, we will create quality of life for all living things.

We'll apply our skills to what we value instead of selling them to the highest bidder.

We'll add muscle to love. And in so doing, we'll create power beyond imagining.

Standing tall in our wisdom of the heart, insisting on manifesting our loving values at every level, we will change the world.

Morgan rose from her bath with the dignity of a goddess being born. She wrapped a terry cloth robe around her body as solemnly as if it were the mantle of the hundredth woman and drew a deep breath.

Just then Serena tromped up the stairs shouting, "These are my love books!"

She had coerced the U.P.S. man into carrying three cartons of books up for her.

That woman goes through books as if they were toilet paper.

Morgan caught a glimpse of her before she disappeared into her bedroom. Serena was oblivious to the fact that the U.P.S. man was getting a kick out of her ravings and thoroughly enjoying her butt in her cutoffs, especially when she leaned down to pull a dust bunny from Beacon's snout.

~ ~ ~

"How did it go?" Morgan was lying on the couch trying to read when Serena breezed in after her first day at the university and threw her briefcase over the back of the love seat.

It was back-to-school day for both Ian and Serena. Ian had dashed in earlier, deposited his books in the dining room, and headed out on his bike. This morning, Morgan had seen Clarissa for her last session in addition to two other clients. It was all she could handle anymore. Then she came home and slept. She'd set her alarm for a half hour before Ian was due back.

"I loved it." Serena stretched her arms high over her head, then placed both hands at the side of her waist and arched backwards.

Morgan pulled her legs in and Serena plopped down on the couch.

"This could become a full time job, it turns out. The professor I'm replacing is relocating. And get this—drum roll, please…."

"What?"

"I got asked out on a date."

"Get out!"

"At least, I think it's a date."

"Dish, girlfriend."

"It's no big deal."

"Yeah, right."

"He's a drama professor."

"Why am I not surprised?"

"Oh stop. I met him at that party at Jane's."

"The guy you talked to practically all night?"

Serena grinned.

"The one with the terrific white sideburns and the to-die-for brown eyes?" Morgan said.

"That would be him. Jeffrey. Jeffrey Hopper. Boy, did you get a good look."

"I always do."

"Am I stepping on your turf?"

"No way. What kind of a name is Hopper? Is he a rabbit?"

"Tell you what, I'm not planning to marry him."

"Serena Hopper. Naw. But go out with him! Save your theories about men for the second date though, okay?"

"Hey, I said I got asked out, I didn't say I was going."

"Why the hell not?"

"Who needs all that right now?"

"You do."

"Yeah, right." Serena laughed, then grew serious. "So. What did the doctor say?"

"Not a whole lot. The lab results didn't show anything. He thinks it's stress."

"In other words, he doesn't know so he wants to tell you it's all in your head. Typical." Serena chewed on the inside of her cheek. "Did he test for Lyme Disease? Epstein-Barr? Chronic fatigue? Fibromyalgia? Thyroid? Diabetes? Hepatitis? A.I.D.S.? Cushing's Disease?"

"Oh, as if I'm going to be outside long enough to get bitten by a tick in this heat. If I saw a tick on me, believe me, you'd know about it."

"What about the others?"

"He said it could be a virus and if I'm not better in two weeks, to go back."

"He's not taking you seriously."

"I'm telling you, Serena, I know what's going on. It isn't physical."

"If that asshole Shadow can make you feel this bad, then he can make something go wrong with your body, too."

She felt herself inwardly recoil. "I don't think he has that much power over me."

Once the words were out of her mouth, she realized this wasn't an altogether true statement. But she wasn't prepared to follow the trail of questions and doubts her fear would lead her on if she revisited her answer.

"What about cancer?"

"Come on, Serena."

"I had a friend who was sick for a long time and they didn't know what it was. By the time they figured out it was cancer, she was terminal."

"Thanks." She hadn't realized she was crying.

Serena swooped down beside her. "Me and my big mouth. I'm sorry."

"It's okay." She buried her head in Serena's warm, bony chest and received the comfort she needed to let go. She cried for a very long time.

"You must be so scared."

"No shit. I even asked the doctor about cancer."

"And?"

"I said I've heard people who go through fatigue, nausea, and weight loss can have cancer."

"What did he say."

"He perked right up. It was weird. He said, 'Oh yeah, it doesn't show up in the lab results and all of a sudden—poof!—they're dead.'"

She cried for a long time.

"What an asshole," Serena said.

"I couldn't have said it better myself." Morgan giggled through her tears. "Look at your shirt. There's mucous everywhere."

Serena pulled her back in and she closed her eyes.

Was it her imagination, or did she hear Shadow snicker?

CHAPTER 21

recognition

1. *I CELEBRATE the abundant gifts I've enjoyed, including…*

    (Insert yer show & tell here)

2. *I OPEN to my higher self and align with Divine Wholeness, trusting in the vast, loving power I'm part of.*

3. *I KNOW Divine Wholeness loves me passionately, lavishing me with opportunities for enlightenment.*

4. *I CREATE my own experience, so I choose a loving, juicy, life-affirming ground of being.*

5. *I CHOOSE to co-create with Divine Wholeness, releasing what doesn't work. I am transformed.*

6. I LOVE and forgive myself and others for
everything. I balance my energy
on every level, releasing any
debris for cosmic composting.

7. I EXPRESS my intentions. Sweet Wildness,
please indulge my adorable
desires, provided they're for
the highest good of everyone
everywhere.

(Insert yer affirmation here—
I now am/have/do…)

And so it is!

8. I ACCEPT the abundant gifts I receive
from Divine Wholeness. Knowing I'm
blessed with all I need, I meet
life wholeheartedly in a spirit
of anticipation, wonder, and
gratitude.

Cumin' 'atcha every day!

—K. G. and her advanced students

"Eighteen hundred dollars?" her mother said.

"Just over." Clarissa was driving her old Ford. Her mother was beside her and the boys were in the back. They were heading to Macon County to do some canvassing.

At first, she'd been reluctant to take her white mother into a black neighborhood where her own status was marginal. But she decided not to let small fears stand in the way of enjoying her mother's support, especially since she'd been willing to buy some normal clothes. Clarissa couldn't see canvassing in either designer originals or those wretched thousand-year-old jeans her mother loved to wear.

"You mean, buy off the rack?" her mother had said when she first broached the subject. She looked shocked, then sheepishly explained she was used to boys' jeans from the Sears catalog or clothing tailor-made to her specifications, all delivered to her door.

"It's because I'm hard to fit," Serena had said.

"Hard to please is more like it," Clarissa said three hours into her mother's first trip to a mall. Serena simply smiled, turned into the next store they passed, and bought three dresses in fifteen minutes. All of which, to her credit, were quite ordinary.

That same afternoon, her mother had returned her rented Mercedes and bought a used van so she could accommodate the boys' friends and blend in with Clarissa's neighborhood.

Now Clarissa was telling her mother about her trip to the mall with Joshua and the boys. Seeing so many coins in the fountain had made her wonder what happened to all that money. So she spoke to the manager and learned they scooped out coins every month when they cleaned the fountains. There were buckets of coins in storage and the mall manager was eager to get rid of them, especially since she liked her cause.

"She turned eighteen hundred dollars over to you, just like that?"

"Combined with the fountains from two other malls, it came to that, yes. Tell Grandy what we did with the money, boys."

Her mother got a kick out of the boys, but wasn't ready for the name "Grandma," so she'd settled on "Grandy" instead.

"We took it to the bank. The car was weighted down really bad," Martin said.

"Very badly," Clarissa said.

"That's what I meant."

"We scraped the, the—" Frankie said.

"The tailpipe hit the road," Martin said, "but we made it to the bank. Three men had to help carry it in."

"Then we got pizza," Frankie said.

"I didn't have to do a thing, and now I have enough money to go ahead with the event."

"I would have given you the money."

"I know. I don't mean to sound ungrateful, but I had to do it myself."

The car rolled into Rosa Brooks' driveway, scattering squawking chickens everywhere. Visiting a house the third and fourth time was even harder than the first. She hated bothering people.

A pretty teenager came to the screen door when she knocked.

"Is Ms. Brooks in?"

"Tameka? Who's there?" Rosa Brooks called from deep inside the house.

"It's that lady. You know, the dump lady."

Thanks.

"Mmm, mmm, mmm," growled a voice nearer the door.

She backed down the steps and stood by her mother.

"Mama, never you mind. I got it." Ms. Brooks stepped outside. She was wearing an apron.

I interrupted her again.

"We're having an event I thought your family might enjoy." Clarissa handed her a flyer.

"'Dump the Dump: Mothers and Others for a Living Earth,'" Ms. Brooks read. She took her time studying the rest of the flyer.

Clarissa's breath caught.

Is she actually going to come?

"We could use some volunteer help. Or you and your family could just come. We're getting quite a few people interested."

Ease up!

Don't push.

"Elder Mary Holden told us about this in church last week. She thinks it would be good for us to get together and stop this dump."

Fabulous.

"We'd love to have y'all join us."

"I don't know—"

"I'm not trying to push you, Ms. Brooks. But I get the feeling people in this community might be afraid to oppose the dump because they don't want to stand out as troublemakers."

"Can you blame us?"

"No. Of course not. But the more people get involved, the less any one person stands out. If you could get your neighbors to come, and they bring their neighbors, pretty soon we'll have a whole community standing together. And that's power."

"I'm sorry." Ms. Brooks tried to give the flyer back to Clarissa. "I appreciate what you're doing, really I do. But I don't want to get involved."

"I understand. Hang on to the flyer, just in case—"

"Excuse me?" Clarissa's mother said. "What do you mean, you don't want to get involved? You live here. So you're already involved. The question is, what are you going to do about it?"

Oh god.

Is my mother going to slam this door I've worked so hard to squeeze one toe into?

"Aren't we all involved? Don't we all breathe this air?" Her mother gestured grandly with her arms. "I'm not just some outsider trying to get you to do something, I'm another woman living downwind from what could be a nuclear disaster. But it doesn't have to be that way. Your church elder is right. Doesn't God help those who help themselves?"

Am I hearing things?

My mother the evangelist?

"And who better than we," her mother said, "the people who live on the land that could be destroyed by this project, to determine what goes on here?"

Rosa Brooks stared at Serena.

But this only fueled her mother's fire. "Don't we have a right to breathe without getting cancer? To drink water, to take a bath without getting sick and possibly dying? Did God create this land and our beautiful children for us to watch it all be destroyed?"

Ms. Brooks glanced at the flyer again. She slowly opened the screen door and went inside. From where Clarissa stood in the still-bright sun, Rosa Brooks' face, now obscured by the screen, was blackness framed by black. Only the whites of her eyes were dimly visible.

"I'll think on it," Rosa said softly.

~ ~ ~

"Do you think Morgan is dying?" Grandmama's hands clutched her heart. She was watching Morgan sleep.

"Great Mother Goddess—she can't be." But Brigid was concerned.

Morgan muttered and thrashed her legs.

"She could be leaving her earth life." Big Mom seldom joined them unless Clarissa was present. Her sudden appearance was both a relief and a signal that Morgan's condition was, in fact, grave. "But I think she could live."

"What gives you hope?" Grandmama sounded desperate.

"She's very brave." Big Mom looked solemnly into Grandmama's eyes. "Even when she's afraid, she keeps going."

Grandmama's shoulders relaxed ever so slightly.

"So far." Shadow appeared out of nowhere. "But surely you don't think I'm finished, do you?"

He made his head very big and shot it out of his neck. It divided into three ghoulish skulls—one laughing in the face of each of them—before he withdrew them and became the dapper gentleman once again.

"I relish the long, slow kill." He ran the tip of his tongue slowly across the tips of is teeth, working his mouth as his eyes became lewd, veiled crescents. "It's my specialty."

"We have to do something," Brigid said, turning her back on him and drawing in close to Grandmama and Big Mom.

Shadow materialized in the center of their huddle. He twirled slowly, looking each of them in the eye. "You don't actually think there's something you old biddies can do, do you?"

He stepped outside their circle and sashayed the periphery of the room, his forefinger tapping his chin. "Your vocabulary word for the day is 'ineffectual.' Look it up. Then look up 'worthless,' 'inadequate,' and, I think," he said, rolling his eyes upward, "let me see, yes, look up 'shit-for-brains.'"

Shadow dipped down and kissed Morgan on the mouth. Her lips turned blue and parted as a pale, smoky substance began to curl from her mouth. It rose toward Shadow, who had positioned himself above her to inhale her essence.

Grandmama lunged at Shadow and tried to push him away while Brigid fanned the smoky substance back into Morgan's mouth with her hand.

"Ignore him," Big Mom said. "Think about it. Everywhere he leads us is the opposite of where we need to go."

"Right you are," Brigid said.

She and Grandmama turned their backs to Shadow and he disappeared.

"We have work to do," Big Mom said. "Big work. It's why I'm here."

"Tell us." Grandmama's voice was urgent.

"If we want to help them move forward, we have to move forward, too," Big Mom said.

"'As above, so below,'" Brigid whispered. How many times had she heard her elders say that? She allowed this thought to penetrate her deepest levels.

"I take your meaning." Brigid closed her eyes and began to sway. Messages were beginning to pour in from her guides. "'Tis in centering ourselves we must begin. We must breathe into our hearts, think of the good things—life's pleasures, great and small—and fill our hearts with love. Then we must go over each point where we gave in to fear, to unworthiness, to self-doubt—these we must examine with the eyes of a hawk."

"If we think only of ourselves, won't that slow us down from helping?" Grandmama frowned.

"No. It's the opposite," Big Mom said. "It's like pulling weeds away from the corn, beans, and squash. We'll be rooting out the poisons so everyone can breathe."

"Aye," Brigid said. "'Tis only when we let go of our past that we can truly support these women of the present. When they want to be bold, we won't be holding them back because we're afraid for them."

"Right. Our fear won't stand over them like a bear." Big Mom raised her head and set her chin. "And we must get others to do the same. The ancestors must all do this work."

"Everyone needs to do this work," Grandmama said. "All the living women need to do it too."

"Aye, it would help them," Brigid said. "Facing the past is a step they cannot skip. They must be clear to become the goddesses they truly are. Morgan laughs at her, but Serena is right. 'Tis not so long before the Great Shift will be upon them."

Big Mom blinked slowly. "It's here now. The prophecies speak of the year 2012, but that's the completion of the cycle." She drew a broad arc in the air with her hand. "It's not a strike of lightning." She clapped once, hard. "This change seems to move slowly, like spring rain seeping into land that looks lifeless until that big moment when the seeds soaking underground burst into life. Women are like those seeds. Each thinks she's alone in her struggle, when really she's the power behind the biggest change to ever sweep the earth."

"'Tis because the ancestors haven't completed our work," Brigid said, "that Morgan is sick, and there's the truth of it. She could easily clear her own feelings. We did the best we could, aye, but we left a legacy of fear. Now she drags around thousands of years of our history. It's too much for her poor body to bear. Much as I hate to give voice to the ugly thought, the strain she's under—it could kill her."

"I won't have that. We're not going to let her die." Grandmama's back became straight as a sapling as she prepared to face her inner journey.

Shadow shimmered in and out of view for a moment.

But then he took a deep breath and launched into a twisted version of *Love Letters in the Sand.* He was dancing the dance of the tide coming in to wash away their efforts, making swishing sounds like waves that drew closer, pulled back, then drew closer still.

"While there's breath in my body, you're not going to win." Grandmama was fierce.

"But that's just it, isn't it, old woman? You have no breath, and you have no body."

~ ~ ~

"The End. Ta da!" Serena grinned broadly.

She was about to burst. It was noon on September second, her sixtieth birthday, and she had just finished reading the outline for her book to Morgan, Clarissa, and the boys. Her working title was *Forgiving the Opposite Sex and Lassoing Your Bliss.*

The book would contain chapters with titles including "Men—Indigenous or Alien?" "Neanderthalus Interruptus," "You Catch More Highs with Honey than You do with Vinegar," "The Hokey Pokey Truth—There's More Than One Way to Turn Yourself Around," and "Backing into Your Bliss."

They were all sitting around Morgan's dining room table. Jake had served a late brunch before he and Ian disappeared on mysterious errands. The women and children were making preparations for her birthday party that evening.

Frankie was tearing up lettuce for the salad, Martin was shelling peas, Morgan was peeling garlic, and Clarissa was mashing butter for the garlic bread. An enormous pot of spaghetti sauce, a specialty of Morgan's and a favorite of Ian's, was simmering on the back of the stove.

Serena had noticed it took Morgan three days to make the sauce because she was too tired to do more than a few steps each day.

"Congratulations! A fine birthday present to give yourself." Morgan looked like shit, but she was trying.

"My mother the *author,*" Clarissa said.

"Grandy, that was really, really good."

"Why thank you, Frankie."

"What are you talking about?" Martin stuck out his lower lip. "I didn't understand it, so I know you didn't."

"You don't have to understand something to know it's good. I'd like to see you write a book outline."

"Maybe I will someday."

"That's right, Martin, maybe you will," Serena said.

Who knew how great it would be to be a grandmother?

A Grandy.

She stood to get everyone something to drink. It was impossible to resist tasting the spaghetti sauce.

"This is excellent."

"Thanks."

"Needs garlic, though."

Morgan looked a little crestfallen, but she took three of the garlic cloves she had peeled for the bread and started to get up to crush them into the sauce.

"Sit. I'll do it."

"Thanks."

"Serena told me you weren't well. How do you feel? You look pale." Clarissa had softened the butter and moved on to shredding cheese for the salad.

"It's this new makeup I'm trying, Mauve Mystery. Doesn't cut it, huh?"

"I'm serious."

"Sorry. I've been feeling a little weak, but I'll be all right."

What an understatement.

Morgan seemed to look worse each day and did less and less. Serena felt as if she were watching her slip away. Why did Morgan keep insisting she was going to be fine, when anyone could see she was getting sicker?

Jake arrived with a bucket of shrimp and a big, flat box he instructed her to stay away from. Then he put a pot on to boil and tasted the spaghetti sauce.

"Tastes great! Needs garlic, though."

Morgan handed Serena three more cloves.

Ian appeared as they were finishing with the salad and the garlic bread, a package under his arm. He grinned at Serena and hid the package with his body.

"Wow! Mom's famous spaghetti sauce!" Still holding the package protectively, Ian grabbed a soup spoon and helped himself to a giant slurp of sauce. "Delicious. Only thing is, it needs a lot more garlic."

~ ~ ~

Morgan started to peel more garlic.

But then again, what the hell.

She pulled herself up from her chair and went to the spice rack. She prided herself on never using garlic powder, but she kept it around anyway. She threw a quarter of the jar into the spaghetti sauce, gave it a quick stir, and poured herself a big glass of iced tea.

At the feeder outside the kitchen window, a mourning dove was frantically feeding her fledglings. The two fat, subtly iridescent youngsters squawked for food and the mother, who was scrawny and dull from the work of raising her second brood of the summer, scrambled to bail seeds into the fledglings' open mouths, never taking a bite for herself. She looked so empty, almost hollow. Morgan worried she might be dying.

When she went out on the deck to take a break and put her feet up, the mother flew off. Too inexperienced to be afraid, the fledglings stayed and fed themselves competently, then began squawking to be fed again as soon as their mother reappeared.

Is this is a message?

A mirror of how women neglect ourselves in order to do for others who can take care of themselves without our noble sacrifice?

Serena, Clarissa, and the boys joined her on the deck. Ian and Jake shot past them, and Jake ran to the far end of the lawn and sailed a frisbee to Ian.

I've been sleeping with the perfect playmate for my son.

"How is your event coming along?" Morgan already knew the answer to that question, since Serena bragged almost hourly about her Pearl's progress, but she wanted Clarissa to tell her anyway.

"We have plenty of funding for the event itself—which is a relief—even without Deep Pockets over here." Clarissa shot Serena an amused smile. "It seems as if more people get involved every day, both from out in the county and from town, so we keep coming up with more ways to expand the project. And we have some great talent lined up, don't we, boys?"

"There's African drummers!" Martin said. "You should see their drums. They're huge."

Frankie jumped into the air and made a big circle with his arms.

"They're rounding up all kinds of noisemakers," Clarissa said.

"Yeah! So everybody can play. Mom? Can we play frisbee?"

"Sure." Clarissa turned back to her. "We plan to get the audience drumming, chanting, singing, and dancing. A women's chorus called *Nobody's Rib* made up a short musical about stopping the dump, and they have choruses for the audience to sing. It's hilarious."

"What fun." Morgan leaned her head back against the top of her chair. Watching Clarissa and Serena move forward, both in their relationship and in their projects, moved her deeply. She drew a deep breath and nourished herself with the satisfaction of knowing she'd helped them become who they truly were. Hundredth women.

"We also have nuclear experts," Clarissa said, "and heads of community groups who'll speak briefly. Emphasize the word 'briefly.' My part is shaping up, too."

"What are you going to do?"

"You'll have to come and see."

"I wouldn't miss it for anything."

"Good. Morgan?"

"Yes."

"There's something I'd like."

"What?"

"I want you and my mother to have a meeting with me."

Morgan raised her eyebrow.

"Not that kind of meeting." Clarissa laughed. "I want to check in about the ancestors and the hundredth woman thing."

"Okay."

"Would tomorrow afternoon work?"

~ ~ ~

Her heart swelling with matriarchal pride and her body—for once—feeling more alive, Morgan took in the scene surrounding her. Serena's party was in full swing.

My brood is thriving.

Ian polished off his fourth plate of spaghetti and Sierra—who was due in two weeks and looked like a ripe seed pod, shiny and bursting—heaved herself off the couch, dug her fists into the small of her back, stretched, and lumbered toward the buffet in the dining room for a second helping.

"Great spaghetti, Mom." Sierra burped. "Way too much garlic, but I love it." She gave her mother a hug, the exertion prompting another belch.

Morgan scanned the room. Jane and Morgan had invited assorted friends to introduce Serena to new people. Jeffrey Hopper, Serena's recent date, was there, keeping a warm, twinkling eye on her.

God, everyone here is a Yankee.

Except Jake and Rich.

And Clarissa and her boys.

And, of course, Aunt Lee, who had arrived with biscuits, marshmallow coleslaw, and cucumber finger sandwiches for her Peach Blossom "to go with the Italian y'all was fixin.'"

Why is it that Yankees in the South seem to know only other Yankees?

We live in a parallel universe, our paths intersecting with native Southerners only in public places.

In her survey of her guests, Morgan's eyes kept returning to an unfamiliar man who'd been observing her with frank curiosity all evening. She held his gaze for a few moments before looking away. Apparently he took this as an invitation, because now he slowly approached her.

Patrick introduced himself with a clasp of the hands—part handshake, part caress—that reeled him in close to her. His skin was cool and soft, but the contact he made was warm. Morgan eased her hand from his and he took a half step back.

Patrick's manner was centered and contained, yet she sensed a gentle zaniness poised to spill forth at any moment.

"Serena talks about you," he said. "Incessantly."

His intelligent eyes were the same color as the soft cloud of clean, well-brushed gray hair that formed a halo around his head and shoulders. He was medium height and lanky, easy in his body.

"She talks a lot."

"No kidding." His eyes were full of fun.

"Do I want to know?"

"I think I would if I were you."

"Tell me. I think."

They laughed together, hard.

"She says you're the most complete woman she's ever known," he said with quiet intensity.

"Serena said that? No."

"Oh yes. What were her words?" He turned and stood by Morgan's side, his shoulder touching hers. Jake pretended not to stare at them from the far side of the living room and she pretended not to notice.

In mock concentration, Patrick framed each adjective with his long fingers before reverently placing it across an imaginary marquee in front of Morgan. "'Intense,' she said. Yes, and 'giving.' 'Bold.' 'Sensual.'" He paused after that word and gazed at her sideways. "Oh," he said, pretending to pull his attention back to the marquee. And 'wise.' 'Profound.' 'Funny.'"

He turned to face Morgan. "A priestess of the wild," he said softly, "a supreme goddess and keeper of the mysteries."

In the air between them, a shimmering energy undulated that connected their entire bodies, from above the crowns of their heads all the way to the space below their feet. It wasn't simply sexual—it was highly charged with the same life force she was coming to know when she connected her body with the earth and sky.

"Indeed?" she said. "You'd better stop. I think I'm falling in love with myself."

Patrick's eyes danced. "Is Serena on medication?"

"No, but maybe she should be," Morgan said. "You must be from the college."

"Part time. I teach a course in the women's studies program called 'What Men Need to Appreciate about Women.'"

"Yeah, right."

"Actually, it's true."

"Seriously?"

"Oh, yes. And humorously, too."

"What do you think men need to appreciate about women?"

"We could take a lifetime on that, couldn't we?" He smiled. "Men's lives are transformed to the extent that they can embrace the feminine—both within themselves and all around them. It's incredible that men can want women so much and appreciate them so little."

"True."

"Most men behave as if lust, spiritual resonance, and emotional connection are mutually exclusive—whereas combined, they're medicine for the soul."

She regarded him evenly. "What else do you do?"

"I run a therapy group for men who batter women. It's a tough job, but someone has to do it."

Morgan raised one eyebrow.

"Nice," Patrick said. "You're very good at that."

"Go on."

"About which?"

"About your work."

"Oh, that. I also facilitate a ropes course and raise my fifteen-year-old son. And I do a little standup comedy and play alternative rock music."

"In other words, you're a force to be reckoned with," Morgan said.

"I hope not. I try to be low maintenance. With no loss of intrigue, of course."

"Really? You have been doing your homework."

Patrick puffed out his chest and grinned. The gesture could have been boyish, but it wasn't. It was grown up and free, spontaneous in a way that most males shut down in adolescence. This was a man who had done the work—and the play—of clearing the obstacles to his own authenticity. And now he was inviting Morgan to dive into his pool of exuberance and have a swim.

Had she felt better—and if she weren't playing hostess—she might have accepted his invitation and added a twist of her own. But Frankie and Martin came bounding up, Beacon and Woof close behind, panting.

Frankie said, "Ian wants to know, are there any jars or plastic thingies that we can't use?"

"No. Why?"

"They're everywhere! Martin, let's go!" Frankie tried to pull his brother away.

"Who's everywhere? What are you guys up to?"

"Fireflies! They're outside. Ian says you can take their butts off and put them on your finger. They glow for a whole day!"

What?

Last I heard, Ian was planning to become a Buddhist vegetarian.

"Hold on," Morgan said. "You're talking about killing those poor fireflies."

"Naw," Frankie said. "Just taking their butts off."

"Think about it," Martin said. "How long do you think you'd last without your butt?"

"Tell you what," Morgan said. "Catch all the fireflies you want, but let them hang on to their butts and release them in an hour."

"Awww… Okay!" Frankie and Martin said in unison and ran off, followed by two very excited dogs.

She turned to Patrick. "If you'll excuse me, I have a birthday cake to set on fire."

She set off to solicit Jake's help. Later, when the last guests were preparing to leave, she pulled Jake aside again.

"I'm having the most delicious fantasy," she whispered.

Jake's jaw dropped and both eyebrows shot up.

"Not that!" Morgan laughed. "But close enough. Why don't you go upstairs, take a shower, put on the tiniest dab of that fabulous cologne you wear, slip into that outrageous black silk robe of yours, tie a ribbon around your favorite appendage, and pay a late night visit to our birthday girl?"

Jake drew away swiftly, but Morgan pulled him back in.

"You can't tell me you haven't thought about it."

"True, but—"

"But nothing. Butt naked is more like it. Serena needs to expand her horizons, and I think you're just the man for the job."

He gave her that long, slow grin of his.

"Hurry up. Just don't let Ian get wind of this."

CHAPTER 22

fire paradise

From around the globe, we gather.
In a pulsing golden spiral, we dance.... .
Woman to Woman
We empower one another.
Woman to World
We bring forth blessing,
As archaic memories swell
In sacred recognition of this
divine responsibility.

—Jennifer Case

Morgan was slicing the last kiwi into a large bowl containing papayas, blueberries, and cantaloupe when Serena and Jake finally emerged for Sunday breakfast, flushed and giggling. She felt the tiniest stab of envy but quickly let it go. Serena deserved this, and it validated the split between Morgan and Jake.

Aunt Lee popped in with hot biscuits and gravy and Morgan fixed omelets. Ian was still down for the count.

Serena and Jake indulged in a little footsie that Aunt Lee—who was late for church and didn't have time for anything but a small glass of sweet tea—didn't pick up on.

After Aunt Lee left and they were seated at the dining room table, Serena blushed like a thirteen-year-old and beamed at her. "I went with the flow."

"Yeah," Jake said, "the flow and flow and flow and flow.

"Good. If you hadn't been able to enjoy Jake, I'd have called in the medics to make sure you were still with us."

Serena jumped up, grabbed Morgan's face and kissed her passionately on the mouth.

Has she finally lost her mind completely?

"How long is this birthday celebration going to last? I don't know how much more I can take," Morgan said.

Serena plopped back down in her chair and grinned at her. "Sorry." There was a brief pause. "I take that lie back. I've always wanted to do that."

"Always?"

"Always."

"Geez."

"My heart is wide open." Serena arched against the back of her chair and ran her fingers through her tousled hair. "Saying yes to Jake was a gift I gave myself. And it was *good.*" She drew a full breath. "Remember how I said the only time I ever felt at home was with Lloyd and Big Mom?"

"Yeah," Morgan said. "I remember that."

Serena's eyes were glistening and she was lit from within with a joy that filled the room with sunshine. "It's no longer true. Thanks to you, Morgan—you and Clarissa and the boys, Jake, Ian, Beacon, Woof—I'm home now." Giant tears splashed down her cheeks.

"You're welcome, Sweetie," Morgan said. "But it's mostly thanks to you. It's amazing how much you've changed. All that anger—it's evaporated."

"Actually, it hasn't. I still feel it. Not as much, but it comes up. The difference is, I try not to zap people with it. Instead, I own it. It's part of me and it's not about anybody else but me."

"Does that help?"

"It does. I found out I always react to the same kinds of things. So obviously what I am reacting to is something in me. I try to find out what's good about my anger in the moment, what messages it offers."

"Like what?"

"Take the other day. I was reading in the living room, and all of a sudden Ian came charging in, threw himself on the couch so hard I thought he would break it—"

"I've got to get him to be more gentle with the furniture. He has no idea how much force his weight carries now."

"Anyway, he grabbed the remote and started channel-surfing with the volume cranked up. At the same time, he was yelling out some joke he heard in school."

"And?"

"And I felt pissed."

"He didn't say anything about you coming down on him."

"That's because I didn't. I laughed at his joke—it was pretty funny—and did my best to accept him. Then I realized what was bothering me. Ian's free and spontaneous. He expects everyone to love him, no matter what he does, and they do. My parents and the nuns punished me for acting the way he does, and I hated it. When I was a kid, I desperately needed to be more like him. I still do. In that instance, I was able to use my anger as a teacher instead of thinking it was something to get upset about."

"That's huge. Congratulations."

"Thanks. I decided I could start being more spontaneous then and there. I picked up the cushion behind me, bashed him with it, and ran. We got into a water fight in the back yard."

"Now that I did hear about. He said you're really cool."

"High praise from the King of Cool. It felt great. Afterwards, I climbed the stairs two at a time and hit the computer. Suddenly, my mind was free and my book concept flew together."

Morgan sank back in her chair, her heart wide open.

Shadow's grip on her spine loosened.

Just a little.

~ ~ ~

Morgan was in bed, the sheets loosely draped across her naked body, resting before her meeting with Clarissa and Serena and working to unravel the mystery of her illness.

Where is Shadow's foothold?

She went back to her training and thought about how psychology defined the inner shadow. It was the unconscious, those parts a person denied and drove underground. She adjusted her pillow and listed the aspects of herself she didn't always accept.

My weight, sometimes.

My fear.

Definitely, my fear.

Not having a book in me like Serena or an event like Clarissa.

Why did that still bother her?

Because I feel as if I'm ordinary, no one special—just another dumb mother trying to keep from looking useless to the rest of the world.

Ouch!

I thought I'd made peace with this.

Why do I still feel as if I don't count because I don't have a goal?

She decided to discover what was wonderful about each aspect of herself she wasn't accepting. She'd find a way to embrace them all.

Starting with her body, she slid her hands over her nakedness. Her waist, even lying on her back, was creased and—since her breasts fell off to the sides instead of saluting skyward, as they once had—her belly mounded with more definition than her breasts.

Morgan laughed out loud. She still loved her body. It was familiar—friendly—and it had been there for her through every moment of her life. What better ally could there be?

Now, what was good about her fat?

I could live longer than Serena without food.

The thought made her giddy.

I'm easy to make love with, hard to push around.

I don't have to run to the gym to keep my body the way it is.

I don't fight with myself to be different from how I am.

When a man is attracted to me, chances are he's thinking with more than just his one-eyed wonder.

Okay. She drew a deep breath.

Now, what was good about fear?

Fear let her know when she wasn't safe, so she could protect herself. At other times, it showed up as a self-limiting belief, signaling her to push beyond her comfort zone and try something new. And being paralyzed with fear is what first drove her into therapy, initiating her journey of self-discovery and spirituality.

Now she wasn't afraid of difficult emotions—other people's or her own—because she knew from experience that each obstacle contained a gift. This knowledge buoyed all her feelings because she'd learned to trust that the journey to self-discovery, lovingly conducted, led straight to the heart of Spirit.

Okay, so what's good about not having a big dream?

Morgan felt herself sinking. She'd already forgotten how anything could be right about feeling undirected.

There was an awful twist in her spine.

Shadow.

Keep going, girlfriend.

You must be getting close to a big one.

She considered the word "goal." It made her think of men with huge padded shoulders thundering across a football field. Or in short-sleeved white shirts, cheap ties, and white socks consuming coffee from styrofoam cups, leaning across collapsible tables with plastic walnut veneer, and going over flip charts at sales meetings.

I don't have goals because I don't want goals!

For me, they aren't necessary.

Goals were contrary to her nature.

She let out a long whoosh of breath. Her path didn't involve bearing down hard on a straight, narrow line to some predetermined destination. What was in her way, then?

I'm drifting.

The thought made her wince. No, she wasn't drifting, exactly.

She was flowing. And listening. There were things she wanted for herself, such as not being controlled by Shadow and not being controlled by the need for a man. Not being controlled, period.

And she wanted to be part of what made life work, what made hearts open and dreams materialize. But these weren't goals, exactly. They were more like... desires, intentions.

Intentions.

She wasn't fighting toward goals, she was gliding toward her intentions. And laughing along the way.

Patrick's mirth-filled eyes flitted through her imagination. He'd been a gift to her, an angel, because their meeting reminded her of something she'd sometimes forgotten in the intensity of that transformative summer—to have fun. Not just to have fun, but to recognize that fun is the heart of spirituality.

There wasn't any point in being the hundredth woman without it.

The ends are the means.

How I get there is what I'll get.

Morgan wriggled pleasantly on her bed. She wasn't some lonely master of her fate. She was linked to all the juicy forces of nature, the higher purposes of her guides, and the Great Laughing Oneness out of which everything oozed.

She inhaled divine love—infusing her body and spirit with grace like warm, flowing honey—then exhaled what she didn't need as a gift to all of creation, her breath connecting her to the limitless love of Spirit, the holy mother earth, and the angels and light beings she could feel gathered all around her.

Now she knew, at a deeper level, that simply being—her heart brimming with love and her desire for the highest good—was as valuable as any book ever written, any event ever conceived. Life was a vast web and her part was as vital as any other.

Not having goals, not expending energy to meet goals, was freeing her to give birth to a new consciousness. She was living the power of the feminine simply by being.

Despite the upheavals of children, lovers, clients, the zany commune her home had become, and her own overworked emotions—or because of them—she was primed to be the hundredth woman. Even now, sick in bed, she had the muscle to insist that the womanly values of connectedness, compassion, intuition, nurturing, and stewardship of the earth take their place of power in the world.

Her expanding awareness generated a more profound satisfaction than she'd ever known. Yawning exuberantly and moving her arms over her head, she indulged herself in a long stretch reaching from the tips of her fingers to the ends of her toes. She arose from her bed with sensual deliberation and wrapped her sheet around her body.

Her image in the mirror was one of an ancient goddess draped in flowing fabric, a radiant being with sparkling eyes and close-cropped hair streaked with shimmering bronze flames.

Morgan lit a white candle and twirled around her room in a slow, celebratory dance in which she bowed low to the parts of herself she had kept in shadow and reached high to the sky places where angels joined her dance.

The doorbell rang. She heard Serena greet Clarissa.

She'd forgotten all about their meeting. Throwing a long, flowing dress over her nakedness and tossing the duvet into easy order on her bed, she called to Serena and Clarissa to bring up something to drink and join her.

They might as well meet in the sacred space she'd created with her dance. Besides, if Clarissa was still thinking of Morgan as her therapist, being in her bedroom would help shift her perceptions.

~ ~ ~

Clarissa carried glasses and her mother brought lemonade up the long stairway. In the depth of color in Morgan's royal purple walls and gold accents, as well as in the relief of white in the trim and the diaphanous curtains, she saw a Morgan's spirit reflected—bold yet airy.

Morgan was perched against her bed in a flowing, ankle-length dress of pale, swirling pastels. In spite of her obvious lack of physical vitality, she rose to greet them, taking the glasses from Clarissa's hands and nodding to Serena to place the lemonade on the table by the window.

Clarissa took in the room, feasting on the easy sensuality with which Morgan had adorned her most private space. There were huge, embroidered cushions and colorful, textured rugs scattered across the floor. Luscious fabrics were draped on the furniture and walls.

A love seat and an upholstered chair were available, but she asked if she could move some of the cushions to the antique crimson and gold rug that lay at an angle in the center of the room. When she and her mother were seated, Morgan closed the door and brought glasses of lemonade for each of them. Morgan began to sit down, then caught sight of the tall white candle burning on her dresser. This she placed carefully in the center of the rug.

For some moments, they stared into the flame, sipping lemonade. Morgan arose with some difficulty and returned with a spiral shell, a feather, and an agate that she arranged near the candle, then smiled at her as she sat down.

Clarissa sighed. In bringing these items to the center, Morgan was acknowledging the reverence with which Clarissa was approaching their meeting.

"Do you mind if we begin with a prayer we each contribute to?" Clarissa said.

Morgan and her mother responded to her request with quiet, accepting smiles.

"You start." Morgan looked at Clarissa.

"Mother Earth, Great Spirit, Grandmother Moon, and Grandfather Sun, please be with us. I call upon the guides, ancestors, and spirit allies who stand behind us.

Morgan spoke. "We thank each of you for your presence in our lives, for your guidance and your gifts. We honor and bless you, and ask that you lift us to our highest place of knowing, gently releasing the cares and worries of our ordinary lives and helping us find the clarity of mind, passion of spirit, tranquility, and groundedness to come into our deepest centers for this meeting. Please gather your circle of protection around us."

"Guide our thoughts and communication for the highest good of all." Serena paused. "Awoman."

They opened their eyes and breathed fully.

"What would you like us to talk about?" Morgan gazed at Clarissa, her eyes clear and shining with love.

"So much has happened, you know? Miracles. I need to touch base. I sense we're part of a movement that extends far beyond us, and I want to understand all I can."

Clarissa looked at her mother, who chuckled and said, "I went for a walk before you came. Aunt Lee was weeding her flowers. She said 'Seek ye first the kingdom of heaven.'"

Morgan snorted. "Queendom."

"Whatever. It was another of those highly instructive, most supportive coincidences."

"How so?" Clarissa said.

"You know, I was raised in a very religious family. What Aunt Lee said, along with 'By my works, ye shall know me,' had already been running through my mind all week."

"What do you make of that?" Morgan looked startled.

"The first one isn't about after we die. I think it means to seek love, here and now on earth. What we've been doing."

"And?" Morgan seemed to find this fascinating.

"And the second one, I don't know, except the obvious. We've been trying to live our visions moment by moment."

"I think there's more," Morgan said. "About Shadow. All the times we've been up against our dark sides, our difficult emotions, we've learned, grown, and become stronger. That has also been our 'works.'"

Clarissa turned to her mother. "Does this bother you—this redefinition of things you learned in the church?"

"It did at first. I've spent a lifetime pretending I wasn't raised Catholic. But what I've been learning this summer runs so deep, all my childhood beliefs showed up, arguing with my new reality. Then I realized that in the Bible, Jesus teaches a technology for transformation through love. He tells people they can be like him. I think Jesus would support what we're doing.

"The Church taught me I was supposed to love others above myself," Serena continued. "But that's out of balance. Especially for women who've used the party line to rationalize their victimization—right? We've been correcting that imbalance by learning how to love ourselves. Yet when that self-love is truly flowing, I have a boundless ability to give to others. It spills over, from an infinite pool."

Morgan smiled. "Sometimes I can hardly believe how far you've come, how far we've all come."

Clarissa's eyes fluttered shut. She was swaying to the sounds of drums from another realm, and the voices of the ancients were coming through her. "Think ahead seven generations, to how your every action reverberates into the future. We are the life givers, so our task is to live our dreams for a planet that works for everyone. We are to let nothing stand in our way." She opened her eyes and gave her mother and Morgan a broad, peaceful smile.

Morgan drew a long breath, her eyes closed, obviously connecting to her own guides. "Take back your body. Own it. Be in your sexuality, your playfulness, your spontaneity."

The next message was from her mother. "But don't compromise the integrity of your soul's path by being with anyone who doesn't support who you really are."

Morgan shifted her weight, straightened her shoulders, and grinned. "Enjoy your body. Stick your breasts out there. Take up space. Let yourself be big and full. Relax your belly, breathe into it, let it be as round as the Earth Mother. Walk tall, use your voice, speak up. Know who you are and give yourself to yourself and to your world. Get back the power you took away from yourself. Be sexy and powerful and who you are because it's fun. Be the woman *you* choose to be."

They laughed together, deep and long, and drank lemonade from their glass tumblers with the sensual formality they might have assumed had they been drinking ambrosia from crystal goblets.

Clarissa raised her glass to Morgan. "My battles with Shadow are behind me. Thank you."

"Mine, too," her mother said. "Thank you, Morgan."

"Hey, you two did your own work. But don't get too cocky." Morgan chuckled. "I'm not convinced Shadow is ever completely gone. Besides, wasn't he our catalyst for miraculous growth? In any case, he's definitely not through with me."

"Isn't it you who must be done with him? It's your call." Clarissa felt a sudden stab of fear.

"He's losing." Morgan's voice was surprisingly compassionate. "I think that's a first for him. I'm sure he's lost battles before, but he's always believed he'd win the war. Now we've recontextualized the playing field. Because we're working on ourselves with love, there is no war. So he's frantic. He doesn't know what to do."

Morgan's voice grew softer still. "The way his mind works—always in hierarchies—he thinks the changes you two have made are my fault. So he's focused on me. Because I'm creating a universe in which his game doesn't work, he thinks I'm dangerous. With my current ill health, he thinks I have an Achilles heel he has his teeth around."

"But as you said, it's not his game anymore." Clarissa was deeply disturbed. What was Morgan saying? "We redefined the terms by following our dreams. He's right about one thing, though. I did the work, but you were my catalyst. You were my hundredth woman."

"Mine, too." Her mother's head was bent, but then she exploded to her feet and began to pace. "Make yourself well, Morgan! You have to! Protect yourself from him!"

"What do you think I do? I clear myself and affirm good health daily. I've changed my diet and started doing some mild exercise." Morgan paused. "Have you ever considered the possibility that my being ill might be for the highest good?"

Her mother's jaw dropped almost to her chest. "How could that be?"

"I don't know. Maybe so I would look inward and grow close to Spirit. Or to help others see that healing doesn't have to be linear and goal-centered, as in the masculine model. Transformation doesn't make you thin, blonde, and twenty. Or healthy, for that matter. Besides, not everyone gets the carrot at the end of the stick. And that's okay. In fact, it's perfect.

"But whatever the reason for my illness, I believe the benevolent force that helped me get this far knows what's best for me and provides it. If I weren't praying daily and taking good care of myself, it would be different. Because of free will, Spirit can't help me unless I ask and follow through. But I do those things. Daily."

"This concerns me—" Serena said.

"I'll tell you what concerns me," Morgan said. "Shadow sees me as a kingpin in the bowling game from hell. I imagine he thinks he can eliminate both of you if he takes me down. And he thinks eliminating you two has a ripple effect because it wipes out a powerful community action with the long-range potential to improve thousands of lives and a book that could do the same."

"Right you are." They all heard Brigid. "He thinks he can defeat us all, the ancestors too, if he can wipe you out."

"Exactly." Clarissa's mother was grim. "He thinks he can prevent the hundredth monkey effect, the leap in the evolution of human consciousness, if he can take down the women who are the catalysts. He's playing us now, trying to divert our energies into fear for Morgan's life."

"And it's working, isn't it, my pretties?" Shadow's stench was asphyxiating, but they couldn't see him.

"Ignore him," Morgan said. It's enough to know what he's up to. There's an important message here."

"What?" she and her mother said in one voice.

"Calm down," Morgan chortled.

How can she laugh?

It was disconcerting. There was nothing amusing in what they were discussing.

"You need to get this." Morgan's eyes glowed in the sunlight slanting across the room and bouncing off the purple walls.

"Spirit has channeled powerful understandings while I've been sick in that bed. I want you to know what I've learned."

Goose bumps raised on Clarissa's arms. She made herself breathe deeply, sensing that what Morgan was about to say could be life-changing.

"There is no kingpin, no pivotal person, no hundredth woman outside yourself. Each time you think someone else is leading you—someone else is crucial, someone else is carrying the ball—you lose in two major ways that will destroy your life if you don't cut it out."

Morgan looked lovingly, maternally, at Clarissa and her mother. "The first loss is you distract yourself from embracing your own magnificence because you give your power away to the person you've placed on a pedestal.

"The second loss is—and this, my dear friends, is so insidious it amounts to an unconscious attempt at soul-suicide—you give up your responsibility, and therefore your power, to guarantee your own transformation and that of your world. The illusion is that someone else is going to do it, so you don't have to.

"But guess what?" Morgan said. "That's the old victim-thinking. Unless you're willing to assume one hundred percent responsibility for being the hundredth woman—whatever that looks like for you—you aren't going to make it because you'll be playing small. You'll still be a victim of what the 'stronger ones' do or don't do. You can—and must—enlist help from others, but you can't assign them the pivotal role. That role belongs to you. Each of us has our own obstacles to clear—you don't have to be perfect—but you must decide that you, and you alone, are responsible for your own transformation."

She and her mother were quiet, their heads bowed.

Then Clarissa squared her shoulders. "I can commit to that."

"Me, too." Her mother turned to Morgan. "But what about you—and Shadow?"

Morgan threw back her head and laughed. "What difference does it make what he does? He's a joke now."

"Morgan, please be serious."

"Do I have to?"

"Yeah."

"I'm not convinced that 'serious' is the way to go, but I'll try to answer your question. I think he's going to make another try for me, and another, until something gives. But we have to detach from the outcome and stay with our intentions. Clarissa, you need to keep your focus on your event and Serena, you need to stay with your book. And I need to keep laughing. Laughing and loving. Shadow is using the same old tired strategy with women all over the world. Can't you feel it? We can't do anything about that. Each of us can only deal with what's in front of us."

"We're unstoppable unless we allow ourselves to be stopped," Clarissa said.

"What about death?" Morgan said. "Are you saying death can't stop us?"

She felt stricken by Morgan's question and couldn't look at her.

"Personally," Morgan said, "I don't think death is a big deal. We can and do keep going, with or without a body."

"But Morgan," Serena finally said, "it's not your time to die. Shadow is inside you, so you can deal with him. You taught me that, remember?"

"Just as you taught me he's on the outside. In my mind, this isn't a contradiction. In any case, it's not over between me and Shadow. That's just how it is. He's been after me all my life, ever since the first time my father hurt me. But there's been no final test. If there had been, he'd be gone. He and I both know I've transformed my life and held my ground. He's seen me make him my teacher, learn the lessons, let go of fear, dependency, and self-doubt, claim my calling, and fill myself with love. Most teachers, even most enemies, would have let go by now."

"He's challenged you and you've prevailed, consistently," Serena said.

"But I'm still sick," Morgan said. "And there's more. You feel it yourself or this discussion would be going in a different direction. If Shadow is our teacher, our servant—then apparently we're not done, so he's not letting us out of class. But if he's an actual adversary, then whatever needs to happen to be complete with him has yet to occur. Remember—I created this whole scenario. But then, so did you. We must each accept full responsibility for creating our own experience.

"What I'm asking you and the ancestors to do," she continued, "is to hold me in the light and in love as I prepare to meet him. My choice is to engage with Shadow in whatever way serves my greater good and the greater good of the whole. Please increase your love and intention to learn from the lessons at the same time that you detach yourselves from me and from the outcome.

"Try to detach with love," Morgan said. "That diminishes the power Shadow has to diminish you and your work by taking me out. We need to have the desire that I'll come through this, but we must also let go of the outcome, trusting to the wisdom of the same Infinite Intelligence that regulates all of nature—and that brought us together in the first place.

"You may find this hard to believe," Morgan said, "but I'm satisfied. I'm full. I'm happy. What remains is simply some earth drama playing itself out through me. Sick or not sick, in a body or not, I'm at peace. I love you more than you can possibly imagine.

"And, above all else," Morgan said, taking the time to look deeply into each of them, "remember you're the hundredth woman. Live each day as if it's your last."

She looked away from the others, apparently studying something in the corner of the room. Clarissa followed her gaze and saw a spider wrapping an insect in thread, around and around and around. Morgan seemed utterly fascinated with this process.

Finally Morgan looked at her. "Have we accomplished what you intended? I'm very tired and want to lie down."

"Please, Morgan, one more thing. Shadow is most in control when we're isolated."

"True."

"Together, we're stronger than he is. So I want us to be together, in our hearts. I want us always to be linked in love."

"We are linked. Always." Morgan rose slowly and cupped Clarissa's face gently with her hand before moving to the edge of her bed and settling herself heavily. "We're one—points on a web that connects us to each other, to the ancestors, and to Spirit.

"Don't worry," Morgan said. "There are those in positions of great power who intend evil. But they're merely frightened souls whose reign of control is ending. They don't know they're going to be all right. Eventually they'll have nowhere to go but to the light.

"So for now," Morgan said, "send them love and show them the light. Please understand how difficult it is for them. They know nothing about the light. And as for Shadow? Send Shadow love."

CHAPTER 23

tendril

This is a YES! Place
Love is a YES!
Not a maybe
Or a will see
Or if you do this & this & this
It's a brisk, clear water, earth, air
And fire paradise!
We are whole and alive
And brilliant and beautiful
And YES!

—Joanie Levine

A car blared its horn, shattering the stillness of Rosa Brooks' home and scattering the chickens. Tameka bolted down the stairs and dashed for the front door.

She nearly ran into Grandma Mattie, who grabbed her arm, held her eyes with a face like thunder, and said in a deep, rumbling voice, "Where you think you're going, flying outta this house like your pants on fire?"

"You gotta let me go!" Tameka said, her eyes grasping for the door and her small breasts heaving. "Jimmy McRae's out there! He's come for me, Grandma Mattie. For *me!*"

"So y'all just going to race out there with your hair a-flyin'?"

"Yes! Let go of me."

"Not until you take a deep breath and count to twelve, Miss Thing."

Tameka relaxed a little, looked into Grandma Mattie's eyes, and tried to suppress a smile. It was no use resisting her. Especially when she told you to count to twelve instead of ten.

"Girl, what are you afraid of?"

"I'm not afraid, Grandma Mattie."

"Yes you are, Baby. You're scared. Why?"

Tameka ducked her head. "I'm afraid if I don't get out there, right now, he'll drive off. And I'll lose my chance to be Jimmy McRae's girl."

"Honey, if you run out there scared, the most you'll ever be is some man's girl. 'As ye sow, so shall ye reap.' Think on it."

Grandma Mattie's voice grew soft. She took Tameka's narrow face in her large, gentle hands. "Let him come up to your front door and ask for you. If you don't respect yourself, Tameka, nobody else will. Especially the Jimmy McRaes of this world."

He honked again, a series of long blasts, and Tameka stiffened. Her eyes were frantic.

"Baby, don't go there!" Grandma Mattie said, moving her hands to her granddaughter's shoulders and increasing the strength of her grip.

Tameka stared at the floor, but Grandma Mattie dipped down low, forcing her to look her in the eye. "If you want to be a strong, proud woman, you go right back up those stairs and think on your future. And by 'future,' I don't mean no man. I mean where is *Tameka* going and what is *Tameka* about. And don't you come back down those stairs until you feel the pride of your dream in your whole body."

Tameka grew thoughtful.

"Jimmy can talk to your old grandma while he waits for you."

Tameka grinned and rolled her eyes.

Grandma Mattie drew a long breath and smiled at her. "It won't hurt that young man one bit to find out you have people behind you."

In spite of the boisterous banging on the front door, Tameka ascended the stairs slowly.

Grandma Mattie called softly after her before answering the door. "When you feel the strength of our people running through your veins, when you know in your heart you're a queen—in other words, when you're good and ready—come back down those stairs. And if you happen to feel like going out in the company of Mr. Jimmy McRae, why then, so be it."

Ten minutes later, Tameka descended the stairs. Her slender form conveying the restrained elegance of a ballet dancer poised for a solo performance, she was silhouetted by sunlight pouring through the large window at the bend in the stairs. A golden aura enveloped her and illuminated the graceful dance of her extended brown arm and the graceful hand that glided down the handrail.

She paused for a moment when she saw Jimmy McRae. Her chin was raised as she regarded him through the thick veil of her lashes.

Jimmy was speechless. He swung the door wide, stammered his good bye to Grandma Mattie, and rushed out after her.

"That was quite a speech you gave Tameka," Rosa said, emerging from the kitchen. "I guess I needed to hear it, too."

"Did you, Baby?" She paused for a moment, then frowned.

"What is it, Mama?"

"I got the goose flesh talking about our people. It's as if they were here."

"I felt them, too. It got me thinking."

"What?"

"How do you suppose our people would have felt about that nuclear dump they're trying to bring in here?"

After a long pause, Rosa's mama said, "I guess they wouldn't have stood for it. Not if they knew what it was and saw it coming."

"That's what I figure. But weren't we dragged over here to do the white man's work because our people didn't see what was coming?"

Her mother hesitated for a moment. "Partly. But there was a whole lot more to it than that."

"I know. But maybe it's time to take the next step."

"What do you mean?"

"Maybe our people stopped where we need to keep on going. And you know what I think stopped them, Mama?"

"What?"

"Fear. The white man had guns. If you stepped out of line, you got shot. So what did our people do? They got on those slave ships. That's what they did. And it's been like that ever since."

"Wouldn't you be afraid if your people got rounded up by men with guns, and you ain't got nothing?"

"Sure Mama, I'd be afraid. But you know what? I've been afraid all my life. And where has it got me?" Rosa spread both arms in a gesture that took in all of their small, dilapidated house. Her spine straightened and she strode back to the kitchen, picked up the phone, and dialed.

"Hello? Is this Miz Clarissa Albright? This is Rosa Brooks. You've been by my house out in the county, remember? Now what I want to know is, how do we stop this damned nuclear dump?"

~ ~ ~

Clarissa took the stairs to Morgan's bedroom two at a time. The boys were engrossed in a board game with her mother and Ian. She decided to take advantage of the opportunity to pop in on Morgan before she got back to work on her event.

"Oh my god, Morgan. I'm sorry. Another time."

Am I spinning so fast I'm blind to everyone else?

Clarissa had been halfway to Morgan's bed before she noticed how bad she looked. Her face—slack, with gray and yellow undertones—was downright scary.

"Don't be silly. Come sit with me." Morgan patted the bed. "I know what I look like. But don't worry. *In Spite of Woman's Sallow Skin, She is Glowing from Within.*"

"That's not funny." Clarissa perched gingerly on the edge of her bed.

"Sure it is. Your event is only a week off, isn't it? What's it called again?"

"Dump the Dump: Mothers and Others for a Living Earth."

"I like that."

She didn't say anything.

"Clarissa, you can look at me. I won't bite."

But she couldn't look.

If I meet her eyes, she'll see my pain.

Worse, she'll see how scared I am of what she looks like.

"What did you have for dinner last night?" Morgan said.

"Huh?"

"You heard me."

She couldn't help smiling. She peeked at Morgan's eyes, which were twinkling fiercely. Suddenly Morgan laughed. It was a familiar sound, layered and infectious. Disarmed, Clarissa pulled her feet up on the bed and sat cross-legged, facing her.

"My mother and the boys wanted us to show Joshua how Big Mom used to feed us. We made bean bread, chestnut bread, fried chicken, cabbage, fatback, beans, potatoes, and corn. Oh, and apple fritters."

"Is that all?"

"Yeah. No calories. After dinner, Josh pulled out his guitar and we sang for hours. And laughed."

"Sounds like fun."

Clarissa smiled. "It was."

"So what's troubling you?"

"Do you have to be a mind reader?"

"I can't help it."

"May I tell you a secret?"

"Sure."

"I'm trying, but I don't feel as close as I should to my mother. I get frustrated with her."

"Whoa. What's this, the shake and bake mother-daughter reunion?"

Clarissa spit out a little laugh.

"Relax." Morgan stroked her hand with cool, silvery fingers. "Everyone gets frustrated with Serena. But it's still okay to let her love you."

"That's just it—I'm not sure she does love me."

"She'd be back on her mountain if she didn't."

"She's good to me, don't get me wrong. But she isn't warm."

"Yet she shows up in a big way, doesn't she?"

Clarissa had to laugh. "Oh yeah. She's taking as much responsibility for Dump the Dump as Joshua and I are."

"That's how Serena shows her love. Warm and fuzzy—that's not her style."

Clarissa grinned. Simultaneously, a tear slid down her cheek.

Morgan looked at her closely. "Now tell me what's really bothering you."

"It's so stupid."

"No, it's not. If you're feeling it, it's not stupid."

Her chin trembled. "Do you remember when that councilman in Macon threatened me?"

"Oh yeah. Is someone threatening you now?"

"No. I don't know."

"Tell me."

"I've been getting hang-up calls. But no one says anything—it might not even be about the dump. And… ."

"And what?"

"I feel as if I'm being watched. But there's no reason to think that."

"Shadow."

Clarissa shuddered. "I don't want him back."

"Here, there, back, gone—what difference does it make where he is?"

"How can you say that?"

"You let go of Spirit's hand, didn't you?" Morgan said.

Another tear slid down Clarissa's cheek.

Morgan smiled. "Do something for me," Morgan said. "Inhale deeply and as you do, breathe in the infinite love Spirit has for you."

Clarissa wept softly and breathed.

"When you release that breath," Morgan said, "having completely immersed yourself in the loving energy of the Infinite, exhale that loving essence out to the entire universe. Good. Now keep breathing like that. Inhale the divine love of Spirit and send it out into the world with each breath."

Clarissa's eyes blinked open.

"I recommend," Morgan said, "you infuse yourself with Spirit's love every day. And not once, like a vitamin. All the time, like breathing."

"You don't ask for much!"

Morgan chuckled. "To the best of your ability." Her face became sober, her eyes warm. "Clarissa, this way of working with the breath is the most powerful tool I know. It helps me broaden my context. By that I mean it lifts me out of my self-centeredness—my victim-thinking, my sense of being powerless and small. When I allow each breath to provide the experience of being fully loved by Spirit at the same time that I support all of creation—I'm safe, I'm in my power, and I'm free."

This rang true. Since Morgan had been so ill, her wisdom had deepened and gained… authority. Now when she spoke, her words carried the resonance of profound spiritual understanding.

"Thank you," Clarissa said.

"You're welcome."

Clarissa's gaze settled on a large feather resting on a silver cloth on a low chest. She crossed the room to look more closely.

"May I touch this?"

"Please."

"Where did you get it?" Clarissa brought the feather to Morgan and placed it in her hand.

"I found it last summer. I gave it to the lover I was with at the time. But when we broke up, I took it back."

"Did you know it's the tail feather of a hawk?"

"Really?" Morgan turned the rust colored feather over and over in the sunlight that streaked across her bed, as Big Mom used to do.

"Some tribes call the red-tailed hawk the 'red eagle.' It's a sacred bird. Visionary. From high above it sees both the whole forest and the smallest detail, the tiniest movement. Like you, it has clarity and perspective."

"Thank you for that." Morgan patted Clarissa's hand.

"Sometimes I feel so stuck."

"We all do. Go into your emotions when you feel that way. Don't act on them. Instead, acknowledge and experience them. Then breathe in the way I showed you. After a time, ask yourself how you would behave if you were coming from your wisest self and acting out of constructive compassion for yourself and everyone involved."

"You make it sound so easy."

"It's not always easy. But it is simple. And it works. Are you ready for the next piece?"

"What?"

"If you want to move forward, you can't be isolated. Not from your mother, or Joshua. Not even from Shadow."

Clarissa recoiled. But Morgan appeared not to notice. She pulled herself up on her bed and arranged her pillows behind her.

"What do you mean?"

"I'll show you. Close your eyes and ask Divine Wholeness—and the angels and guides who love you and work for your highest good—to protect you at every level. Good. Do you see Shadow?"

"Hey, I'm not looking for trouble."

"Bear with me. I'm not asking you to search for him or call him in. I'm asking if he's already there."

Clarissa did as Morgan requested, shuddering when she finally felt the contact with Shadow.

"Do you see him?"

"Yeah."

"What's he doing?"

"I don't know. He's looking at me with pure hate, as if he wants to do me in and he can't wait. He has this big black ball and he's getting ready to throw it at me."

"Okay, now freeze the action. Good. What you described is what Shadow does. When he's not trying to take our energy, he's trying to give us his negativity."

"I don't want to just stop the action. I want to block him."

"Not this time. Let him throw the black ball at you. But control the rate. Let it come slowly."

"I don't want to."

"You'll be all right. See him release the ball and see it coming toward you in very slow motion. What does it look like?"

Clarissa drew a jagged breath. "It's like a black stone with streamers trailing behind, or a harpoon with a rope attached to it."

"Good."

"Good?"

"Yes. Now, instead of protecting yourself, open your heart to Shadow. Simultaneously, work with the color of the energy coming your way. Turn the black energy into brown. Have you got that?"

"Yes."

"Now change it to red, then orange, then yellow, then green, then blue—"

"The colors of the rainbow."

"Yes, and of the energy centers in the body. Then indigo, then violet. When the whole energy field he's hurling toward you is violet, change it to white."

"White?"

"Yes. A gently glowing, golden white light. Pure. Radiant with love and peace. Receive this energy lovingly in your arms until you've gathered all of it. Embrace it. At the same time, experience both loving compassion for Shadow and the clear understanding that he chose darkness and evil out of his ignorance and fear. Never underestimate his capacity to do great harm, yet allow your heart to be moved by his suffering. Communicate to him that you understand and accept why he feels that he has to do what he's doing."

Morgan paused. "You're doing beautifully. Now, look at the energy he's sent you and see that it's fully converted into a glowing golden-white ball into which you project pure love. Got it?"

"Yes."

"Good. Now, with the deepest respect, send the ball of energy back to him. Do this gently and with great care, as though you were sending him a blanket containing God." Morgan paused. "How's it going?"

"He looks confused, but he's taking it."

"Exactly. You didn't fight him."

"He's walking away. He's disappearing. He's gone." Clarissa opened her eyes and blinked, looking at Morgan with amazement. "He's really gone! That's fabulous. I can do that next time he shows up."

"Not necessarily. Be careful. Choose the approach that feels right at the time. This time, he was confused enough to accept the light. Another time, he could draw energy from that approach and use it against you. We're being challenged to intuit our way through this, to find the tools that are right for the moment."

"That's so complicated," Clarissa said.

"Not really. It's about shifting awareness into the heart and belly—the feminine centers—and from that position, balancing the masculine, the mind. Learn to use all you faculties and you'll be fine."

"How are you dealing with Shadow these days?"

"Mostly, I laugh at him and let him know I think he's ridiculous."

"You're kidding."

"Nope. Hey, this thing with Shadow is getting old and my interests lie elsewhere. When he's really persistent, I open my body to him and say, 'Come on in! Have a look around! But remember, I'm saturated from head to foot with the divine light of love."

Morgan laughed heartily. "He doesn't stick around long when I remind him of that."

Clarissa could hardly believe her ears. How could she taunt Shadow like that when the stakes were so high?

As if she'd read her thoughts, Morgan said, "It helps to lighten up. Try it. But since your pressing concern of the moment is safety, remember the best way to be safe is to ask Divine Wholeness to protect you at all times. The other realities aren't allowed to help us unless we ask. It's divine law. And do the practical things you're called to do, of course. If your gut is telling you to work with the phone company to trace or block those hang-up callers, do it.

"We also need to realize," Morgan continued, "that since what we're attempting is new, not only our minds but also our bodies are changing. Our cellular structures are responding to our emotional and spiritual changes—which isn't always a comfortable process—and we need to allow for that."

"Is that why you're so sick?"

"I don't know. Maybe. I've wondered if my body is equipped to do the work I'm doing. I'm asking it to learn."

Morgan stretched her arms over her head. The current of air created by the A.C. was playing with the gauzy white curtains at her window, causing them to billow rhythmically like waves.

Clarissa closed her eyes. Her shoulders relaxed. With the love she inhaled with her next breath, she embraced the clean satisfaction that came with the integrity she'd gained from reaching for her best.

There would always be enough love available to bathe and buoy her spirit. When she opened her eyes again and looked around Morgan's room, she noticed even the air looked brighter, cleaner.

She gazed at Morgan. "What about you? With all this infinite love you're breathing in and out, shouldn't your body be getting stronger instead of weaker?"

Morgan's laugh was almost a bark. "There you go again, 'shoulding' all over the place."

"Sorry." She ducked her head playfully, and Morgan reached out and gently lifted her chin with one finger.

"Awhile back, we got the message that once you set your intention, if you don't get what you asked for, either your request wasn't for the highest good at that moment, you're trying too hard, or you're working against yourself with some conscious or unconscious core belief."

"I remember."

"I set my intention to be well, and I've gotten sicker. I looked to see if any core beliefs, conscious or unconscious, were blocking me. I got help. I went to my therapist and to an astrologer. A colleague did a clearing technique on me. I talked to friends.

"Through those experiences, I discovered the unconscious belief that I don't deserve to have a good life. My unconscious mind thought all the horrible things that have been done to me throughout my life were my fault. Therefore, I deserved them and needed to be punished. I had created a powerful, unconscious, self-imposed requirement for suffering."

"Oh my god—"

"It's not uncommon. Most people have a whole slew of unconscious beliefs gumming up their works. I figured mine might be keeping me from getting well, so I did some very deep clearing and now I feel lighter and more joyful."

"So how come you're still sick?"

"I don't know. Maybe I haven't yet cleaned out enough of my inner sewer." Morgan laughed. "Or maybe my body doesn't speak the language of New Age 'presto change-o.' Or perhaps being ill is for my highest good at the moment."

"How could that be? I still don't get that."

"It's a mystery, isn't it? Look at it this way—we're enough, Clarissa, exactly the way we are. Sick or lonely or afraid, we're enough. We can love ourselves, receive the love of Spirit, live our dreams, do our best—one day at a time—and turn over the results *in our present condition.* Nothing's missing. In all our imperfections, we're exactly where we need to be to learn and grow today. Don't they say in Twelve Step programs, 'I can't do today's work with tomorrow's recovery?'"

Clarissa grinned. "Yeah."

Spiritual growth is a process that can't be measured by worldly results. The experience of profound satisfaction can be attained regardless of circumstances. It's an inside job." Morgan smiled. "Big Mom helped, too."

Clarissa's heart gave a little leap. At the sound of Big Mom's name, she somehow knew everything was going to be all right. Morgan was rotating the hawk feather, which was almost the same color as her spiky hair, round and round as she spoke.

She could accept Morgan wholeheartedly now—exactly the way she was—which meant she could see the glowing vitality beneath Morgan's sallow skin and the inner light that spilled from her eyes.

"Big Mom told me that since the beginning of time," Morgan said, "all over the earth, the gifted ones—the shamans, the healers who travel between the dimensions—are often very ill. Typically their illness lasts seven years, but often it's much longer."

"She never told me that. Did she give you a reason for it?"

"So they can learn. So they can leave their daily concerns behind, go inside, and learn in the other dimensions—usually when they're asleep, in the dreamtime."

Morgan smiled. "Big Mom said those who seek wisdom don't always get sick. But they all have something wrong with them. Like Serena, with her anger—or you, with your self-doubt."

"Why is that?"

"Because our culture has taken a wrong turn. People think if they're very good, things will turn out well. They're like children in this way and need to learn what Big Mom calls 'coyote medicine.'"

Clarissa laughed. "The coyote is the trickster. He teaches us—through jokes, challenges, and humbling experiences—that black isn't black and white isn't white, but all is in degrees of shadow."

"Did you hear what you just said?"

"Oh my god."

"It takes all those lovely nuances and shadings to make the whole. The lessons come and make us more complete, not better. If our circumstances or behaviors improve, it's because we're dancing to a different beat, not because we're morally superior."

"I think I understand," Clarissa said. "Wisdom doesn't come only to the buff, white, righteous heroes in the movies, It comes equally to the wounded, the sick, the unsuccessful, the ugly, the invisible."

"Exactly. All is perfect in its imperfection."

"I still keep thinking we can have it all."

"A very dangerous concept, in my opinion."

"Why?"

"Think about it. How many women have driven themselves and their kids nuts by birthing babies at the same time they scrambled up the career ladder two rungs at a time, attempted a daily workout, expected themselves to maintain the seductive allure of a movie star, and secretly measured their homemaking successes against Martha Stewart?"

Clarissa laughed. "You have a point, but—"

"I could have tried to 'have it all'—a relationship with Jake, my health, my calling, a major immersion in the little commune my home has become. But to get where I am, I needed to pull back and focus. I have friends and clients who want it all and they're slaves to their calendars. Is that life? Mostly they scatter their energies—then feel guilty. I think that approach leads to a loss of self.

"I say," Morgan continued, "pick one thing at a time and go for it. I picked my calling, my path—me—and was rewarded beyond my wildest imaginings. Health is wonderful, don't get me wrong. I want health, I welcome health. But having a solid inner core is so much sweeter, so much more valuable. It's sublime. My soul didn't incarnate so I could have a healthy body. I came here to create wholeness, so I expanded beyond being mother to my children and lover to my partners and became mother and lover to myself and, from that powerful base, to all of creation.

"No matter what happens," she continued, "now that I picked the thing I most wanted and went for it, I'll be satisfied. Since I can't have everything I want, I'm going to make damned sure I get what I most want. That's what works for me."

"Yee-haw!"

"I think so. I set my intention and taught myself how to receive the gifts creation wants to give me."

Clarissa felt her eyes welling with tears of joy. "I can see it now. If you never left this bed, you'd still be the hundredth woman. And so am I." A sob caught in her throat.

Morgan drew Clarissa in and held her. "Yes, Clarissa, you are the hundredth woman."

"In spite of all my imperfections."

"No, my darling, because of your imperfections, and because of the amazing heart and courage with which you meet them." Morgan took Clarissa by the shoulders.

"But I am getting out of this bed, Clarissa. I have a very important event to attend and a dump to dump."

When Clarissa left, Morgan moved to the love seat to enjoy the peach and iris hues that stained the sky as dusk deepened. Everyone had gone out to eat and the house was quiet. As the light faded, she slipped easily into the meditative, twilight world in which she listened to Divine Wholeness and met with her angels, her guides, and the ancestors. She asked for divine protection and requested a ripening of her wisdom.

Gradually, she became aware of Brigid's welcome presence in front of her.

"Tell me, Luv." She felt Brigid's words within, "what is it that makes you the hundredth woman?"

"Is this a pop quiz?" But Brigid didn't answer, so she focused on her question. "I came to be the hundredth woman because I committed myself to love."

"How did you do that?"

"I embraced myself."

"How?"

"I was honest. I allowed all my feelings. I recognized how I'd been looking outside myself to find satisfaction."

"And?" Brigid's voice contained the music of the light.

"I let myself be. I decided it was time to fall in love with myself, exactly as I am now."

"And?"

Morgan chuckled. "You sound like me, conducting a therapy session."

She heard the bell-like tones of Brigid's laughter before she repeated the question. "And?"

"And I reached into my soul. I allowed myself to experience the love and purpose pulsing there, and how that resonates with a greater love and purpose. When I did that, I found spiritual satisfaction. Even the challenges became infused with joy."

"Which made you more available to the promptings of Spirit."

"And the love of Spirit."

"Aye."

"Thank you for guiding me, Brigid."

"In for a penny, in for a pound."

Morgan laughed. The familiar scene outside the window, the dark shapes of trees who were more like friends, comforted her.

"Brigid?"

"Child?"

"I'd like to know what's happening with the power you drew into your belly and carried into the sea."

"Would you now? Soon you shall see for yourself, Luv. But this much I can tell you. In you, in Serena, in Clarissa, in women all over the earth—that power is being released into manifestation. 'Tis leaders of a revolution, you are. Your hearts are growing lighter, more full of love. Soon you shall see that without even thinking about it, you'll be breathing in the love of the divine and exhaling it out into the world around you with every breath.

"All you have to do," Brigid said, "is to continue on the path you have begun and everything will change for everyone, everywhere. What were once problems will evolve into challenges, and working through those challenges will become divine play. The mantle of the hundredth woman will slip onto hundreds, then millions of shoulders. As naturally as you breathe, you'll claim your authority to usher in, on a global scale, the powers of the feminine—the powers of compassion, connectedness, intuition, nurturing, and stewardship of the earth. You're creating the matrix that will free women to lead humanity into a more humane future."

Brigid laughed. The sound was like the tinkling of thousands of bells.

The trees outside Morgan's window stirred in the evening breeze as though they were waving at her. She rippled her fingers in response, arose from the love seat, and removed her nightgown.

Naked in the darkness and still very weak, she lit four candles around her room and several more near the full-length oval mirror standing in the corner.

She put on three long, shimmering necklaces and the purple feather boa she once wore to a costume party and wrapped a rainbow-colored silk scarf around her head, its ends hanging long on either side of one shoulder.

In spite of her weakness, Morgan reveled in her naked body. She stroked her body with the boa, her hands, and the silk scarf, making glorious love to herself in front of the mirror.

This is it, Grandmama, isn't it?

She sleepily blew out the candles and fell back on her bed.

It's having your sensuality, your love, and your power, all at the same time.

It's not a Southern thing.

It's a woman thing.

Morgan began to understand that another facet of her life purpose was to be one of those who consciously set the intention for the new human journey. She was to feel the calling of the human spirit all around her—the collective higher consciousness—so she could sense humanity's greater purpose and dream the outcome into reality with her heart and mind.

To do this required penetrating the layers of fear, cynicism, powerlessness, and apathy that enshrouded the human heart so she could arrive at the center of goodness at the core of each individual and, hence, the collective. She was to dream the collective purpose, to imagine it and to send her intention out into the future like a flying anchor that would pull humanity toward it. And that collective higher consciousness was all about sacred stewardship, love, cooperation, sharing, and creativity. It was about reverence for all life.

In the outer world, I'm like a mountain climber who has established a base camp on the side of a mountain after a long, hard climb.

I tend the camp, extend my hand to others who want to reach the point I've attained, offer a place to rest and gather strength, and give them a leg up when they want to climb higher—all the while inwardly dreaming a loving future for us all and projecting ahead, into the time yet to come, the guidelines that connect us to that dream, the ropes we'll use to pull ourselves forward.

Without warning, Shadow's sinister presence snapped into Morgan's awareness. He tried to grab her throat and strangle her.

She found his antics to be so absurd she shook with laughter and he bounced backward, rolling through the air, end over end.

At first he was stunned, then he regarded her evenly for one long moment and disappeared.

But before he was gone, she saw in his eyes his decision for an immediate showdown. From Shadow's point of view, Morgan knew, the scales had just tipped in her favor.

He was going to have to get rid of her.

Quickly.

CHAPTER 24

spider webs unite

I can feel the mental tendril of
a mind close to mine,
and suddenly distances are spanned
and I am surrounded by beloved spectres,
their ghostly lips brimming with
  womynly wisdom,
kind thoughts and expanding visions
that fill me with hope, courage,
  and the
knowledge of a million earthbound years.

—Trisia Eddy

Morgan eased herself into a chair a full ten minutes before Dump the Dump was scheduled to begin. An electric hum filled the hall as people greeted friends on their way to the few remaining seats.

It was a kaleidoscope of humanity. Morgan's eyes gravitated toward the sound of hearty laughter and found an older black woman, dressed in magenta satin from her heels to her hat, sharing a hearty handshake with a dark-suited gentleman. She recognized faces from the university and from the environmental community. Children were interspersed with the elderly and clusters of old hippies greeted each other enthusiastically. Attire ranged from elegant to casual. Racially, the mix was roughly equal.

To attract media attention, one woman carried in her arms, like a baby, a doll painted iridescent orange with nuclear warning symbols decorating it. Two others—who looked like astronauts on a moon-walk—were dressed in white plastic suits and headgear, as though prepared for a nuclear incident. There must have been at least three hundred people, an impressive turnout for a non-mainstream political event in Hopewellen.

Jane waved at her from across the room. She was sitting with her husband and some of their friends from the university.

I'll give her a call next week.

She'd played such an important role in bringing them all together.

Morgan tried to find a way to be comfortable in her steel folding chair. Simply getting to the event had been an act of will. She wasn't feeling worse, but she wasn't feeling better, either.

At least Ian was spending the night with a friend, so she could look forward to uninterrupted rest. Lately he'd been getting up in the middle of the night to compose music. He was quiet, but she had a mother's ears. Even with him away, she didn't want to push herself. Sierra's baby was a week overdue, and she didn't want to be at low ebb when her grandchild finally arrived.

And then there was Shadow. She was keeping herself on an even keel so she'd be ready for him.

~ ~ ~

Backstage, Clarissa slid her fingers along the edge of the stage curtains, drawing comfort from their black velvet heaviness. She maneuvered a small opening and scanned the crowd, relieved to find there wasn't a menacing face in the room.

She'd tried to forget her fears about being threatened, but they'd crept in more each day as her event approached. Yet now it was the big night, and—to her amazement—the hall was full and people were smiling.

So what was this fear that gripped her spine?

Stop it!

No one is going to hurt me and I won't let fear prevent me from savoring each moment of this triumph.

Like a wet dog coming in from the cold, she shook off her fear.

You're flying now, girlfriend.

All you have to do is stay the course and nothing can ever hold you down again.

~ ~ ~

Slowly, the lights dimmed while the last people scurried to their seats. Morgan hurriedly finished reading the program and noticed her own name in the acknowledgments under "Moral Support."

Sweet.

The hall darkened. Someone walked out onto the stage and sat on a tall stool in front of the microphone, tapping it to be sure it was on. A spotlight gradually illumined Clarissa, who wore tight-fitting black from head to toe. T.V. cameras to either side of the hall began to roll.

"Welcome. This is Saturday night, a time you could be kicking back and relaxing. If your life is as stressed as mine, giving up a Saturday is giving up a lot. I appreciate that each of you is here because you care about the quality of life for yourself, your children, and your children's children."

There was a light sprinkling of applause that swelled pleasantly. Clarissa smiled. She raised a note card and studied it for a moment, then dropped it to her lap.

"I prepared a speech, but I'm not going to give it. Let me tell you how I got on this stage. For two years, ever since I first heard about it, I've wanted the proposed nuclear waste dump to go away."

Soft, sympathetic laughter undulated through the hall.

"After a year, I realized it wasn't going to. I got angry because no one was doing anything about it. Then, several months ago, I had to ask myself why I wasn't taking action.

"After some excruciatingly painful soul-searching, I realized I wasn't doing anything about the dump because I didn't think I could. I grew up with the kinky hair and full nose and lips of a black child on an Indian reservation in the mountains. I didn't fit in the Indian world, I didn't fit in the black world, and I sure didn't fit in the white world."

The hall became silent—hushed—except for Clarissa's voice.

"Besides that, I was a girl. By the time this nuclear dump came around, I was a single working mother raising two boys. I was shy, and I was scared. No way was I going to go out there and knock on your door and ask you to help me fight a multimillion dollar project. Indians don't do things like that—in case you didn't know—and I grew up Cherokee.

"Then I found out women haven't been doing things like that for a whole lot of years, either. Only a century ago, even white women were enslaved—their only real choices were marriage and prostitution."

She paused. There wasn't a sound in the hall.

"When I realized fear and powerlessness were in my genes, in every cell in my body—not only because I'm Indian and black, but also because I'm a woman—I began to see I'm not some crazy person who can't get her act together. I was used to being soft and unassuming, like a caterpillar." She used a gentle gesture, hands cupped, to describe a small creature. "But then I was thrown into the chaos inside a cocoon that became my jail.

"I was lucky. I met someone who knew how caterpillars become butterflies."

Clarissa grinned, and Morgan smiled inwardly at the acknowledgment and at the strength in Clarissa's voice, the power in her erect posture, and the energy vibrating from her body.

"About the time I began to find my wings, I heard about a woman named Dr. Alice Stewart, now in her nineties. She's the one who discovered, over fifty years ago, that x-rays aren't good for pregnant women. She bit down hard on that one and never let go, fighting the nuclear industry most of her life.

"I started looking around, and I saw the Alice Stewarts all around me—women who were taking a stand—whether in a big way, like Dr. Stewart, or in their daily lives.

"I began to think, why not me? Why can't I take at least one small step to stop a nuclear dump that could poison our land and water for millions of years? I got a picture in my mind of this event, and I found the courage to knock on your doors."

Clarissa was met with applause combined with a few hoots and a long whistle from Joshua.

"Thank you. This is a predominantly female audience, but there are a lot of men out there tonight. Perhaps some of you are wondering why I called this evening 'Dump the Dump: Mothers and Others for a Living Earth.

"I did that because I believe that—for one night at least—we need to consider the precious earth we walk on with all the tenderness of a young woman nursing a child at her breast. For one night, I invite you to become a mother lion who would stop at nothing to protect her young.

"We're accustomed to the phrase, 'Mother Earth.' But every mother was once a child, and until we can honor the tender vulnerability of the earth, how can we honor the life she nurtures so abundantly?

"So, just for tonight, every man in this hall is an honorary woman, all of us are mothers, and we have this baby to take care of, this earth. How are we going to do it?"

She introduced the first act of the evening, the Golden Glams, three gay men in gold lamé singing and dancing to their own rollicking anti-dump version of *Stop in the Name of Love.* Audience participation was not simply encouraged, it was "required, Honey."

When the applause and laughter died down, Clarissa outlined the hazards of nuclear waste. She spoke of the necessity of developing ways to minimize nuclear waste and to store what is created in a safe manner on site; the impossibility of guaranteeing public safety when nuclear waste is transported; the potential for another Three Mile Island, Chernobyl, or terrorist attack if the proposed nuclear dump were to be built; and the devastating impact when the human body is exposed to even the most minute traces of radiation.

A hush fell over the audience. Shoulders slumped and faces looked solemn.

"This is the day of the fall equinox. For the ancients, the hard work of summer was over, the harvest was stored, and this was the beginning of the quiet time of the year, the time of long, dark nights and an opportunity for reflection.

"So let's forget for a moment about the perils of nuclear waste. Imagine a waterfall of light is washing away the image of the dump and all it stands for. Take this opportunity to close your eyes, relax, breathe, and ask yourself what you want in your life. Let your mind go and imagine all the blessings you desire are raining down on you." Clarissa paused for a few minutes.

"See it all clearly. Imagine everything you want for yourself and your world. Reflect on every detail. Let yourself experience exactly what it would feel like to live in the world you want." Clarissa waited for another minute. "Now let me ask you this. Did any of you find yourself longing for a nuclear dump in your future?"

"No!" The response was loud and laughing, in spite of the silence the meditation had created.

"Thank you. Come on back to this hall and open your eyes. Could the house lights come up a little?"

Morgan enjoyed how Clarissa was putting the techniques she'd taught her to good use. Clarissa caught her eye and winked.

"Is everyone comfortable?"

Some audience members responded in the affirmative.

"Come again?"

"Yes!"

"What did you say?"

"Yes!"

"What about the honorary women?"

There was laughter, and a few men said, "yes."

"I can't hear you!"

"Yes!"

"Can we stop this dump?"

"Yes!"

"Are you sure?"

"Yes!"

There were more and louder affirmative responses until Clarissa teased the whole audience into shouting, "Yes!" over and over.

Just look at her!

She's a natural leader.

And she's actually enjoying herself.

It required charisma, confidence, and unmistakable humanity to inspire such a diverse audience to participate so willingly.

And the power of the times.

"Now tell me again, are you comfortable?"

"Yes!"

"No wonder you're comfortable. Look where you're sitting! Surrounded by your friends, in little clusters defined by color. Bring the lights all the way up, please! Although this is a racially mixed event, the seating you have self-selected is almost completely segregated.

"But this community, this planet we're trying to protect, belongs to all of us. So maybe it's time to work together. Do something for your baby, please, the precious, tender earth. Gather up your belongings, stand up, move away from the folks you came with, and sit down next to someone of a different race, someone you don't know."

When the audience reassembled, Clarissa asked people to introduce themselves to those around them and find out why they were here and how they felt about the proposed dump. Soon an electric buzz filled the hall and people had to raise their voices to be heard. The atmosphere that resulted from shaking things up by creating "honorary women" and the new seating arrangement was charged, thrilling.

Morgan eased back in her new chair as a power surge engulfed her body, causing her to pull her fan from her purse. She was profoundly satisfied.

Clarissa proceeded with the evening, bringing in a variety of lively acts, nuclear experts, and political and religious speakers, each of whom actually managed, as promised, to be brief. She engaged the audience with humor and inspiration.

As Morgan watched, she felt she had passed on a baton to Clarissa, who had geometrically magnified its force, so that now the baton had grown into a staff of enormous power. The audience was being swept up by the strength of this force—uplifted—and the evolutionary change in consciousness she and Serena had discussed so many times was happening right before her eyes.

Surveying the hall, Morgan witnessed in those around her the eagerness of children combined with the integrity and focus of adults who were firmly on course. Faces were lit from within, eyes were bright, and spirits were glowing.

"It's amazing, isn't it Luv?" The voice was Brigid's. Suddenly she saw what Brigid saw.

The hall was full—not just with people, but with the shimmering shapes of the ancestors, tier upon tier of them, wise women from every time and culture. Light illumined them from within and they suffused the hall with their brilliance.

The guides were there too, on the perimeter, creating an undulating glow like the northern lights.

Big Mom was there with her clan, stretching back into antiquity. Grandmama was standing erect and proud, her lineage behind her.

The wisewomen from Brigid's tribe were gathered, the underwater women, embracing one another and reuniting with their children and their men, the fire in their bellies blazing bright.

A little girl holding an infant pushed her way through the underwater women and faced Brigid.

"Flidias! Skatha!"

The girl began walking slowly toward them. As she did, she grew taller and older, and the baby in her arms became a toddler, then wriggled down to her feet and grew along with her sister. By the time they embraced their mother, they were the strong women they had become. Seamus, their father, emerged from the crowd and pulled Brigid close.

The ancestors were massing. African and Native American drummers moved into place behind Clarissa. Pioneer women, women who had been tried as witches, women from every place and time moved into position, forming concentric rings around the hall and filling the aisles in a great, unified, vibrating throng.

Male spirits came from behind, respecting and supporting them. The imbalances of the elders, the pockets of pain and fear and confusion, were being replaced with love, harmony, and strength.

The underwater women fanned out and formed a larger circle around and above the group. They breathed like bellows, intensifying the fire in their bellies and bringing it to full force. Then each drew the fire from her womb in a sacred act of birth and held it in her arms for a moment before tossing it up.

The fireballs exploded in midair, like fireworks raining down on the crowd below. The audience seemed to draw a collective breath, drawing in the energy.

Brigid was the last to go, tossing her ball high into the air from the center of the hall. As the glorious rainbow sparks showered down all around her, Morgan breathed deeply, inviting them into her heart and belly. Their energy moved through her, revitalizing her body and the earth beneath her.

She felt a profound shift occurring in the audience. Somehow she knew—intuitively and with certainty—that similar shifts were occurring throughout the world. She wondered how many such events were taking place at that very moment, and how many women like Clarissa, Serena, and her had transformed themselves so the change could happen.

She knew the way was being cleared for a new awareness to infuse the spirit of humanity—a womanly love for earth and for life that would equip humankind for conscious, sustainable living. Everyone in the hall was being rearranged at a cellular level, and the same thing was going on in other places, as well.

She began to see beyond her immediate environment, as though a solid movie screen in front of her was transforming into a thin gauze veil that revealed a kaleidoscope of scenes behind it. She saw other women throughout the world turning and changing, moving toward what they loved.

The first scene was a senior citizens' dance. The few men present were dancing with partners. The women on the periphery were looking at the center of the floor with hungry eyes, their feet tapping. Suddenly a woman grabbed another to dance, and they grabbed two more. Soon the whole dance floor was packed with frolicking women.

The scene faded and Morgan saw a small room in which four dark women were preparing a young girl for a clitoridectomy. One of the women was wielding a sharp piece of glass. Another woman hugged the one with the glass shard, then smiled broadly and took the piece of glass away, throwing it into the fire. The other women embraced the girl, who sobbed in her relief.

This scene gave way to a woman directing traffic around a road construction site. She tossed her 'SLOW' sign to a male coworker and grabbed a shovel.

Across the globe a woman with a pick was tearing up her driveway, preparing the ground for an organic urban vegetable garden.

Closer to home, teenage girls hung in a nervous cluster in a mall, scanning for boys. "I don't want to be here," one of them said. "Let them find us if they want to. Let's go do something we like!"

A woman cuddled next to a man on a sofa, her face slack in the flickering blue light of a television as the man robotically clicked the remote. All at once she bolted off the couch, turned off the T.V., and pulled the man to his feet. "We're going out," she said, "to walk and talk in the moonlight. I want to tell you about my plans to run for Congress."

In a hospital delivery room, a woman pushed a baby into the world. "It's a girl! Oh my God! It's a girl! It's a girl! It's a girl!"

Abruptly, Morgan was back at Clarissa's event, tears streaming down her face.

In an audience participation piece, richly costumed women holding tall, white candles high in the air were taking up positions in the four corners of the hall. Clarissa instructed the audience to imagine a white light vortex on the stage, the same whirling vacuum Morgan had taught her to use to remove Shadow. Then she had them shout out all the negative things they wanted the vortex to sweep away, past, present, and future, including the dump and and all the forces behind it.

Then each person was given a small, white candle and asked to think about what they wanted for the earth. The bearers of the tall candles approached every row and lit the candle of the person in the aisle seat. Each member of the audience received a light from the person next to them, until eventually everyone was standing with a lit candle.

"Please gaze into the flame you're holding," Clarissa said, "knowing the web of life on earth is as fragile and as powerful as that flame. Think of one thing you'd be willing to do to help stop the dump. Then look around this hall at the beauty and power of so many flames together and create a vision in your heart of how we can cooperate to stop the dump.

Morgan drew a long breath.

I'll do as she asks.

I need to give substance to my commitment to the world I want by taking some kind of action.

It doesn't have to be big.

But it has to be real.

Clarissa asked everyone to gaze into their flames and affirm their willingness to create change before extinguishing their candles for a short break. She directed them to refreshments and to a table for information, donations, and a raffle.

"And please continue to talk to people you don't know. Share the ideas you have for stopping the dump. If each of us does one or two simple things to help prevent this dump from happening, we can stop it. After the break, we'll have more entertainment, the Golden Glams will be back—" She paused until a ripple of whistles and giggling subsided. "And we'll gather the ideas you've generated."

❧ ❧ ❧

Clarissa grinned broadly while the audience roared. The electricity in the hall was palpable. Concentric circles of ancestors had supported her throughout the evening, and now she felt their light filling her heart and drenching every fiber of her being.

Her boys were so excited they were running across the base of the stage. Joshua was beaming and tears streaked Serena's face. Dump the Dump had been a fabulous success. Dozens of ideas had been generated in the second half of the program. Working together, they had quickly refined the best of these into such a sweetly simple plan and most of the audience members had been able to commit to at least one concrete action.

A fund-raising team was put in place and a task force had been organized to work with politicians at state and local levels.

The two network television stations and three newspapers covering the event had sent staff who appeared to be sympathetic, so they were off to a good start with the media.

Within the week, a web page would be created. Telephone trees were organized and addresses were gathered. Two pastors agreed to do outreach to churches, and Rosa, her mother, and Tameka Brooks agreed to head up organizing out in the county.

A committee had been established to plan the next gathering—which would probably be a demonstration—and audience members had agreed each of them would be responsible for getting at least three new people to attend.

Clarissa waited for the audience to quiet.

"Look around you at the faces who will change the world!" Applause and laughter filled the hall.

"There are some special people I want to thank. Without their help, this event wouldn't have been possible. My sons, Frankie and Martin, helped me canvass, make flyers, and keep the home office running."

Frankie and Martin hopped up on the stage and bowed dramatically several times before throwing their arms around their mother. The applause surged.

"Every time I hit a hurdle I couldn't jump, Joshua Jones had a fresh idea and the energy to carry it out."

From the side of the hall, Joshua's grin took over his face.

"My mother, Serena, was my eleventh hour angel. Her instincts for what to do and how to do it saved the day again and again."

Her mother, who was standing beside Josh, was shaking, overwhelmed by tears. First she covered her mouth, then she buried her face in Josh's shoulder. Joshua winked at Clarissa and applauded her mother while his arms encircled her.

"I will always be grateful to Big Mom, my Cherokee grandmother, who supports me from the other side.

"I want to thank all our speakers and talent, as well as the volunteers who made this event possible. Please take a bow. And I want to thank each of you out there in the audience. You are my heroes.

"And there's one woman without whom we wouldn't be here tonight. She heard about my dream to Dump the Dump when I was still too scared to take the first step. She believed in me before I could believe in myself, and she never stopped believing in me.

"Morgan Forrester, I love you."

~ ~ ~

Morgan waited in her chair, her eyes closed in rest, for the volunteer cleanup crews to finish so she, Clarissa, and Serena could grab a bite to eat.

There was going to be a party for everyone who worked on Dump the Dump. But it was scheduled for next week because Clarissa wanted the events of the evening to sink in and her team to be revitalized so they could brainstorm new possibilities at the party. Tonight, Clarissa had told her, she simply wanted to unwind with her mother and Morgan. If she was up for it, of course.

Someone sat down next to her, someone who leaned comfortably against her and had a warm shoulder and cool forearms. She knew before she opened her eyes it was Patrick.

"It was magnificent, wasn't it," she said.

"Yes. I cried."

"Me too."

"Did you see the ancestors?" he said.

"Oh yeah."

"The shift is happening."

"I know."

But at the periphery of her awareness, Shadow sniggered.

CHAPTER 25

gold dancing

When spider webs unite,
they can tie up a lion.

—Ethiopian proverb

"You're brilliant!" Morgan said.

Clarissa did that little dip of her head Morgan had grown so fond of, then met her eyes.

"I've never seen anyone engage a crowd that size so fully," Morgan said. "What a creative concept! And you pulled it off! But that's how a meeting should be run, isn't it? Don't harangue them about the problem, which leaves them no choice but to fog out. Uplift them, get them laughing, moving, talking. They were having fun and setting the world on fire at the same time!"

"Teaching school taught me that."

"Dump or no dump, you were teaching people that what they want and what they do means something. You created an experience that allowed them to drop their powerlessness and take charge."

"I learned that from you."

"Thanks, but whatever I taught you, you took the ball and ran. You reached inside and found the magic in yourself. Your event was inspired—a miracle—from beginning to end."

"Literally." Clarissa stepped back and locked eyes with her in a rapt, shimmering gaze. "I had more help than I knew existed."

With a fluid gesture of her willowy arm, Clarissa swept the room—both at the parallel, human level and above, indicating Spirit and the guides and ancestors.

"So you saw them?" Morgan said. "The ancestors?"

"Oh yeah."

Serena came bounding up. "Are you still up for going out? Clarissa and I were thinking about breakfast at the all night diner."

"Sounds great."

She longed for her bed, but this was not a moment to be missed. Joshua had taken the boys home to give Clarissa a celebratory girls' night out.

The three women strode out into the humid night air and piled into Serena's van. They weren't out of the driveway before Serena was going off about how the hierarchal archetype of the patriarchy was giving way to collaborative dreaming and action. Dump the Dump was proof of that.

Out of the blue, Serena hit a hard right and took a shortcut through a neighborhood Morgan avoided at night because of its dark intersections, high crime rate, and crack houses. But Clarissa didn't seem to mind, so she decided not to protest Serena's choice.

"Mother," Clarissa said. "Your gas light is on."

"So it is!"

City people can be such a pain in the butt.

They were so accustomed to being unsafe they thought it was normal and didn't take precautions. Statistically, this section of Hopewellen was as dangerous as most urban crime zones.

The closest gas station would take them deeper into the neighborhood Morgan wanted to avoid. But what choice was there?

Shadow gave her spine an unmistakable yank.

This is it.

The showdown.

God I hope I'm wrong.

Serena rattled up to the gas pump and Serena and Clarissa piled out. She had assumed they would stay together. But the pump didn't accept credit cards and before she knew it, Serena and Clarissa were headed toward the convenience store. To save time, she started pumping gas.

When she returned the nozzle to the pump, Morgan heard a muffled sob coming from the shadows at the far end of the parking lot. She peered into the darkness. A man had a woman pinned against a car and was hitting her. She couldn't see anyone else—anywhere—so she moved towards the couple, placing herself midway between them and the convenience store.

The man had his enormous back to her. He'd stopped beating the woman and was towering over her, spitting words in her face Morgan couldn't understand.

She could see the whites of the woman's eyes flash—crazed, like a cornered animal's—when she noticed her.

"Come inside the store with me!" Morgan's voice broke the heavy night air with a strength that surprised her.

The woman turned away.

"Do you want your life to be about this?" She ignored the man, creating her world instead of fighting him.

But the man backed away from the woman and took a step toward her.

"You fat pig!" He threw his head to the side and spit.

"Cunt! Whore! I'm gonna to fuck every hole you have and I'm gonna make you bleed!"

She ignored him. She sensed this woman wasn't ready to leave this man. But she was there for her anyway, using her imagination to create a world in which violence didn't exist. Simultaneously, her pulse throbbed in her ears and she was calculating what it would take to make it into the convenience store.

Could she get there before he got to her?

Probably not.

The woman was looking at her.

"Come with me." She extended her hand toward the woman and backed slowly toward the store. "Your life can be bigger than this. Choose. You deserve it."

The man took three long, easy steps toward Morgan, swinging his arms wide, menacing her.

"I'm going to call the police. Come with me," Morgan said.

But the woman was frozen in place.

"You can end this anytime. If not now, please make it soon." Clarissa and Serena appeared out of nowhere and pulled her into the store.

A petite woman with fierce, frightened eyes said, "I called the police." It was the night manager.

"How long ago?" Morgan said.

They were the only ones in the store.

"About a minute."

"I hope they get here fast," Morgan said. "He's crazy." It was common knowledge that the police could take forever responding to a call in this part of town.

"You're right," the night manager said. "I know him. He's been in prison most of his life. Rape."

The door behind her flew open. Morgan whirled around. It was the woman. The flesh on her face was raw and her eyes were wild with terror. She bolted across the store and locked herself in the restroom.

The night manager fumbled for keys and rushed out from behind the register and toward the door. The man was moving closer. His manner was deliberate, menacing.

Like Shadow.

The night manager locked the heavy glass door and turned to her with big eyes.

That door was not enough to protect them from this man.

Moving as one, the four women grabbed the nearest display shelf and tipped it inward. Its contents scattered across the floor. They pushed through the debris and dragged the shelf to the door, where they wedged it under the lip of the door frame.

The man struck the door with his hands, hard. His screams pierced the glass and resounded throughout the fluorescent interior of the store.

Morgan heard the woman in the bathroom. "Oh God, oh God, oh God. Help me! He's going to kill me. He's finally going to kill me. Oh God."

Morgan was all adrenalin. Her body was suddenly strong, as though she'd never been ill.

The man moved sideways to the floor-to-ceiling window and bounced his fists against the glass, taunting them.

She finally looked at him. He was boring into her with his eyes and his entire body was twitching reflexively. Even from outside, he towered over her.

He was sweaty with agitation, huge muscles rippling beneath his wet tee shirt, the meat of his forearms glistening in the green glare of the outside lights. Eyes bulging, he stripped each of them, one at a time, with his eyes. Then he spat, threw back his head, and laughed.

The man relaxed and regarded them calmly, as if to say the locked door and shelf were no obstacle to him. It was only a matter of determining the most enjoyable way to finish them off.

All at once Morgan realized that although the man's form was human, his eyes were demonic.

Shadow.

A bolt of terror shot through her spine, freezing her in place.

Shadow answered her fear by licking his lips and easing into a slow smile that said his victory, over her at least, was assured. He kissed into the air toward her casually—pointedly.

The chill from that kiss wafted through the glass between them and stole her breath. She felt the contents of her stomach collecting at the base of her throat.

He rocked back on his heels, tossed his head, and laughed. It was an ugly, rasping sound. Then there was a small explosion of smoke and, where Shadow had stood, there was nothing. The night manager's eyes bulged and she flew across the store, screaming, and locked herself in the other restroom.

The electricity popped off, both in the store and outside.

Instinctively, Morgan, Clarissa, and Serena sought one another's hands in the darkness. A deafening silence permeated the store. But then they detected a subtle rattling sound that increased eerily in volume until it was deafening. It was the merchandise on the shelves, shaking more and more violently before hurtling across the room.

Somehow, even in the darkness, the three women managed to pull one of the smaller display shelves behind the register and prop it against the counter. They took shelter beneath the shelf while a hurricane force wind gathered in the store, pitching objects against the walls and ceiling.

Serena's body was convulsing with tremors and Clarissa was crying for Big Mom.

"Clarissa," Morgan shouted above the roaring wind, "the ancestors can't stop this. But we can." Suddenly she knew exactly what to do. She took Clarissa's fingers and laced them through Serena's.

"This is what I need you to do," Morgan yelled.

She could barely make them out in the swirling darkness, but she sensed Serena and Clarissa forcing themselves to attend to her words.

"I need you to help with this storm, so I can deal with Shadow." Morgan gripped the two women's clasped hands. "Settle into your love for each other. That will calm the storm. It's what you've been on your way toward, but now you need to get it totally. Embrace in your hearts that you love each other and are loved—that you deserve it and it's real."

She rubbed their hands. "Can you do that for me?"

"Yes!" they shouted above the din of the storm and huddled closer.

"Good. It's time for me to go out there and meet Shadow. But remember—this isn't about him. It's about us."

She pulled out of their makeshift shelter and entered the storm, protecting her head with her arms, closing her eyes, and willing herself to find Shadow. Following a pull from her heart and belly, she soon found herself outside the darkness of the storm, which was now focused in a tight sphere around Serena and Clarissa.

The electricity was on again and—except in the tight area where Serena and Clarissa still fought the storm—everything was in order, as if nothing had happened. She blinked in the fluorescent light and saw that Shadow was still outside, about ten feet away, grinning at her through the floor-to-ceiling window.

Rage filled Morgan's head and she wanted to lunge at him through the glass and force him to leave Clarissa and Serena alone. But indulging in anger at any level, she realized, would play into his hands. It would give him free access to her reserves of energy.

Breathing deeply, she grounded herself and inhaled the limitless love of Divine Wholeness, held it for a moment, and released it into her world. She continued to breath in a circular, even flow of love. Her shoulders, jaws, knees, and belly softened. Invoking protection from Spirit, she continued to breathe until she was at ease.

She looked into his eyes. "I love you, Shadow," she said softly.

He looked stricken.

"I love you," she said, "and I no longer need you. I've released my self-imposed requirement to suffer. Thank you for standing by me when I still needed that. You're free to return to the light now."

She prayed to Divine Wholeness to bring a golden white pillar of love into view so Shadow could see the light.

But he turned his back on it and began to hyperventilate, working the bellows that stoked his dark power.

Shadow whipped around, crouching, searching for a means to get at her. His arms were outstretched, fingers quivering, as though they were detectors that could draw a weapon to them. Throwing his head from side to side, his motions spastic and erratic, he scuttled across the ground, spittle flying from his mouth in long loops, and picked up a large rock. He waved his weapon at her gleefully, running his tongue over his lips.

Moving with the springy step of on an athlete, his body barely able to contain his energy, he stepped back, taking his time to gauge the optimum distance from which to throw the rock.

Like a pitcher, he took his stance, penetrated her with his eyes, and aimed the rock at her head. Then he strutted, re-aimed, and strutted again.

Shadow's agitation didn't touch Morgan. She was perfectly calm.

Rooted in the mineral strength of the Earth Mother, I stand in the love of Divine Wholeness.

My guides and angels surround me.

Let this play out as it will, for the highest good of all.

She simply looked into his eyes, making no effort to duck or to raise her hands to protect herself.

It was almost in slow motion that he drew back to pitch his weapon through the glass and her skull.

As she watched him move, she was curious. It was an old scene, timeless, like a movie with a closed loop running for the thousandth time. This was Adam, this was her father, this was the Scots. As she observed the mean-spirited gesture, the smallness, the self-centeredness, the fear, Morgan felt something move in her heart.

It was compassion. Her eyes locked with his. She smiled, feeling loved by Clarissa, Serena, the ancestors, everyone.

When he saw kindness in her eyes instead of fear, Shadow hesitated. He looked confused. But then he became angry, as if someone had tricked him. He drew back his arm, then jerked it forward, hard.

Time froze, then jolted into slow motion with the halting lurch of a film being shown one frame at a time. He was projecting something at her from the rock. Ahead of the stone, a sinister ray of energy was moving toward her. All at once, she knew what it was. It was the energy he had penetrated her with her whole life, whenever she felt afraid or unsure of herself.

Morgan renewed her focus on her breath and relaxed more deeply. Without knowing why, she reached out to the warrior angel. "Archangel Michael, protector of all who seek the light, please come now."

In the split second before Shadow released the rock, Morgan's gaze fell on the glass between them. She saw a small spider, whose web had miraculously survived the storm, methodically wrapping her latest captive in a ball of silk.

Thinking with her belly and her heart, Morgan raised her hand. Her palm deflected the ray of sinister energy Shadow projected ahead of the rock, sending it back to him at the same time that her whole being settled into alignment with Mother Earth and Divine Wholeness.

"Dear Shadow, I wrap you in your own energy," she said aloud. In her mind, she stretched the ray out, winding it lovingly around and around him, until he was entirely encircled in a ball of his own energy.

Simultaneously, she withdrew from him all the energy he had ever sapped from her, pulling long ropes of it toward her and washing it in a shower of tinkling, rainbow-hued light before taking it back into her own body. Then she withdrew the lifetime accumulation of his energy from her body, rinsed it, and returned it to him.

All at once the familiar strength and vitality—the power that was Morgan's essence—settled into her body and charged her with a profound sense of well-being.

Shadow dropped the rock as though it had stung him, then looked at his hands. Disoriented and uncomprehending, he staggered toward Morgan. He put his hands on the window between them, pressing his face to it. His legs gave way and he stared at her as he slowly slid down the window, his face contorting against the glass as he fell.

He was on the pavement now, paralyzed, his face still pressed to the glass. His eyes, which were curiously open and almost childlike, were locked with hers.

She kneeled so it was easier for him to see her. "I forgive you," she told him. "I forgive each of us for everything and for all time."

He had crumpled even lower now, his head skewed so one eye could still meet hers.

~ ~ ~

Inside the storm of their own creation, Clarissa and Serena held each other. At first their bodies were rigid, but as each clung to the slender frame of the other, murmuring words of acceptance, forgiveness, and love, a curious thing happened. The softer they became, sinking into love and allowing it to work its magic, the more the storm around them eased. Soon they were surrounded by undulating pastel light and the gentle singing of angels. Their bodies relaxed into a full embrace and they smiled, at peace with themselves, each other, and all of creation. They were home together at last.

~ ~ ~

The police pulled up and Morgan straightened. They yanked the man to his feet and handcuffed him. One officer read him his rights and interrogated him while the other questioned Clarissa, Serena, the night manager, and the woman he had beaten. Morgan also gave a brief statement.

All the while, she and Shadow were gazing into each other, and she was telling him things in her mind the others couldn't hear. But she knew he was registering every word.

"We're not so different, Shadow, you and I. I have also been controlled by fear. In a moment, Archangel Michael will take you up to a place where you'll have the opportunity to learn from all this, if you want to. You'll be allowed to experience love and to work with the light. I advise you to take advantage of this opportunity. Find a new way of working with your fear.

"Own your fear," she said, "instead of attempting to protect yourself by trying to control everything around you. That game always leads to failure—don't you see?—because everything we try to control ends up controlling us. Instead, bring your fear back inside, where it belongs. Deal with it, so you can learn how to work for something bigger. Otherwise, it won't be long before there's no place for you. Anywhere."

A power surge hit Morgan hard and she pulled out her fan, which she felt herself wield with the grace of a queen.

The officer grabbed the arm of the man Shadow had inhabited and shoved him into the back of the police car. Shadow's form remained behind, faint but still sharply delineated. Archangel Michael drew near him. It was time for them to go up.

Subtly yet distinctly, Shadow bowed to Morgan.

She breathed deeply, inhaling and exhaling love, taking into herself the boundless love of the infinite, then gently releasing what she didn't need to the universe.

Even to Shadow.

Archangel Michael swept Shadow up in his embrace. Suddenly she saw the possibility of Shadow as an angel of the light, a magnificent being with the capacity to become a great healer. Shadow's form glowed brightly, then disappeared as Archangel Michael drew his wings in around him and rose slowly toward the light.

Morgan felt the restorative powers of the earth filling her body as profoundly as if she were lying on the grass, meditating in her own garden. She released into the earth all the hurt Shadow in his many forms had caused her. The earth, the Great Mother, would know what to do with it.

❧ ❧ ❧

Later that night, embraced by the protection of darkness, Morgan rocked on the glider on her veranda. Earlier, she'd unbuttoned her dress and twirled in the petal-soft air, offering her bare breasts to the full moon and consciously drawing the silvery lunar light into her flesh. Now the heady scent of four-o-clocks, their color nearly piercing the night, enfolded her as she rested.

"So you're not going to die on us, Luv?" It was Brigid.

"Who, me?"

"I'm serious."

"You of all people—uh, spirits—asking me that? Brigid, you know I love you, but I have to tell you—that question proves the old saw that just because someone's dead doesn't make them smart." She laughed hard, slapping her palm on the slats of the glider.

"Cheeky woman!"

"I'm sorry. It's been a long night and I'm losing it. Forgive me."

"Done. You do feel better?"

"Yes. I have more energy than I've had in weeks. But what difference does that make?"

"How can you say that?"

"What matters is, I've got myself. I'll never trade that for anything again. Not a mate, not my kids, not my job, not my health—nothing."

"But who says you have to trade—"

"By standing up to Shadow, rooted in the truth of who I am and what I stand for, I prevailed. I didn't attack, I didn't sink into fear. I simply asked for help and did what came to me. In so doing, I freed myself and the world of a powerful dark force and I enabled a being who taught me a great deal to move on.

"And that," Morgan said, "is perhaps the greatest accomplishment of my life."

"Sure, and—"

"And I'm not about to diminish myself or my accomplishment by assuming an outcome, such as health. This isn't a whitewash, all tied up in a bow like a movie with a happy ending. This is real."

"Aye, but—"

"I don't regret for one moment having been sick. It's taught me exactly what I needed to learn. Anyone can lose their health, lose the ones they love, lose their job, lose their home. None of that is the point. Being whole is." A light breeze lifted Morgan's hair. She stretched her legs, pushed her toes into the cool wood of the glider floor, and drew a long, refreshing breath. "Now that I'm on my path, I'm forever exactly where I'm meant to be."

"I take your meaning." Brigid thought for a long time. "Why didn't we think of that before, wrapping him in his own energy?"

"How could we? For so long, we let him name the game. But the technique isn't what got rid of him, anyway."

"What, then?"

Morgan paused. "We weren't ready before. Until tonight, we never really got it that the whole of Infinity supports us."

"We talked about it."

"I know. And that was an important start. Awareness is the first step. But tonight, at Clarissa's event, we finally lived it."

"Even though the ancestors let you down?"

"How can you say that?"

"We never stood up to Shadow. We never told him to take his bloody hands off us. In the end, you had to face Shadow alone."

"It's not a race. You did the best you could with what you had. You were beautiful!" Morgan turned and grinned in Brigid's direction. "And I thank you with all that I am. How could we have gotten there without you? Besides, everyone faces Shadow alone. But the deeper truth is, we were never alone. That's the whole point."

"I know, but at the event… ."

"What?"

"Big Mom, Grandmama, and I wanted all the ancestors there. But only some would—or could—get far enough in their work to show up."

"But it was enough, wasn't it? It was perfect." Morgan patted the place where she felt Brigid's hand on her shoulder. "You were perfect." She released a burst of raucous, sleepy laughter.

"What's so funny?"

"You're the hundredth ancestor."

"Dumb as I am. . . ."

"Hey, nobody's perfect."

"Holy Mother Goddess. You need some sleep."

"Brigid, a person can chip away at their barriers for a long time before they see a big shift. Regardless of the time required, the thing that guarantees a personal transformation is the decision to do whatever it takes to make it happen, no matter what that looks like. The energy of that commitment—when combined with the action that flows from it—ripples through the soul and out into the world, long before the results become visible. The ancestors were more successful than you know. Intention moves energy. You moved a lot of energy."

"I hope so," Brigid said.

"Count on it. You were fabulous. Thank you."

"You're welcome."

Morgan yawned and indulged in a full-body stretch from her toes to her fingers. "Besides, until recently the women of the present didn't understand the hardships you endured, We didn't have our history straight, so we couldn't see you for who you were, and that was dangerous. It blocked you—and us—because we couldn't love each other the way we can now."

"I suppose that's true." Brigid seemed to be breathing more easily now.

Morgan let out a snort of a laugh.

"What is it, Luv?"

"*Shrink Shrivels Shadow, The Self-Created at Last Abated.*"

"You didn't create Shadow!"

"We don't know that. Yet even assuming he's real, I'm the one who told him 'Hey, here's my life, take it!' But I'll tell you what—no teacher ever served me better. Because I took on Shadow, my life is now my own. And I'll tell you something else."

"What?"

"I love him."

"Have you gone daft? How can you say you love him?"

"Can you imagine the sacrifice he made? To help me become whole, he became a soul whom all fear and none love. Can you imagine giving up so much in order to serve another? I wouldn't do it."

"I scarce believe what I'm hearing. There was true darkness in that soul."

"Perhaps. But it doesn't bring me peace to dwell on how twisted he became. When I think of Shadow as a teacher who showed me my weaknesses—a teacher who wouldn't let me off the hook until I was strong and whole—then my heart is full and my mind is easy."

"Don't underestimate the treachery his kind is capable of."

"I don't pretend evil doesn't exist. But I'm sure I wouldn't even have noticed him if he didn't reflect a part of myself."

"But now you've shown him the boot and he can't come back."

"I don't think that's how it works, Brigid. I'm human. Of course I'll experience fear and self-doubt again. I don't think any of us ever sees the last of Shadow. But he'll never own me again, not as long as I remain true to myself and my path."

"So you're ready for life now, no matter what it throws at you?"

"Bad joke. You've been down here too long."

"I don't know about that."

"What will you do now, Brigid?"

"Get on to my next life, I suppose. I see myself in some new and shining world, a place where everyone has the opportunity to grow and love and be free."

"How lovely. That place is in your heart now so you'll take it with you, wherever you go."

"Yes, I suppose I shall. And what about you?"

"I think I moved into that world tonight. My only plan is to root myself in the earth and inhale and exhale love throughout eternity."

~ ~ ~

The next morning, Morgan awakened deeply refreshed. Sunlight filtered through the breeze-tossed branches outside her window and pranced along the floor. She danced across the rippling play of light and shadow, free at a level she'd never known.

Her grandchild was born.

She knew it.

She'd dreamed about Sierra giving birth and had even awakened briefly, when the room was still velvet with night, clutching at her own belly as if she herself were bringing new life into the world.

It was too early to phone, so Morgan decided to walk to Sierra's and see if she could figure out whether they were awake. It wasn't far, only half a mile, though it had been months since she'd made the journey on foot. She picked chrysanthemums from her garden, in shades of gold and burgundy, before she headed out. The morning was blissfully free of humidity and refreshingly moderate in temperature.

She paused in front of her daughter's home. The living room curtains were open and she detected movement behind the black glass. A figure was pacing—Rich? Was the flash of white a small bundle in his arms? Morgan moved up the sidewalk slowly, reverently, smiling to herself. She thought Rich saw her.

"Wait just a minute, okay?" His voice was muffled.

"Okay!"

Time paused, then she heard movement inside and the door opened.

Rich was beaming. He had his arms around Sierra to steady her. Mere words could never describe her daughter's gleaming radiance. Sleeping in her arms was the most exquisite baby Morgan had ever seen.

Except for her own, of course.

"This is your granddaughter."

"She's precious." Morgan extended her hand and gently lifted a tiny forefinger. Ever so tenderly, Sierra placed her baby in her mother's arms. She was so light, so warm, and she smelled like angels, like vanilla, like rain.

In response to the first rays of sunlight to ever touch her face, the baby's little cheeks squiggled until she worked her eyes open. They were bluer than blue.

Morgan found herself gazing simultaneously into the stillness of ancient knowledge, the laughing good humor of a confident spirit, and the sleepy innocence of new life.

"Does she have a name?" Morgan said.

Sierra looked up at Rich and smiled. "We've tried to be objective, to keep experimenting. But only one name seems to fit, so we've made the choice."

"Or she has!" Rich laughed and stroked his daughter's cheek with his forefinger.

"What is it?" Morgan said.

"Brigid."

To the Reader

I wrote this book out of respect—and awe—for the myriad ways so many of us are questing for our own unique paths and spiritual truths. There is so much nonfiction out there to assist us. Yet nothing beats fiction for its power to strike a deeper chord by allowing us to step into the myth, try it on, and take what fits as our own. I felt it was time to celebrate the pioneering heroism of women as we take on life's biggest challenges and claim from the richness of our lives our own quests and spiritual adventures.

The hundredth woman is a new model, an option for embracing our wholeness more fully—our laughter, our courage and frailty, our steeliness and love. And especially our power to transform and our fear of doing so, for if we can face our fears and combine the worldly strengths we've claimed over recent decades with our innate powers as lifegivers, nestlers, and nourishers, we can harness the alchemy of that wondrous mix to turn this crazy world around.

The possibility still exists for sustainable life and fulfillment for everyone—but only if more women insist that our immediate worlds are life giving for ourselves and for all who share them with us.

Though I'm techno-impaired, I have hopes that my website, **hundredthwoman.com** can become a place where we can exchange information—and some laughs—about the kinds of ideas that appear in this book, as well as our experiences along the way.

See you in cyberspace!

Best to you in every way,

Kate Green

0-595-27958-9